FROM THE LIBRARY OF

ISBN 978-1-958164-02-0

First Edition
First Printing October 2022

Published by The Postmodern Press LLC
www.ThePostmodernPress.com

Printed in the United States of America

Names: Leah, Shan, 1980- author, illustrator.
Title: Bands of a small hurricane / Shan Leah.
Description: Dunedin, FL : The Postmodern Press, 2022.
Identifiers: LCCN 2022936125 (print) | ISBN 978-1-958164-00-6 (hardcover) | ISBN 978-1-958164-02-0 (paperback) | ISBN 978-1-958164-01-3 (ebook) | ISBN 978-1-958164-03-7 (audiobook)
Subjects: LCSH: Fathers and daughters--Fiction. | Girls--Fiction. | Families--Fiction. | Hippies--Fiction. | Florida--Fiction. | Bildungsromans. | BISAC: FICTION / Literary. | FICTION / Coming of Age.
Classification: LCC PS3612.E25 B36 2022 (print) | LCC PS3612.E25 (ebook) | DDC 813/.6--dc23.

Bands of a Small Hurricane

SHAN LEAH

Also by Shan Leah
Thieves, Beasts & Men

POSTMODERN

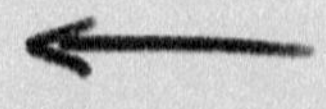

SOUTH

Bahia Honda Bridge (18 miles)
Key West (50 miles)
Mallory Square (52 miles)
Cay Sal Bank (55 miles)
Havana, Cuba (138 miles)

Quade's Boathouse

Roaming Grounds of
Mister Brownstone

Seaside Motel

Boot Key

Sombrero Beach

Seven Mile Bridge

Hippie Beach

The Botel

The Haunted House

Sombrero Reef & Lighthouse

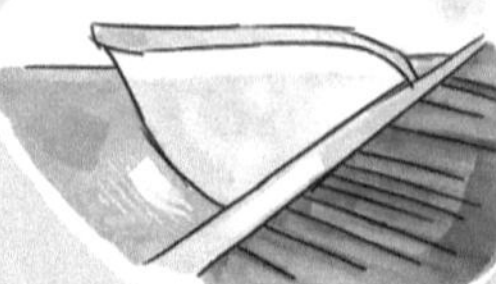

Quade's Boathouse

The Armada

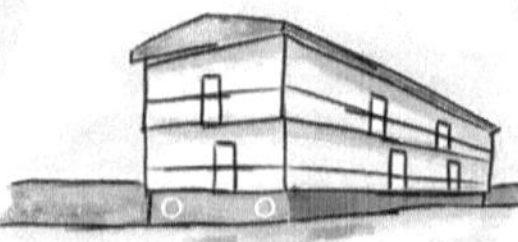

Marathon, Florida

Dedication

For Danny.

Danni helped me learn your name, and now I'll never forget.

Prologue

A father loses his daughter in three distinct phases.

The first is when she begins menstruation. This is no place for a father. A stain in the panties so obscene that it casts dad into a state of intentional blindness. A contract signed long before birth. Because when that time comes, she's no longer his little girl. Every month, her womanly body now ripens, then opens, then purges. An expectation unfulfilled, a cervix weeping.

The second phase is when she loses her virginity. If she's lucky, there is love.

I was not so lucky.

When a girl loses her virginity, her entire world is forced open alongside her body. A boy looming larger, larger, eclipsing all others. There is pain, too. My God, is there pain. And your father, the man who's protected you, loved you like an extension of his own heart, his own skin, is woefully vacant. Here, there grows a new secret. A new estrangement.

And then the third phase.

There comes a time in every child's life when they begin to see their parents for exactly who they are. Clouds part. Illusions dissipate. Mom is no longer the picture of domesticity. She's a caged animal, fighting for survival. A self-made victim of willful ignorance. And dad is no longer the superhero he once was. He's a liar, a cheat. And the truth hits you like a stone to the face: your father can't protect you. He can't even protect himself.

My entire life changed the night of the hurricane. It was also the night of the Halloween dance. Dad told mom he'd be chaperoning the dance, but he wasn't there. He was with that blonde woman from the bar.

I met her once. She had an accent, a slight drawl I couldn't place.

That was the night I lost my virginity. It happened in the band room, behind the tubas.

Where it smelled of brass oil and spit.

He was a nice boy, but he wasn't the right boy.

The carpet was sticky and rigid. My clothes were in a pile by the music stands.

I stared at the ceiling, to the exposed piping with chipped paint next to a small yellow skylight, as a wound exploded from the softest part of my body.

My fingers clawed at a carpet too dense to grasp. My heels sought ground, but they were trapped beneath his body.

It was then that a flash of lightning filled the skylight.

A crack of thunder soon followed, and as it faded away, a reverberation was left behind. All around us, the instruments began to ring and hum like wine glasses stroked by wet fingers. As though in the sudden absence of sound, they had begun to panic.

Part One

INNOCENCE IN THE SEASON OF EDDIE

A SCORPION OF STARS

JULY 1967
3 MONTHS BEFORE THE HURRICANE

Richard Quinn stands at the helm of the Valkyrie, dwarfed by the stars above, and exalted from the waves below. They lift him higher and higher, cresting tall, capped with salty foam that lashes his face. He bares his teeth and screams into the gale whipping in from the Atlantic. He loves every second of it.

The lights of Marathon and her surrounding islands grow smaller behind him. It won't be long before even the most nocturnal of residents snuff their lamps.

At the bow, Danni bounces on her toes. Like her old man, she craves the sea.

By summer's end, she'll be a freshman in high school. But her eyes still hold the wonderment of a child, and for that, Richard is grateful.

The cool breeze is a welcome reprieve from the Florida heat. In a matter of hours, the sun will rise, the air sagging with moisture. But at this moment, everything is crisp, dark, perfect.

Nearly thirty miles from shore, Richard relies solely on the landmarks of his own memory. No buoys, no maps, no revolving lights. Only the black ocean below, with Saturn and Jupiter beaming down from the night sky. And the watchful gaze of a glittering scorpion, if the atmosphere is clear enough. Tonight, it is.

Danni points ahead and shouts to her father.

She's spotted it.

Richard cuts the motor, and the Valkyrie coasts across broad swells and closer to the churning waters of the Humps. He descends the ladder to stand beside his daughter.

"The range is right under our feet," he says.

Danni peers overboard like she's expecting to see the mountain peak beneath the surface.

Richard hands her a flashlight, and Danni holds it against the rail.

The ocean is more smoke than water, dense with swirling clouds of foam and krill. Something darts through the light, a flash of silvery yellow.

Danni jumps. "What's that?"

"Barracuda."

"And that?"

"Dolphin. Or tuna. Hard to say. She was fast."

"We're on top of the mountain right now?"

"Yep. You see how the water is smooth, and then all of a sudden, it's choppy, like two completely different oceans?"

She nods.

"That's where the peak is. The current hits it and wham!" Richard claps his hands. "Instant waves."

Richard surveys the water. Perhaps this is the night he will finally spot Mister Brownstone navigating the current.

Mister Brownstone is a Florida Keys legend with more sea tales attached to his name than Richard himself. A dinosaur of the sea, somewhere between a thousand years old, or a million, depending on who you ask. Men say the beast is enormous, upwards of twenty feet long.

Many times, Richard has insisted, "Longer. Thirty feet. Wide as a sailboat. I've seen 'im myself."

But Richard has never seen Mister Brownstone. He's only heard the stories of other men. Of tarpon pilfered from fishing lines, the mammoth hammerhead shark springing from the depths to snatch fish from the air, startling the fishermen as much as the tarpon.

Richard throws a glance toward the islands, but as always, the giant shark remains concealed beneath the infinite black.

"Be careful, pumpkin," he says, grasping his daughter's shoulder. "If you fall in, I might not get to you before the sharks do."

∼

I lean over the railing as though in flight, illuminating underwater galaxies.

The ocean churns like water on a stovetop as the waves crest above the submerged mountain range, arcing into a circle before melting into the calmer swells beyond. I imagine a sea monster sleeping far below, his snores creating sound waves that travel up, up, up, rippling the surface.

A school of small white fish funnel into the flashlight beam, circling and darting as though unable to escape the boundary.

Only one brave soul breaks free, leaving the rest imprisoned.

Dad takes the flashlight and turns it off, placing it on the deck. He clicks on a small lantern and whispers, "Come with me."

I follow him to the stern where the lantern exposes a mere crescent of his face, like a crime noir comic. He stands there for a long moment, chiseled by moonlight and smelling of salt and leather, and I beam with pride.

Richard Quinn. My dad.

He spreads his arms and winks at me. And then, like an anchor he falls backward, crashing into the water below.

"Dad!" I yell, running to the edge, peering into the depths. "Daddy!"

I search for his shirt, his hair, *anything*. We're miles from shore. No neighbors to call for help. Not even a full moon to light the way home.

My mother's voice floods my head: *One day your father is going to get on his boat and never come back. Poof. Just disappear.*

Mom always says this. A self deception she can't escape from. And every time she speaks these words, I want to slap my hand over her mouth and pinch her lips shut before she wills her own worst fear into existence. My worst fear, too.

But dad would never do that, and I wish she would stop saying it.

I hear something splash in the distance and rush to retrieve the flashlight, begging the stars above to let it be my father and not Mister Brownstone.

By the time I return, dad's hands are grasping the stern, his body bobbing up and down like a buoy. He flings his head backward to the rid water from his face.

"Get in," he urges.

"No way! There's sharks!"

He scoffs. "Sea puppies."

"Sea puppies with *teeth*!"

He grins up at me, a gaping, lopsided smile that looks absurd on his face. "Mine are bigger."

And then dad kicks away from the boat, floating high and low atop the ocean.

"Get in, pumpkin," he says. "It's the only way to see the stars."

I think of all the things that could be below us right now. Not real sea monsters, of course, but tuna and swordfish, giant groupers and barracudas, stingrays and sea turtles, mountain ranges and an endless abyss. And yes, sharks.

"I'm scared," I confess.

"I won't let anything happen to you."

And I know he's telling the truth.

I step closer to the edge.

Hold my nose.

Count to five.

And jump.

The ocean is warmer than I expect, and I float on my back, casting a celebratory, "Woohoo!" into the night before paddling closer to dad.

I think once more of all the scary and dangerous things that are surely waiting in the darkness. But the swells quickly soothe my fears.

Because dad was right—this is the only way to see the stars.

~

Richard Quinn collapses onto the couch in his study, depleted, yet still greedy. Already, he misses the sea.

The pillow has long ago gone limp, so he folds it in half before wedging it into his neck.

On his desk is a small bronze statue of a whale. It's heavy, practically a paperweight, and stacked beneath it are lesson plans for his upcoming American Lit class.

Danni isn't the only one anticipating the commencement of a new school year.

Richard adjusts his assignments periodically to alleviate his growing boredom. This year, he's decided to assign *To Kill a Mockingbird* as their reading requirement, since *Catcher in the Rye* was removed from the library for profanity and sexual situations. If he is ever to assign *To Kill a Mockingbird*, it has to be now. Already, parents across the nation are beginning to speak out against it. A recent protest described the book as "damaging to integration," and accused schools of "institutionalized racism."

Richard listens to Miriam toss about in the next room. She won't be pleased with his late-night arrival home. He should buy her something pretty. Maybe that electric skillet she's been wanting—in pink, to match her hand mixer.

Richard mashes his face into the pillow, and the fabric snags his whiskers. He closes his eyes.

When he can't sleep, Richard imagines he is fishing, the pole rigid in his hands, the line swaying from side to side.

Winding.

Pulling.

The clacking of the reel.

But tonight, sleep eludes him, and his thoughts return to the upcoming school year.

Though his lesson plans vary from year to year, one thing remains unchanged: on the final day of school, Richard Quinn enters his classroom without a word and drops a heavy book onto his desk to get their attention. He waits for silence, reverence.

He waits until the hum of anxiety fills the room.

It used to be easy, but word has been passed down. Last year, students eagerly awaited him on that final morning—and other students cut their classes to sneak into his room—just to hear his book slam against the wood. To hear Mr. Quinn recite, entirely from memory, the first chapter of Moby Dick, his voice roaring so loudly that neighboring teachers pounded on the walls.

Tucked into the couch in his study, Richard recalls his favorite lines, one by one, drawn out and deliberate.

Call me Ishmael. Some years ago—never mind how long precisely—having little to no money in my purse...

Miriam continues to slumber in the bedroom, and as she shifts beneath the sheets, Richard pictures her body shifting as well, thin and tan, and he is suddenly erect.

Deep into distant woodlands winds a mazy way, reaching to overlapping spurs of mountains bathed in their hill-side blue.

Richard adjusts his erection against his leg and hopes it goes away; he's almost to his favorite line.

…two and three there floated into my inmost soul, endless processions of the whale, and, mid most of them all, one grand hooded phantom, like a snow hill in the air.

Miriam coughs in her sleep, a gentle and feminine sound. Richard strokes himself through pants still damp with seawater, and licks the salt from his arm, just to taste the ocean.

And when he can take no more—when his body is ready to burst like a wave over the reef—he leaves his study and takes his wife.

JIMMIE AND THE HUT

The bathtub water covers my nose and mouth as I try to erase the sounds that woke me.

But even underwater, I can still hear dad's voice. Lower than usual. Grunting. Wheezing.

I don't want to picture dad doing *that*. Naked, sweating.

Gross.

I shove my feet into the tub and slide into a sitting position. I could throw up right here in the bathwater, and I consider crawling across the tile so I can vomit in the toilet like a lady, but I swallow it back. I'm not a kid anymore, but they should still have some respect.

I can't picture mom that way. Maybe because through all of dad's grunting and wheezing, and the sound of the squeaky springs, she never made a peep.

By the corner of the tub is a pink box of Mr. Bubble —a forgotten remnant of my childhood—and I shift it around with my toes. High school girls don't use Mr. Bubble, so neither do I. But I sometimes miss the smell.

Mom's in the kitchen, bustling about. Too early for baking, but there's nothing else for her to do.

I hear spatulas and bowls being moved from one location to another. The refrigerator door opening and closing.

And the whir of her hand mixer, pink like Mr. Bubble. Her old one was an outdated olive color, and she wanted a new one. So dad bought her a new one. She keeps it next to the old olive one now, which she refuses to throw away.

I stand and approach the mirror, though I'm careful not to study my reflection too closely.

Sometimes my features melt across my face like a frosted cupcake in the sun. My nose swells. My eyes shift. Shadows slip down either side of my chin and red splotches spread like gasoline across my cheeks, vibrant enough to rival the acne patches at my temples.

And for just a moment, I see what I truly am—what no one else will tell me.

I'm deformed. Practically a monster.

Maybe nothing is ever meant to stay the same. Defying this concept of permanence, reliability, every little thing—even your nose and eyes—will eventually grow restless and declare mutiny. Rebellion is, after all, the natural order of things.

People tell me I'm pretty, but they're lying. That's just what adults are supposed to say to kids.

I push away from the sink and wrap one towel around my body, making sure the scars on my thighs are covered. I twist another towel atop my head before dashing to my room, because I don't feel like hearing about whatever it is that mom's cooking this morning, baking this morning, blending this morning.

And I don't want to hear mom say, again, that one day dad is going to get on his boat and never come back. Poof. Just disappear.

My clock blazes 6:05 am.

Outside my window, the sky is still black, and I clap a mosquito buzzing past my ear as I lean into the fan. Then I shrug off my towel, pull on my favorite blue and red striped shirt and my overalls, rolling the cuffs above my calves.

No shoes. No need.

And I step into the living room and collapse into dad's special chair.

Above the television hangs a wooden oar. *VALKYRIE*, it says, etched deeply into the wood and stained in blue. Below that, in small white writing: *Marathon, Florida, 1963*. It's from dad's first set of oars aboard the Valkyrie. He had new ones made last year by a local woodworker. The old ones were just fine, but a student from his American Lit class was from a poor family and her father needed the work.

Mom hovers above a mixing bowl, her hair in rollers and hidden beneath a headscarf. Later, she'll look like Jayne Mansfield, her golden hair curling around her ears and dusting her shoulders. But right now, she just looks bored.

Mom turns to me, noticing my presence for the first time. Her eyes drink in my outfit, and I hold my breath.

"Where do you think you're going, young lady?" she asks. "It's still dark out."

Dad emerges from the hallway, skin flushed and damp. His belt is still unbuckled, and the images I tried to drown in the bathtub are swiftly resuscitated.

"Jimmie's," I say, trying to make myself small.

"At this hour?"

"He's up."

Mom looks to dad, begging for reinforcement.

But dad is always on my side, and he just smiles. "Yes, I s'pose he is."

I hustle down the stairs to circle the building, turning at the dock and following the path that skirts the water. My bike is leaning against a post behind the apartment, and my legs are anxious to ride. I know the way. I barely look up.

It feels good to race in the morning, in the stillness before the sun rises and the day officially begins. Like I'm stealing something that wasn't meant for me.

Of course Jimmie will be up. His whole family will be awake and bustling about the hut.

And today is going to be a good day. Today, Jimmie and I are going to make some money.

The wind whistles through the spokes as I pedal hard and fast, and the rising sun illuminates the clouds on the horizon.

Whenever I watch the sun rise or set, I hear dad's voice: *Red sky at night, sailors delight; red sky at morning, sailors take warning.* It sounds beautiful and dangerous all at the same time, like a giant hungry fire could surge from the ocean to swallow you whole.

This morning, the sky is a little yellow, a little orange. Beautiful, but not dangerous.

I follow the center line of US1 and veer onto the road that leads to Key Colony Beach. The first rays of the sun skewer the lowest clouds like roasted marshmallows, but despite the allure of desserts in the sky, all I can smell is fish.

I pedal past houses dwarfed by mountains of crab traps. The wood has been bleached gray by the sun, gnarled by saltwater, blistered by barnacles. The traps release a briny stench that will only grow stronger as the temperature rises.

Jimmie's a Conch, like me. That's what folks call people who were born in the Keys. *Native Conchs.* His parents are Conchs too. So is my dad.

But not mom.

Mom was born somewhere on a Kansas farm. She says that when the sun sets just right, and the ocean takes on a golden hue along the horizon, she can squint her eyes and see an endless field of sorghum.

Native Conchs are the luckiest kids in the whole world. Here in the Keys, there's no pressure to adapt with the times. We move at our own pace, protected from outsiders. That's what dad says.

Jimmie's house is just ahead, one of the many whose lights are already on at this hour. I race toward the hut in his front yard—the one with the smokehouse behind it. During season, Jimmie's parents sell perfectly gleaned and blushed fish fillets to the tourists, but the locals come for the crawfish and smoked fish spread.

Jimmie waves and I skid to a stop, walking my bike the rest of the way.

"Hiya," he says.

"Hiya."

Jimmie listens with bulging eyes as I tell him about my parents' early morning shenanigans.

"Gross," he says.

"*So* gross."

"*My* mom and dad don't do that."

"Maybe they're just really quiet about it."

Jimmie considers this and shudders.

Mrs. Yearling walks toward us carrying a wooden crate of fish from the smokehouse. Steam obscures her face.

"What are you two gossiping about?"

Jimmie looks to me, waiting for an answer. I look to him, waiting for the same. And suddenly we can't stop laughing. Mrs. Yearling rolls her eyes and continues toward the hut.

Jimmie's mom always looks beautiful, all long skirts, maroon lips, and fancy bandanas in her black hair, even though she has no one to impress but dead fish.

Jimmie's dad stands before the fire in the smokehouse, his body a wedge of shadow lined in orange.

"You're here early today," he says, tossing another log onto the fire.

"My dad woke me up."

"Not another one of his *adventures*, I hope."

Mr. Yearling says this in a way that makes me feel like I'm in trouble.

I've always liked Mr. Yearling. He has kind eyes that look as though he might weep every time he smiles, and big arms that are always wrapping Jimmie up in bear hugs.

But I don't like the way he asks about my dad.

"No, sir," I say.

A sort-of truth.

"Good," he says, wiping his hands on his pants. His eyes burn into the top of my skull, like a fire on the ocean.

Red sky at morning.

I understand why Mr. Yearling would think dad reckless. Mr. Yearling would never wake Jimmie in the middle of the night to float atop savage seas, shark-infested waters. But it's not Jimmie's life—it's mine. And he's not Jimmie's dad—he's mine. And it all suits me just fine, thank you.

A silence widens, and I wonder if Jimmie feels it too, but I don't think so, because he's grinning and hopping up and down, a net in each hand.

"Ready?" Jimmie asks.

I look at Mr. Yearling. Am I?

He tilts his head, apologetic-like, and smiles. "You two have fun. Catch lots of crawfish. And stay in the shallows."

"Here he comes," Jimmie whispers, like the crawfish might hear him from beneath the surface.

I watch the alcove in the coral as Jimmie prods the sand with a snapped tree branch. A red body jets from its hiding place and squirts across the reef.

"I got 'im!" I say.

"I got 'im!" Jimmie says.

We splash after the crawfish, sea anemones recoiling in our wake. It darts this way and that, tail flapping, beady eyes accusatory.

I lunge forward, nearly colliding into Jimmie. He laughs—until he sees the crawfish in my net.

"Aw, man."

"You'll catch the next one," I say, dropping the crawfish into a plastic bucket.

We move from one coral cluster to the next, shuffling our feet through the sand to scare off any stingrays lying in wait. A school of Damselfish races across the sandbar. They would look like flattened sapphires if not for the blazing yellow of their tails.

I point to a mass of seaweed snagged on a lone rock, and when we approach, a small crawfish—this one pumpkin orange with yellow stripes—bursts from the hiding place and darts across the sand. We give chase, and I let Jimmie lead.

He dashes through the shallows, heading toward a large body of coral.

Jimmie throws himself at the crawfish, but it makes a quick turn, heading right for me.

I shove my net through the water, pushing him back toward Jimmie closing in from behind. But Jimmie loses his balance, falling into me, and together we tumble onto the sandbar.

My hair is a wet clump against my face, and Jimmie can't stop laughing as I pull strands from my mouth and eyelashes, and then I'm laughing too. When we finally catch our breaths, we're left with a few minor bruises, a cyclone of sandy water spinning around us, and a crawfish in my net. Pumpkin orange with yellow stripes.

Jimmie scowls and chucks his net into the water. "How many we got?"

I consult the bucket.

"This is lucky number seven," I declare, holding the crawfish aloft.

"This is a bummer," he says. "Let's do something else."

Mr. Yearling pays us $3.00 for ten crawfish. He'll probably give us $2.00 for seven, and that's still a dollar each.

"We can go to The Sundry Store and get candy," I say, dropping lucky number seven in with the others. Minnows trail behind, nibbling scum from the bucket.

"You just wanna go to the Botel," he says, "so you can ditch me for Eddie."

The Botel is exactly what it sounds like: half boat, half motel. It's as large as a real building, and I've always marveled how it stays afloat.

"That's not true!" I insist, resigning myself to sneak out and see Eddie later.

Eddie and I met a few weeks ago at the abandoned lighthouse, and he's a real hunk. He comes to the Keys with his family every summer and stays at the Botel. He's in high school already, and from a big city somewhere in Ohio. Sometimes we'll spend a whole afternoon together and I'll listen as Eddie tells me about city buses and trains and 24-hour diners and the lights of dance clubs sparkling across the sidewalk at night, as I try to imagine what the world looks like outside of the Keys.

Jimmie ignores the school of Parrotfish evading us, even though I point them out.

"What's wrong with you?" I ask.

"Nothing."

Jimmie slaps his gloves against the waves, and it's the only sound in the shallows.

"It's just that…"

I wait.

"You're gonna be in high school," he says. "You'll forget all about me."

Oh.

Jimmie's a year behind me, but we rarely talk about it. We'll still be under the same roof. The only difference is that I'll be with the high schoolers while Jimmie remains sequestered in the middle school wing with the other sixth, seventh and eighth graders.

I can't help that I was born a year earlier than Jimmie. And I don't like it any more than he does. Jimmie's my only friend, and now I'll be forced to expand my social circle before I'm labelled a *total* skuzz.

What was a verbal kind of silence only moments ago now feels like a physical kind of silence, like there's an entire ocean separating us. Or an entire year.

"You're gonna be on the same side of the school as your dad."

That's Jimmie's attempt to change the subject, which I appreciate.

"I'm not in his class 'till senior year," I say.

"It's still weird. You know all the girls have a crush on him, right?"

"*That's* weird."

We laugh, and everything is okay again.

Jimmie takes the bucket from me and climbs the rusted ladder.

Mrs. Yearling meets us at the dock and extends her hand, helping me up. She wraps her arms around both of us at the same time like I, too, belong to her.

Our wet feet collect dirt and pine needles until it feels like we're walking on shoes made of carpet.

Mr. Yearling is barely visible, toiling away inside the hut, and I follow Jimmie inside so we can hand over the crawfish and collect our money.

Already, there's a line of locals snaking toward the road for orders of smoked fish spread.

TO BE LUCKY OR UNLUCKY
UNDER THE VACA CUT BRIDGE

The Sundry Store is only a short ride from Jimmie's house, and we drop our bikes in the bushes by the front door as a customer exits.

"Ma'am," Jimmie says in courtesy, but she's already walking toward her car.

The Sundry Store is the only store in town, aside from the grocery, that has air conditioning. Walking into The Sundry Store is like walking straight into the North Pole.

"Good afternoon," says the clerk. He's thin as a stick of gum held sideways, and so tall he has to duck beneath the REGISTER sign when he takes a customer's money.

The store smells of milk and coconut, and we pass cases of fresh mangoes, limes, bananas, and avocados; coolers of milk, juice, and orange Fantas; and a dozen varieties of gum—Bazooka and Chiclets and Teaberry.

As Jimmie and I approach the candy section, we grab our penny bags and rush to fill them until the scale tells us we're at a dollar each. Like always, Jimmie's bag is filled almost exclusively with Mary Janes. They're his favorite.

We're almost to the register when Jimmie smacks my shoulder, pointing to the magazine rack. Someone has left a Playboy magazine right in front of the Times and Lifes and Good Housekeepings.

On the cover, a woman stands before a sea of sunflower yellow. Her lips are perfect loops, like Christmas ribbons in bubblegum pink. The camera has caught her in a moment of feigned shock as her yellow polka-dotted bikini unhooks at her spine. Luckily, she's grasped her chest just in time, protecting her modesty.

I want to grab the issue and flip through the pages until I find more of her pictures, but I don't want the clerk to yell at me: *Playboy is not for children.* We aren't children. And it's not our fault someone left it in front.

As we make our way to the counter, I peer one last time at the bathing beauty on the sunflower cover.

I hope I look like her someday.

The clerk weighs our bags and takes our money. "Don't eat it all at once," he says.

Jimmie and I hustle to our bikes and select our first treats from our penny bags.

"What should we do now?" Jimmie asks. "I don't wanna go home."

"Let's go to the bridge and watch the boats!"

The Vaca Cut Bridge is only two blocks away. We don't *hope* for a boating accident, but we race the whole two blocks anyway, because you never know.

And we wouldn't want to miss a thing.

The guardrail cuts into my hips as I lean over to watch the swirling water below. The tide is coming in, and that's the most perilous time. The current churns, smashing against the pilings and cresting into peaks unlike anywhere else on the islands.

This is the most dangerous place in the Florida Keys. This bridge. This current. It's less than a block long, but claims more lives each year than all the US1 accidents from Key Largo to Key West. Dad told me that, so it must be true.

The lunch crowd seethes in the diner behind us, thick and rowdy—likely already drunk—and we tuck between two benches for a better view.

The tourists come for fish sandwiches and margaritas. But the locals come to watch the boats.

Boaters have to go fast, and they have to time it just right, in between the swells, to pass through unharmed. But tourists don't know our waters, and accidents are frequent. Hit the surge too slow, or at the wrong time, and the boat is airborne, slamming into pilings and busting to bits, the current sweeping everything and everyone into the ocean.

Last year, I saw a boating accident with my own eyes. Mom was in one of her manic phases and pulled me out of school for a pilgrimage to the Dadeland Mall in Miami. We stopped at the diner for lunch on the way home, arms stuffed with Burdines bags. We could've left them in the car, but mom wanted to show off. As we ate, a small boat drew closer, bouncing on the waves. From a nearby table, a man said, "No, no, no." From another table, a man rubbed his hands together and said, "Here we go."

On the boat was a father and his little boy, and when the current smashed them against the piling, I couldn't tell what was human and what was splintered wood flying through the air. Everyone gasped in horror as if they weren't hoping for excitement only moments earlier. The boat sank, and the father and son never surfaced.

The diner called my dad, and he circled the island on the Valkyrie. He discovered the father and son washed ashore at the harbor on Key Colony Beach. Injured, but alive. The boy was unconscious, and the father wouldn't stop screaming while dad gave the child mouth-to-mouth. The boy ultimately lived, and our local newspaper called dad a hero. He didn't disagree.

They were lucky. If they'd been *unlucky*, the current would've taken them straight out into the Atlantic.

I pop a Fireball in my mouth and draw a breath across my tongue to ease the burn. I look around, but no one is on the water today.

"Do you think Mercy Turner's boobs got bigger?" Jimmie asks.

"Not possible. She'd fall over."

Jimmie laughs. "I bet she's somewhere, falling over *right now*."

Mercy's going to be a freshman, like me. Every summer, she goes on vacation with her family, and by the first day of school, her hair has gained an inch and her bra has gained a cup.

Jimmie always says, Gross. So I say, "Gross."

But this year, Jimmie shrugs and says, "I don't know."

Oh.

And suddenly I don't want to talk about Mercy Turner anymore.

The current foams and laps at the seawall below our feet. If the concrete were to bust apart, Jimmie and I would instantly plunge into the cyclone, washed out to sea. *Unlucky*.

"I bet Timmy Katz got taller," Jimmie says.

"No way. He'd hit his head on the ceiling."

"I bet he's somewhere, hitting his head on the ceiling *right now*."

A STRANGER ARRIVES IN KEY LARGO

A woman who has never seen the ocean arrives in Key Largo.

She drives faster than the posted speed limit, keeping vigilant watch through the rearview mirror.

The woman saw the Gulf Of Mexico as she crossed from Alabama into the Florida panhandle, and again somewhere near Tampa, but the water was dark and solemn, as was the weather. She continued south until Miami ushered her into the blinding summer sun. The woman finally saw glimpses of sparkling turquoise water through the slim gaps between the mangroves while traveling the barren expanse of the 18-mile stretch. But she is not here to see the ocean and should not revel in such things. Shame floods her cheeks every time she smiles at the water.

She is not used to this heat, and she shoves her hand against the window crank, but it goes no further. A few inches of fresh air is all she'll be granted on this journey.

A strange smell fills the car. Something like oil, something like cut grass. She's never smelled anything like it. And by the time she stops for gas midway through town, she realizes the stench is everywhere. This is just the way it smells here: brine and asphalt and seaweed and scorched mangroves.

The woman asks the gas attendant how many miles to Key West, but her tongue is thickly accented, and the man appraises her for a long, silent moment before waving her off.

She pays for the gas without another word and slides back into her car.

When she stops for lunch in an hour, she will again ask someone about Key West, so she practices her English. Her words do not fail her, only her pronunciation.

The woman pulls out of the gas station, and the salty air whips her blonde hair into a fury; she pulls the strands from her throat.

In the back seat, her suitcase thumps to one side as she makes a heavy turn back onto US1.

On her dashboard is a Polaroid of a young man. The photo was taken some years ago, when he was still a teenager. The boy does not smile. His haunted gaze pleads at her through the emulsion, keeping her focused on the road as she drives south. When the wind snatches the photo, hurtling it toward the open window, the woman leaps to catch it, nearly steering her car into a roadside bait stand. She tucks the Polaroid against the passenger seat where it's safer.

She grips the wheel as she passes over a narrow bridge and into Tavernier.

The water is the color of jade, coating the sandbar below, glistening like a melted candle. The horizon reflects the sun and the clouds so flawlessly that it's hard to tell where the ocean ends and land begins. Like a picture in a glossy magazine. Like a watercolor painting.

She tries not to notice.

A MISEDUCATION OF SPIRITS AND SEX

My street is a long one, with room for at least ten houses on either side, but there are only two. The trees grow thick and tall, Slash pines and palm trees and coconut trees all dueling for light. When the sun is low in the sky, the shadows create a tunnel, keeping the air moist and cool.

As I near our apartment complex, I pedal faster and jerk my body upward, hopping the ledge of the walkway. Our door is all the way at the end and up the stairs, so I have five apartment-lengths of wheeled freedom. The salty air whooshes by my ears like whispers of a conch shell.

I want to let go of the handlebar, spread my arms, and close my eyes, like Travis Misker does on his way to school. But he's a boy, so he's braver than me.

The faster I go, the tighter I clench the handlebar.

As I near the stairs, I veer left, coasting toward the dock where I hop off and nudge the kickstand.

Though I should be thinking about the new school year or planning what Jimmie and I will do with our last days of summer, all I can think is: Eddie, I'm on my way!

I open the front door, hoping for an empty kitchen and stealthy escape. But there's dad, smiling down at me.

I rush to my bedroom, but his voice barrels through my door, as if there were no door at all. "You and Jimmie have fun?"

"Yeah."

"You go crawfishin'?"

"Yeah."

I shrug out of my clothes because Eddie deserves better than wet, fishy overalls. I overturn my drawers, seeking my dark jeans. The tight ones that are high on the calves.

"You goin' back out, pumpkin?"

"Yeah."

I wait for dad to demand more answers, but it seems the interrogation is over.

I smell my armpits and cringe. I don't have perfume, but there are incense cones on my dresser. I crush one between my fingers and buff the chunks into my wrist and under my arms. Most of it falls to the terrazzo, and I pulverize the evidence beneath my foot, kicking it under the bed.

I roll up my sleeves and tie the front panels into a knot so that if I reach above my head, Eddie will get a peek of my belly.

As a final touch, I choose a gold owl necklace, fastening it around my neck. Little nuggets of rubies shimmer in its eyes.

I admire my reflection in the mirror, careful to look away before those familiar shadows form on my chin and my face begins to melt.

And then it's time to go.

My heart races.

Dad will take one look at me and *just know*.

That's what dads do.

I crack open my door, anticipating more cross-examination, but dad is already in his study, and I quickly make my escape.

I skid to a stop at the Botel, spotting Poppy, Eddie's little sister, playing in the grass.

I expect her to run over and hug my knees like she usually does, but she's preoccupied today.

"What have you got?" I ask.

"Wessy Wessy!"

Poppy's still learning her words, and what she really means is *Betsy Wetsy*. Apparently, I speak preschooler.

"And Play-doh, too?"

Poppy grins, returning to her growing pile of blue, yellow, and white lumpy things.

Eddie must've been watching from his window because he's already walking toward me. I want him to run over and scoop me into his arms, twirl me around. But I know he won't.

"Hey," he says.

"Hey," I say, forcing my sloppy grin into a normal position.

Eddie's taller than me, which is unusual for boys. He's so tall he could pick me up, throw me over his shoulder and run away with me right now. But I know he won't.

Eddie has a backpack over one shoulder, which makes him look like he's heading off to school. He's wearing gray pants with a white V neck tee shirt, and I try to imagine him pulling it on, stretching his arms, adjusting the tuck—all those secret rituals no one gets to see.

"Take your sister," his mother hollers from the dock before adding, "Hi, Danni."

"Hi, Mrs. Green!"

Eddie whispers, "Follow me," and he runs, clutching the backpack as it slips from his arm.

"Eddie, take your sister!"

He grabs my hand.

Oh my God.

His hand is so big. His palm is sweaty and strong, and all the other things a boy's hand should be.

He could bend down and let me climb onto him, piggyback-style, my arms draped around his neck, face buried in his hair.

But I know he won't.

"Eddie!" Poppy cries.

"Edward Green, get back here!"

That's the last thing I hear as we near my bike.

I hop onto my handlebar as he takes the seat, and I don't even find it funny that Eddie's pedaling down US1 on a purple bike with rainbow streamers and a white wicker basket. I find it wonderful.

"Where are we going?" I ask.

"The haunted house. I have a present for you."

I squeak a little and hope he didn't hear me. If he did, I'll blame it on a seagull.

I smile into the wind and let go of the handlebar, spreading my arms wide, just like Travis Misker on his way to school.

With Eddie behind me, I can be so brave.

We pass over the Boot Key Bridge and pedal down a dirt road lined with mangroves. I've taken Eddie to the haunted house before, so he knows the way. He once told me he can see it from his bedroom window at the Botel, and that on some nights, he sees lights flickering on and off. I told him there's no electricity, so it's not possible. He told me it's the ghosts, and it's hard to argue with that.

The trees and mangroves grow sparse until the ocean suddenly opens up before us.

"Your water is so blue."

Your water. He says it like it's mine. Like I've allowed him to see a super secret part of myself. Maybe I have.

This water birthed me. I've swam in this water, swallowed this water, peed in this water. Somehow, Eddie has summed up my entire existence in one short sentence: *Your water is so blue.*

I want to say, Yes, it is, and I'm showing you all of me and please don't go home and I love you.

But instead I say, "Yeah."

Eddie makes a sharp turn, and right there in front of us is the haunted house. I hop off the handlebar, and Eddie drops my bike to the ground.

The old mansion is unlike any other house on the islands. Three stories tall, and abandoned for generations. It's a giant cube with sloping supports on each corner, covered floor to ceiling with native coral. Pitted and jagged, the coral is like calloused skin, curving and wrapping around old bones. The roof is rimmed with individual coral spikes pointing toward the sky. A primitive fence against prying eyes.

"C'mon," he says, so I c'mon.

I follow him through the arch that once had a door as he dashes up the crumbling staircase and leans through an opening that once had a window. He's so close to me that I can smell his cologne.

This is the perfect spot for our first kiss, so when Eddie points out how small a lizard looks from up here, I want to kick him in the shin.

Kiss me.

Below us is a small strip of beach with a few inches of water lapping across the sand. Our own private ocean.

Kiss me. Kiss me. Kiss me.

"Look," he says, pointing to a seagull coasting toward land. "It's a bird, it's a plane…" Eddie chuckles as if he's said something truly funny.

I've never been kissed by a boy my own age. I've only been kissed by a grownup, and I need to know if it's any different.

This, right here, is my deepest, darkest secret. If my parents, or anyone else, ever found out, I'd surely die from shame.

Eddie *has* to kiss me today. I need a new definition of romance. I need a boyfriend I don't have to hide from the world. I need someone who will love me and protect me. I need someone to think I'm beautiful. I just…need.

KISSMEKISSMEKISSME.

But Eddie wanders to another window, captivated by something below, so I stomp back downstairs, where the desolation matches my mood.

Dad once told me that long before I was born, a man murdered his wife in the old mansion and her ghost lives on, roaming the grounds at night.

Sharon Wolinski's dad told her that the mansion was built on an ancient Indian burial ground, and their spirits terrorize anyone who tries to live here.

But Scott Waller's mom said it was a gas explosion that killed that poor man and his wife all those years ago. A terrible accident, and nothing more.

As I trace the blackened coral walls to tidepools of charcoal on the ceiling, I realize Scott Waller's mom is probably right, if a little short on imagination.

I turn when I hear Eddie bounding down the steps, two at a time. Finally.

"I have a present for you, remember?" he says, sloughing the backpack from his shoulders. "It's far out."

"Close your eyes and open your hands," he says, wrestling something from the depths of his bag.

My grin practically splits my face in two.

Eyes closed.

Hands open.

He places an object in my grasp, and I can tell immediately that it's a book.

"Open 'em."

I look down but can't read the words. They're in Spanish or Russian or—

"It's French," he says.

I turn the book over, but the back is in French. And the spine too.

But then I see the cover. An illustrated man cradles a woman who is losing her dress.

Oh.

The woman on the cover is nearly exposed, and I raise an eyebrow at Eddie.

"It's *The Kama Sutra*," he whispers, and though I don't know what that means, his smile tells me I won't be disappointed.

Eddie didn't kiss me today, but he sent me home with *The Kama Sutra*, which is almost as good. He said he swiped it from his mom's book collection, and he talked about it as though I'd heard of it. As though *everyone* had heard of it. I nodded along and pretended to be impressed when he looked impressed. I giggled when he giggled. All the normal stuff.

I sit on my bed, clutching the book to my chest like foreign treasure.

There are large bodies of text I'll never be able to read, but that's okay. It's the illustrations that hold me captive. Figures dancing, laying, sprawling, standing, bending. I've never seen anything like it. Women's breasts are ringed, protruding, their legs spread open in a way that grosses me out and makes me nervous and warm all at the same time. And it's not just women— men are also exposed, their penises hanging low, swinging high, rigid as a snorkel. The men, too, are leaning, arcing, suspending, contorting. Sometimes there are a man and woman together. Sometimes two women, painstakingly recorded in paint, tongues plunging into each other's mouths. Fingers in places. *Toes* in places. I'm horrified. And I can't look away.

Eddie was right. This is *far out.*

I'm so engrossed in the pages that I fail to notice my mother standing in the doorway, running a towel across a glass, until she says, "What are we reading tonight?"

I'm paralyzed. My fingers grip the cover so hard it bends backward in my hands as she steps closer, closer still.

A handful of lies cross my tongue: Nancy Drew, Good Housekeeping, the Dictionary.

I'm terrible at this.

I keep the cover bent so she won't see the front image. Maybe she's never even heard of *The Kama Sutra.* I'm likely the first person in the entire Florida Keys to receive this outsider knowledge.

But then mom gasps, and I realize what's in my lap. The cover may be folded over, and the text may be in French, but the illustration needs no translation.

On the page, a woman leans backward over a cushion, her most intimate parts spread open for the man pushing into her while also fondling a second woman crouched beside him.

Mom shrieks, but it's all in slow motion. She calls out, "Richard!", but dad's already gone, wherever it is that he goes. Fishing or drinking.

The glass and hand towel are in slow motion as they leave her grasp, twisting and spinning through my bedroom.

The book is in slow motion as my mother plucks it from my hand and flings it through the door.

Her open palm draws closer to my face.

And then she does it. The unthinkable. She slaps me. And nothing is in slow motion any longer. It's utterly frozen.

We regard each other in silence—me, stunned, clawing at my burning cheek; mom, trembling, eyes wide, pushing her knuckles against her lips. Neither of us know what to do, what to say.

I would never hit her back, but mom needs to be punished, and dad isn't here to rescue me.

So I let the tears fall.

My cheek *does* hurt, but I'll tend to that later. Right now, this performance is all for her.

I sob and pull a pillow to my chest. I bury my face into the sheets like a child. I curl into a ball in the middle of my bed, cradling my cheek like an injured little girl. And I stare at her. I want her to see the tears. I want to make sure that for as long as she lives, mom never forgets this moment.

Only when she rushes wordlessly from my room, shutting the door swiftly behind her, do I cry for real. Even though I'm not a little girl anymore, lying in a ball still feels comforting, so I stay that way for a long while, until my tears deliver me to sleep.

A STRANGER ARRIVES IN KEY WEST

A woman who has never been fishing arrives in Key West to rent a boat.

The woman parks in a sand lot near Mallory Square and hurries toward the water. She weaves through throngs of people staring idly at the setting sun.

Tied to the docks are charter boats—speed boats, sailboats, yachts. It does not matter to the woman which boat she rents. But as she rushes from dock to dock, encountering only empty vessels with no captains, she begins to worry.

The sun dips below the ocean, and the crowd on the Square erupts into applause. There are couples holding hands, families dragging limp children behind them, and a group of young people twirling, kissing, and calling for Atlantis to rise.

The woman arrives at the final dock where a fishing boat stacked with traps and poles sways with the waves. She knocks on a small door, but there's no answer. She turns back toward the parking lot, preparing to weave through the crowds one last time, when she hears a voice behind her.

"Can I help you, Miss?"

The woman spins to find a tall, lanky man standing before her. His skin is slick with sweat and salt, and he chews a reed of something she cannot identify.

"I need to rent a boat."

She practiced this line for the last twenty miles of her drive, and her pronunciation is perfect.

The fisherman studies her and looks around.

"Whatcha fishin' for, Miss?"

"Please," she says, "I need to rent a boat."

"I heard ya." He appraises the line of docks and all their varieties of crafts. "But what kind of boat do you need?"

"Tonight," she says.

The fisherman leans into his heels and scratches his abdomen. "It's mighty late. We best be off in the morning. You meet me here at quarter to nine, and I'll get you on the water. You visitin' long, Miss?"

"Please," she says, rummaging through her bag and withdrawing the cash she saved especially for this moment. She hopes it is enough. "Tonight."

The fisherman considers the roll of bills in her hand and whistles through his teeth. He looks to a bar just beyond Mallory Square. Already, the chairs are filling up, and a warm amber glow floods from the open shutters. The sound of a lone guitar echoes from somewhere within. The woman knows there's a drink waiting for him in the bar; it could be in his fist in less than five minutes. But the stack is thick in her hand and could buy the man a hundred drinks tomorrow.

He leans back, staring down at her through waterlogged lashes. He accepts her payment, counting the bills, one by one.

"Tonight it is, boss. Let's get you on the water."

THE CALM BEFORE THE STORM

It seems the old lighthouse has always been abandoned, standing like a broken statue on the coast just past The Armada, dad's favorite bar.

Eddie balances on the coral as he walks ahead of me. Unlike us Conchs, he isn't used to the uneven footing, and more than once, he's had to save Poppy from a fall. Eddie's gentle with her, and she gazes up at her big brother with adoring eyes.

"It's on the other side," I call to him. "The door faces the water."

The tide is rising, splashing the coral with surfer's waves more suited to California than Florida.

The walls of the lighthouse are rough, calloused by textured peaks. Immortal fingerprints of the men who built it. The paint has long ago been eaten away by salt, but the stripes are still visible, like palm frond shadows slashed across the gray.

We wait for a break in the waves before funneling through the lighthouse door. Inside, everything echoes, even our breaths.

Eddie bounds up the staircase, and I bend down to Poppy's height. When she smiles, her face turns redder than rouge, and her lips curl into her gums, showing off all her baby teeth.

"Don't go fast like your brother," I say. "Hold on to the railing."

The steep spiral staircase ascends like a nautilus shell above our heads. The walls were once green, but the plaster peeled away over the years and now lolls from the concrete like moldy tongues.

Eddie gasps, and Poppy rushes up the remaining steps to catch up with her big brother. I take the last two steps in one stride.

The glass of the lighthouse bulb is enormous. Held in place by metal rods, the glass bulges like couch cushions, facets sheared onto every curve. Eddie whistles as he runs his fingers across the design.

On the balcony, there are no walls, only a narrow walkway and guardrail around the giant bulb. I keep my hand on Poppy's shoulder so she doesn't go sliding off the edge and into the coral below.

Eddie and I don't have much time left together. I need him to kiss me before he goes home. Poppy's cute, but she's ruining my last chance at romance.

I sit beside the bulb and Poppy tucks in beside me.

"Tomorrow's my birthday," I say.

"Happy early birthday," Eddie says, still gazing out to sea.

I have to ask him something, but it feels like a girl asking a boy out on a date, which is against the natural order of things.

"I'm having a party at my house tomorrow," I say. "Can you come?"

"You told your folks about me?"

"I'll say I know you from school."

Eddie chuckles. "We can't. Dad's renting a boat. We're snorkeling for our last day."

Like I need reminding.

"I love boats," I say, staring at his mouth.

"I love snorkeling," I say, staring at his neck.

He's not getting it, so I stand and join him at the railing.

"Will I see you at all before you leave?"

The look on his face says it all.

"You're a real groovy chick," he says.

I'm groovy!

"A real fox."

I'm a fox!

"And if you lived in Ohio, you'd be my girl, for sure."

I nearly fall over.

"You still have my address, right?"

I know exactly where it is—folded in half and tucked beneath my record player, where no one will find it. Lined, yellow paper, torn from the upper right corner of a pad. His handwriting in blue pen, the words embossed from his heavy hand. Some of his letters are loopy, like a girl's. He forgot to dot an *i*.

Kiss me. Kiss me. Kiss me.

"Actually," Eddie says with a smile, "I think you should be my girl right now."

He towers above me, his face becoming serious.

It's finally going to happen. I just know it.

I can sense it in the way the air changes. I close my eyes and wait. *This* will be the best birthday present ever.

I wait.

And wait.

"I gotta go potty," Poppy says.

She's not cute anymore.

"That's my cue," Eddie says, helping his little sister stand.

She toddles down the steps, holding onto Eddie's pants. I kick the railing, following behind, one step at a time and slower than before.

When we emerge in the sunlight, Poppy hugs my knees.

"You can come by in the morning," Eddie says. "Dad rents the boat at 10, so—"

"I'll be there."

When Eddie turns away, the smile melts from my face.

I'm trying to figure out how to make the day go by faster when Eddie sprints back to me, leaving Poppy alone on the coral.

"She could fall!" I call out, but Eddie runs fast and is suddenly standing above me.

"I forgot something," he says.

"What did you forget?"

Eddie grasps my face, pulls me closer.

Oh.

And then his lips are on my lips, between my lips. My feet are liquid, spilling through the fissures in the coral. My throat opens as though gasping to steal his breath. The scent of his cologne is all around me, his sweat. I feel every individual tastebud. A sheet of warmth falls from my temple, flooding my skin.

It's everything I wanted it to be and more. Kissing a boy is way different from kissing a grownup. I know that now. The mechanics of a kiss are the same, but the way my body melts against his is unlike anything I've experienced. Like I am pudding and he is pudding. Like we are salty ocean water.

I hope he never stops kissing me.

～

Richard Quinn enters The Armada, and for a brief moment, the interior is aglow with sunlight before the door closes behind him, returning the room to darkness. But there's enough light to spot his friend at the bar.

"Andy," Richard bellows.

"Ishmael," Andy says, his voice quieter than usual. Slower, too. Andy's been here a while.

Moments later, the bartender appears, setting a frothing beer and shot of warm whiskey in front of Richard, who nods his thanks.

The men sit in silence, pretending to gaze past the liquor bottles and out the small port windows that merely hint at the abandoned lighthouse and vast ocean beyond.

The Armada is steeped in colors too serious for tourists. This is a locals' bar. What isn't wrapped in leather or cast in bronze, is painted maroon, brown, or left as raw wood. The seat fabric is sticky with boat wax and spilt drinks. It's perfect.

Richard pulls a cigar from his pocket, brown and sweet as honey, and chews the tip away, spitting it into an ashtray. He reaches for a box of matches on the counter, and the smell quickly fills the space between them. It's enough to get Andy talking.

"Cuban?" Andy asks.

Richard pulls the smoke on either side of his tongue.

"How do you get your hands on those?"

Richard considers his drunk friend and smiles. "You don't want to know."

"I imagine I don't."

Near the end of the bar sit two men that Richard recognizes, but doesn't know by name. A rarity. To his other side sits Gabe, Marathon's mailman, draped across the counter, his face tucked beneath his elbows. Three empty shot glasses before him. Richard anticipates an empty mailbox today.

On the far side of the inebriated mailman is a woman Richard has never before seen. Not a local. Cute. Thick auburn hair. Lips as brown as his cigar, likely as sweet. She orders two coffees to go, apologetically, as though worried she's in the wrong place. The bartender stumbles over his words but eventually tells her he can brew some, though it may be a few minutes. The bartender is slow to turn away, and Richard can't blame him. When the woman shifts her hair behind her shoulder, Richard spots white lace peeking out from beneath her shirt.

She turns as though summoned, and when she smiles, Richard Quinn slips his wedding ring off his finger and into his pocket.

Richard declines a second round from the bartender and returns his attention to Celeste.

He compliments the simplicity of her earrings, and when he learns she's studying to become a teacher, he regales her with war stories: students smoking in the bathroom or necking in the gymnasium. Celeste is captivated as he tells her about the Valkyrie, and deep-sea fishing at night. How he saved a father and son from the harbor at Key Colony Beach after a terrible boating accident under the Vaca Cut Bridge. And he slips easily into a monologue of *Moby Dick*, Chapter One.

Richard does not tell stories about his wife or daughter.

While explaining to Celeste how he uses constellations to guide his boat to shore, Andy nearly chokes on his beer, and Richard kicks his friend's chair from behind.

"Well, Ishmael, it's time I took off. I'll catch up with you later," Andy says, waving his fingers through the smoky air, "under the stars."

Andy hobbles—somewhat efficiently—toward the front door. Richard would've offered his assistance if Celeste hadn't asked him if he also knows Chapter 2, ignoring the coffees set down before her.

"Of course," Richard says. "I know the whole book by heart." He pauses for effect. "But I'll never share more than the first chapter."

"And why is that?" she purrs, the steam from the untouched coffees moistening her cheek.

Any other man would stop here, suggest they go some place where they can be alone. But Richard Quinn is not *any other man*. His knee may be nestled between her legs, but his desires lie elsewhere. And he almost has her.

Richard moves toward her ear, forcing his breath over her collarbone. "Always leave them wanting more."

Celeste lets out a heady breath, as if he's caressed her, kissed her, pushed his weight into her, though he's done none of those things.

She clears her throat and buffs a palm across her neck to banish the goosebumps. Her grin is different now. Crooked. *Honest.*

Almost there.

"Well, Richard Quinn," she says, "I'll be in town for a few more days. Maybe you could take me fishing. As long as I don't get too wet."

Richard touches her ear, spinning the small stud earring, and her breath catches in her throat.

"Maybe I can change your mind about that."

Sometimes it's too easy. Not even fun.

"I wish I didn't have to go," she says, fanning her flushed cheeks. "I think you might be the most interesting man I've ever met."

And with this, Richard's heart slows as if medicated. *There it is.*

He suspects she may lean in for a kiss, so he brings the cigar to his lips.

Celeste slumps with disappointment before pulling a pen from her pocket. She scribbles on a napkin, folding it like a secret. "This is me."

Richard presses the napkin flat on the bar.

Seaside Motel, Room 14.

Below that, the motel's direct line. He recognizes the number. He's seen it before.

"You'll have to beat me off with a stick," he says.

Celeste plucks her drinks from the bar and stumbles toward the door as if drunk, though all she ordered was coffee.

Richard spins back to the bar and its deceptive port windows. He smooths the wrinkles of the napkin and snuffs his cigar against the room number before sliding it into his pocket.

When he gets home, Richard will tuck the napkin into the bottom drawer of his desk with all the others. But he won't call Celeste. He never calls any of them. He won't knock on her motel door or take her fishing. There's nothing more she can offer him.

Richard replaces his wedding ring and walks out of The Armada.

A STRANGER SEEKS A PILOT

A woman who has never celebrated the sunset pulls a sheet over her tired eyes to block the morning light.

Already the town has grown boisterous, as if nothing bad ever happens here. Maybe it doesn't. Maybe she will stay forever.

When the woman closes her eyes, she recalls the night before. The hard plank of the ocean, black and vast. The sky, too, had been black. The only lights were the stars reflected on the surface. She had not anticipated such an absence of sound.

Once she told the man she wasn't there to fish, and after she faked poor English, he stopped flirting. The woman stood on the bow of the boat and asked him to show her Cuba. He pointed and said, "About 90 miles that way." When she asked the man to show her Key West, he pointed in the opposite direction. "That way, about 10 miles or so."

Perfect.

The woman studied the water, paying special attention to the height of the waves. She scanned the horizon for other signs of land, ocean liners, cruise ships, official vessels of any kind.

The man grew anxious and suspicious. He asked questions she did not want to answer. So the woman told him she was ready to return, and he sped off toward Mallory Square.

The woman knew she would have to find a boat captain and pilot upon her arrival in Key West, but as she watched the skinny man struggle to turn the wheel against the whitecaps, she began to doubt her plan.

Maybe nothing would go right.

Maybe she'd come all this way for nothing.

The woman turns in her bed, unable to find sleep. She throws the sheet from her body, walks to the open window, and breathes in the surf. On the street below, a musician blows into a wind instrument unlike any she's seen before. Another bangs his hands on a steel drum, decorated with bright red streamers. A couple walks by, stopping to dance and spin around each other. The musicians nod their approval.

The woman runs her tongue over fuzzy teeth and pushes her fist to her forehead. She lugs a satchel from her suitcase and stumbles into the bathroom, tucking the Polaroid of the young man into the frame of the mirror so she doesn't lose focus.

Her mission to find a suitable boat captain has been unsuccessful so far. Perhaps she'll have better luck finding a pilot. Not far from her motel is a small airport. She will start there.

THE END OF EVERYTHING

I wake at 7:10 am, with plenty of time to spend with Eddie before their snorkeling trip on his last day here.

I dress quickly and grab my swimsuit, in case Eddie invites me along, and tiptoe through the kitchen, past a new electric skillet—in glossy cream—displayed on the counter like a bouquet of flowers, before slipping out the front door.

No shoes. No need.

The sun is a mere crescent along the horizon, and the color is unmistakable: red. The ocean is aglow, more blood than water.

Red sky at morning, sailors take warning.

I continue toward The Sundry Store, weaving across the center line like a braid.

When I buy myself a chocolate bar, planting a nickel on the counter, the clerks scolds, "Not an ideal breakfast for a growing young woman." He lets me off the hook when I tell him it's my birthday.

I pause outside The Armada to lick chocolate from my fingertips, but it's no use—I'll be sticky all day. But at least I'll taste like candy when Eddie kisses me again.

I veer into the parking lot to find Eddie standing by his folks on the dock, a rental boat already roped to a post.

"Dad got the boat early," Eddie says.

"Danni!" Poppy yells, wrapping her spindly arms around my knees.

I look to them all, one by one, unsure of what to say. I want to yell at them for being early. I want Eddie to stay onshore and go to the haunted house with me, walk on the flats with me, *anything* but leave. A year will go by before I'll see him again. *A year!*

Everyone stares at me, so I spit out, "Today's my birthday."

Mrs. Green clasps her hands together. "That's wonderful. How old are you today?"

For a moment, I forget.

"Danni?"

"Fourteen."

"Well, isn't that something. Poppy will be four next month."

Poppy beams at me, shows me four fingers, and mouths the word *four* like it's a secret she's keeping from the world.

Mr. Green muscles a heavy cooler down the ramp of the Botel, tucking it between the boat seats. Already he's red and sweating. The sunlight reflecting off the water will not be kind to him today. That'll be his punishment for leaving early. But it's not good enough. Not even close.

Eddie pulls me through the parking lot and sits on the curb. I join him and stare at the rocks. He owes me an explanation.

"I'm sorry I can't come to your party," he says.

My party. I nearly forgot.

I want to take his hand, but don't. I want to grab his face and kiss him, but don't. That's *his* job.

I kick a rock in his direction. "What about later?"

Eddie just shakes his head.

I push myself from the curb and try to wipe the dirt from my palms, but it sticks to my hands in chocolate bar shaped blotches.

"Danni," he says, but I'm already walking toward my bike.

"It was nice meeting you this summer, Danni!" Mrs. Green calls out. "I hope you have a wonderful birthday."

I pretend not to hear her as I swing my legs over my bike and head for home, punching my swimsuit into the corner of my basket where I don't have to see it.

The bathroom is a good place to hide. No one knocks on the door. No one asks what's wrong.

But today, my reflection offers no reprieve. Those familiar shadows have begun to stain my chin. My forehead swells. My eyes droop.

I don't understand why people say I'm pretty. Lying to kids should be punishable by law.

I'm deformed, practically a monster.

It's no wonder Eddie didn't ask me to go snorkeling.

It's no wonder Eddie doesn't want to come to my party.

I turn my face from side to side, trying to buff the redness from my eyes, as if sorrow can be wiped away so easily.

Eddie will go back to Ohio and tell his friends all about the hideous freak he toyed with on his summer vacation. They probably already know. They're probably in on it.

The razor glints from the ledge of the sink, and even though I promised myself I'd never do this again, I snatch it into my fist.

I roll the cuff of my shorts into my hip and press my thumb into the scars hashed across my thigh like a game of hopscotch. The welts blanch and tighten.

There's an invisible line that needs to be crossed when you hold a razor in your hand. When you bring it closer to your flesh. When you're injured somewhere deep inside, and nothing else will soothe the wound.

I imagine it's like a man on the ledge of a building, one foot in the air, pushing his weight from the wall. Doubt in the moment before he leans forward. And a nanosecond of time when he knows *this* is his last chance to back out, change his mind, before he freefalls toward the pavement. That's *his* invisible line, and this is mine.

I clutch the razor tighter.

It hovers above my leg.

Closer to the ledge of the building.

Closer still.

And I begin to push away from the wall.

There's a knock at the front door, and I freeze as though caught.

"Jimmie!" dad says. "Come in, young man."

Blood only moments from spilling.

"She's in the bathroom, but she'll be out any minute. Are you excited for school? Go crawfishin' today?"

Dad's voice is like a tether. A board I can walk on to find my way home. And I return the razor to the sink where it belongs.

"How are your folks?" dad continues. "My, you've gotten taller."

As I listen to dad bind Jimmie in a web of questions and observations, I straighten my shorts, secret concealed, and wonder what mom did with The Kama Sutra. Did she throw it away, or did she save it for a private late night read?

I'll never know. The mysteries of The Kama Sutra will be forever filed away with all the other things we don't speak of in this house.

I open the door and spot cake on the dining room table, and a large glass bowl, punch tiding from side to side.

I wave to Jimmie, who looks uncomfortable with dad towering above him.

"Hiya," I say.

"Hiya."

Mom chimes in from the kitchen. "I used my hand mixer."

We all stare at her like she's scribbled a message in hieroglyphics.

She holds up the pink enameled appliance, proof of her domesticity.

"That's wonderful, my love," dad says.

Mom beams and returns to the sink, satisfied.

Jimmie hands me a wrapped package and it's the best thing that's happened all day.

I tear away the paper, and in my grasp is a new record with three beautiful women framed in blue squares.

The Supremes. *A' Go-Go.*

"This one's my favorite," he says, tapping a title on the back that reads, "Hang On Sloopy."

We hop from the couch and put the vinyl on my record player. I find the groove for "Hang On Sloopy" on the first try.

We're only one verse into the song when there's a knock on the front door.

I peer outside my bedroom to see Andy enter the kitchen, and I duck behind the wall.

"Who's that?" Jimmie asks.

"No one."

"Is he mean or somethin'?"

I consider this. "No."

Jimmie arcs over me for a better view. "He looks nice."

"I don't want Andy here," I whisper.

"Why not?"

I kick the wall, hoping the music muffles the sound.

"I just don't."

"Then I don't want him here, either."

I smile at Jimmie.

That's what best friends are for.

There's a strange vibe in the air as we gather around the dining room table for cake.

"Make a wish, Daniella," Andy says as I lean over the candle.

"I already did."

"Take your time! Make it a good one," he says. "You only turn fourteen once."

Mom and dad nod in agreement, so I close my eyes and make the same wish I did a moment ago. But I wish slowly, with feeling, that Andy will go home. And then I blow out the candle.

Andy hands me a present, and Jimmie leans over the table to get a better view as I peel away the paper.

"Neato," he says.

In my hands is a Troll Doll.

Oh.

The doll's puffy-cheeked grin is pressed against the packaging, tragically optimistic in its confinement.

Jimmie snatches it from my hands. "Lucky!"

The adults chuckle as mom slices into her homemade cake.

"I'm glad you came," dad says, clapping Andy on the back. "Where's Dottie?"

"She's not feeling well. She sends her love." Andy slurps loudly from his punch, which is darker than my own—he must've added something extra.

When Jimmie announces he has to be home for supper, I walk him to his bike, parked near the dock.

"When does Eddie leave?"

"Tomorrow morning."

Jimmie tries to look sad for me. I appreciate it.

He nudges my shoulder. "Bya."

"Bya."

I watch him pedal away until he's out of sight.

When I return to the apartment, I slip past mom, dad and Andy, and into my bedroom.

"Don't forget your doll," dad says.

My doll. Like a little girl.

"And don't forget to thank Andy."

Andy smiles and opens his arms for a hug. He smells of salt and dead skin, but just beneath that is the familiar spice of his Yardley aftershave.

Once released, I hurry to my room and shut the door, tossing the Troll Doll into the corner.

My bedroom is a time capsule of my childhood, filled with things long forgotten. Mr. Potato Head, topped with a hearty dollop of dust. Old Barbies, hair lopped, lips still a glossy pink, holding strong through years of neglect. My collection of Troll Dolls eager to welcome a new acquisition, as though a fresh face may reignite my interest.

Sometimes I feel lost in somebody else's life. These items belong to a little kid.

The sky outside my window is already blurring with shades of cotton candy, and from the kitchen, I hear chairs moving and voices saying, Goodbye, and, Thank you, and, The cake was delicious, Miriam.

And then Andy is gone.

I crash onto my bed and wrap my arms tightly around myself. An imaginary hug from Eddie.

I don't hate Andy. Not really. Nothing was his fault. Things are just a little weird between us now.

Because last year, Andy was my secret boyfriend.

The telephone rings, and mom answers. "Quinn residence."

Silence.

"Just one moment. Richard, telephone."

Dad's heavy footsteps pad into the kitchen. When he greets the caller, it sounds serious.

"How long ago did this happen, Peter? Who've they got on this?"

"Richard?"

"I'm on my way. Tell them to stay put."

I rush into the living room as dad snatches his boat jacket from the hook near the door.

He's heading out to sea! Another adventure, just the two of us!

I rush to my room to grab my windbreaker. It can be chilly on the water at night, and who knows how late we'll be. Dad receives calls like this all the time. If something happens on the water, *everyone* knows to call Richard Quinn.

Dad's eyes are pained when he says, "Not this time, pumpkin."

And I see in his face that the matter is settled.

Dad slips his boat keys into his pocket and looks to mom.

"There's been an accident at the Vaca Cut Bridge."

"That's terrible," she says.

It *is* terrible. I've seen what can happen under that bridge.

"A local?" mom asks.

"A family here for the summer," dad says, shaking his head. "We shouldn't rent boats to visitors. They don't know our waters."

Dad's right—tourists are usually the only ones to find trouble on the water.

"They've been staying at the Botel. Hit the bridge on their way back in. The Greens, or something."

Dad's voice is farther away than it was a moment ago.

"I might be awhile, Miriam. They washed up at the harbor on Key Colony Beach. They're okay, but—" He coughs, and his voice cracks. "Well, most of them. Their little girl was taken out to sea."

I pedal my bike down the long walkway of our complex. I want to pound on all the doors, beg someone to tell me it's a bad joke.

I never warned Eddie about the bridge.

Why didn't I warn Eddie about the bridge?

This didn't have to happen.

I could've stopped it.

If Poppy dies, it's all my fault.

My wheels hit a rock, and it takes all my strength to keep the handlebar under control.

The sky's darkening. It'll rain soon, and I beg it to fall on me now, flood our street and wash me away.

By the time I reach US1, I'm out of breath, and have nowhere to go, so I spin my bike around and stare down the long road back to the apartment.

Headlights approach, and the car rolls to a stop beside me. Dad cranks down the window.

"Why'd you run out in such a hurry, pumpkin?"

I open my mouth, but words fail me. I want to tell dad that the little girl he's hoping to rescue is my boyfriend's sister. That my guts feel like they're tearing apart. That little girls can't die. And if she *is* dead, I don't understand that either, because we don't just disappear. *Poof.* We had to be *somewhere*.

Dad nods as if I've said this aloud and offers his hand through the open window. I take it.

"We must be grateful for every moment of our lives. That's what you have to tell yourself in times like these."

His words are meaningless.

"I've gotta get to the marina. You head on home. Looks like we're due for a storm. Some timing, huh?"

Some timing.

Then dad turns onto the highway, his red taillights vanishing from view.

I hope water takes me one day.

No sickness, no pain, no terrible accident.

Just beautiful, peaceful drowning.

I said this to dad when I was just a little girl.

I don't know why I said it. I don't even know if it's true.

We stood side by side on the bow of the Valkyrie, gazing across a sandbar. It was a sunny day, low tide. A Horseshoe crab jostled across the sand.

Dad's eyes glazed, and a smile tugged at the corners of his mouth. He put his large palm atop my head, dwarfing me.

I giggled beneath dad's heavy hand that day, on the bow of the Valkyrie, and said no more. I didn't have to. His grip on my head told me everything I needed to know.

I will never drown, because dad will always save me.

And I know dad will save Poppy too, so I wipe the tears from my cheeks and pedal toward home as rain begins to spill from the sky.

A STRANGER AND A PINK SQUIRREL

A woman who has never been drunk orders another Pink Squirrel.

The bartender splashes her cup with liquids of pink and white and snatches the cash from her hand before she can count it one more time.

She'd wanted something strong but made the mistake of asking for something sweet. A Pink Squirrel was what she got. Three drinks later, they're finally getting the job done. And she can't deny it—they're delicious.

The woman spotted this bar yesterday, upon returning from the barren strips of the Key West Airport. There had been a few open hangars, a couple of planes, and a man who pretended not to speak English. When she spoke to him in her native tongue, he pretended not to speak German either.

The woman's vision is fuzzy, and she rubs her eyes, spilling her drink onto her lap.

"Everything okay, little lady?"

She swings around to find a large man leaning over her. She can smell all six feet of him.

"Little lady?" she scoffs. "Who do you think I am?"

"Well, I don't know who you are, but I'm willin' to find out."

He smiles, and she's surprised he has all his teeth.

"Where's that sweet little accent from?" he asks.

She peers across a pinched nose, shaking her head. "You have not heard of it."

He laughs. "Fair enough. Tell me your name, at least."

She sticks out her tongue.

"Looks like you need another drink."

The man signals the bartender, pointing his fat finger in the woman's face.

"I do not need another drink," she says, shoving his finger aside. "What I *need* is a pilot. Not another *Pink Squirrel.*"

The man laughs.

"What is so funny?"

"I think we could all use a little pink squirrel every now 'n again, don't you?"

The woman balks. "You are making fun of me now? How do you say? Coming on to me?"

The man straightens, smiling at her outrage. "Wouldn't dare. So why do you need a pilot?"

"A pilot is for flying."

The man burrows his fingers into his beard. "Maybe you *don't* need another drink."

The bartender pours one anyway.

"I'm Shane," the man offers, extending his hand.

The woman does not accept it. She slumps in her chair and rolls her head against the edge of the bar. "I do not need a Shane," she says. "I need a pilot."

"Then it must be your lucky day. I'm at your service."

The woman sits up and appraises Shane. She shakes her head. "You are no pilot," she declares, taking large gulps of her sweet drink.

"Is that right?"

Spittle mists from the woman's lips. Shane wipes it from his arms.

"A pilot," the woman says. "Maybe you are a spy, too, yes? Or a wealthy bachelor come to marry me? No. There are no pilots here. Only fools."

"Can't argue with that," Shane says, taking the seat beside the woman who has never before been drunk.

"I've got to go," she says, dropping her motel key and a few American dollars from her back pocket. Shane scoops them from the sticky floor, cleaning them with a napkin before handing them back. "I need a boat captain and a pilot, and I am not going to find them sitting here."

"You never answered my question," Shane says. "What's a nice lady like you need with a pilot?"

She shakes her head. "I cannot tell you this," she scolds. "Only a boat captain or a pilot I can tell. I am sorry."

The woman stumbles, and Shane grasps her arm.

"Let go of me."

"Please wait."

Shane pats his jacket, feels up and down his pants. The woman steadies her weight against the bar as he pulls a folded piece of paper from his back pocket.

He opens it, holding it so close to her face that she has to take a step back.

The woman reads aloud, sounding out the English words she's never before spoken: "Federal Aviation Agency." Her eyes grow wide. "You are a pilot," she states.

Shane exhales. His breath smells of beer. "Do I look like a liar?"

The woman searches his eyes, his face, his clothes for further evidence. "Yes," she confirms.

But she returns to her seat.

"The only pilot in Key West, and *you* find *me*. In a bar. Impossible."

Shane smiles, bobbing his head. "There are *many* pilots in Key West. You probably passed ten of them today and didn't know it."

"But there were no pilots at airport."

"I s'pose not," he says, spreading his arms. "Look where you are. No place in the world like the Florida Keys. No one ever leaves. All arrivals, few departures." He raises his drink in a toast she does not return. "And we're all out of work for it."

The woman mulls over his words and watches his face for evidence of untruths. She finds none, signaling the bartender for another Pink Squirrel.

"Well, Shane The Pilot," she says, "now that you have found me, I shall tell you about my brother."

UNLUCKY

Richard Quinn pilots the Valkyrie to shore, memorizing the stars reflected on the black water. Men wait on the dock. Some speak among themselves, while others wave him in, keeping an eye on the pilings.

Someone takes the rope from Richard, and he leaps onto the dock.

He ignores their questions. He ignores their paperwork. Richard Quinn walks through the small crowd, past the dirt lot, and into Quade's Boathouse.

"Peter?"

The Boathouse is the only thing that makes Richard feel small. It towers over him, hushed and deserted. The only sound is the slapping of waves where the floor would be if this were any other kind of storage facility. Three stories of open space loom above him, every nook housing a boat of one type or another: skiffs, airboats, cruisers. Even sailboats and catamarans on the lowest levels. Just outside, near the docks, are dinghies, dories, a stack of canoes. As formidable as Quade's Boathouse is, Peter doesn't have a slip big enough for the Valkyrie. Once the officials are done with Richard's boat, he will pilot her to The Duck Key Marina, a few miles north of town.

He calls again, "Peter?"

Nothing but the waves.

Richard retreats from the boathouse and its docked, towering giants, and circles the warehouse. He finds Peter Quade on the other side, hunched over an old Boston Whaler skiff, sanding its newly painted mustard yellow hull.

Richard steps into the light of a work lamp, and Peter jumps.

"Jesus H. Christ, you scared the piss outta me."

"A bit late for boat work."

"A bit late for a lot of things."

Richard grunts.

The two men regard each other in silence, waiting for the other to speak. Fiberglass dust drifts through the light like a plume of cigar smoke. Peter lays the sandpaper block on the ground as a lone car travels south on US1, illuminating the Boathouse as it passes.

"I'm sorry, buddy," Peter says, grasping Richard's shoulder.

"I know."

"If there were anyone else..."

"I know."

~

I've been up for hours when the front door finally opens, and slow, heavy footsteps plod into the kitchen.

Dad's home. Maybe he found Poppy clinging to debris or washed ashore at the harbor on Key Colony Beach, alive.

Lucky.

"Richard?"

Mom's voice is muffled, and I listen for her sigh of relief.

It doesn't come.

I tiptoe to the door and press my ear against it.

Mom and dad speak in low voices in the kitchen.

I peer through my door. Dad collapses into mom's arms as she struggles to hold him upright.

Dad didn't save Poppy. She's gone.

I ease my door shut and run back to my bed, pulling the sheet tightly around my ears.

I wish I'd never opened the door.

In the morning, I rush to the bathroom and don't think about what I'm doing. I just act.

Leaving no room to reconsider, I snatch the razor from the ledge of the sink and slam the blade onto my thigh, line after line.

Blood speckles the bathroom tiles.

I bite my lip, my tongue, to keep from crying out. Not from pain, but from something else. Something no words can describe.

I cut until I'm out of breath.

Until blood flows like a river across the grout.

Until my heart grows still and there's a blankness in my mind. If I could find this kind of peace any other way, I would. I really, really would.

This time, there's a lot of blood.

It streams down my calf, pooling in the cleft of my ankle. I rip a towel from the hook and press it into my thigh.

When the bleeding slows, I appraise my leg—it's sore, but will heal. The towel, on the other hand, is a goner. I pull a clean one from beneath the vanity and wrap it around my body, holding it away from my thigh. I crush the bloody towel into a ball beneath my arm and hurry to my bedroom before mom and dad wake up.

After dressing, I sprint to the docks, and with little ceremony, chuck the ruined towel into the water where it unspools on the surface. But the tide will soon retreat, taking my evidence with it.

I hop onto my bike and soar up my street and onto US1.

My heart races with thoughts of what I'll find at the Botel.

My mind races with what I will say.

The Greens might be angry at me for not warning them about the Vaca Cut Bridge. But I'm Eddie's girl, and he needs me now more than ever.

By the time I skid to a stop at the Botel, blood has seeped through my shorts.

There are voices up ahead, and I hide within the trees, telling myself it's because of the blood on my shorts, but I think it's because I'm a coward.

Eddie is stacking suitcases against the curb.

He looks different. No expression on his face, and his eyes are dark and hooded. He struggles to lift even the smallest bag.

The Greens are on the dock, talking to a group of officials. A young man in uniform hands them a small cardboard box.

Mrs. Green looks like a crumpled piece of notebook paper. Mr. Green just looks mad.

Mrs. Green takes the box from the officer and reaches inside, lifting a piece of clothing. She lets out a sudden scream, and I jump, nervous I'll give away my position. Eddie is unaffected by his mother's outburst, as if this happens all the time now. The new normal.

I grip my handlebar, hoping for a surge of bravery, but the lines I practiced on the way here dissolve on my tongue, and I hobble my bike closer to the road, turning onto US1.

The last thing I hear is Mrs. Green as she releases another merciless scream before falling abruptly silent.

Once home, I run to my room and push the pillow into my ears. But I can still hear Mrs. Green screaming, as if she were right outside my window.

MOM'S MANIC DAY

I wake to thoughts of Poppy. And Eddie. And the Greens. My body is heavy as I peel away the damp sheets and hold my face to the fan.

All I want is to curl up in the bathtub, let the water cover my face, and stay there all day.

When the water is a few inches from the ledge, I step in and immediately disappear beneath, wondering if I could die right here in the bathtub. And I force myself to stay beneath the water. For Poppy.

Is this what she felt? Was she scared? Did she cry out for her mom and dad? I see her little limbs—the same ones that hugged my knees—swirling through the waves, spinning beneath the current. I hear the boat slamming into the bridge, and for a moment, I think I might be drowning too.

But then I rocket from the bathtub, gripping the porcelain and coughing water from my throat. I'm trapped in the tub, a fish in a tank that's too small, a box of Mr. Bubble tapping maliciously on the glass.

This is how my morning begins.

Mom's morning began differently. She woke in a manic phase, and as I enter the living room, she announces we'll be driving to the Dadeland Mall today.

"School clothes," she says in a sing-song voice, as though with this annual ritual, everything has returned to its rightful place.

But mom isn't the only one trying to move on, trying to forget.

Dad storms through the apartment.

"Miriam, where's my folder?"

"On your desk, dear."

Dad stomps into his study, rummaging through the mess on his desk. He grunts, satisfied. "Pens?"

"Top drawer, dear."

A drawer opens and closes. Dad grunts once more.

The cuts on my thigh still burn, and my mind clutches to hope that Poppy's death was only a bad dream and nothing more.

But it wasn't a dream.

What kind of person could think about school clothes at a time like this?

Dad rushes from the living room to his study, over and over, stuffing items into his bag. School starts on Monday, and today's a planning day for teachers. I don't know why mom and I haven't left already. It seems she's waiting for something.

"Richard, I can stay in town if you'd like. Bring you lunch."

Dad rolls a stack of oversized papers into a tube. "Another day, my love."

"Always another day."

"I can't do this, Miriam. Not now."

Dad struggles with the zipper of his school bag and looks up at me, forcing a smile.

We say nothing. We just stand there for a moment, dad and me. Like no one else is in the room.

"You smell good," mom interrupts. "Very sharp. Very *dapper*." She purrs the last word.

Dad ignores her and rubs my head. "Let's go, pumpkin," he says. "School clothes won't buy themselves."

It's a long, quiet walk to the parking lot.

Normally, mom's happy when she's manic. But not always. Sometimes she's *mad* manic.

"I'm excited for school," I say to break the silence.

"I'm excited too," dad says.

"I bet you are," mom says under her breath.

I sink into my seat and count the trees as we turn onto US1.

We park in the gravel lot of the high school, and when dad pulls his seat forward to let me out, mom slides behind the wheel, slamming the door behind her.

"Is mom mad at you?" I whisper.

"No, but she thinks she is."

I nod as if this makes sense.

"Hey, pumpkin," dad says, putting his whole hand atop my head. I stumble under his weight as his fingers slide up and down my scalp like an octopus. "What's this?"

This is our thing. A treasured souvenir from my childhood that neither of us want to leave behind.

"I don't know!"

"It's a *brainsucker*. And what's it doing?"

I laugh, nearly toppling over from his giant fingers bobbing up and down on my skull. "I don't know!"

"It's STARVING."

Dad weaves his arm through the strap of his school bag, and I circle the car, sliding beside mom.

We watch as dad waves to the gym coach, Mr. Lansing, leveraging a flag up the pole.

From the other side of the building, we hear, "Mr. Quinn! Happy returns!"

Mrs. Berrett, the guidance counselor, runs to catch up with dad before he enters the front office. Her carrot hair glows in the morning sun like a campfire, and she flashes him a smile as brilliant as a mirror catching light. Dad holds the door for her as she tucks beneath his arm, vanishing into the building.

And then mom spins out of the lot, peppering nearby cars with little bullets of gravel.

Buildings whiz past my window as mom tunnels south on US1. The Armada, the lighthouse, and the boathouse fly by in a parade of colors.

Mom's going the wrong way, and I'm afraid to tell her. I assume she'll realize her mistake once we hit the Seven Mile Bridge.

She doesn't.

I hate driving over the Seven Mile Bridge. The lanes are so narrow that the mirrors of passing cars sometimes click against each other. Dad always pulls the mirror against the car before getting on the bridge. Mom doesn't.

I spot an oncoming car and clutch the edge of my seat. The mirrors don't click, but the rushing air pushes our car toward the guardrail like the wake of a passing boat.

Another car flies by and I grab my thighs, anticipating a click that doesn't come.

My hand is warm and wet—my leg is bleeding again. I look to mom in panic, but she hasn't noticed.

Knights Key hurtles past my window, growing smaller in the rearview mirror.

Today isn't turning out as planned.

Mom's manic, but not happy manic.

It's hard to predict, and if there's a pattern to it, I haven't yet figured it out. During one happy manic phase, mom pulled me out of school in the middle of the day to go on a candy shopping spree. We giggled all the way to the register, arms full of Mary Janes and Yum Yums and Marshmallow Sandwiches. And then we feasted in the living room, laughing at episodes of *Leave It To Beaver*.

But during another manic phase—a *mad* phase—we drove to the Bahia Honda Bridge, and I watched in horror as mom threw all of Nana's jewelry into the ocean. Gold and emeralds glinted one last time before disappearing forever. When I asked mom why she did it, she just stared into the horizon and said, "It's time I stopped hoping for things to be different." She spun her wedding ring around her finger. I was scared she might toss that into the water as well, but she didn't. I guess throwing away one family member was enough for one afternoon.

When we emerge onto the next island, mom realizes her mistake and spins the car around in the middle of the road.

We're back on the Seven Mile Bridge, this time going north.

A flock of pelicans circles above the waves, spiraling one by one into the ocean. The water explodes on impact as feathered bombs drop from the sky. Some birds emerge victorious, bobbing on swells, their throats distended from the thrashing fish within. Others take flight once more, soaring like prehistoric parrots before careening back into the Atlantic.

"We're making a stop," mom announces.

Maybe lunch, I think.

A red sedan speeds toward us on the bridge and I'm thinking about grilled cheese sandwiches when the mirrors go *click*.

The school is quiet. It's strange to see a place I know so well look completely different.

Today, we're intruders. Mom parked in the mangroves across the street to avoid detection.

We sit in silence, observing teachers bustling about a student-free school, sharing bagged lunches on a bench.

Mom's breaths are slow and severe, like she's meditating in a hurry.

"There," she says, leaning over the steering wheel, her eyes wide as sand dollars.

Dad emerges from the library accompanied by Mrs. Saylor, which isn't odd because Mrs. Saylor *is* the librarian. But mom's expression is pinched and accusatory.

I watch Mrs. Saylor speak with dad in the hallway, searching for signs that mom's fears are justified.

They exchange papers, and dad says something that makes Mrs. Saylor laugh. But dad makes everyone laugh.

Mom's hand trembles on the steering wheel.

She opens the car door.

"Mom," I plead.

She stands beside the car, gently latching the door shut behind her.

"Mom!"

Dad smiles as she approaches, and Mrs. Saylor waves a greeting before changing her mind and retreating to her library.

Mom yells, but I can't hear her words. She flails her hands, hitting dad in the head. His face is red, but not angry. He just looks sad.

I can't watch.

I spin around in my seat and stare through the mangroves toward the beach.

I've heard rumors you can see the beach from one of the high school classrooms. The boys claim seats closest to the window so they can spy on scantily clad sunbathers when the teacher isn't looking.

There are no sunbathers today. But there *is* something unusual tucked into the mangroves.

A tent. And beyond that, another.

I look everywhere, from mangrove to mangrove, and as far into the water as possible. Nothing moves except a thin colorful sheet on the sand.

The car door opens, and I flop back into my seat.

Mom's eyes are wet and pink when she says, "Let's go home."

I watch the peak of the tent disappear in my side mirror, and I don't ask about the mall.

Later that evening, when mom is distracted by dinner prep, I make my escape, biking to Jimmie's.

"Hiya," he says as I skid to a stop in front of the hut.

I want to tell Jimmie everything. About mom's delusions, growing worse by the day. About the fresh cuts on my thighs (or all the old ones like wallpaper across my skin). I'm an overfilled balloon ready to burst.

Ask me anything; I'll tell you anything.

"It's pretty late," he says. "We're about to have supper."

And then I think of the one thing I *can* share with my best friend.

"Guess what?" I say. "Someone's living on the beach by the high school."

Jimmie's eyes go wide, and I'm about to elaborate when Mr. and Mrs. Yearling emerge from the hut and walk toward me, their faces solemn. Mrs. Yearling folds her hands against her long skirt of yellow and white flowers.

"We were so very sorry to hear about that little girl," she says.

Oh.

I hadn't told Jimmie about Poppy, but word travels fast on an island.

"I understand she was a friend of yours."

My mouth is dry. "The sister of a friend."

"How awful. Is your friend okay?"

I shrug, and it's an honest answer.

Mr. Yearling wraps me up in one of his huge bear hugs usually reserved for Jimmie. I collapse into him, and for a moment, I pretend that he's *my* dad. That he knows how much I'm hurting, and he's going to love me through it, even though I never told him about Eddie. I pretend he forgives me for all the other bad things I've done that he doesn't know about, too. And when Mr. Yearling tells me everything's going to be okay, it's as if dad's own voice is in my ear.

Mr. Yearling releases me and I force a smile.

"What are your plans tonight?" Mrs. Yearling asks. "Can you stay for supper?"

"I wanted to go to the beach with Jimmie, but I guess it's too late."

"Nonsense," she says. "School starts tomorrow. Go have some fun while you still can."

I grin at Jimmie as I hop onto my bike. "Thanks, Mrs. Yearling."

"Of course, Danni. You're family," she says.

And I know she's telling the truth.

"Right *there*," I say, my finger straining through the mangroves.

We sneak onto the sand, gripping the roots that run parallel to the ground, the foliage swaying with our weight. We duck down as a man sprints across the beach.

Completely naked.

"Woah," Jimmie says. "What was that?"

"I'm pretty sure it's called a penis."

He sticks out his tongue.

We stay close to the mangroves, hopping from shadow to shadow until we spot a bonfire.

Bodies—some dressed, some not—lounge and laugh on the beach. A naked woman rushes into the waves and water crests around her. Her breasts glint in the fading light as she becomes still, staring into the sunset, her hands clasped beneath her chin as though in prayer. For a moment, she reminds me of the cover model on the Playboy magazine at The Sundry Store, doe-eyed and pink-lipped. But this woman on the beach is *nothing* like the Playboy model. She poses for no one but herself, primitive and natural.

I've never before realized women could look this way. No makeup. No perfectly coifed hair. Just their raw, perfect selves, and nothing more.

And I no longer want to look like the woman on the cover of that Playboy. I want to look like *her.*

She frolics back to the fire and someone passes her a cigarette. The smoke wafts our way, but it doesn't smell like a cigarette. Or a cigar. I gasp.

"Is that marijuana?"

Jimmie shrugs. I cover my mouth, trying not to look so shocked.

"Hippies," Jimmie says.

The word multiplies and spins around my skull. A dozen colors and shapes and feelings arise from this single word. *Hippies.*

"We should go," Jimmie whispers, looking to the darkening sky.

I don't want to, but he's right.

We return to our bikes, and I listen to the shifting rhythms of their drums for as long as I can, trying to hold the sound in my heart as I pedal away.

The apartment is quiet when I arrive home. There's a plate of supper waiting for me on the table, but mom's nowhere in sight.

On the kitchen counter is an electric tea kettle in silver and sage, still in the box. A gift from dad. Now mom won't be mad about Mrs. Saylor anymore.

I tiptoe through the quiet house and slip into my bedroom, tapping drumbeats against my hip.

~

Richard Quinn leans forward on his stool, squinting through the port windows of The Armada.

Andy grunts. Richard grunts back.

Behind the men, the door swings open and the setting sun ignites the room before the door closes, snuffing it out once more.

"We goin' fishin' next weekend?" Andy asks.

"I'll let you know."

"Sure, sure." Andy tosses back the rest of his drink and signals the bartender for another.

The men sit in silence, broken by occasional clips of conversation from the other patrons.

"What's goin' on?" Andy asks. "Things okay with Miriam?"

Richard snorts. "I never know, my friend."

"Buy her a necklace. Or earrings. Always works with Dottie."

Richard shrugs. "I bought her a kettle."

The men burst into laughter and the sound erupts through the bar. Andy claps a heavy hand against Richard's back. "Don't forget about the skillet!"

Richard cries through his laughter, tears streaming down his cheeks and disintegrating against his unshaved whiskers. Spittle rains from his lips.

"I needed this," Richard says, wiping the dampness from his scarlet face.

"Me too, old friend. Me too."

When the merriment subsides, the men are once again alone with their inebriated silence.

Andy speaks first. "I was real sorry to hear about that little girl."

Richard sips his beer.

"Had to be you," Andy says. "Always has to be you."

Richard stretches his long arms behind his neck. "Somethin' like that makes you wanna give up the sea."

Andy scoffs. "I know you, Ishmael. You don't mean that one bit."

Richard spins Andy around on his stool, his finger against the man's throat, his hot breath on his face.

"Jesus, Richard…"

"You didn't see it, Andy," he says through clenched teeth. "You didn't *see* that little girl." Richard slams his finger into his own chest, feeling the puncture of it like a harpoon. "*I* saw that little girl. *I* pulled her dead, purple body from the ocean. *Me.* That could've been my own goddamn daughter out there. Don't you dare tell me what I mean and what I don't. Fuck the ocean."

Richard spins back to the bar, tossing the rest of his beer down his throat, and Andy signals to the concerned bartender that everything is under control.

"I don't know if I have much left in me, Andy," Richard says. "When something goes wrong in this town, they call *me.* If someone's in trouble, they call *me.* I'm not the goddamned authorities."

"You're better than the goddamned authorities. And who the hell else are they gonna call?" Andy swings his arms wide, displaying the sleepy Marathon bar. "You're a hero in this town."

"Nothing's exciting anymore, Andy. We're not young men. I'm starting to think there's an expiration date on happiness. One day, we're just too old and too wise to get excited about anything anymore."

And with this, Andy is out of responses.

The room fills with the day's dying light as the door to The Armada opens and two women enter the bar. They're out-of-towners, and they peer around nervously as though hesitant to approach the counter. One of the women makes eye contact with Richard, and when she blushes, he knows that by the end of the night, he'll have another phone number for his collection.

He nudges an adjacent barstool with his shoe, giving her an opening. She elbows her friend, and as the two women draw closer, Richard slides his wedding ring off his finger and into his pocket.

A STRANGER PAINTS A PICTURE

A woman who has never been an artist paints a picture.

She sits by the open window of her motel room. Before her is a pad of watercolor paper, the top sheet covered in her handwriting, her words disappearing with every descent of the paintbrush.

Tonight, she paints a sunset.

A thick smear of maroon watercolor paint, hardly diluted, conceals the first line: Hallo, Bruder.

Hello, Brother.

The sun, of course, is not maroon, but this is of little concern to the woman, who adds a smudge of purple as well, because yellow will not do. She dips the brush into a glass of water and creates a thick paste from blue paint, streaking it across sentences that read, Ich habe einen Piloten gefunden—*I have found a pilot*—and, Wir werden bald zusammen sein—*We will be together soon.*

There are no words on the paper about her failure to find a suitable boat captain. She could not bear to write it. Not yet. The woman still has hope.

Greetings for their mother are quickly swallowed by the paint, as are her inquiries about the state of his documents.

Line by line, her handwriting is transformed into a rickety boat on the sea, the black silhouette of a stout bird in the sky, and the thick, gaudy rays of an abysmal sunset.

No one on Mallory Square would celebrate the atrocity the woman has painted.

She looks it over, holds it to the light to check the opacity. Nods her approval.

The woman turns off the lamp, leaving the paper on the table to dry in the warm breeze, before forcing herself into bed.

Tomorrow, she will press the painting within the pad of paper and bundle it with the art supplies.

Tomorrow, she will package it, address it, and deliver it to the Key West mail service building.

Tomorrow, the package will be sorted into International Post, bound for a small mail room—tucked between a shuttered diner and an abandoned library—in the impoverished city of East Berlin.

THE NEW GIRL

The very first thing I notice about high school is how tall the seniors are.

I tuck against the wall of the hallway and watch them strut past. Superstars. Most of the boys look like grown men, grabbing and flirting with the senior girls as they twist by in their skirts and headbands.

A pair of students are necking outside the library, practically climbing on top of each other. It's hard to look away, and even after Mrs. Saylor waves them off, I watch them scurry hand-in-hand toward the gym until they're out of sight.

A tall, thin girl with strawberry blonde hair shuffles past me, leaving me spinning in her wake. She has the longest stride I've ever seen, her legs wrapped in flowered fabric that hugs her hips, like a fleshy heart pulsing with each step. She wears a simple coral tank and wide leather belt, and she strolls by a group of senior boys, provoking wide-eyed stares and an impromptu duel of rock-paper-scissors.

I look down at my plaid skirt and saddle shoes, feeling like a toddler by comparison. I should've worn pants. And a wide leather belt. Maybe then boys would've been dueling for *me*.

Clutching books against my chest, more shield than academia, I brave the bustling hallway.

Travis Misker darts by, shouting, "Hi, Danni!" before ducking into the cafeteria. Travis got cute over the summer. His hair is darker, and there's a shadow along his chin. I wonder if he still rides his bike to school—hands held out, eyes closed—or if he's too grown up for that now.

Sharon Wolinski skips toward me.

"My summer was so dreamy," she purrs.

Sharon's eyes are mere slits in the morning sun, and she's about to elaborate on her dreamy summer when she sees Mercy Turner at the end of the hallway.

Sharon runs toward Mercy, who's already hopping up and down, her giant breasts oscillating as a single entity. The two best friends struggle to hug each other over their piles of schoolbooks. As I approach the east wing, I spot Jimmie.

I want to run to him and hug him while books fall out of our hands, like Sharon and Mercy, but we don't have that kind of relationship.

New middle schoolers file in behind him, glancing over their shoulders to nervous mothers hovering in the parking lot.

They look so small. Infantile. *We* didn't look that young on the first day of middle school. No way.

My first class is Environmental Science, and half the desks are already full. The room smells of chalk and paper. *MR. LOVITZ* is scrawled on the chalkboard in messy handwriting.

"Hello, Miss Quinn," the teacher says.

How does he know my name?

"Take a seat near the front, please. I expect a lot from the daughter of Richard Quinn."

Oh.

I want to tell Mr. Lovitz that I don't want to sit in the front, and shouldn't be punished just because my dad is a teacher, and this empty seat in the back is just fine, thank you.

I say none of this as I choose a seat near the front—but in the *second* row, in rebellion.

All around me are familiar faces, slightly altered by three long months of teenage evolution.

Someone taps my shoulder and I turn. It's Margaret Leech, and I struggle to hide my disappointment.

"I had so much fun this summer." The words whistle through the giant gap in her front teeth.

"That's nice, Margaret."

"We spent a whole month in Niagara Falls—that's in New York! My aunt lives there, and she has a *basement*. That's a room that goes *underground*."

We don't have basements in the Keys. Beneath every home is a thick layer of coral and limestone. Beyond that, the vast Atlantic. I want to ask her what people do in an underground room, but I don't want to encourage conversation. I'm too distracted by her teeth, and the way her lips are open *all the time*. I've never figured out how she keeps from drooling all over her shirt.

"What did *you* do this summer?" she asks, rocking back and forth, anticipating a grand tale to rival the basement story.

A hundred images flash through my mind.

"I like your necklace," she says.

I run my fingers along the dainty chain of my gold owl necklace with the ruby eyes. The one I wore when Eddie first kissed me outside the abandoned lighthouse. I haven't taken it off since.

Behind me, the door opens, and everyone turns to watch an unfamiliar girl enter the room, books held casually at her hips.

The new girl scans the room, choosing a seat in the back corner. She's short but moves with the confidence of a six-foot tall model, and I swear I smell cinnamon apples as she passes my desk.

Her pants are black, her shirt is black, and her hair is black, cropped just below her earlobes. The only color on her is the pink glow of her skin, and a yellow bandana tied against her bangs.

She's not from around here. No one in the Keys wears all black, and none of the girls have hair that short.

The new girl shuffles papers beneath her books, placing the stack under her chair. She pulls a pen from her bag—not a pencil—and begins doodling on the cover of a notebook.

"Good morning, new freshmen. Graduating class of '71!" Mr. Lovitz barks from the chalkboard.

I'm about to face the front—a mere second from turning away from the new girl—when she suddenly looks up. Our eyes lock.

When she smiles, I spin forward in my chair before deciding whether or not to smile back.

My finely-honed socialization skills on full display.

I'm barely listening as Mr. Lovitz drones on about his expectations for Environmental Science because I'm picturing the new girl's face in my mind. Her icy blue eyes and peach mouth.

She's different.

So different that she frightens me.

Different from all the other girls at school.

Everyone is going to call her weird, I just know it.

And I know one other thing for sure.

I desperately want to be her friend.

I wait all morning for Mr. Lovitz to call attendance so I can learn the new girl's name, but he never does. I keep pace with her as I walk to my next class, but she disappears through a different classroom door.

I choose a seat in English—the back corner—and hope to see the new girl later, in Social Studies or Algebra.

The English teacher is new to Florida, and he talks about himself for the entire class. The snow in Colorado, and how he was about to marry the woman his parents wanted him to marry when he had a psychological break.

He makes a psychological break sound like fun. An excuse to run away from your life. No one can be mad at your decisions if you have a disease. Like cancer. Or tuberculosis. Or a psychological break.

He's talking about his adventures on the road, hitchhiking to Florida, when I notice his socks—yellow with red polka dots. This guy can't be a teacher. He's barely a grownup. His thick, dark hair swoops forward, nearly covering his eyes. He wears bold Clark Kent glasses, but has too many muscles to be a nerd. I look to his name on the board, printed in block letters: MR. MALLORY.

If I had known Mr. Mallory was going to be such a hunk, I would've sat in the front row *by choice.*

When the bell is a few minutes from ringing, our new English teacher becomes serious.

"I may be new here, but we're following the same rules, the same curriculum. But," Mr. Mallory says with a smile, "I want this class to be fun, too. Education doesn't have to be boring. Learning is *fun.* Learning *elevates* us. It *betters* us. It makes us *men* and *women*, rather than little kids."

I like the way he emphasizes certain words to make his point.

"Every little thing we learn brings us closer to the person we're destined to become." He spreads his arms. "So take it in. Don't do it for me, or for a grade. Not even for your parents. Do it for *you.*"

Mr. Mallory waits for applause but has overestimated our level of academic enthusiasm.

"I also plan to introduce you to the magic of poetry. Normally, that's in the sophomore arena, but I think we can handle it."

Mr. Mallory is about to elaborate on our upcoming poetry studies when the bell rings.

Like a current, the students sway from their seats in a single motion, heaving books into their arms, before surging through the open door, a deluge spilling into the hallway.

As I pass the window, I catch a glimpse of the beach beyond.

This is the infamous view all the boys clamor for. Two distant figures sprawl across the sand, though this time, they're clothed.

Hippies. In my hometown.

"Better hurry along," Mr. Mallory says.

I look at him, and his large, sweet smile. I blush.

"Can't have you running late on my watch. Mr. Quinn would have my butt."

Oh.

My blush disintegrates. I feel as though I have a spotlight on me. Or a scarlet letter Q emblazoned across my chest.

I slink past Mr. Mallory and through the classroom door without another word.

I look for the new girl at lunch but don't see her. I hope she's not sitting with the popular girls. Mercy Turner or Sharon Wolinski or Darlene Kipp. If Mercy gets to her first, I'll have no shot at all.

Mercy's really nice. Smart and funny, she blends into every clique seamlessly. All friends and no enemies.

Dad once told me that you can't trust someone who doesn't have an enemy because you don't know what they stand for.

As I search for a new face in a sea of familiar ones, I wonder, do *I* have an enemy?

I'm leaning against the wall and peering into my lunchbox when Margaret Leech calls my name. I resign myself to sit at her table. Just for today.

I pour something thick and gritty from my thermos, and Margaret sneers, her front teeth bursting from her gums.

"What's that?" she asks.

"Pear juice."

"Gross," she says, turning away like the matter is settled.

"It's sweet, like a popsicle."

"It's gross," she declares again, raising an eyebrow and leaning over the cup. "But it *does* smell like a popsicle."

I smile at my small victory and take a sip, scanning the cafeteria.

"Did you see the new girl?"

Suddenly, Margaret has my full attention. "The girl in black?"

I search Margaret's eyes for details and try to ignore her teeth.

Margaret nods. "She's *weeeiiirrrd*," she says, elongating the word because 'weird' in its basic form just won't do. "And she's not even that pretty."

Yes, she is.

But I say, "Definitely not."

At the other end of the cafeteria, Sharon Wolinski joins Darlene Kipp, Timmy Katz and Ronald Weller, who are pointing through the window at something on the lawn.

"I need a napkin," I say, leaving Margaret behind. As I approach, they usher me into their clutches.

Sharon points to the new girl sitting on the lawn, eating lunch alone.

"Why is she out there by herself?" I ask.

"Why *wouldn't* she be?" Sharon says.

"Go sit with her, Sharon," Timmy says. "I dare you."

"*You* sit with her."

"I dared you first."

"No way. I'm no skuzz."

Dad was right—you can't trust someone who doesn't have an enemy. And I must be *super* trustworthy because right now, I have four: Timmy Katz, Ronald Weller, Sharon Wolinski, and Darlene Kipp.

I spot Margaret's fuzzy hair through the crowd and return to my lunch, wishing someone had dared *me* to sit outside with the new girl.

I would've done it. Honest.

"You were right about the pear juice," Margaret says, nibbling her sandwich. "It *does* taste like a popsicle."

My thermos cup is empty, only a smudge of pear grit remains.

I sneer at Margaret Leech.

Now I have *five* enemies.

I don't see the new girl again until my last class.

She's the first student in the room, and though all the other chairs are empty, I sit right in front of her, hoping it looks natural.

Miss Mason writes *Algebra I* in big loopy letters across the chalkboard, leaving little room for anything else.

I wait for her to assign classwork or dictate notes, but scrawling *Algebra I* across the board is all she intended to do today. Miss Mason sits on the edge of her desk and asks about the most exciting thing we did over summer.

Mercy Turner says she went to Ghana with her family. A mission, whatever that is. Miss Mason looks impressed, which doesn't surprise me. People are always impressed with Mercy Turner.

Debbie Lawrence says she spent all summer at the beach, and now her tan is deeper than her sister's. I glance over and don't doubt her.

"How about you, Danni?" Miss Mason asks.

Oh.

All eyes are on me.

Do I tell everyone that I fell in love, and that we kissed in the shadow of the old lighthouse? Or that my mom slapped me, and we never spoke of it again? Jimmie and I stalked naked hippies on the beach? A little girl died in a boating accident under the Vaca Cut Bridge and I still dream about her, lost in swirling waters, night after night?

"I—"

The bell rings.

Thank God.

"Wait," Miss Mason commands, raising a hand to the wave of students spilling toward the door. "I need to take attendance."

Later that evening, as I sit down for supper cooked on mom's new electric skillet, dad asks about my day. What are we studying in Environmental Science? How am I feeling about Algebra? What's the required reading for freshman English?

I shovel a lump of mashed potatoes into my mouth to buy myself some time.

I could tell him that Mercy Turner's boobs got bigger. Or that the new English teacher wears colorful socks and had a psychological break.

I could tell him about the new girl at school with short black hair and icy blue eyes who eats lunch on the grass and does her classwork with a pen.

And that her name is Audrey Lipke.

"Richard," mom scolds. "It's only the first day."

"Okay," dad concedes. "Did you have fun, pumpkin?"

I nod.

Dad reaches over and places his heavy hand across my head. His fingers wriggle behind my ears, and I rock back and forth beneath his weight.

"Stay very still!" he says. "I think I spot a brainsucker."

A STRANGER SEEKS A MADMAN

A woman who has never known a pilot waits for Shane at Mallory Square.

He's late, and she paces in the darkness, trying to convince herself that she hasn't made a mistake. That he *is* a pilot. That he *does* know many boat captains. She buffs the exhaustion from her eyes and hopes she hasn't been made a fool.

The ocean is nothing more than a black tub of seething saltwater foam. Below her, the waves bring offerings of seaweed. A nest of tangled clusters churns and chafes against the seawall. She gags on the smell. A dead fish bobs atop the seaweed, its eyes veiled with white slime, its tail chewed clean off.

She was wrong—Key West is no paradise. Not for a woman who arrived with a Polaroid of her brother on her dashboard, and an eye toward the sea at night.

"I'm late," a voice says, approaching quickly from behind. The woman jumps and spins around, wary of falling into the stink below. Shane extends his hand and helps her off the ledge.

"Yes," she confirms. "You are."

He pulls his thick hand down his face, drawing the skin toward his chin. He doesn't meet her eyes.

The woman waits, picking at the edge of a chipped fingernail.

After a long minute, Shane says, "I'm sorry, but I can't help you." He hangs his head, running his hands through his hair.

"But you *want* to help me," the woman says. "I can see this."

Shane looks over the top of her head to gaze mindlessly at the water, finding the view more of a comfort than she does.

"Yes," he says.

"*Then help me*," she pleads. "Did you find a boat captain?"

"This is Key West. There are more boat captains than mangroves."

"This is good, yes?"

"But none of them are madmen."

The woman peels off the tip of her fingernail and it flutters through a gap in the dock, disappearing into the abyss below.

"They're just men," Shane says. "Family men, working men, *good* men. What you are asking of them —and of me—is ludicrous."

"Ludicrous?

"Yes, ludicrous. Crazy. Insane. Impossible. You know these words, right?"

The woman turns back to the ocean. Yes, she knows these words.

And she knows the danger of what she asks, but she has no choice.

"I have something for you," Shane whispers, as though they may be overheard.

In Shane's hand is a folded bar napkin. She reaches out to take it, but he pulls it to his chest.

"You're a nice lady," he says. "You should leave here and go home, wherever that is."

"I have no home."

"Then go make one. Find a husband, pop out some kids. Forget about all this. You could be killed. Your brother could be killed. *Anyone who helps you* could be killed. Only a fool would take this on."

The ocean crashes against the seawall as families and lovers weave around them.

Finally, Shane speaks. "October?"

"Yes."

He fingers the napkin in his hand. "I'm not going anywhere. I'll be here."

"You will be my pilot?"

"You need to secure a boat captain yourself. You do that, and maybe."

Shane holds out the folded napkin and she plucks it from his fingers.

"No promises," he cautions. "Just a name. And a place where you can find him."

"A boat captain?"

Shane nods. "No one else is gonna touch this." He looks around, scratches his chin. "You get *this* guy to say yes, and I'll be your pilot."

She runs her trembling fingers across the fold, remembering Shane's warning. She could be killed. Her brother could be killed. Anyone who helps her could be killed.

"He's your only shot," Shane says.

"But is he a madman?"

"That's what they tell me."

The woman smiles. "Good."

She opens the napkin, inspecting the handwritten letters printed within.

Richard Quinn
The Armada, Marathon

A DAY TO RIVAL ALL OTHERS

It's Friday, and the first week of high school is nearly over. I've spent all week trying to talk to Audrey Lipke. And failing. She sprawls on the lawn during lunch like she's the only person on the planet and doesn't seem to notice the stares from the other students.

I enter Environmental Science and change my approach, heading to a seat near the back, in front of Audrey.

Mr. Lovitz watches me bypass the first two rows and choose the third.

I avoid his gaze.

But Mr. Lovitz has nothing to say to the daughter of Richard Quinn this morning.

Audrey's behind me. I can smell her—cinnamon apples. Like a cobbler. Like the Fourth of July.

I want to say something. Turn around right now and just say *anything*. Why is this so hard?

"Alright," Mr. Lovitz says, "take out your notebooks and write this down."

He scrawls, *MONDAY: MODELS OF THE EARTH* in all caps on the chalkboard.

I pull a pencil from my bag. Behind me, Audrey fumbles through hers.

"The following week," Mr. Lovitz says, "is—"
EARTH'S STRUCTURE AND ENERGY.
"Psst."

Audrey taps my elbow and my pencil skips across the page.

I turn around to find Audrey Lipke leaning over her desk, grinning at me. Her head is tilted so far to one side that her short black hair folds like origami onto her knee.

Mr. Lovitz's voice drifts away.

"I forgot my pen," she whispers. "Do you have one I can borrow?"

A moment passes in silence.

Another.

"I have an extra pencil," I stammer.

Relief floods her face. "Fab."

Fab.

We share a smile—at the exact same time. I can't even tell who smiles first, her or me. It just happens.

"Miss Quinn," Mr. Lovitz bellows across the classroom, bringing all eyes to Audrey and me. He taps the board with a wedge of chalk before writing, *EROSION AND DEPOSITION.*

I give Audrey my pencil without another word, and we share an eye roll.

But I lied. I don't have an extra pencil. That was my only one. So I sit through the rest of class pretending to write notes on Environmental Science while reliving our conversation in my mind. Every word, every smile.

It was fab.

In English, Mr. Mallory discusses the elements of basic poetry. Rhythm and meter. Line structure and stanzas. I don't have a pencil to take notes, so I try to remember everything. But I quickly forget what he said about stanzas. Four lines? Three? I look around for someone who could lend me a pencil, but the only student in earshot is Margaret Leech, and it's not worth the risk.

When the bell rings for lunch, I enter the hallway and see dad walking toward me, flanked by the tall, strawberry blonde I saw on the first day of school. And this time, I can see more than the back of her head. Her lips are juicy as grapefruit pulp, and her auburn lashes burst from her eyes like flames. She laughs at something dad says. Touches his arm. Fumbles with her hair.

She's flirting.

With dad.

As they draw closer, I don't know whether to wave or hide as famished freshman surge toward the cafeteria.

I worry dad might hug me and make a big scene in front of everybody, but he offers only a smile, and the subtle threat of a brainsucker, his fingers flexing at his hip.

The strawberry blonde isn't wearing a bra, and her nipples bulge from her tank like the nubbins of Key limes. A boy passes her, running into a trash can. She pretends not to notice.

Dad walks by without further acknowledgment, and I'm grateful he didn't embarrass me. But also jealous as the beautiful senior coos at him. She's always wanted to read *To Kill a Mockingbird*, she says, and she's simply thrilled he's assigned it.

A tall brunette—another senior—enters the hallway. "Hi, Mr. Quinn," she purrs as she spins past him.

A curvy girl runs after him. "Mr. Quinn, can I help you with your books?"

All the girls bat their lashes as dad walks past. All the boys puff their chests.

As dad and the strawberry blonde vanish through the library doors, I wonder what mom would think if she were here, watching the great Richard Quinn patrol his hallways. I wonder if dad will regale his student with tales of bravery on the sea, or night swimming under the stars.

I wonder if he's noticed her nipples.

After school, I'm supposed to head to Jimmie's house to go crawfishing, but as I approach the Vaca Cut Bridge, I skid to a halt.

At the entrance to the bridge, mere spitting distance from the diner, is a bouquet of flowers tied to a post.

Beside the post, a pink teddy bear.

A memorial for the little girl who died here.

And I can't do it.

I can't cross the bridge.

I walk my bike in a circle until the memorial is out of sight and take a few deep breaths until the urge to vomit disappears. And then I go home.

~

Richard Quinn lets the door slam behind him, and the few patrons of The Armada turn to see who has entered. They return to their drinks as if he is nobody at all, and he chuffs, strolling to an empty seat.

"Regular?" the bartender asks Richard.

"Yessir."

He soon returns with a beer and whiskey.

"Thank you, my friend," Richard says. "Quiet in here today."

The man leans against the bar, surveying the modest crowd. "Barely enough to make a living." He taps Richard's wedding ring. "You're married," he says, more statement than question.

"Love of my life."

"I'm surprised," the bartender says. "Quite the ladies' man."

Richard chuckles, pulling a cigar from his jacket. He spreads his arms. "We are what we are. You married?"

"Nah. Gave that up a long time ago."

The man pulls a box of matches from behind the bar and lights Richard's cigar. Smoke billows like an apparition before melting into the air.

Richard offers it to the bartender.

"Thanks, but I gave that up too," he says, walking away as he pushes a wet rag across the counter. The stench of dirty bleach strangles the sweet perfume of the cigar.

Richard pulls his car keys from his pocket, tangled with his boat keys. He lays them both on the bar and feels the Valkyrie calling to him. Crying for him. But she'll have to wait. Tonight, there are lessons to plan.

Richard tucks the floating wedge back into his pocket and paints his tongue with the last drops of whiskey.

The bartender sprints from the far side of the bar. "Richard, I almost forgot. There was a woman here yesterday. Looking for you."

"Oh?"

There are always women looking for Richard, but he never tires of hearing it. "What did she look like?"

"Tall. Blonde. She had an accent."

Richard smiles. "I like blondes."

The bartender fiddles with some paperwork below the edge of the bar and finds a small piece of paper, handing it to Richard.

Seaside Motel, Room 2. Below that, the motel's phone number. He recognizes it instantly; he's seen it before.

No name.

"Blonde, you say?"

The bartender nods. "Love of your life?"

"So many loves, so little time."

And then Richard exits The Armada, tucking the paper into his back pocket.

~

"Danni's home!" mom broadcasts as I walk through the door. She takes my hand, adding, "Dottie's come for a visit today. Isn't that lovely?"

Mom's hair is perfectly curled around her ears, dusting her shoulders with golden wisps. Her cheeks are particularly rouged, and she wears a white cotton dress with tiny red flowers all over. A gold clip-on earring dangles from the edge of one earlobe. The other earlobe is bare.

"C'mon, silly," mom says, pulling me into the living room and gripping my shoulders like I'm a prize-winning pie.

If only she beamed like this when we didn't have company.

"Daniella," Dottie says. "you need to stop growing, young lady. You're taller than your mother! So pretty, too." She looks to mom. "Apple didn't fall far, did it, Miriam?"

Mom's cheeks puff with sweetness, and she releases me, retreating to the kitchen to brew more tea with her sage and silver tea kettle.

"Where's dad?" I ask.

"I don't know, dear."

And I can tell by her tone that she has better things to do than think about dad. Tea won't pour itself.

Mom places the kettle on a cloth napkin on the living room table and sits next to Dottie. It's nice to see her smile again.

I wave a quick goodbye and slip into my bedroom.

Right away, I notice something on the bed.

A letter from Eddie!

I think of mom's hands on my letter, and my cheek stings as though I've been slapped, but it's only my guilty conscience.

I stare at his name on the upper left-hand corner.

Edward Green.

I squeal behind my teeth and nudge my finger carefully beneath the flap so as not to tear it—so I can save it—and smell the dried glue along the edge. Eddie's tongue was *right here*. I hold the glue to my lips. I lick it, but can't taste Eddie, only the sweet tang of adhesive.

Inside is a sheet of yellow paper, and the first thing I notice is that it's not very long. Just a few short paragraphs. I'm his girl, (his groovy fox, remember?), and he should have more to say to me.

Danni,
School started this week, but nothing is the same anymore.
Everything's different. It's like Poppy's just taking a nap or
something, and we're all waiting for her to wake up.

Mom and dad don't talk anymore. Not to each other, or to me.
They're real downers. I think they wish I had died instead.

That's it, I guess. It's pretty gnarly here. Thanks for being a good
friend. I won't ever forget you. Maybe I'll see you next summer,
but I don't know. It's not a good time to ask my folks.
Later.

Eddie's letter, once full of promise, is just a sheet of paper with a few meaningless sentences. A tear lands on his words, puddling into a lagoon of blue pigment.

I stare at his sentences as though prophecy can be read in the ink.

I tear a sheet of paper from my notebook and write, *Dear Eddie.*

I pause, not knowing what to say.

But there's really only one thing I need to know: *Just tell me,* I write, *am I still your girl?*

SOMEWHERE IN GERMANY

A man who has never left Germany hurries toward the train station with a package from America tucked beneath his coat.

He glimpses to the wall, watching the lights of West Berlin glitter off broken bottles embedded in the mortar. The shards of glass cannot be seen from where the man stands, but the reflective glisten of life beyond betrays their hiding place.

The man hears footsteps behind him, heavy and languid, and he hustles forward without looking back. The sky is pale, though it's almost night, and he descends the platform steps, not greeting anyone who walks past, who might look into his eyes, or ask what is stashed beneath his coat.

The station is hazy.

Here, smog surges up, filling the sky, but it also pushes toward the ground, pervading the tunnel, as though in rebellion against the very laws of physics. He finds a gap between a lone man and a coughing woman with her coughing child. It's the only sound in the tunnel until the jangle of rails and a shower of brick dust announce the arrival of the next train out of the city.

The man funnels inside and finds a place to stand, leaning against a wall so the bulge of the American post will be hidden behind his body.

Beyond a small discolored window are passing shapes of industry and settlements. The shadow of a forklift like a goose snapped at the neck. Windowless, doorless buildings, the pale night bursting through their openings like fog lights. The man watches the landscape morph from small houses and villages to the remnants of farmland, their rows of soil vacant and parched.

He feels as though he's being watched, and he scans the downcast faces of his fellow riders as the parcel digs into his hip like a broken bottle in the mortar. He forces himself to look ahead, outside the small window and into a night choked with opaque factory smog. The man hasn't seen a dark sky since he was a boy. How he longs to see the stars.

When the train lurches to a stop outside his village, the man with the American package hurries home.

He calls out, "Mama," as he bends down to step through the door, "ich bin zuhause."

I am home.

A much shorter woman emerges from the shadows of the kitchen, her round face silhouetted by soft candlelight. She places a plate of bread on the small wooden table and sets a candle beside it. She cups his cheek, pushing her finger into his dimple, as she's done since he was a boy.

The man pulls the parcel from beneath his coat and places it on the table beside the bread. His mother clasps her hands beneath her rosy chin.

"Von deiner Schwester?" she asks, hopeful.

From your sister?

The man nods, his smile natural and easy.

He turns over the brown lump, looking for evidence of government inspection. No torn corners. No re-taped edges. The paper seems to be in its original condition, undamaged and unmarked, although one can never become complacent. He rips open the package and fans out the contents: a pad of paper, a pencil, a pan of watercolors with the brush inside, and a new painting. The man stares at the painted sunset—the terrible composition, the garish colors—and hopes that when his sister looked out her window for inspiration, she was surrounded by beauty.

His mother coos at the painting as though it's the loveliest one yet.

Is she prosperous in America? she asks.

"Ja."

How is art school? she asks.

The man's sister is not in art school.

Good, he says. Best in her class.

His mother beams, her eyes glistening in the candlelight.

Eat something before you sleep, she says, standing and kissing the top of his head before she walks away.

"Gute Nacht, Mama."

The man waits until his mother's breath grows heavy before walking to the sink, painting in hand. He hunches over the basin and scoops cold water from the bucket beneath. He holds the painting under the stream, watching the colors run together in a muddle of pigments before circling the rusted drain. The first sentence emerges: Hallo Bruder.

And then the next.

I have found a pilot.

LAST DITCH SUMMER

It's Saturday morning and Jimmie and I bike to the haunted house for a good old-fashioned Key lime fight, just like when we were kids. It feels good to play again.

A few of the limes we brought with us have spilled out of my basket during the ride, but there's still plenty for a fight. I'm slipping the last few into my pocket when a Key lime hits me square in the back.

"Cheater!" I yell, running for cover.

"Am not!"

Another whizzes past my ear, and I duck behind the coral supports of the haunted house to catch my breath. Jimmie's nowhere in sight, probably hiding on the other side of the mansion.

A lime barrels through an empty window and catches my forehead, leaving sticky, sour liquid dripping down my face.

"You're gonna get it!" I yell, chucking a lime back through the window.

It must have made contact because Jimmie yells, "Ow!"

I run behind the haunted house, to where the water meets the sand, and where there are fewer windows. I throw a lime to the ocean gods for good luck and creep around the side of the fortress.

A Key lime explodes against my butt, and Jimmie laughs so hard that I'm able to empty half my pocket before he finds the strength to stand and run away.

By the time our battle concludes, the haunted house is covered in Key limes—whole limes, busted limes, stringy scraps of limes, and the sweet, sticky juice of limes. We collapse along the beach, grabbing fistfuls of seaweed.

With every shake, tiny critters drop to the sand: crabs, shrimp, sargassum fish. If we're lucky, we might find a seahorse.

"That's a big one," Jimmie says, as I scoop a fish from the shore, releasing it back to the water.

I toss the depleted seaweed behind me and scoop up another batch, shaking it over my hand. Four baby shrimp squirt across my palm.

Jimmie unpacks a bag, pulling out smoked fish dip and crackers. Already, seagulls circle us.

I toss the second batch of seaweed back to the water and sprawl against the hot sand.

"What are you doing?" he asks.

"Getting a tan, dummy."

"Gross."

"Don't call me gross."

"Don't call me dummy."

And with that, it's settled. Jimmie busies himself with a thermos of lemonade.

"Why do you want a tan, anyway?"

"All the high school girls have tans."

Jimmie rolls his eyes, and I feel no need to explain further. Middle schoolers just don't understand.

When I flop onto my stomach, Jimmie stands and glowers down at me.

"You're different lately," he says.

"Nuh-uh."

"You lied to your parents about Eddie, and now you're tanning. And what's with the necklace?"

I'm still wearing the gold owl necklace. The one I wore for Eddie.

"None of your business," I say.

Jimmie grabs his thermos, crackers and fish spread all at once, shoveling them back into his bag.

I flip over and push onto my elbows. "Where are you going?"

Jimmie slings the bag across his shoulder and snatches his bike from the grass. "I'll see you Monday," he says. "At school."

"Bya," I offer.

He pedals away.

"Bya!" I yell again.

Lately, something's changed between Jimmie and I, and I feel it more and more every day. Maybe he's still upset that I'm a high schooler now, and he isn't. Maybe being born a year apart makes a big difference, after all.

CONTACT

Richard Quinn stumbles into The Armada and collapses into a barstool. He lights a cigar, buffs the chalk from his pants, and as the bartender sets a cold beer and whiskey before him, Richard nods a wordless thanks.

Behind him, the door to The Armada creaks open. Warm night air rushes inside as a blonde woman pauses at the entrance.

She scans the bar, meeting Richard's gaze. He spins his wedding ring around his finger and waits. It'll happen any minute. He's a patient man.

Richard smiles, but the woman does not return it.

The cigar in his mouth, typically sweet as honey, has lost all flavor, and Richard snuffs it against a napkin, dislodging a piece of tobacco from his teeth. He indicates the empty barstool beside him, sliding his wedding ring over his knuckle, but the woman approaches the bartender, and Richard pushes his ring back onto his finger.

The woman has legs long enough to shame a sailboat mast. Her skin, shimmering with Florida heat, reflects the sunset through the port windows.

The bartender points at Richard, and the blonde suddenly turns toward him. She approaches with small steps, as though not entirely sure she's in the right place.

Richard stands.

To regain some height, some power, perhaps. Or to get a better look at a beautiful woman.

"You are Richard Quinn."

Her tongue is heavily accented.

Richard smiles. "The one and only."

"I left my number but you did not call."

Richard searches his memory for a neglected phone number, but there are too many to recall. And they are all neglected.

"You are the madman?" the woman asks.

Richard takes a step back and looks around, but there is no one to overhear.

After a moment of deliberation, Richard laughs. "I've been called worse."

Richard tries to listen as the blonde woman tells him about her brother, but her eyes prove distracting. They're the palest of blue in the center, perhaps a little green, defined by a dark ring of indigo. Like a sandbar at the edge of an ocean trench. On more than one occasion, his hand has moved to his wedding ring. Though he has not removed it, he places his right hand atop the left, hiding the evidence.

The woman passes him a photograph. In the Polaroid, a young man stares out from the black-and-white image, his dark hair slicked away from his face. He wears no smile, but his eyes are kind and pale, like his sister's. A single dimple notches the bottom of his cheek.

"Why are you showing me this?"

"So that you see why I ask the things that I do. I do this for him. For my bruder."

Bruder. This one word cripples her, shattering the mirage of perfect English. A single chink in the armor.

Richard smiles at the woman, the kind of smile that softens his eyes, flashes his teeth. The kind of smile that always gets him what he wants from a beautiful woman in the bar. He spins his stool until they're facing one another. His thigh brushes her knee.

The woman readjusts, separating them once more. "I can pay."

Richard straightens, returning to his drink. He stops covering his wedding ring.

"Your brother is defecting, is that right?"

"I do not know this word."

"Escaping. Running away from his country."

The woman pinches her nose. "Yes."

"Your English is good. I'm willing to bet you've been here a while. Why didn't your brother come with you to America?"

"He was just a little boy when I left."

Richard rolls his snuffed cigar back and forth on the countertop, watching the leaves unfurl.

"How did *you* get here? Did you defect too? Escape?"

"Yes, but that was before the wall. Police watched for people crossing over, but it was not difficult if you carried little. I live in West Virginia now."

"Long drive."

"Please, Richard, will you help my bruder?"

"Lady, you're in dangerous territory here. How many guards are on a ship like that? 10? 20?"

"More."

Richard exhales through his teeth. "Armed?"

"Yes."

"You could be killed."

"Yes."

"*I* could be killed."

"Yes."

"And you expect me to risk my life for a little money?"

The woman leans onto her elbows, cradling her forehead with her palms.

"You can have all of it. All the money. Everything I have."

Richard balks. "I don't want your money."

"So will you help me?"

Richard wants to be her hero, her champion of the sea. He wants so badly to say yes.

"No."

"But you are the only one," she pleads.

Richard thinks of that little girl he pulled from the water, her body bobbing motionless on a dark and endless ocean.

"Nothing goes as planned on the water. It's not like on land, like you and me, sitting right here. This," he says, picking up his shot glass, "is predictable. Stable. This," he says, spinning her barstool left and right, "can be controlled. Out there," he says, pointing to the port windows and the darkening sky beyond, "you control nothing. There are no laws. Guards will shoot you dead and you will sink to the bottom of the Atlantic and no one will ever know what happened to you. And that's if we could even get close enough. They built a wall for a reason."

Richard Quinn pushes his empty shot glass across the counter.

"I'm sorry," he says, "but even a madman wants to live another day. This is crazy, lady. You waltz in here, ask me to do this great big thing, risk my life, and for what? We're not friends. I don't even know your name. You're a *stranger* to me."

The woman spins her barstool, facing Richard. He's taken by her confident gaze, her blue eyes. A sandbar at the edge of an ocean trench.

"My name is Galina," she says, "and we are no longer strangers."

Part Two

EXPECTATION IN THE SEASON OF AUDREY

PRETTY GIRLS

By the end of September, Audrey and I are fast friends. She lets me borrow her bandanas, and I *always* do classwork with a pen.

Today is Friday, and Audrey's already waiting for me on the grass at lunchtime.

I run to her and we hug and squeal, like Sharon Wolinski and Mercy Turner, and then I collapse beside her and open my lunch box. I'm *starving.*

Audrey falls onto her back, stretching her arms above her head. "I can't even think about food on a day like today," she says. "I just wanna go to the beach, ya know? They shouldn't keep us locked in this place. It's like jail."

I've never thought of school like jail, but Audrey's right. "Gray, concrete walls," I say. "We have to ask permission to go to the bathroom."

"And we get in trouble if we try to escape."

"It's unreal," I say. "Criminal, even."

"*Especially* on a day like today."

I push away my lunch box and join her in the grass. I wasn't that hungry anyway.

"There's a bridge party tomorrow," Audrey says. "You ever been?"

Under the Seven Mile Bridge, where large rocks sit half-in and half-out of the ocean, are secret parties, and no one tells their parents. I've heard about these parties but have never received an invitation. Apparently, Audrey has.

"Sure," I say. "All the time. It's far out."

"Wanna go?"

So badly. But tomorrow's Jimmie's birthday party and I can't flake on him.

"Who invited you?" I ask.

I need to work on my subtlety.

"Mercy," she purrs.

Mercy Turner.

My heart sinks.

"Everyone's going to be there," Audrey says.

I didn't realize Audrey knew *everyone*.

Until now, the relationship between Audrey and I has been confined to school. A bridge party would be a big step for our relationship, and I consider giving Jimmie my finest excuse before admitting, "I can't."

"Bummer," she says, tucking a strand of her black hair beneath her bubblegum-pink bandana. "I'll tell you all about it on Monday."

"You're going without me?"

"If you can't go, then I'll have to go stag, won't I?"

"I don't think you and Mercy will get along," I spit out, regretting it instantly.

Audrey turns to me, her face mushed against her forearm. "Why not?"

"You know how girls are."

Audrey shakes her head as I stroke a blade of grass, playing it cool.

"It's just that Mercy was the prettiest girl in school until you moved here," I say. "She might be jealous of you is all."

Somebody, please make me stop talking.

"I don't think Mercy's the prettiest girl in school," Audrey says.

I glower at Audrey and her adorable ignorance. "Of course she is. Who else would be?"

Audrey leans forward. "*You*, silly. *You're* the prettiest girl in school. Everyone thinks so."

I throw a blade of grass at Audrey.

"Stop it," I say.

Don't stop.

Mercy Turner is close to stealing Audrey away from me. I can feel it.

"Do you wanna go snorkeling with me and my dad this Sunday?" I ask. "We're going to the Sombrero Reef."

"I get seasick."

Oh.

"Have you ever caught crawfish?" I ask. "If we catch ten, Jimmie's dad will pay us $3.00!"

"Ew. They look like bugs."

Oh.

I throw another blade of grass.

"Did you know that hippies are living on the beach?" I ask.

Audrey sits up, staring down at me with eyes big and round as a sand dollar.

"Where?"

I point toward the east wing which houses the band room. It's the oldest part of our school, with exposed piping, chipped walls, and yellowing skylights that paint everything a vibrant gold.

"No. Way," she says, wriggling to get comfortable. "Lay it on me."

I sit up and tell her all about the tents and bonfires and drum circles. And the nudity, of course. Her eyes drink in every scandalous drop.

"No way," she keeps saying.

And I keep saying, "Yes."

"I have to see," Audrey says, scooping her uneaten lunch into her bag. "Right now."

"I can't ditch class. My dad would kill me. Legitimate murder."

"Do you wanna be a hostage your whole life, or do you wanna be free?"

Audrey's right. I want to be free.

We grab our lunch boxes and sneak past the cafeteria, through the east wing, past the empty band room and its wide circular steps, beneath a yellow skylight offering a view of nothing, and through the back doors, into the breeze. We run, laughing and covering our mouths, toward the cover of mangroves.

The two prettiest girls in school.

Audrey turns to me slowly, like her head operates on well-oiled gears.

"Way. Out."

We watch the small gathering through the empty places between the mangrove roots. No one's naked, but they might as well be. A tall blonde man, lanky as seagrass and just as fuzzy, prances across the surf in women's panties.

"They're smoking marijuana," Audrey whispers.

A dozen bodies sprawl across the sand, and as I lean over a root for a better look, something rattles above me.

All across the thicket, ornaments hang from yarn. Shells of all kinds, from the broken bits that wash ashore with the tide, to full size conch shells, their open lips glossy peach. They're strung together with squares of macramé, unraveling like psychedelic spaghetti onto the beach.

"Just so you know," Audrey says, "they don't like to be called *hippies*. They're *Love Children*."

I peer across the sand as they share drinks and brush each other's hair—the girls *and* the boys. They laugh and smile at one another like they're all sweethearts. Love Children, indeed.

"That's her," I say, pointing to a blonde woman in a red swimsuit. "The one who was naked."

Today, she's wearing the tiniest crocheted triangles, held together by yarn so thin it's practically imaginary. Blonde wisps poke out from beneath her bikini bottom.

Beads are woven into her long hair, and they sway and clack against her shoulders when she turns her head. A living, breathing musical instrument. When she laughs, her voice is like a wind chime made of seashells.

Audrey and I spy on the hippies all afternoon, and when the end-of-school bell tolls in the distance, it's official. I've ditched my last two classes of the day.

"Let's stay a while longer," Audrey says. "My mom won't mind if I'm late."

I want to, but Jimmie's waiting. Mr. and Mrs. Yearling have finally agreed to let Jimmie ride his bike to and from school this year, as long as we ride together. He meets me at the top of my street every morning at 7:25 sharp, and at the bike rack as soon as the bell rings.

"Next time?"

Audrey rolls her eyes, but I can tell I haven't let her down too badly.

"C'mon," she says. "I'll race ya."

Jimmie's already waiting at the bike rack, and as I approach, he pulls a thick wad of napkins from his pocket.

"Ellie Walker brought brownies to class for my birthday," he says. "I stole one for you."

I devour the treat, spitting out a garbled, "Thanks," as we walk our bikes toward the road.

"You'll be at my party tomorrow?" he asks.

My shoulders drop. I've finally received a bridge party invite, and a chance to hang out with Audrey outside of school. And Mercy Turner and Sharon Wolinski and Darlene Kipp and all the other popular girls.

But I nod, forcing a smile. It's not Jimmie's fault that his party is on the same day. It's not his fault that his birthday is ruining my entire life

I change the subject.

"Dad's taking me snorkeling on Sunday," I say, wiping my hands on my shorts. "Wanna come?"

"No way. My dad would never let me."

"Why doesn't he like my dad?" I ask.

Jimmie leans his bike against his knee as cars funnel out of the gravel lot behind us.

"It's not that he doesn't like your dad," he begins.

A minute passes. Maybe more.

I wait.

"He just thinks he's…" Jimmie trails off, choosing his words. "Irresponsible."

"So? That's the fun stuff. My dad isn't dangerous. He *saves* people. Everyone knows that."

"He didn't save that little girl."

He's talking about Poppy.

"I'm sorry," Jimmie says, and I can tell that he is. "I didn't mean it," Jimmie says, but I know that he did.

I ride behind Jimmie in silence, the harsh shadows of the Slash pines like a road map leading me home.

I've never known anyone who died before. Sometimes I try to forget, but that feels awful, too. As though forgetting is a second loss, the permanence of which is unbearable.

Poppy's death is still as fresh as unearthed soil, dark and moist, teeming with worms. It's always there, beneath the surface of my skin, a scab waiting to be picked.

SOLITUDE KNOWS NO FRIEND

Richard Quinn stares at the bronze whale paperweight on his desk and leans back in his chair as morning light surges through the window.

He shakes the Polaroid as though it's still developing. As if mysteries can be solved by agitation alone, their truths revealed in the emulsion.

Galina left the photograph on the bar last week. On purpose, he imagines, so that he'd have no choice but to take it with him, ponder it, dwell on it, from the comfort of his home. As though the photograph alone might cause him to change his mind.

Because he had said no.

Richard has his family to think about. His daughter. His wife. He can't leave them to fend for themselves should the plan turn deadly. What Galina asked of him was foolish and dangerous. Every boat captain from Key Largo to Key West has already turned her down. She's a stranger, here, in the Florida Keys. A stranger in this country. She secured a pilot, she told him. Someone to buzz the ship as both signal and distraction. Richard doubts this. It was only a ruse—a life raft for him to cling to, so he felt justified in saying yes.

But he said no.

October.

Not nearly enough time to prepare for something like this. The ship, she said, will travel south, between

West Palm Beach and The Bahamas. It will then skirt South Florida before making its turn for Cuba.

Richard knows the route well. Foreign ships hit the shallow Cay Sal Bank, where they're forced to slow their engines over shallow water. Just beyond is The American Shoal—an unmanned lighthouse some 6 or 7 miles south of Sugarloaf Key, east of Key West. The lighthouse stands as a landmark for a sharp southern turn. Next stop: Havana.

An unarmed man leaping from a ship in the middle of the night, and into the black Atlantic. If the German Police don't shoot him dead in the water, the sharks will surely finish him off.

The telephone rings, and Miriam's gentle footsteps plod across the terrazzo.

"Quinn residence."

Richard buffs the sleep from his eyes and leans over the photograph. The young man's name is Gunter. Galina told him that. Over and over. *Gunter. Gunter.* As though hearing the name would make him human. Family. But he is not family. Gunter, like his sister, is a stranger.

"Richard," Miriam calls. "There's a woman on the phone for you."

His wife walks from the kitchen toward his study, her footsteps no longer gentle.

"Who is this woman, Richard?"

"I don't know, my love. I've only just stood up."

Richard pushes past Miriam standing at rapt attention in the hallway and plucks the receiver from the counter.

A familiar voice on the line.

Richard looks to his wife and tries to hide his alarm. "How did you get this number?"

Galina's voice hums through the receiver, and Richard cups the mouthpiece, his palms growing sweaty with her every plea.

You are the only one, she says.

She begs, *Please.*

I won't leave until you say yes, she says.

"This is my home, need I remind you." Richard lulls his tone to something like compliance as the scowl on Miriam's face deepens. "We've already spoken on this matter."

Please.

"Don't call here again."

Richard hangs up the phone and makes a show of untangling himself from the cord to buy some time.

"Richard?"

Shit.

"It's nothing, my love. Just school matters."

Though dwarfing her by a full foot, Richard feels like a child beneath Miriam's gaze.

She thinks he's having an affair. Of course she does.

"My love, it was only Carolyn Saylor. We had an issue this week with a book shipment."

"It can't wait until Monday?"

He bends down, kisses her blonde curls. "It certainly can, my love. Monday."

And then Richard hurries away, retreating to his study.

⌒

The Yearlings have a big family, and I'm instantly dwarfed by them. Jimmie's aunt is a large woman, waddling around the picnic table to lean against the hut, with a smile as kind as Mr. Yearling's. She looks like she could give a bear hug to rival the best of them. His uncle is a waif of a man, stiff and studious. Not at all the type to give bear hugs, even if he'd been blessed with larger arms.

Jimmie's grandmother is there as well, caring for a gaggle of cousins. One of the little girls reminds me of Poppy, and I find myself drawn to her and trying to avoid her all at the same time.

Jimmie's cake is smothered in candles, and we sing the Happy Birthday song as flames dance in his eyes.

"Make a wish!" everyone says.

"Make it a good one," I say. "You only turn thirteen once."

That's what Andy told me at my birthday party over the summer. It annoyed me at the time, but as I watch Jimmie close his eyes and blow out the candles, I hope he made it a good one.

After cake, Jimmie plays with his cousins, wrestling them one by one into the pine needles. Mrs. Yearling gabs with her sister-in-law and braids her hair into two long stalks that hang over her ample chest.

The men gather in the hut, discussing man things.

And before I know it, I'm sitting all alone at my best friend's birthday party. No one could blame me when my thoughts turn to the party under the Seven Mile Bridge. *Everyone's* there. Everyone but me.

If I hurry, I can still make it.

I bite my lip and walk toward the road, pacing by the hut where customers wait in line for smoked fish spread. I straighten the basket on my bike and fiddle with my streamers until Jimmie approaches.

"Are you leaving already?"

I shrug, and Jimmie's shoulders drop. "Why?"

"There's a party under the Seven Mile Bridge," I say. "I told a friend I'd stop by."

"Well, let's go," he says. "I've always wanted to go to a bridge party."

Oh.

"I don't think you can."

"Why not?"

"You weren't invited."

"But," he says, scratching his head, "didn't you just invite me?"

I open my mouth to respond, but nothing comes out. I must look like a fish on a line because my eyes bulge and my mouth gapes open.

"Danni," Mrs. Yearling calls, walking toward us with a cracker in her manicured hand, "do you wanna join us for a board game?"

"She's leaving," Jimmie says.

"So soon?"

"There's a super important *high school* party today," he says.

I take a deep breath and pray I'll keel over right here, dead in the dirt.

Mrs. Yearling looks pained, or maybe she's only mirroring the look on her son's face. "Can you come back afterward?" she asks.

But Jimmie says nothing at all as I ride away from the Yearlings and their confused eyes burrowing into the back of my skull.

I hop off my bike and walk it down the large, rocky slope that dips under the Seven Mile Bridge. Stones and shells slide beneath my feet as I begin the steep descent beneath the highway.

This is our equivalent of a mountain. The Great Marathon Summit.

But today, there are no voices. No laughter.

I skirt further down the incline, but there's not even a towel draped across a rock.

Maybe I'm too late, and everyone's already gone home.

Maybe they went swimming and were swallowed whole by Mister Brownstone.

Above me, the bridge arcs like the ribcage of a whale, passing cars like a roll of indigestion. The ocean barrels through the openings between the support beams, crashing against the concrete, waves like lashing tongues.

No bridge party.

Did Audrey lie to me?

I force my bike up the hill and don't look down until I'm standing at the top.

In my mind, another scenario plays out: Audrey Lipke and Mercy Turner and Sharon Wolinski and Darlene Kipp all run to me and clap me on the back, and we share beauty tips and giggle over cute boys.

"Hi Danni!"

I turn around to see Travis Misker and Timmy Katz fishing from shore. It was Travis who spoke.

He hands Timmy his pole and walks toward me, his hands buried in his pockets.

"Are you here for the bridge party, too?" I ask.

"You mean the one at Bahia Honda?"

Oh.

Audrey never said which bridge. I just assumed.

The Bahia Honda Bridge is a few miles south of the Seven Mile Bridge. The *other* side of the Seven Mile Bridge.

A whole ten miles from where I'm standing right now.

"Wanna fish with us?"

Travis smiles at me. A real genuine smile that goes into his eyes.

Behind him, Timmy huffs with annoyance.

"Maybe next time," I say as I swing my leg over my bike.

I pedal away from the Seven Mile Bridge and try my very best not to cry.

ANDY, THEN AND NOW

A car slows beside me as Andy coasts to a stop.

"Hop in," he says. "I'll give you a ride home."

He exits the car and takes the bike from me, slipping it into his trunk.

We regard each other in silence until he returns to the car and shuts the door.

My streamers are caught in the latch of his trunk like severed fingers.

The sun is already setting, the highway empty, and I could bike all the way home on the center line. All I have to do is say, No.

But a decision was made, and it wasn't mine to make.

I accept my fate and sink into the passenger seat. As we head toward home, I wonder if Andy will put his hand on my knee like he used to, his fingertips tracing little circles on my skin.

But today, Andy's hands are at a perfect ten-and-two position on the wheel.

~

I'll always remember the first time Andy told me I was beautiful.

He passed me on my way home from school and offered a ride.

"What do you think of Dottie?" he asked when the small talk faded.

"She's nice."

"Do you think she's pretty?"

Andy studied me, analyzing every move I made. But somehow his scrutiny felt comfortable and safe. Like he already knew me, already knew what I would say.

"Dottie doesn't think she's pretty," he continued. "Between you and me, I think that's why she doesn't like having you around."

I wanted to leap from the car and run all the way home. *Dottie didn't like me?*

"That didn't come out right," Andy corrected, dipping his head in apology. "We both love you. You and your folks are like family. It's just that…"

He trailed off, readjusting his grip on the wheel. He swallowed so loudly it echoed across the car. I'll always remember that, too.

"It's hard for women of a certain age," he continued. "And you don't even know how beautiful you are. That's the scariest part."

Women of a certain age. I mulled this phrase around in my mind, trying to imagine what it might mean. But I never asked.

About a week after Andy called me beautiful, he found me on the dock behind my apartment and sat beside me. We watched seagulls battle over the crust of my sandwich. He offered me a sip of his beer. I declined. We laughed like two best friends. Like me and Jimmie.

He talked to me for a long time that day. About friends and school and life at home. I told him everything. All my silly middle school secrets vomited from my throat. When he asked me what I wanted to be when I grew up, I told him the truth about that, too—I didn't know. And he said that was perfectly okay.

He leaned forward to wipe a crumb from my chin, and when his fingers touched my face, I froze like a Key deer in headlights.

And then he kissed me. Just like that. It wasn't a big deal. He kissed my forehead at first, and I giggled, like when dad jokes about brainsuckers. Then he kissed my nose, which tickled.

But when he kissed my lips, something bloomed inside my gut, like my limbs were falling off. Like I was shrinking, slipping through the gaps of the dock.

I could taste his beer on my lips.

"You only did that because you were drunk, right?"

Andy slumped beside me. "Alcohol doesn't make you do things you otherwise wouldn't," he said. "It just gives you the courage to finally do them."

And with that statement, the fabric of my world unraveled. I was brand new. Someone interesting. Someone who was adored. Someone that a grown man desired.

We didn't talk about school after that. And we didn't talk about what happened. We just went upstairs.

Inside the apartment, mom and Dottie were curled up on the couch with ice cream and spoons. No bowls. Like two kids at a sleepover.

"How was the sandwich?" mom asked.

I couldn't speak with Dottie sitting there, smiling at me like she loved me. Like I was family. Because I knew the truth.

It's hard for women of a certain age.

〜

With tourist season over, Andy's headlights are two small lanterns ushering us through a ghost town. Familiar buildings reach for me like the spindly fingers of storybook witches.

"How's freshman year?"

"Fine," I say.

Andy turns and we lock eyes. For just a moment, he looks at me the way he used to before turning back to the road.

"You got a sweetheart now that you're in high school?"

Is he allowed to ask me that?

"Kind of," I say, "but he doesn't live here."

Andy laughs. "Then where does he live?"

"Ohio."

"I see. Does this sweetheart from Ohio have a name?"

"Eddie."

"And where did you meet this Eddie from Ohio?"

"Over summer."

"Sure, sure. Summer love."

"I'm not making it up."

"I didn't say you were."

"But I know what you're thinking."

"No," Andy says, clearing his throat, "you don't."

We drive past a cluster of Slash pines, their needles casting speckles of moonlight across US1.

"A boy your own age, I hope. Does this summer sweetheart have a last name?"

"Green."

Andy's grip stiffens on the wheel.

"The Greens? Like that little girl at the bridge?"

More silence as we drive past vacant motels and empty parking lots and closed restaurants.

I inch up the cuffs of my shorts and trace my scars.

If Andy asked about the cuts on my thighs, I'd tell him. I wouldn't lie one bit.

Ask me anything; I'll tell you anything.

Street after silent street.

Andy pulls into the lot, and I stare at my apartment complex, a dozen windows like fireflies in the woods.

"You can kiss me if you want," I say.

"Oh, Daniella."

Kiss me.

"Daniella," he says, shaking his head.

Please kiss me.

Andy's eyes are sad, his face flushed. And he won't stop shaking his head.

I'm a mess.

Deformed.

Practically a monster.

I don't know why I said it.

I don't even know whether or not I meant it.

But please, please, *just kiss me.*

I want to cry, and Andy looks like he wants to cry too, and he keeps saying my name, "Daniella," as if I'm supposed to know what that means. But he doesn't come closer. He doesn't put his hand on my knee, and he doesn't kiss me. So I guess that means no.

I shove my palm against the handle and spill out of the car.

"Daniella, we can't," Andy says, but I've already slammed the door, relegating his voice to a place where it doesn't hurt so much.

⌇

After that day on the dock, Andy and I were an item. Sometimes he'd catch me outside the apartment on my way home from school or meet me in the mangroves by the water. We pinkie-swore to never tell a soul.

Romance is more fun that way.

But then one day, he told me we couldn't see each other anymore. He said it was wrong. And then he walked away without saying anything else at all. No more meeting outside the apartment or in the mangroves by the water, and for days, my heart was a boulder in my gut.

This new kind of hurt was immersive. Like I was slipping into the deepest, darkest ocean, never to be seen again. And there was no tether, no board to walk on to find my way home. For the first time in my life, I was completely alone.

I slapped my cheeks. I sobbed, clutching the rim of the bathroom sink, watching my tears slip through the drain as if they never existed at all. As if they didn't even matter. I pounded on my thighs, scratched my skin. But it wasn't good enough. Not nearly.

I wanted to tell dad everything. Collapse into his arms and confess my heartache. I needed dad to tell me everything was going to be okay. That he loved me. That he was never going to get on his boat and disappear, poof, like mom always says.

But if dad knew the truth, he would never look at me the same way again. I could barely look at myself.

I also had mom to consider. She could never be friends with Dottie again after such a confession. Dottie's her only friend in the whole world, and I couldn't take that away from her.

I knew in that moment that this secret would have to die with me. I could never tell a soul.

That was the first time I reached for the razor.

SOMEWHERE IN GERMANY

Gunter stares into the milky night sky. It might be lovely, were it not for the ever present plumes of pollution and coal emissions.

"Nimm einen Mantel," his mother says from the small doorway.

Take a coat.

Gunter accepts, shrugging his arms into sleeves he long ago outgrew. He bends down so she can kiss the top of his head and then steps into the night.

He strolls the streets of his hometown and kicks at the paths grown weedy and dusty. Rusted vehicles lie strewn about, missing tires and engines, shattered windshields, chipped paint. In the distance, the shadow of a factory stack spits fresh cream into the sky.

Tonight, his mother had so many questions.

When do you leave, my son?

Do you have your papers yet? Your stamps?

How long will you be gone, my son?

Such an important man now.

I'm so proud of you, my son.

After working for the German shipping combine for the last two years, Gunter has finally been granted travel approval through the union. His background check was thorough: workplace efficiency, loyalty to the GDR, relation to party, draft status, past interactions with mass organizations, alcohol use, moral conduct. When asked if he had friends, colleagues, or relatives in

Cuba—or America—he said no, and officials determined Gunter to be a loyal member of the Communist Party. A low flight risk. The union will arrange his travel documents, and a month from now, he'll be on a ship bound for Havana.

Gunter pulls his coat against his neck and walks toward an empty farm near the edge of town, where there are no neighboring houses. Where the passing trains drown out his screams.

He waits patiently by the tracks. It's coming. He can see it. The train grows louder, burning coal spewing forth like vomit, smog against smog.

It draws nearer—nearer—and is passing now, a flashing tornado of train cars and the dark vacancies between them. The rails quake like chattering teeth. The noise is thunderous, and as Gunter contemplates the last time he will hug his mother, he screams.

His jaw unhinges, and spittle rains from his throat, but the sound is swallowed by the cacophony and heard only in his mind.

He thinks of his sister gazing out across infinite blue water, and not these desiccated farms and decaying homes, and he screams.

He thinks of the ship guards that will be all around him, armed and ready—the Volkspolizei and the plain-clothed Stasi—as he leaps into the black ocean, and he screams.

And only when he has fully exhausted his breath does he weep, watching the train grow smaller in the distance.

Gunter turns toward home. He walks past factory stacks and rusted vehicles, through gravel streets grown weedy and dusty, toward the only life he has ever known. Where, in a home that hasn't been repainted in decades, under a roof that leaks during a dense fog, he will sit by a candle at his mother's small kitchen table and draft a letter bound for America.

And then, to be sure their plan is not discovered by the German police should they search the package, he will mask his words under a veil of watercolor.

LITTLE DISTRACTIONS

Richard Quinn surveys his students like he's scouting a fishing hole. He hates Mondays. Thank God for pop quizzes.

He returns to his special edition of Moby Dick in his lap, the title gilded along the spine. Inside the front cover, a simple line drawing of a sperm whale. Twisting ribbons of ocean waves. Billowing clouds atop the horizon line. The printed letters: FROM THE LIBRARY OF. And the scrawl of his name in blue ink, penned in Miriam's delicate handwriting.

But he's not reading. Plaited among the pages is Galina's Polaroid. He couldn't risk Danni or Miriam finding it and asking questions.

So the Polaroid lives here now, tucked within the bulkheads of The Pequod, an ever present eavesdropper on the musings of Captain Ahab.

"Mr. Quinn?"

"What is it, Marjorie?"

"I don't understand number 24. Did we go over that?"

Richard doesn't have to check. He doesn't make mistakes.

"Just do your best."

Marjorie flashes him a smile. Not a child's smile, but a woman's smile, curved and puckered, before returning to her paper.

Two students throw wadded paper at each other in the back corner, but Richard doesn't say anything. Why bother? It's not the bad students you corral, it's the good ones. The ones for whom a little extra attention will actually make a difference.

Richard scans the room. Sweaty faces study scribbled answers. Knuckles pop and feet tap. They're so nervous. It's just American Lit. You'd think they were about to plead their case to a jury.

Or leap from a ship into shark-infested waters.

In the front row sits the strawberry blonde. She's chewing gum even though gum is against school policy. No harm done. Her name is Sara, and whenever Richard calls attendance, he has to force himself to say it loud and blunt, because a name like Sara just begs to be whispered.

Richard tries to look away, but her shoulders are so pale, hardly any color at all, just a spattering of freckles across her collarbone. Her long legs stretch well beyond her desk like downed tree limbs wrapped in lavender. Her hair is like a red sky at night. *Sailors delight.*

She wears a blue sweater. The fabric is thin, fuzzy, and coats her skin like paint. It's too hot for a sweater, but comfort is of no consideration to girls like her.

She suddenly looks up, meeting his gaze, and Richard jumps, dropping the Polaroid to the floor.

The bell rings, and students file into line, stacking their exam papers atop his desk as they rush to their next classes.

The room quickly empties, and Sara is the last one to turn in her exam. She blows a bubble, and when it pops, Richard is lost in a cyclone of warm sugar that vanishes all too quickly.

Sara walks away, her long legs covering the distance in mere seconds before her lavender stride disappears from view. Richard inhales the air, searching for more of her scent, but detects only chalk and ink from the dot matrix printer.

As he shuffles the papers into a neat pile, Richard spots a note at the bottom corner. He checks the name, Sara Racine, then follows the scrawl of her answers like a nautical map until he anchors on her handwriting.

If there's anything I can do to earn extra credit, let me know. My parents are out of town this weekend.

Below that, an address.

This is a bold move. Aggressive and highly inappropriate. He considers marching the paper directly to the principal, scheduling a conference. No need to get her parents involved at this stage. Just an honest conversation between the three of them. What's expected of students at this school, and what won't be tolerated.

But her invitation is too tempting a trophy, and as his next class files in, Richard tears Sara's note from the paper, and tucks it into his pocket. When he gets home, he'll stash it in the bottom drawer of his desk with all the others.

～

Mondays are Lovedays.

So are Fridays.

We begin the week with the love, and we end the week with the love. It was Audrey's idea. And since it's a Monday, we meet for lunch under the yellow skylights of the east wing, on the circular steps of the band room.

"Happy Loveday," she whispers, but it's so quiet in this part of the school that even those small syllables are caught in the acoustics, stretching to impossible lengths. We cover our mouths and explode out the back door.

This weekend, I'm sleeping over at Audrey's house, and we only have four days to figure out all the amazing things we're going to do.

Audrey already has big plans. She says we're going to listen to music, make fruit leather (whatever that is), shave our legs, and expose our deepest, darkest secrets. And then we're going to channel the spirits on her Ouija Board and find out who *really* killed Kennedy.

Like every Loveday, we head toward the mangroves that line the beach so we can spy on the hippies. We stay well-hidden, tucked into the shadows where the mangroves meet the Slash pines. A covert operation.

As I pull out my peanut butter sandwich, Audrey withdraws a glossy purple box. "Wanna see somethin' *far out?*"

Always.

She arcs dramatically over the mysterious box, and I watch her slide back the lid, inch by excruciating inch. I bite my lip and lean forward as she reveals the contents with a flourish.

I'll admit I'm disappointed.

"Rice?"

"And fish!" she says.

Audrey grabs a hunk of rice which has been mushed into cubes and cylinders. When she turns it over, I see all the colors. Green and pink and red and yellow.

I poke a sesame seed and lick it from my finger.

"It's called sushi," she says. "It's Japanese. My mom made 'em."

"What's inside?"

"Mostly raw fish and seaweed."

You shake baby shrimp and crabs out of seaweed. You aren't supposed to eat it.

"Is your mom Japanese?"

"No, silly. Her guru taught her how to make it."

I probe my teeth with my tongue, trying to dispel the sesame seed that's been sitting on raw fish all day, and I resist the urge to ask what a guru is.

After school, I walk to the bike rack, spotting Jimmie in the crowd.

But he's not alone.

Ellie Walker is with him, swinging her books in front of her waist like an Easter basket. She's wearing a navy-blue dress with polka-dots, and small white shoes that blaze like the sun against her tanned skin. Jimmie whispers to her, and Ellie's lashes flutter against her cheeks.

I creep closer, trying to overhear their conversation as Ellie places books in a bike of her own. I never noticed that she rode to school, too. I hear something about math homework, and something about smoked fish spread, and Ellie saying she's never tried it before. Jimmie tells her that she just *has* to try it. It's the best.

He's right. It is.

And then Ellie Walker throws her leg over her bike and waves.

"Bya," she says.

"Bya," Jimmie says.

Bya?

BYA?

This is the ultimate betrayal.

I stomp to my bike and drop my books into the basket, smashing a shell into the ground with the tip of my shoe. But when I find the courage to look Jimmie in the eye, he isn't looking at me at all. He's watching Ellie Walker pedal through the gravel lot and out of sight. A drop of sweat rolls down my ribs, and I smother it into oblivion with my shirt.

"Ready?"

Jimmie asks this in a voice that makes it seem as though nothing has changed between us, and somehow this enrages me even more, because I haven't heard the normal Jimmie voice since before his birthday party. And today, it's not for me. Today, it's for Ellie.

The breeze whistles through my spokes as we turn onto US1, rattling the playing card Audrey tucked in between them last weekend.

I follow Jimmie in silence toward my street, distracting myself with thoughts of school.

In Social Studies, there's a giant map of the world pinned to the wall, and this morning, I located the Florida Keys, a mere crescent arcing into the ocean. Then I found Marathon. Just a dot in a long string of other dots. My entire world, no bigger than a speck of dirt.

In Environmental Science, Mr. Lovitz taught us about The Butterfly Effect, and how one little thing—such as a butterfly flapping its wings—could have a drastic effect on something else. Like causing a typhoon on the other side of the world. He said it's scientific fact, but it's hard to believe something so small could change anything at all.

I stay a few bike lengths behind Jimmie the whole way home, and when I turn off at my street, he just keeps riding. He doesn't even look back.

～

Sometimes Richard Quinn doesn't need the sea.

Sometimes a sandbar is good enough.

The Valkyrie is too large to navigate onto the sandbar itself, so Richard cuts the motor along a deep trench, the water teal and burgundy beneath the hull. Liquid gemstones lighting his path.

Richard buffs his hand down his face and the skin draws toward his chin. He's changing. Getting older. It happened after all. He pushes against his whiskers and licks the salt from his fingertips.

In his jacket pocket is Galina's Polaroid. Though it doesn't belong to him, it's become as precious to Richard as an heirloom. When he holds the photograph, he trembles with anticipation, as if this adventure were his for the taking. An untapped memory. A map of places he could have traveled. And it is, he imagines. But he had said no.

If the rescue were a success, just imagine what the papers would say.

LOCAL HERO, RICHARD QUINN, BRAVES GREAT WHITES AND GUNSHOTS TO RESCUE GERMAN REFUGEE FROM BEHIND THE IRON CURTAIN.

And the news stations. Local, of course, but maybe National, too. International.

The ocean is fairly uninhabited this afternoon. In the distance, a sailboat. Beyond that, a freighter of some sort, heading south toward the Cay Sal Bank.

He pulls a cigar from his jacket pocket.

It's nice, just he and the Valkyrie on the sea. Richard runs his hands along her fiberglass hull and brass railing, watching a school of Parrotfish braid through the languid current.

American dream, indeed.

He bites the tip of his cigar, spitting it overboard, and strikes a match.

The good, old-fashioned American dream.

He holds the smoke against his tongue.

A mundane, uninspired American dream.

If Richard were being honest, sometimes he just wants to get on his boat and never come back. Poof. Just disappear. Beneath Saturn and Jupiter and a scorpion of stars, into the great watery beyond.

Richard stares at the Polaroid.

Sometimes he anticipates an empty wall will have formed in the emulsion, the man having moved on, grown tired of waiting for a hero.

His name is Gunter, and he stares at Richard, his gaze never wavering, his lips never speaking. Richard returns the photograph to his pocket for safekeeping and will not think of Gunter or Galina a moment longer. Their struggles are not his burden.

Richard thinks instead of the absence of sound at night, out here on the ocean.

Of insomnia.

The couch in his study.

Swells of deep water luring him to sleep.

And the first lines of Moby Dick: *Call me Ishmael. Some years ago—never mind how long precisely…*

Winding. Pulling.

The clacking of the reel.

And then he pictures Sara in the front row of his class. Her sweater. Her freckles. Her indecent invitation. She's waiting for him right now. He just knows it.

If he closes his eyes, he can still smell her bubblegum breath.

Richard pitches his cigar overboard. If he thinks about one more goddamned thing, he's likely to leap off the stern right now, swim for the unreachable horizon. Something has to change.

Fuck the American Dream.

All he has to do is show up. All he has to do is knock.

Damn the consequences.

Richard climbs the stairs to his cockpit, fires up the engine and makes a sharp turn toward The Duck Key Marina.

Richard stands before her door. He double-checks the address, trying to summon the nerve to knock.

This is wrong.

He shouldn't be here.

Doubt taps an endless percussion on his skull.

What is he thinking?

He knows better.

He can still change his mind. He hasn't done anything yet, and no one would ever know he was here.

If he just walked away.

Right now.

Richard Quinn pinches his brow between his fingers, rolling the skin. Trying to buff away his excuses.

Richard runs his hands through his hair and smooths a wrinkle from his shirt before giving a light knock on the door.

Maybe she won't hear it, and he can skulk back to his car, go back to his good and decent life with Miriam.

But the door swings open, and she's suddenly there before him. No turning back now.

She stares at him with eyes that are the palest of blue, perhaps a little green, defined by a dark ring of indigo.

Like a sandbar at the edge of an ocean trench.

Richard steps forward. "You still lookin' for a madman?"

Galina opens the door wider, her face flushed, and she nods. It's all she can do as Richard steps into the darkness of her motel room and disappears. Poof.

SOMEWHERE IN GERMANY

Gunter wonders what it might be like to seize the guard from behind, snatch the weapon from his shoulder and fire into the wall.

But he knows the truth—he would merely notch the brick before he was shot dead in the street.

There's only one guard before him, but there could be others. Anywhere. Everywhere. He walks past the armed man without a glance from the ground.

It's a short walk from the shipping combine to the post office, but his coat is not thick enough to obscure the parcel hidden beneath, and the stroll feels more like a death march.

From a lookout post, a woman's face emerges above the west side of the wall, and Gunter pauses, meeting her eyes.

Other than her plump rouged cheeks and vibrant yellow shirt, she looks like anyone else Gunter might pass on his walk. Just a woman.

With a camera.

She raises her arm and captures a photograph, the sound of the film advance lever ricocheting off the brick like shots fired.

Gunter ducks instinctively, and then hobbles away, shielding his face with the collar of his striped coat. Behind him, the guard hollers, "Komm runter von dort, du abscheuliche Fotze!"

Get down from there, you vile cunt!

The guard throws rocks and chunks of brick at the woman. She hollers as one strikes her, and then disappears beyond the wall.

When Gunter arrives at the post office, he hands the parcel to the attendant and requests international post. The young man drops it into a box beside a half wall.

When the package arrives in Key West, Florida, his sister will unveil a pad of blank paper, a pencil, a pan of watercolors with the brush inside, and a painting of a cornfield—the sky purple, the corn black.

And hidden beneath the paint, the words he almost couldn't write for fear he may wake tomorrow to discover it's all been a dream: Ich habe meine Dokumente. Wir werden bald zusammen sein.

I have my documents. We will be together soon.

The man rushes to the train station, failing to hide the grin on his face. As the sun falls, the sky morphs to a faint shade of decay, and he recognizes the color from the watercolor pan: Davy's Gray.

He descends the platform steps and wonders what the sky will look like in America.

A KINKS KIND OF NIGHT

The week slogged by in slow motion, heavy and lumbering, and Friday couldn't have come fast enough.

Mr. Mallory assigns our end-of-the-year project, but it's not due until June. I don't care that we have to write a poem about what home means to us. I don't care that Mr. Mallory wants us to *dig deep* and find the true meaning of home within our hearts.

Because the Halloween Dance is just two weeks away. Even Margaret Leech has a date, and it's all anyone can talk about. I overheard Darlene Kipp tell Sharon Wolinksi that Margaret was asked to the dance by Ronald Weller. The hems of Ronald's pants are always dirty, and he smells like baked chicken.

I'm going to be a witch for Halloween and Audrey's going to be a black cat. None of the boys are brave enough to ask Audrey to be their date, so we're going stag, just the two of us. Like real sweethearts.

Audrey meets me on the band steps for Loveday. Her mom's picking us up after school for our sleepover, so I brought an overnight bag. I told Jimmie I couldn't bike home with him, and he promised not to tell his folks.

We slip through the exit doors and toward our special place by the beach.

The mangroves are seeding, and long fleshy darts jostle in the breeze. I look up to see more seeds dangling above my head, some over a foot long. Audrey strokes the length of one, and it falls from the branch, cleaving the sand with ferocious accuracy.

There's music on the hippie beach—a lone man slaps a drum while others lounge in the shadows, passing a joint.

Audrey bops her head to the sleepy beat of the drum as she opens her box of sushi. She doesn't offer me any, which suits me just fine.

"What's in the bag?" she asks.

"Clothes and records, mostly."

"Far out." Audrey nods her approval. Or maybe she's still lost in the drumbeats.

Audrey's *really* into music. So I brought my entire record collection: The Shirelles, Wanda Jackson, The Beach Boys, Lesley Gore, Patsy Cline. And The Supremes, a birthday gift from Jimmie. And because my collection was meager when stacked together, I swiped some of mom's as well: Woody Guthrie, Chuck Berry, Miles Davis, and Bruno Walter.

I'm about to take the first bite of my sandwich when we hear footsteps approaching through the mangroves. Audrey and I freeze.

The hippies!

We've been caught!

"Audrey?"

"Mom?"

"Where are you?"

Audrey bolts to her feet, waving, and I turn to see a woman, slender and graceful as an anole weaving through the roots and seeds.

"This is quite the hideout you've discovered."

Audrey's mom is stunning, and I force my mouth closed. She's not pretty in a normal "popular" girl kind of way. Her beauty is different. Odd. Her eyes are dark and complex, and her eyebrows are overgrown, which somehow makes her even *more* beautiful. Now I understand why Audrey stands out from the crowd. This kind of otherworldliness could never blend in.

"You must be Daniella," she says.

"Nice to meet you, Mrs. Lipke."

"Please, call me Katia."

KAW-tiya.

"That's a real pretty name."

She smiles, her lashes like palm fronds sprouting from the lids. "So is Daniella."

"What are you doing here, mom?"

"I thought you girls might want to start the fun early. Anyone opposed to playing hooky, just this once?"

Unreal.

Audrey shovels her sushi back into its box.

I'm too stunned to answer, but I follow her lead.

As we walk toward a car hidden in the shadows, and not parked in the lot with the others, I ask, "How did you know where to find us?"

"It's a Loveday," she says. "Where else would you be?"

My bike is wedged into the trunk of Katia's car, its streamers whipping through the air. I try to imagine what mom would say if I told her that Audrey and I ditch lunch twice a week to spy on strangers. She'd gasp in shock. Blame my deviant behavior on peer pressure. She might even slap me, the action no longer immune from consideration.

In the front seat, Audrey and Katia giggle, leaning into each other like best friends. They take turns peering into the rear-view mirror to adjust a bandana, a stray hair. Katia licks a finger, smoothing her eyebrows as though they've gone rogue since leaving the mangroves.

I've been forgotten, stashed out of sight alongside my bike. I need to find a way in.

"I like your necklace, Mrs. Lipke," I say, before correcting myself. "Katia."

I don't like her necklace at all, but I'd never say so. Shriveled and misshapen, her necklace looks like a string of dehydrated rat testicles, the color of that sludge dad hoses out of the waste can at the marina.

Katia fingers the strand, grinning at me in the rearview mirror. "Thank you, Daniella. These are rudraksha seeds, but I'm sure you knew that."

Audrey turns to face me. "When you wear them," she adds, more aware of my ignorance than is her mother, "you're blessed by Shiva."

I shrink into the gaps of the upholstery.

"Plus, the sun is in my seventh house, you see," Katia says plainly, bringing a dehydrated testicle to her lips.

Audrey looks to her mom. "Very inauspicious."

"*Very*."

I stare out the window as we pass my street, peering through the canopies and searching for a glimpse of something familiar.

The diner flies by the glass, and then we're hurtling toward the Vaca Cut Bridge.

I gape through the window at Poppy's memorial. At times, it feels like a lifetime ago, but there is the teddy bear, still tied to the post. Its fur is sun-bleached, no longer vibrant pink. The flowers are gone, long ago crisped by the Florida heat, consumed by rot and humidity.

When we pass the turnoff to Key Colony Beach, I realize where we're going: Coco Plum, where rich houses are built right onto the beach.

Katia makes a sharp turn, and my ordinary landscape transforms into uncharted luxury.

The roads are newly paved, and all the houses have fancy new cars in circular driveways.

Audrey's house is no exception, built right onto a private strip of beach.

It's not a two-story house—it's a *three*-story house, painted white and green, with two balconies visible from the driveway alone.

I trail behind, throwing a glance to my simple bike strapped to a fancy car. Her rainbow streamers dance in the breeze as though pleading in sign language. As I near the house, my bike accepts her fate, streamers slumping beneath her.

Katia bounds up the steps, her rudraksha seeds swaying from her neck. She pushes open the large wooden door, and a gust of air conditioning envelopes me, as cold as The Sundry Store. The sweet scent of citrus blossoms burgeons from the opening.

It's lovely and inviting, and…

I just want to go home.

But I say nothing as I haul my overnight bag up the steps, and the large wooden door slams shut behind me.

I stand in the kitchen, leaning against a large, independent counter they call an *island,* trying to decide which part of Audrey's house is the strangest.

Near the front door is a small sitting room. It's not their living room, which is just past the kitchen. According to Audrey, this room is only for *sitting.* But the furniture is covered in thick transparent plastic.

"You don't sit on it?" I asked.

"Never. It's the *good* furniture. You can sit in the living room, but not the sitting room."

So there's an island in the kitchen, and plastic-wrapped sofas in a sitting room you can't sit in.

Audrey even has her own private balcony attached to her second-floor bedroom, with a hammock suspended across. The tide surging against the sand creates a constant roar of white noise.

And in the living room, *a color television.*

The screen is large, luminescent, and it draws my attention like the sunrise against the Atlantic.

I can't look away from all the colors housed in a shiny wooden frame, rich and luxurious. All the hues reflect off of Katia's white rug at once, transforming the living room into a dance club. I imagine Katia as a secret Go-Go dancer at night, swishing the fringe of her white halter top, the plume of her false lashes.

"Fruit leather's ready!" they announce in tandem, as though sharing vocal chords.

Audrey picks at the corner of something that was applesauce only a few hours ago but is now hardened and marred by striations of a plastic shelf.

I want to say, No, thank you.

But instead, I peel the fruit leather from Audrey's sticky fingers and nibble at the corner.

I glance into the living room where a newscaster is speaking of rare footage just received by the station—a photograph taken over the Berlin Wall by a French photographer.

An image flashes across the screen.

Audrey's television may be in color, but the photograph is still in black and white, a stark contrast to the newscaster's honey brown suit and sandy blonde hair.

On the screen is an image of East Berlin. No mangroves, no water, no coconut trees. Just pasty rubble, a swirling pale sky, and a man in the foreground, cloaked by the black and white stripes of his coat. In the distance, a guard rushes toward the viewer while gripping a gun. His body is small within the frame, but his mouth is a dark, hollow cavern.

The young man in the striped coat shields his face from the camera with frayed fabric like iron bars cloaking his identity. Only his chin is visible, a veneer of stubble recorded forever in colorless gray.

Richard Quinn shoves back from his desk and the springs of his chair howl beneath him.

He stares at the stack of books Carolyn Saylor ordered for him under the guise of new library acquisitions, no questions asked: Laws and Guidelines of the Federal Maritime Commission, Merchant Ships of the Federal Republic Of Germany, and a rare manual on the construction of turbine engines. The last one is written in German, which Richard didn't anticipate, but he's been studying the schematics, hoping translation can be detected in the lines.

Apparently, it can't.

The final class of the day begins to file into the classroom, but Richard can't concentrate. Not on the books in front of him, nor the lesson plan he scribbled on a bar napkin over the weekend.

The room spins and Richard kneels forward, feeling his face blanch.

"You alright, Mr. Quinn?"

Who said that?

Richard holds up a hand, keeping his eyes on the floor to assure himself he hasn't yet fallen over.

Beneath the books on his desk is a large topographical map of the Atlantic Ocean with a special concentration on the southeastern edge of the United States. A corner of the paper sags from his desk like a cerulean blue tongue, and he wills it to swallow him whole.

This was a mistake.

He never should have knocked on her door.

He should never have said yes.

"Mr. Quinn?"

How did his socks get so dirty? He can smell them from here. Sour, dank. How many times has he worn this same pair?

The bell rings, signaling the beginning of class, and a hush fills the room.

He's to meet Galina in Key West tonight. Galina *and* Shane. That's right—both of them. Richard looks forward to meeting the man who will locate the ship, signaling Gunter to jump while buzzing the passengers for distraction. Better be one hell of a plane.

Miriam's dining with Dottie tonight, and Danni's at a sleepover. That girl with the short black hair, whatever her name is.

Good. No one to question his whereabouts.

Richard wants so badly to confide in Miriam about the rescue. About his doubts and fears. But he can't risk another downward spiral. It's better this way. Better for them all.

Someone clears their throat in a ploy to get his attention, but Richard Quinn can't stop staring at his socks. And the hems of his pants, which are stained brown with God-knows-what.

"Can someone please open the door?" Richard bellows across the room, a little too loud.

He watches the stockinged legs of a young woman pad toward the door and prop it open with an extra chair. A breeze tunnels into the small classroom.

Finally, he looks up at his students.

In their wide-eyed stares, their slack mouths and furrowed eyebrows, he sees his own lunacy mirrored back at him.

Murmurs spread across his classroom like a plague, hazy at first, but he plucks a few words from the racket: What's happening? Is he okay? Face is pale. Sick? Cuckoo. Totally unglued.

In the front row, Sara Racine stares at him too, her gaze sharper than those of the other students. It's been this way since her invitation went uncollected. She crosses her long legs and bounces her foot in irritation.

Did she really think he would consider such a proposition? She's a goddamned *child*. She should be grateful he didn't call her parents immediately.

Richard fumbles with the books on his desk, stacking them to the side, and folds the map. Refolds the map. Opens it and traces the established folds with his finger before trying again. He then tucks the mostly folded map under the books, and stands.

He can do this. He can teach his classes. He can protect his family. He can make himself presentable for his meeting with Galina and Shane tonight. And he can save a man from the Atlantic Ocean.

He is goddamned Richard Quinn.

Richard clears his throat. "Open your books to chapter 3, please."

A timid voice says, "Chapter 3 was last week, Mr. Quinn. We're on Chapter 4 now."

Fuck.

Richard stalls at the blackboard, chalk in hand. He squeezes his eyes shut and takes a deep breath before facing his students once more.

"Then open your books to chapter 4."

After our fruit leather snack, I show Audrey my records. She scans the titles.

"Who's this old guy?" she asks, pointing to the Bruno Walter record I swiped from mom.

I shrug, and it's an honest answer.

"Wait here," Audrey says, her icy blue eyes aflutter as she rushes to a record shelf near her dresser. She must have a hundred, and I stash my feeble stack into my overnight bag, waiting for her to return with something more hip than a bunch of old guys.

She skips back to me and spreads the albums across the floor like a deck of cards.

The Beatles: *Revolver*. The Kinks: *Face To Face*. The Yardbirds: *Over Under Sideways Down*. The Byrds: *Mr. Tambourine Man*. And Jefferson Airplane: *Surrealistic Pillow*.

"Pick," Audrey says.

This is a test, I just know it. There's a right and wrong answer to be offered, and it's *dire* that I answer correctly. The only band I recognize is the Beatles, so I point to *Revolver*.

"Yeah," she purrs, "they're groovy. However…"

I've answered wrong.

"It's really more of a Kinks kind of night, don't you agree?"

I nod, unsure of what that means. But yes, I agree. I really, really do.

~

After school, Richard saddles into an empty barstool beside Peter Quade, and the two men exchange a quick acknowledgment as Richard signals the bartender. He then lights his cigar, offering an extra to Peter, who accepts with a large exhalation of gratitude.

"How's that little skiff you're workin' on?" Richard asks. "The yellow one."

"Issues with the fuel line. Engine. All of it."

"Stroke engine?"

"Tiller."

Richard takes a long pull of the Cuban, relishing the smoke like a long-awaited sedative. The sun coming in from the port windows is high and sharp, and paints The Armada in a harsh, cold light.

Richard faces his friend. "You know anything about German vessels?"

"You plannin' an invasion?"

Richard burps. "Not on a Friday."

He looks around the bar. Empty, save for himself, Peter, and Gabe, the mailman, slumped against the corner of the countertop, a pouch sagging from his shoulder and spilling undelivered envelopes onto the floor.

"Just a little project I'm workin' on," Richard continues.

"Battleships?"

"Passenger ships, freighters, that sort of thing."

Peter tilts his head and squints against the sunlight. "I can't even fix a tiller engine, my friend."

"Fair enough."

In a few hours, Richard will drive to Key West—the southernmost city in the United States—and meet the other madman in Galina's life: Shane, the pilot. Richard wonders why Shane would agree to something so reckless. Shane probably wonders the same of him.

Richard can smell himself. Even over the smoke and dirty bleach rags, his scent emerges victorious. Sour and peppery. He needs a good shower. And a shave.

The bartender returns with drinks for the two men. Peter holds one up to Richard. "To man's grueling quest to fix the unfixable."

Richard Quinn lifts his glass. "I'll drink to that."

Richard weaves through Mallory Square. Groups of young people lounge near the docks. The sound of an untuned guitar echoes from a lounge.

He scans the crowd for Galina's tall, blonde frame and sandbar eyes.

A drunk woman stumbles into Richard. He grasps her elbow, helping her to her feet, and she laughs at her clumsiness, glancing back to her friends. When she meets Richard's eyes, the woman tries to compose herself, repositioning her disheveled hair.

"Well, hi there," she says, her voice light and smooth. "You saved my life. Looks like I owe you one."

Richard releases her elbow and walks away. He does not answer. Does not look back.

The woman yells, "Asshole."

Richard pockets his keys and withdraws the Polaroid for good luck. It works. Just ahead, he spots Galina sitting across from a tall, stocky man draped over a half-wall.

As he approaches, the pilot stands, dwarfing Richard by a few inches, and Richard pushes his shoulders back and raises his neck before extending his hand.

"Shane," the man says.

His grip is harsh, and Richard squeezes back.

"Richard."

Their fists bob between their bodies, neither man willing to break first. The veins in Richard's hand begin to throb.

"So you're the pilot," Richard says.

"And you're the boat captain."

Shane releases his grip, and Richard pushes his hand into his pocket where the circulation can recover in privacy.

"What are you drinkin'?" Shane asks, signaling the bartender.

"Whiskey," Richard orders from the blushing girl who seems to have lost her words, retreating with only a nod and a lopsided smile. "So," he begins, "your plane is equipped with a VHF radio, yes?"

"Plenty of time for that," Shane says, reaching across the tabletop and giving Galina's thumb a squeeze.

"But that is why we are here," Galina interjects. "We should delay no longer."

Shane ignores her, but it reads as compassion rather than disregard.

"So, Richard, tell me about yourself. It seems you're something of a local legend. I've heard many stories."

The bartender returns with drinks, retreating with a pout when Richard does not meet her gaze, offering only a curt nod of thanks.

"That so?" Richard says. "I've heard nothing about you."

Shane laughs. "I suppose not."

"How many hours you got in the sky?"

"Stopped counting long ago."

"Sounds like pretext to me."

"Pretext?"

"An excuse. The groundwork lain to explain away one's deficiencies," Richard lectures. He tosses the whiskey past his tongue in one swig. "Deficiencies. Shall I explain that as well?"

Shane shifts his weight from one foot to the other. "Now I may not know all the fancy words," he says, "but neither am I an idiot. And you'd be wise to recognize the difference."

Galina's brows furrow, a seed of distrust germinating in her expression, and Richard settles back into his seat. He chews the inside of his lip and strokes the Polaroid through the fabric of his pocket.

Shane is youthful, but he's no child. Perhaps only a few years Richard's junior. Though his beard is thick and unkempt, his hair is cropped short. Ex-military? Possibly.

Shane straightens in his chair as Richard is making no effort to hide his scrutiny.

Richard clears his throat, begins anew. "Shane The Pilot," he says.

"And Richard The Boat Captain."

Waves lap the sea wall, saltwater foam rushing in beneath the dock at their feet.

"You've heard many stories." Richard says. "I assume you have stories of your own?"

Shane belts out a hearty laugh.

The sound is infectious, and Richard can't help but join him.

Galina lets out a long, appreciative breath.

"Regale us, then," Richard says, "with a grand tale of the sky."

Shane slams both hands on the tabletop, his eyes frenzied and aglow.

"A wonderful idea," he declares, signaling the bartender. "But first, we're gonna need a lot more liquor."

⌒

It was, indeed, a Kinks kind of night, and I wake to the tune of "Sunny Afternoon" bouncing around my head.

Audrey stirs beside me, stretching her arms and tussling her hair. "Breakfast?"

"Breakfast."

I follow Audrey to the kitchen where Katia's mixing grains into bowls from a dozen glass jars. I recognize oats and pecans, but the other ingredients are a mystery.

"What's that?" I ask, pointing to small beige pellets.

"Millet. And this over here is flaxseed. Wheat berries. Chia. The normal stuff."

I raise an eyebrow.

"So," Katia says, pouring milk over the grains and seeds, "who killed Kennedy?"

Last night, Audrey set up her Ouija board, and we went hunting for answers.

Audrey shrugs. "The spirits weren't cooperating. Unless his initials are Y-7-M."

Katia places a bowl in front of me, and I dip my spoon into the slurry, segregating the grains, while beside me, Audrey shovels it into her mouth.

After breakfast, I lock myself in the bathroom to change into day clothes, and when I enter her bedroom, Audrey's naked, donning only a pair of yellow cotton underwear.

I spin around, shielding my eyes.

"What are you doing?" she asks.

"You're *naked*."

"So? It's just a body."

Oh.

"You're being silly. Help me pick something."

I hover against the door, deciding between flight and friendship.

Friendship wins.

"Okay," I say, staring at the floor, "but I won't look."

"Suit yourself. Purple pants or red skirt? It's very mod, don't you think?"

"Very mod."

"Danni, you didn't even look."

I look up, trying to keep my eyes on the skirt.

"I like the buttons," I offer.

"They're fab, aren't they?"

Audrey steps into her red mod skirt with the fab buttons, and I peek, even though I promised not to.

Audrey's pale as a sandbar. She has small breasts like me, but she isn't shy like me. She has pimples on her butt like me, too.

But no scars on her thighs.

She bounces up and down, wedging the skirt over her hips.

Just a body.

But it's Audrey's body, and I want to keep looking.

Audrey tucks a soft white shirt into her skirt and ties a navy bandana in her hair. She looks like a cover model.

Audrey and Katia are having a mother-daughter day, and no one has asked me to join.

By the time we make our way downstairs, Katia's already waiting by the front door, wearing the same mod skirt as Audrey, in baby blue.

"This is for you," Katia says. "They're in bloom. Aren't they lovely?"

She hands me a hibiscus flower so large and colorful it belongs in a gardening magazine. The center is dusty lavender, fading to pastel pink along the rippled edges of each petal.

"Something to remember us by."

Like I could forget.

"Try it like this," she says, tucking the flower behind my ear where it sags against my cheek. I grin, feeling foolish and beautiful all at the same time.

"We place it behind our right ear to let the world know we're open to adventure," she whispers with a wink, as if this is a secret code I'm familiar with.

The heavy wooden door swings closed behind us as we emerge into the real world.

Audrey pulls her seat forward, but as I walk past my bike still trapped in the trunk, the streamers graze my arm.

"Actually," I say, "I'll bike home from here."

"Are you sure, Daniella?" Katia asks. "I'm happy to drive you."

Audrey nods her agreement.

"I'm sure. It's a beautiful day."

I walk my bike down the circular driveway, holding the flower against my cheek so I don't lose it.

When Audrey and her mom pass me on the road, they offer one final wave from the windows before their arms vanish from view.

I feel as though I've emerged from a parallel universe, where everyone dines on mysterious foods and speaks in foreign tongues. Sushi? Rudraksha? Millet? I can't keep up.

Audrey's a different species.

And somehow, I hate her, and want to *be* her, all at the same time.

On my way home, I pause at the Vaca Cut Bridge to visit Poppy's memorial.

I touch my gold owl necklace, twisting it around my neck. Even though Eddie is states away, it keeps him close to my heart. I'll wear it forever.

I kick the dried-up flowers over the side of the bridge where they're swallowed by the hungry waters of the Vaca Cut, unlucky, and pull the hibiscus from my ear, tucking it into the ribbon around the bear's neck.

The current slams against the bridge, splashing high enough to soak my feet. In the distance, a small boat cuts its motor, making a slow approach. I can't watch. I fling my leg over my bike and pedal away so fast that my feet are dry by the time I reach my street.

SOMEWHERE IN GERMANY

Gunter wraps a microfilm of his diploma in plastic. He does the same to the letters he's received from his sister, and a small stack of photographs he couldn't bear to leave behind. Once everything is watertight, he places the small stack atop his identification papers and travel documents.

His mother calls from the other room.

My son.

"Ja, mama?" he answers, pulling clothes from a narrow drawer while appraising the hollows beneath his eyes in the dresser mirror.

Will you take many photographs for me? she asks.

When Gunter answers, he closes his eyes so as not to face himself in the mirror.

"Ja," he promises.

And his mother's lilting voice sings, Oh, that's wonderful. I do long to see ocean.

Today, Gunter procured something special for his mother. The gifts were difficult to find, and favors were promised, but he'll be on the other side of the world soon and has little guilt. When he finishes packing, he'll make his mother a fine supper: a slab of ham, two potatoes, and a small honeycomb for dessert.

Gunter carries a stack of folded clothes to the suitcase lying open on the bed. The garments tremble in his grasp as he tucks the microfilm, letters, and photographs within a clump of socks, and then zips the suitcase closed, placing his papers and travel documents on top. He sits on the mattress and his luggage slumps against him like an anchor already sinking and dragging him to the bottom of the ocean.

Gunter boards a ship in the small port town of Warnemunde, the air smelling of dead fish and piss. He buries his face against his sleeve to smother the stench. Below the gangplank is the commencement of the Baltic Sea, and though the weather is harsh—the skies dark and bitterly cold—it's the first time he's seen the sea, and he cannot look away. He bumps into another passenger, apologizing with a silent raise of the hand, a dip of the head.

The man before him turns and smiles. He wears a faded blue shirt, a brown coat frayed at the elbows, and a belt much too long, now tied in a knot around his waist. The man's hands tremble, barely able to grip the railing as they wait to board. The men exchange one more glance before Gunter thinks better of it, returning his attention to the guards ahead, who are rifling through the suitcases of each inbound soul.

Gunter wipes the sweat from his brow despite the chill and looks to the sky, giving silent gratitude to whomever may be looking out for him. Last night, before boarding the first of many trains that would take him from a small farming village outside of East Berlin to a bustling port town on the northern coast, he'd changed his mind. He removed the microfilm, letters, and photographs wrapped in plastic from his suitcase, opting instead to strap them flat against his body.

He can feel them now beneath his coat, where he once hid a package from America.

HURRICANE

We learn about the hurricane on a Friday, one week before the Halloween Dance.

Audrey and I file out of Algebra with the rest of our class as soon as the summons is declared over the speaker: *All students, please report to the gym for a school-wide announcement.*

I hate the gym. It reeks of old sweat, cheap deodorant and the spicy tang of Brut cologne swiped from fathers' dressers. The bleachers are never washed, forever gilded in dried mud, ketchup and snot. The ripped basketball net sways like a dead jellyfish snagged on a branch of Staghorn Coral.

We shuffle between two rows of bleachers, stepping over a heap of something squishy and unrecognizable.

On the court is Mrs. Berrett, the guidance counselor. Her carrot hair blazes with sunlight every time a fresh surge of students opens the door.

"Hello students and faculty," she begins. "I know it's the end of the day and you're all eager to get home."

A round of applause fills the room.

"Just a quick announcement, and we'll have time for questions in a moment. No one in this room is a stranger to hurricanes."

Now Mrs. Berrett has everyone's attention.

"The National Hurricane Center has released an update for the southeastern U.S. that I'd like to share with you."

Audrey snaps toward me, her eyes like magnifying lenses, her bottom teeth exposed in a nervous wince.

"Last week, a Navy reconnaissance plane spotted a potential threat forming off the coast of Africa. Over this past week, the storm has become better organized, and an eye has developed. As of now, it's still a tropical storm," she assures us, "but they predict it'll intensify within the next 48 hours."

Ooohs and *Ahhhs* ricochet from every bleacher, as though we've just witnessed a fireworks display.

"This is a serious matter and should not be taken lightly. The storm has already done major damage over Barbados and St. Lucia and will pass over Puerto Rico and the Dominican Republic in the next couple of days. Mr. Lovitz will have a map posted in his classroom tomorrow morning and will be tracking the storm. Keep an eye on those pins, and we should know more after the weekend. Does anyone have any questions?"

Mrs. Berrett points to a student behind me.

"Is it gonna hit us?"

"I don't know, Michael. We'll keep everyone updated as we learn more. Yes?"

Audrey stands to speak. I didn't realize she raised her hand.

"What about the dance?"

A swarm of hushed chatter fills the room, and Mrs. Berrett nods as though anticipating this very question. "Yes, the Halloween Dance is only a week away, and nothing is cancelled at this time. You're not the only ones looking forward to a little revelry," she adds with a mischievous smile. "I've been working on my costume as well."

Mrs. Berrett looks around to gauge our interest, of which we have none.

"I'll give you a hint," she says, rubbing her hands together. "I might just have some 'splaining to do."

I file out of the gymnasium, neither worried about the storm, nor interested in picturing Mrs. Berrett as Lucy. But when I arrive at the bike rack, Jimmie's already gone.

I look up just in time to see him riding out of the lot, Ellie Walker biking beside him.

⁓

Richard Quinn presses into the corner of his chair and watches the news.

He also watches his wife. She's turning again. He can see it in her dull gaze, her pallid skin.

Miriam folds herself into the armrest furthest from her husband, fiddling with the hem of her skirt.

"You look beautiful today, my love."

No answer. Only the slightest dip of her head.

On the screen, a man speaks before a map showing the southeastern United States, Haiti, Cuba and The Dominican Republic. The land masses are rendered in simple gray shapes, punctuated by latitude lines and crisp gridded dots. This is not a map of artistry; it is one of necessity. The man on the screen places a pin just east of Puerto Rico.

The television is muted, and neither Richard nor Miriam have stood to correct the volume. The weatherman orates in silence, while outside the window, a light rain ushers in the sunset.

"Supper was delicious, my love."

Supper was a heap of overcooked pasta mixed with tuna, peas and canned mushroom soup. Tonight, Miriam did not use her electric skillet and she did not brew tea with her sage and silver tea kettle. Richard picks the skin of a pea from between his teeth, wiping it on his napkin.

"I hear Danni wants to be a witch for Halloween," Richard says. "Have you started her costume, my love?"

Miriam pushes back a cuticle. "No, dear."

Richard peers out the window, watching the rain fall. "I'll be chaperoning the Halloween Dance next Friday, and—"

The telephone interrupts Richard, and he waits for Miriam to stand and answer the call.

On the television, the camera clips away from the weather to show a video of protesters in Washington DC, a colony of ants surging toward The Pentagon. Richard leans forward, narrowing his eyes at the screen, while in the background, the telephone continues to drone.

Young men shout at the camera in muted silence. The crowd is uproarious, tussles of elbows and fists between youth and authority. The Memorial Bridge clogged with bodies, like a tangle of hair in the bathtub drain.

The phone stops ringing.

Clashes and arrests on the screen. Banners and signs. Military men with rifles and bayonets file down the bone white steps, creating a barricade against the chaos. Long-haired boys draped in blankets, smiling and flashing peace signs at the camera as though thriving in the mayhem.

When the phone rings once more, Miriam flinches as though hearing it for the first time.

She stands, straightens her skirt, and steps toward the kitchen, answering on the fourth ring.

"Quinn Residence." Her voice is like an impression left in an old mattress.

On the television, a newscaster stands before a photo showing a young man in a thick sweater slide a flower down the barrel of a gun.

"Richard," Miriam says, laying the receiver on the kitchen counter.

He stands, and when he passes his wife, he cannot smell her perfume, her body lotion, the powdery tang of her lipstick. All he smells is the dewy musk of unwashed hair. He can't fault her for that, he thinks, wiping the sweat from his brow. It's been a sticky October.

"This is Richard."

Galina's voice bursts through the receiver, agitated with talk of hurricanes and wind and repeating her brother's name over and over, like a meditation. Gunter, Gunter.

Richard covers the mouthpiece, but Miriam has already retreated to the bedroom without another word, the scent of her scalp like a trail of breadcrumbs he cannot follow.

AURORA BOREALIS

Mom left hours ago for brunch with Dottie. I'm starving, so dad makes sandwiches.

Whenever mom spends time with Dottie, I fight the urge to tell her everything that happened between me and Andy. I pinkie-swore to never tell a soul, yet the confession threatens to burst from my throat, nonetheless. What I want to say is: Mom, there's something I need to tell you. I don't want it on my conscience anymore.

But I say nothing as she walks out the door. Every time.

I sit at the dining room table, my chest heavy and solid, as dad severs my crust.

"You don't have to do that anymore, dad."

"I know how my little girl likes her sandwiches."

I'm not a little girl anymore. The crust is the best part!

But I only smile.

I wait for him to grab plates and join me at the table, but he wraps the sandwiches in two napkins, stacking them atop the counter.

"Pumpkin," he says, "how about a little adventure?"

I don't ask dad where we're going. Adventures are more fun that way.

When we arrive at Quade's Boathouse, I follow dad past the warehouse and its docked, towering giants, to where fuel tanks are stacked in the back. Peter Quade hunches over an old skiff, fiberglass dust drifting through the sunlight like plumes of cigar smoke. Dad waves a hello.

"Grab that one," dad says, pointing to the smallest tank.

When I lift it, the liquid pulls to one side, nearly knocking me over, and I have to use both hands to steady it.

"Atta girl."

Dad grabs a second and third tank, and I follow him back to the car.

The fuel pillaged from the boathouse sloshes in the trunk as we tunnel south through Marathon and over the Seven Mile Bridge.

When we reach Big Pine Key, dad halts in the middle of the road to allow a Key deer and her fawn to cross the highway. They're in no hurry, and the small doe delays in the headlights, dipping her head and shimmying her tail as though thanking us for our consideration. I laugh, and the doe rushes forward, startled, turning back for only a moment before ushering her little one into the trees and out of sight.

We're almost to Key West when dad suddenly slows to a stop in the middle of the highway. There's nothing around us but mangroves.

He looks in the rearview mirror and waits until a car traveling north turns out of view before stepping on the gas and driving straight into the mangrove thatch.

The path through the roots is narrow. A few choice mangroves have been slashed to allow easier passage, but the car still thumps over sand pockets and tide pools. I cling to the dashboard as we lurch over a root that's begun to grow across the trail.

And then suddenly we emerge into a secret clearing.

A peninsula of sand juts into the Gulf, shrouded from the mainland by thick mangroves, their seeds heavy and pendulous, swaying like little bombs awaiting launch.

A young man approaches the car, dressed head to toe in camouflage. Even his boots are the color of sand. It's odd to see someone dressed this way considering the heat. I imagine he must get very warm.

He has thick dark hair, and eyes big and brown as a walnut. Black stubble peppers his neck before curling out from beneath his shirt.

He would be quite a hunk if not for the gun strapped across his chest.

I sink into my seat.

It's a machine gun, like the kind you see in war movies. Gray metal, with dirt and dents marring the surface. Bullets are draped around his throat like a candy necklace.

"Quinn?" the man asks, his voice thickly accented.

Dad nods, and the man points his gun toward the beach, approving our access.

Extending beyond the sand and into the water are a handful of makeshift docks. Not at all like the docks at the boathouse. These are crafted of tires and spare wooden planks, strung together by rope and fishing line.

Two small boats are tied offshore, machine guns atop tripods mounted to their bows.

Dad grabs my knee and gives it a little shake as we pull onto the sand.

"Everything's okay, pumpkin," he says.

Is it?

Four men, dressed like the first, approach dad as he steps from the car.

"Roll up your window," he says to me as he shuts the door. I'm quick to obey.

Their voices are muffled, but I can still hear them querying dad in Spanish.

Dad raises his hands and points to the trunk. "Fuel," he says, before adding, "gasolina."

"Gasolina?" a man asks.

And dad says, "Sí."

The men follow him to the trunk, and though I want to keep an eye on dad, I face forward to see a lone man emerge from one of the docked boats. He stands, watching us from the stern with binoculars.

I feel his eyes on me, and I duck down.

Unfamiliar voices speak in unfamiliar tongues all around me.

I'm lost.

I need a tether.

I need dad.

But dad is out of sight, and right here, on a secret beach behind a slashed mangrove path, surrounded by men with guns and binoculars, there's no board to walk on to find my way home.

I am completely alone.

Sugarloaf Key is a blur, as are Cudjoe and Little Torch Key.

The sun is setting fast, bathing our faces in crimson light.

Dad's quiet. Too quiet.

Sweat beads along his hairline. He nibbles his bottom lip.

"I shouldn't have brought you," he says.

I fidget with a seam unravelling on my shirt. "Who were those men?"

"They needed help."

"For what?"

"I don't ask questions."

We drive through unnamed habitation, just clusters of empty land masses and islands beyond the road.

In the Florida Keys, bridges are like stitches holding it all together so nothing washes away.

Dad withdraws a brand-new wooden box of cigars from beneath his seat.

He bites one end, spitting it out the window. The car fills with smoke as dad lights it and nurses the tip.

He rolls the cigar in the air before him. "Sweet as honey," he says.

But all I detect is the chalky odor of a stale ashtray.

"This stays between us," he says. "Just me and my girl. They didn't scare you, did they?"

Yes.

"No."

We continue over the Bahia Honda Bridge with an eye toward the ocean.

Dad arcs through the window, peering at the water below. "Do you see him?"

I know who he's looking for, and I study every swell, every reflection, for Mister Brownstone.

But as always, the giant hammerhead is nowhere to be found.

Dad collapses back in his seat as we reach the end of the bridge, slamming his palm against the wheel.

"Next time, dad."

"What would you do," he says, "if you were swimming in the ocean, and saw Mister Brownstone?"

"Just a sea puppy, right?"

"A sea puppy with teeth!"

"Yours are bigger."

Dad grins at me. A gaping, lopsided smile that looks absurd on his face. "Thirsty, pumpkin?"

"Yeah."

"Me too."

It's been said that at the very moment the sun vanishes below the horizon, it emits a flash of brilliant green. A natural anomaly of sorts. Our own private aurora borealis that happens so fast you'll miss it if you blink. I've never seen it, but dad says it's real, so it must be.

The sun is almost gone, only a sliver of light above the ocean, growing smaller, smaller still, and I force my eyes to stay open.

Almost there.

Almost.

And then the sun is gone. No flash of green. No flash of anything.

"Did you see it, pumpkin? The flash?"

I shake my head. "No flash."

"Sure there was," he says. "Lit up the whole bridge. You must've blinked."

We coast past Quade's Boathouse and the Botel before turning into the gravel lot of The Armada.

Oh.

We're not going home.

Dad comes to a stop and smiles at me as if this were a special treat.

"It's not a problem," he says. "You're with good ol' dad."

My lucky day.

I follow him to the entrance but can't take my eyes off the lighthouse in the distance. The very place on the rocks where I shared my first—and last—kiss with Eddie.

Dad leans his weight into the heavy wooden door, and as it parts for us, all I see is smoke.

Blurry lights hang over a smoky bar, where men speak smoke and breathe smoke and laugh smoke.

I cough into my arm as dad locates two seats below circular windows with a view of nothing.

"Andy," dad says.

"Ishmael," he greets. "And Daniella."

Dad waggles his fingers at the bartender, which must be some kind of private language, because the man delivers exactly what dad wanted. I feel like I'm spying on a secret brotherhood, all covert handshakes and smoke signals.

It stinks, and my thighs meld to the seat cushions, peeling off like a bandage every time I move. Can't dad see that I'm tired and just want to go home?

"Get my little girl some pretzels, would ya?" dad says to the bartender. "And a Shirley Temple."

I wish dad would stop calling me his little girl.

But it *does* feel good to bite down on something crunchy. And there *are* extra cherries in my Shirley Temple.

"You go fishin' today?" dad asks.

"Thought about it," Andy says, nudging an empty shot glass with his knuckle. "Didn't."

Dad nods. Another secret code.

"Dottie's waiting for me at home," Andy says, pushing himself from the barstool. "She's makin' my favorite."

Andy's two completely different men rolled into one: Ishmael's first mate, and the *other* Andy. Listening to him talk about his wife cooking dinner is like eavesdropping on an imposter. A bodysnatcher.

I crunch down on another pretzel and figure that if I finish my Shirley Temple quickly, we can go home. I take a big sip.

Behind us, the door to the Armada opens, and warm night air rushes inside.

In a room full of barrel-chested men, the beautiful blonde is easy to spot. Dad sees her, too. Can't look away. His eyes dart from the woman, to me, and back again. He lays his hands flat on the counter as though a gust of wind may blow him away.

And then the woman is standing before us, silent, her expression one of…expectation?

"Andy," dad says, "would you be so kind as to take my daughter home?"

Mom worries about dad with other women, and I try to picture him with someone other than mom. Calling her *my love*. Touching her, kissing her. The image is unconvincing. Dad would never do that. But I find myself clutching my Shirley Temple in defiance.

"Let's go, Daniella," Andy says.

As we approach the old wooden door, I hear the blonde woman say, "Everything is in place for Friday night."

I hear Dad swallow the contents of his shot glass before striking it against the bar top. "My wife thinks I'm chaperoning a dance."

And then Andy's hand is on my shoulder, pushing me into the night.

~

Richard Quinn extends his hand to help Galina onto the Valkyrie, stepping back to allow inspection. She walks cautiously, grasping for balance each time a small wave rocks the vessel. Richard tries not to smile.

"Radio?"

Richard indicates the ladder leading to the cockpit.

He follows behind, his hand hovering at Galina's back to catch her should she fall. Galina grips the wheel, attempting to turn it left and then right, but it's heavier than she expected. He wrestles the mouthpiece from the VHF radio. Galina takes it from him, holding it in her palm like a looking glass. As though with this single item she holds the future in her hands.

"Hello," she speaks into it, and Richard laughs. "Why do you laugh at me?" she demands.

Richard takes the mouthpiece from her and flips on the radio, adjusting the squelch knob. Static fills the small cabin, and Galina sinks into the captain's seat, pressing her fingers to her lips.

"When it's time," he says, "this is how Shane and I will communicate. We press this button and speak. Simple as that. You'll hear me from the air."

Galina slumps in the seat.

"I will not," she laments. "Shane says I am to wait onshore. He says it is too dangerous."

"He may be right."

When Galina begins to protest, Richard says, "Everything will work out just fine. Your only job is to have cold beers ready and waiting."

"And this hurricane?"

"A small one," he says. "It should pass south of us. We'll get some wind, some rain, but nothing serious. We're prepared, Galina. Shane is precise, well-trained, and you've found yourself the best boat captain this side of the Iron Curtain."

She grunts, unimpressed.

"Friday," he says.

"Friday."

"Did Gunter receive the letter? Does he know what to do?"

"Yes."

Richard checks his pocket and withdraws the Polaroid, returning it to its rightful owner.

Galina holds the Polaroid to her chest, turning back to the ocean, silent.

Richard gives her this moment and says no more.

KITCHENWARE

Richard Quinn grits his teeth and shields his eyes against the fluorescent assault of the Dadeland Mall as he breaches the threshold of Burdines.

Just inside the entrance, shackled to a pedestal, stands a woman molded of plastic. Her arms are rigid, emaciated, palms twisted at peculiar angles, fingers pointy as the snout of a marlin.

Her face is painted with joyful optimism, and Richard hopes it is contagious.

The crowd pulses and shifts around him like ocean waves, ebbing and flowing as he approaches the nearest counter.

"Can I help you find something, Sir? For your wife, perhaps?"

Standing before Richard is a raven-haired young woman with lipstick so pale her lips disappear into her chin.

"This is our bestseller," she continues. "Isn't it lovely?"

Richard accepts the lipstick, peering down the tube.

"Peach-a-Boo," the woman says.

"God-bless-you."

She giggles. "Peach-a-Boo. That's the color. It compliments every skin tone."

"Is that what you're wearing?"

The woman dusts her fingertips across her lips. "As a matter of fact, it is." Her lashes flutter against her cheeks.

Richard knows he could have the woman's number in his pocket before she could properly spell *Peach-a-Boo*.

He returns the lipstick. "I'll pass."

Richard browses the jewelry counter, finding nothing of interest.

He dodges an effervescent salesgirl on a mission to saturate him with orange peel and musk.

In the ladies' section, Richard fondles chiffon nighties and tightly woven girdles. His calloused fingers snag the soft satin of an evening gown.

He's here to find his wife a gift before he dives headlong into the abyss. Something that will prove his eternal love for her, even as he sneaks off into the night.

Something to remember him by, should he not return.

His gaze lingers a little too long on a garter set modeled by a rigid mannequin, and Richard begins to detect the sneer of judgement on the faces of nearby shoppers.

Overhead, the fluorescent lights flicker. They may as well be flashing stars over a nighttime ocean, because Richard is lost and adrift at sea.

His clothes are too tight, and he tugs at the belt biting into his waist. He gulps for air, seeking the familiar tang of salt.

Richard spins around, seeking direction, exit, anything.

Women gather in clusters among the seemingly endless aisles of silky undergarments. They cross their arms and whisper, content to watch from afar as a drowning man is caught in the clashing currents of communal shopping and brutally lit ladies' fashion.

Richard Quinn needs a safety buoy. He needs a lifeboat.

And then he sees it. A small sign offering reprieve.

Richard has never been so happy to see eleven black letters printed on a striped banner: KITCHENWARE.

BLACK VELVET

Monday morning, we all stared at the map Mr. Lovitz posted to track to hurricane.

Little red pins connecting lines of red thread like Pick Up Sticks across the Atlantic. The first pin was placed just North of Saint-Marc, Haiti.

Tuesday morning, a new pin, a new line of thread, positioned directly through the city of Baracoa, Cuba. A beast creeping closer. A savage nomad atop the waves. We were still hopeful.

But on Wednesday, the mood grows solemn as Mr. Lovitz places the most recent pin on the northern edge of Cuba, just west of a small town called La Boca. The hurricane has picked up speed and is predicted to continue west-northwest, eventually making a northern hook toward Louisiana. It's only a Category 1, and dad says it'll weaken further, but Mr. Lovitz thinks it'll intensify. Something about converging winds and excessively warm waters in the Gulf.

Dad says the school will make a decision today about the Halloween dance. I told Audrey, and Audrey told Mercy, and Mercy told Sharon, and Sharon told everybody. The tension is undeniable. Everyone wants to know if the dance will be cancelled. Everyone is waiting to learn their fate.

Mr. Lovitz is trying to lecture on fossil fuels, while outside, a cleaning crew pressure-washes the wall after someone spray-painted, *Hey, hey, LBJ. How many kids did you kill today?* across the east wing. Mr. Lovitz has to shout above the racket, and we're enjoying that about as much as he is.

I glance out the window. On the hippie beach, a man chases a woman through the waves, and when they tumble onto the sand, he kisses her.

I stroke my gold owl necklace and think of kissing Eddie. Sometimes this necklace is a carrier pigeon, transporting sweet nothings all the way from Ohio. But sometimes it's an albatross clawing at my neck.

Margaret Leech taps my shoulder. "Sharon told Darlene that Travis likes you."

I turn around, and the sunlight through Margaret's fuzzy hair makes her look like an angel on fire.

"Travis Misker? No way," I say, though my cheeks flush.

Tell me more.

But Margaret changes the subject. "I'm gonna be an astronaut for Halloween," she says. "My mom's even making a moon out of papier-mâché."

"We never got to the moon, Margaret. Apollo exploded. Astronauts *die*."

"Not always."

"Uh-huh. Besides, only boys can be astronauts. Everyone knows that."

Margaret's eyes narrow, and for the first time ever, her lips close over her teeth, concealing her mouth completely. And she no longer looks like an angel on fire. She just looks mad.

It's not until the last class of the day that the intercom buzzes to life.

Good afternoon, students and faculty.

Even Miss Mason turns an ear toward the speaker.

After the most recent update from The National Hurricane Center…

Please.

...it seems the hurricane is continuing a western path. We're still anticipating strong showers as the storm moves into the Gulf. Possible inland flooding, strong winds, and rain...

Just say it. Break my heart.

The speaker crackles and falls silent. We hold our breaths.

...so don't forget your umbrellas Friday night!

Every classroom erupts in applause, and we hoot and holler in solidarity.

I collapse into my chair, depleted with relief.

As Miss Mason struggles to refocus the students, Audrey hands me a box.

It's an at-home hair dye kit by miss Clairol. In Black Velvet.

"I can't. My mom would kill me."

Audrey groans. "You *have* to. Witches have black hair. Your mom will understand."

I lift the flap with my thumb, peering at the mysterious bottle within.

Audrey's right. It's Halloween. Mom will understand.

When I arrive home, mom doesn't even glance up from the couch. She stares intently at a catalog in her lap, running her thumb along a page.

"Audrey's helping me finish my costume for the dance," I say. "I'm going as a witch," I add, because she hasn't asked.

"The dance," she says, her voice even and robotic.

"Yeah. This Friday. It's not cancelled."

She nudges the page. "Your father will be there."

Mom doesn't know. She doesn't know that dad met with a beautiful blonde woman at The Armada last weekend. She doesn't know that the woman told dad she has everything ready for Friday night. Or that dad told the woman, "My wife thinks I'm chaperoning a dance."

But *I* know.

I want to scream at mom that if she smiled more, this wouldn't be happening.

But instead I make my way to the bathroom, a box of hair dye burning a hole in my hand.

I don't recognize myself.

With my hair parted down the center, hanging loose and heavy before each shoulder, I look like a cover model. I look like a hippie on the beach, ready to burst into the waves at sunset.

I look like Audrey.

If Eddie could see me now, he'd sprint across every state line for the honor of escorting me to the Halloween dance.

But Eddie won't be there.

I wonder if Travis will like my new hair.

Maybe mom won't be mad once she sees how beautiful I look. In fact, I'm sure of it. Mom's a woman too, and can appreciate another woman's desire to reinvent herself.

I walk into the kitchen, waiting for mom to look up.

On the counter is a brand-new Sunbeam Mixmaster. The box is unopened.

I'm not hungry, but I open the refrigerator, close it.

Open a cabinet, close it.

Nothing.

Then I turn around to find her staring right through me. I regret everything.

The silence widens as I shuffle my feet, awaiting punishment.

Mom's mad. She hates it. She hates *me*.

It's amazing, this power she has over me.

I had planned to stand tall and proud and tell mom I'll be dying my hair black from now on, whether she likes it or not.

But mom says nothing and returns to her catalog.

I stand speechless in the kitchen, wondering if I should say something. Mom isn't mad. She didn't yell, and she didn't punish.

She didn't even notice.

I wake the next morning eager for school.

I love my long, black hair. I'm confident and beautiful and everything else a woman should be.

But even so, I wait until I hear dad bustling about his study before sneaking out the front door undetected.

Jimmie spots me as I skid onto the gravel at school.

"Um. Hiya?" he says.

I shrug. No big deal. "Hiya."

"What did you do to your hair?"

Ellie Walker approaches, swinging her books in front of her waist. When she sees me, she laughs, covering her mouth.

It doesn't bother me one bit. Honest.

I look to Jimmie.

Please don't laugh.

"In the sunlight, it almost looks blue," he says. "It's neato."

"*Very* neato," Ellie adds with a slight twist of her lips. Bitch.

"C'mon, Jimmie," she says, spinning toward the middle school wing.

I want to say, Don't go. Don't follow Ellie Walker. Be my best friend again. Let's have Key lime fights behind the haunted house and catch crawfish and buy penny bags of candy, a dollar each.

But then Audrey's voice bellows down the hallway. "Oh. My. God."

She runs toward me, mouth agape, and I can think of nothing better.

"It looks. So. Fab!" she says, fluffing my hair and hopping up and down. "We *have* to show you off!"

She pulls me toward Environmental Science, and Jimmie watches me sprint past the middle school wing, a look of torment on his face.

Mercy says I look amazing and should dye my hair black for the rest of my life.

Sharon adds nothing herself but nods along with Mercy.

Margaret asks what brand I used because she wants to dye her hair black too. I lie and say I don't remember. I don't want Margaret copying me and Audrey. This is *our* thing.

Later, everyone stares at me as I walk to my next class, and I hide from dad when I see him in the hallway. I'm not ready for that. Not in front of everybody.

Audrey beams and twirls around before departing for her next class. She points at me and walks backward in a delicate choreography only Audrey could pull off. "You're my spirit guide," she hollers. "I wanna be *you* when I grow up!"

$\sim$

Richard Quinn pushes his knuckles into his jaw and turns back to the mess in his study—to the books Carolyn Saylor ordered for him on German vessels spread across his desk.

He struggles to focus on the texts, but the lines are like an Etch-O-Sketch, his scribbled calculations like Braille.

Richard closes his eyes and imagines he is fishing on the deep swells of a black ocean, a pole rigid in his hands, the line swaying from side to side.

Winding.

Pulling.

The clacking of the reel.

Tucked in the corner of his study is a brown twill suitcase. Inside is a change of men's clothing for Gunter, a windbreaker, and an old spare towel from the back of the bathroom closet.

He recites the first few words of Moby Dick in his mind, *Call me Ishmael. Some years ago…*, before letting the rest die away, resigned to his melancholy.

It's of no use. Tomorrow is the big day, and tonight he will find no peace.

Richard closes the books on his desk, concealing them beneath lesson plans, and makes a quiet retreat down the hallway, pushing open Danni's door.

He perches on her bed, careful not to press too deeply into the mattress and wake her.

The room is dark, and he places a hand on her back, feels her breaths rise and fall beneath his touch.

Richard sits with his daughter for a while, remembering her as a young girl wrapped in a yellow ducky towel, eager for dad to recite another story. Her blonde pigtails. The year she lost all four front teeth at once, and the ensuing lisp when she spoke.

He sees it all in his mind, like a filmstrip projected on the wall. Richard wants to believe he will return tomorrow night with another grand story for his daughter. To see her elated and proud of her old man.

To see the newspaper articles that will surely be written.

And hear the adulation of their friends and neighbors.

The whole goddamn town.

Richard strokes Danni's hair and leans forward, breathing her in. She smells like a woman now. But beneath the fragrance of White Rain and Clearsil, Richard can still detect the scent of his little girl.

Tomorrow.

Dear God, tomorrow.

Richard feels for the Polaroid in his jacket pocket, but it's no longer there.

THE MADNESS OF CROWDS

Gunter has lost all interest in seeing the ocean.

In the neighboring bunk sleeps the man Gunter met upon boarding. After days spent at sea, he still wears that faded blue shirt and a belt knotted around his waist. The two men have crossed paths many times, nodding like old friends, though no pleasantries have been exchanged. Gunter knows nothing of the man other than his shortage of clothing.

Gunter pushes from his bunk and steps into the hallway.

Men part for him, and no one meets his eyes as he approaches the starboard side of the ship, gazing toward the horizon. The moon is large, its reflection smeared across the ocean like a gangplank to the sky.

A man leans beside him and Gunter tenses. His documents are still wrapped in plastic and strapped to his body. He feels them like a knife to his back.

"Hallo Freund," says the dark figure.

Hello, friend.

Gunter sees the man's belt first, a loose knot tied around his waist, and he relaxes. Gunter has a good sense for people. This man is not a guard. He is not Stasi.

"Hallo," says Gunter.

The man leans against the railing and Gunter joins him. Together, they stare at nothing.

"Christoph," the man says, introducing himself.

"Gunter."

Christoph nods. This is not the place for handshakes.

A silence falls between them, but it is not disinterest. The silence is dense, filled with conversation they would have had if this were another place, another time. Gunter sighs. Christoph sighs. Just two men admiring the sea.

Behind them, staff bustle about—maids, servers, ship guards and passengers alike. But there is little conversation.

"America?" Christoph asks with a flick of his finger, his voice hushed.

"Irgendwo."

Somewhere.

There, he says.

Gunter appraises the spattering of lights—pinpricks on the horizon.

Gunter has studied the maps. It is not America, but likely a small cluster of islands called Bermuda. He considers saying as much but doesn't want to disappoint the man.

Gunter shrugs. "Vielleicht."

Perhaps.

Christoph leans toward Gunter and whispers, When we get closer, I'm going to jump.

Gunter coughs, swallowing it back. This man is a loon. He knows nothing of Gunter or his affiliations. Gunter could be Stasi for all Christoph knows. Or an informant. *Anyone* who is a loyal member of the Communist party could have this man's head right now.

Come with me, Christoph says. We can go together.

Gunter does not take his gaze from the horizon when he says, "Nein," with a curt shake of the head.

Christoph points to the pinpricks of light, and Gunter squeezes his eyes shut, aghast at the man's lunacy.

"America," he says.

"Es ist nicht Amerika!"

It is not America!

Christoph pushes into the railing and runs his hands through his hair. The ship rises on a wave, and when it crashes down, saltwater drenches the two men. Christoph laughs, and all is forgiven.

Do you have a wife? Christoph asks. Children?

"Nien," Gunter says. "Nur eine Schwester."

Only a sister.

"Schwester?" Christoph says with a smile. "Ist sie sehr schön?"

Is she very beautiful?

Gunter does not remember, but is about to tell the man, yes, when a sharp horn sounds behind them, followed by a voice exploding from a hidden speaker.

This is your captain.

Christoph stops speaking. Maids and servers and ship guards and passengers all stop their activity to await the unexpected announcement.

Due to a weather disturbance, the ship will reroute. We will take a southeastern path around the storm. Arrival will be delayed. That is all.

The speaker hums before returning to silence. The only sound is the slapping of waves against the hull.

The ship lurches, making a sudden turn, and Christoph sprints toward the stern, following the pinpricks of light as the ship changes course.

Gunter wants to holler, Don't worry, friend. That is not America anyway.

But even if he could shout such a thing without penalty, his thoughts have already returned to Galina.

His sister. In the middle of the ocean. With a boat captain and a pilot, and no brother to save.

The sound of a splash fills the otherwise sleepy deck, and a guard runs past Gunter, rifle in hand, toward the stern.

Gunter leans over the railing and spots something glowing in the water. Something like moonlight. Or a pale blue shirt.

The speaker crackles to life once more, this time with a siren.

The ship crew halt their tasks to stand rigid against the railing, a human fence constructed of maids and servers and guards and passengers—not real passengers, but plain-clothed officers. Gunter freezes, and a woman places her hand on his back. He hollers, spinning toward her.

Sir, she says, return to your cabin at once.

He can still feel the pressure of her fingers near his spine, a mere inch from the plastic-wrapped documents.

Gunter nods, but when she turns away, he peers between two men at attention against the railing.

Christoph struggles through the waves. He kicks the water with his boots, finding little traction.

Searchlights scan the Atlantic, trapping Christoph in their glow, the nighttime waters as brilliant as a summer morning on the farm.

Gunter wants to see his new friend dive below the waves, resurface farther out, beneath the moon.

Sir, return to your cabin.

A guard fires into the water.

But Christoph still swims. The guard missed.

Sir.

Another guard joins the first.

Sir, return to your cabin.

"Ja," he says, taking a step toward the doorway.

And then the man in the pale blue shirt and knotted belt finds his stride, propelling himself through the waves.

Passengers are herded toward the doorway, and Gunter is caught, pulled from the railing. He resists, pushes back, as overhead the siren continues to soar.

A line of guards marches toward them, batons in hand. But Gunter withstands the surge of bodies, weaving in between them to keep his eyes on the ocean.

He has to see. He has to know.

When a second guard fires into the water, Christoph stops swimming.

Gunter watches the pale blue shirt rise and fall, listless atop a deep sea swell. A third shot is fired, painting the wind red.

There's a clip of utter stillness, as though every soul on the ship stops breathing, stops speaking, stops moving for a small moment of unity before the searchlights power down, returning the deck to blackness.

RAPUNZEL, SNOW WHITE, AND A BLACK CAT WALK INTO A ROOM

Tonight is the Halloween Dance, and I will be the best witch anyone has ever seen.

I buff white makeup across my face and smudge my eyelids with charcoal. Then I swipe mom's red lipstick over my lips and smear a dollop of dad's Brylcreem across my hair before slipping a black witch's shawl over my head.

Audrey says I'm the prettiest girl in school, and I search my reflection for evidence. My eyes droop a little at the corners. My nose is too big. And those shadows have returned on either side of my chin, emerging like moon craters right before my eyes.

And I no longer look like a cover model. I'm no longer a hippie goddess.

The box of Mr. Bubble mocks me from the bathtub ledge, so I turn on the faucet and dump it down the drain, watching it struggle to foam in its final moments.

I shove my toothbrush into my mouth and brush. Hard. I brush until saliva drips down my chin, pooling in my neck, and don't stop when my teeth are clean, or when the bristles smash against my gums, or when my teeth begin to ache from the pressure. I brush so I don't look in the mirror again.

So I don't think about Eddie and his stupid letter, or worry why he never wrote me back.

Or wonder if he still thinks about me at all.

So I don't feel sad that Jimmie likes Ellie Walker best.

Or that dad would rather be with that blonde woman from the bar than chaperone my dance.

I brush so I don't reach for the razor again.

At least I still have Audrey.

The one good thing in my life.

It's not until I spew a mouthful of blood across the drain that peace finally finds me.

When I step out of the bathroom, mom says nothing about my costume, turning back to the television.

Dad's in the kitchen.

"Look at you," he says, beaming at me. "You're a vision in black. Wait. Did you dye your hair?"

Oh.

I push backward, wishing for an island in the kitchen to conceal me.

I twirl the ends of my hair, staring at the floor, because I know how dad must see me.

Raggedy shawl with unfinished seams, like some kind of drifter. Cherry red lips like a harlot from 1950s Hollywood. It's 1967, and only sluts wear red lipstick. Everyone knows that.

Right now, dad's looking at me and thinking, She's not my little girl anymore.

But I am. I really, really am.

Dad places his hand on my head and I nearly topple over from his weight rocking me back and forth.

I smile, but it's not until dad places a finger under my chin, lifting my face that I look up, finding nothing but tenderness in his gaze.

"Pumpkin," he says, "you look beautiful."

I arrive early, but already the school hallways are slashed with orange and black streamers. Members of the dance committee are tacking a HALLOWEEN DANCE banner to the cafeteria doors. Mrs. Berrett is attempting to place small candles in the mouths of jack-o'-lanterns lining the walkway, but the outer bands of the hurricane are moving across the Gulf, the wind severe, and her efforts are wasted. She flaps her arms in frustration before stomping away, her gingham dress clinging to her thighs, exposing the clasps of Lucy Ricardo's stockings.

I scurry into the cafeteria before I lose my hat, and Margaret Leech runs toward me in a spaceman suit, her teeth burgeoning from behind a dome of plastic. A papier-mâché moon sways from her shoulder like a purse.

"Far out," she says with a smile to rival a barracuda. "You look great, Danni."

"Is Audrey here yet?"

"Haven't seen her."

I head toward a long table where cups are arranged in a grid and filled with something cold and sweet.

"Danni! Wow. You look…"

Travis Misker strolls toward me.

"Just, wow," he says.

Travis is dressed as a policeman, which makes sense since his dad works at the station. He isn't wearing a real uniform—just black pants and a black shirt. Pinned to his collar is a badge made of tin foil. But I'm pretty sure the hat is real. Travis looks like a grownup in his costume, and I take a big swallow of my punch, wiping away a spill as it falls down my chin. Quickly, before he notices.

"You're a policeman," I state.

Smooth.

"Every year. My mom doesn't like to sew. Do you have a date tonight?"

I shake my head and toss the rest of my punch down my throat, like dad at the Armada, about to signal the bartender for another.

"Me neither," he says.

The cafeteria doors open, and two students dressed as wolves march into the room.

"Well," Travis continues, "see you around."

I would've complimented his hat, or at least said goodbye, but the doors swing open once more, and Audrey glides into the room, a cat ear headband atop her head, long shaggy tail bouncing behind her.

This is *our* night—the Halloween dance!—and it's going to be amazing.

But then I see Mercy Turner and Sharon Wolinski beside her, and pause mid-stride.

What are they talking about?

And why is Audrey laughing?

She spots me, grasping hands with Mercy and Sharon as she runs toward me. "You. Look. Amazing. Sorry we're late," she says with a pout.

"We?"

"Us, silly."

"Mercy kept messing up her braid," Sharon says.

"Did not!"

"Did too! Katia had to cut a piece off because it was tangled."

"Just a small piece."

"It was. Just a small piece. But still."

Sharon reaches over, smoothing the ends of Mercy's Rapunzel braid.

"It's fixed now."

"Totally fixed. Can't even tell."

"But it was gnarly."

"Totally gnarly."

Sharon's dressed as Snow White in a long skirt of yellow and blue. On her hand is a corsage with a bird figurine tucked inside the flower.

"So," I begin, trying to mold my thoughts into actual words, "you all got ready together?"

"Yeah," Sharon says. "At Audrey and Katia's house."

"Punch!" Mercy says, sprinting toward the table. Sharon follows.

I look to Audrey for an explanation. She didn't ask *me* to get ready at her house. I picture her undressing in her bedroom during our sleepover, standing naked before me. That took real trust. Love. Did she do that with Mercy and Sharon, too?

But Audrey says nothing as she releases my hand and bounds toward the drink table.

I want to cut off Mercy's braid and smash Sharon's bird corsage against the ground.

They all look back at me, and when I force a smile, my injured gums break open, pink saliva pooling against my lip.

GRAND FALSEHOODS

Richard Quinn presses against the helm, pushing the Valkyrie through clashing waves. He bares his teeth, hollers into the wind, licks the salt from his lips.

Richard shakes the rain from his eyes and examines the sea, the wind, the looming shelf of clouds ahead.

It doesn't look good.

He reaches for the VHF mouthpiece and dials into the channel Shane specified.

Using authentic identification over the radio made Richard nervous—and he said as much during their last meeting—so Shane suggested alternatives.

"This is the Pequod, headin' south for some Amberjack. Wailing Bird, what's your twenty? Over."

Richard listens to the silence that follows, buried beneath an endless expanse of static.

A gust knocks the Valkyrie to one side, slamming Richard against the wall of the cockpit. He struggles to right himself, peering up at his antenna, a hissing rattlesnake whipping back and forth above the boat.

"Goddamn it," he mutters, stumbling forward to grasp the wheel. "Wailing Bird," he yells into the mouthpiece. "Wailing bird, do you copy? Over."

The waves are bloated and angry, thrashing against the hull. The wind screams and bellows as Richard steers into a gust so as not to be capsized by it. Rain hammers the thin roof as Richard makes one more attempt on the VHF.

"Wailing Bird?"

No response.

Hail peppers the deck, but this is no deterrent to Richard Quinn. He gnashes his jaw and leans into the helm, pushing the motor to full power. This hurricane will not take his victory.

Richard slams the mouthpiece onto the radio and grips the wheel with both hands. He's late. But tonight was the Halloween dance, and he wanted to see his daughter one final time before charging into battle.

When he left shore, Richard was a boat captain. But tonight, he shall return a warrior.

~

Watching the news with mom on a tiny black and white television is more fulfilling than watching Audrey dance with Mercy and Sharon to the final chorus of "I'm A Believer." Audrey doesn't even like The Monkeys. She likes The Kinks. And The Yardbirds. And Jefferson Airplane. I know this because we're best friends.

The wind whistles over the first chords of "Ruby Tuesday" as they all sway in a three-way slow dance. Audrey waves at me to join, sticking out her lower lip when I refuse.

We were supposed to go stag, just me and her. But I've been stood up.

Even Margaret Leech is having a better time than me, leaning her head on Ronald Weller's shoulder. Ronald's dressed as a skeleton, in a black jumpsuit that's too long, painted with white lines. I hope Margaret's astronaut helmet protects her from the stench of baked chicken.

I have to calm down. I don't want to push Audrey farther away from me and closer to *them*. I hope she hasn't told them about our secret spot on the hippie beach.

The hippies! In this weather!

I have to check on my Love Children. They're probably losing their tents, their wind chimes ripped to shreds by the harsh wind, tangled in the mangroves.

I glimpse one last time to Audrey before slipping out of the cafeteria unnoticed.

Into the storm.

The rain batters me from both sides of the overhang as I run toward the east wing. I look to see if Audrey has followed, but the hallway is empty except for the water flooding in from the lawn.

When the door to the east wing slams shut behind me, it sounds like I'm inside a tornado. The rain falling on the skylights, paired with the acoustics of the band room, create a pounding echo, and I rush to the exit door, peering through the small glass window. I can't see the beach. Or anything at all. Only the rain.

"Hi," someone says, and I jump. "Over here."

I recognize Travis's voice, but he's tucked within the shadows of the band room steps.

"Where are you?"

I smell him before I see him. Marijuana.

The band room door is unlocked, cracked open and throwing warm light across Travis's feet.

"Janitor left it open," he says. "Flake."

"What are you doing out here?"

Travis shrugs. "You're soaking wet."

I look down to assess the damage. My shoes spew rainwater with every step. My stockings are ripped, and my shawl droops with moisture, my nipples plainly visible through the fabric. I gasp, horrified, and yank the costume from my body.

"Far out," he says, taking another hit off his joint. He passes it to me. "Sharing is caring."

"I didn't know you smoked that stuff."

"There's a lot about me you don't know," he says.

I pluck the joint from his fingertips.

"Have you ever?" he asks.

I shake my head.

"It's super easy. You just take a hit—that means inhale—and hold it in your lungs until you can't hold it any longer."

I bring the joint to my lips and wish that Audrey were here to see me. But she's not. She's dancing with Mercy and Sharon. Happily ever after.

The smoke stings my eyes as I hold it to my lips, feeling the wetness of Travis's saliva on the paper. We're practically kissing.

Inhale.

Hold it in your lungs.

The smoke razes my throat, hotter and harsher than I expected, and I choke, hacking smoke into the empty corridor.

Travis chuckles. "Keep coughing. It helps the high."

My lungs have collapsed. Turned to ash and cinder, crushed into charcoal by the pressure of my ribs. I could very well die right here on the band room steps, where my body won't be discovered until *after* the dance. *After* the weekend. And no one will even notice my absence because Mercy Turner and Sharon Wolinski are *Just. So. Fab.*

Travis places his hand on my back, his touch like an electric eel. And I don't tell him the urge to cough has passed, because his knuckles are working little circles on my spine.

"This is more fun than the dance," he says, plucking the joint from my fingers and taking one final hit before pinching it out.

Travis withdraws his touch, and my body pulls with it.

He leans forward and looks at me beneath the shroud of my witch's mane. His gaze is so wet I could drown within it. Beautiful, peaceful drowning. I could disappear forever.

And all I can think is, kiss me.

A crack of thunder explodes above us, and I grasp my chest. Moments before, my lungs were charred and lifeless, but they've been revived. Plucked from the brink of death.

The shawl melds to my skin once more. I feel the coldness, the wetness, but I don't care. I want him to see me.

Kiss me. Kiss me. Kiss me.

Because right now, on the circular band room steps, in the empty east wing, Travis Misker is wearing all black, a real policeman's cap on his head, and a tin foil badge pinned to his collar. And he rides his bike to school every morning with his arms spread wide open.

KISSMEKISSME—

And he does.

~

Richard Quinn stumbles across the cockpit, the Valkyrie caught between two opposing gusts.

He screams into his VHF radio. "Wailing Bird!' and then drops the mouthpiece to veer into another squall.

The ocean is ominous, the waves increasingly unstable and impossible to predict. So much for a small hurricane.

The wind tunnels around him, his boat jacket like a sail strapped to his back. He wraps his elbows around the spokes of the wheel in defiance.

A click fires from the radio, followed by a voice perforating the static.

Richard drops the boat to idle speed and collapses to the ground, bracing his legs. He snatches the mouthpiece from the air.

"Wailing Bird! You copy?"

Static.

"Wailing Bird?"

Another band of rain soaks the Valkyrie, gone as quickly as it arrived. Richard swipes his forehead, clearing his eyes.

"Answer me, goddamn it!"

Shane's voice echoes through the radio: *Pequod?*

Richard seizes the mouthpiece, wrestling the cord to his chest.

"I'm here! Behind schedule but makin' up time. Just south of Bahia Honda. What are your coordinates? Over."

The radio clicks once more, and Shane's voice fills the cockpit, his words fractured and erratic: *Pequod, this is…Bird…read…over.*

"I've got you, Wailing Bird. Can you hear me? Over."

We got…fly…wind and…over.

Richard grasps the wheel with his free hand and is about to power up the motor when the rain stops falling and the wind grows still. A silence settles atop the water and the waves throw the Valkyrie forward. And then he sees them: two cones—one of sky and one of sea—lengthening and pulling toward each other, morphing into a single funnel of saltwater wildness.

And as suddenly as the wind retreated, it returns with haste, bristling with sounds that prickle Richard's skin: train whistles, beehives, rumbling waterfalls. The waterspout contorts atop the waves, a cyclone of water spewing from its base. It widens and twists into the sky, coiling into the clouds like a severed power line, trembling with trapped energy, desperate for release.

Richard watches the clouds swirl around the funnel, and barely hears Shane's voice through the radio, and the words he'd hoped would never be spoken.

Can't fly. Turn back. Abort.

~

The band room.

In the back, behind the tubas, where it smells of brass oil and spit and no one will find us, I peel off my wet shawl.

He asks if I'm sure.

He says we don't have to.

He says he's never done this before.

I'm Audrey's spirit animal, she said so herself. I'm who she wants to be when she grows up. So just wait until she hears about *this*.

I drop my shawl to the floor.

Travis is the first person to see me naked.

Andy touched my body—long ago, when we were an item—but he never *saw* me. Somehow, this is scarier.

Travis steps back to look at me, and I cover myself.

He pulls at my elbows.

I'm going to vomit. Maybe from the joint. Maybe not.

My breathing grows heavy and fast, echoing from the bells of the tubas.

Travis moves his hand from my elbow, and I stay like a well-trained dog as he touches my chest, right in the center. Just below the gold owl necklace.

I can't swallow. My mouth is dry, like his kisses have sucked all the moisture from my body. My lips are pressed together, glued forever shut.

"Wow," he says.

Oh.

And suddenly I can breathe again, swallow again.

When his palm slides over my breast, I am sea grass, idle and limp.

I'm scared, and I think he can see it.

He tells me we can stop. Just go back to the dance.

I want to say, Yes. But I shake my head no.

For Audrey.

I never thought it would be like this. Not here, on the floor of the high school band room. Not with Travis Misker dropping a real policeman's cap to the ground. Unbuckling his pants. Not kissing me anymore. Not looking at me anymore.

Look at me.

Don't look at me.

I'm on the floor beside the French horns. The carpet is sticky and rigid, and my clothes are in a pile by the music stands. All of them.

Please don't ask about the scars.

He doesn't.

I lie on my back and wait.

Push my legs flat to the floor, squeeze my knees together. And wait.

I look to the ceiling, to the exposed piping with chipped paint next to a small window leaking light like twinkling breadcrumbs into the east wing.

Travis crouches on the floor beside me, naked, his penis hidden beneath the arc of his body like a secret he won't share. I have no such secrets.

When his hands grip my legs, I close my eyes.

When he pulls my knees apart, then my ankles, I'm grateful for the shadows.

His abdomen pushes against the underside of my thighs, and I suck in my breath, hold it, like a hit off a joint.

"Are you ready?" His voice is small and uncertain.

No.

"Danni?"

No.

"Please talk to me. Do you want to stop?"

"No."

"Are you sure?"

I can't say it. Too scared to say it.

"Do you still want to do this?"

I open my eyes because it's all I can do, but I can't look at Travis Misker. I look to the window above us, to lightning plunging like an avalanche across the sky.

When I finally say, Yes, I expect more hesitation, more conversation. But what I receive is immediate pain.

A sharp, rigid wound explodes from the softest part of my body, and all I want to do is scream.

My fingers claw at a carpet too dense to grasp. My heels seek ground, but they're trapped beneath his body.

I grimace, gnashing my teeth against the pain, and turn my face to the side so he won't see the saliva foaming from my lips like a mouthful of rabies.

I'm deformed.

A monster.

Travis rocks into me, over and over, his face turning red, then purple. I've never seen Travis's eyes like this before. His mouth is different too. This person is a stranger.

I wrap my arms around my face, burying my nose in the crook of my elbow so I don't have to watch.

I can't breathe, but I don't care.

Please stop.

I don't want to do this anymore.

I've changed my mind.

No!

But I say nothing as he slices into my body.

I want to hit someone.

Run away.

Rip off my skin.

But I can't stop it.

So I disappear.

In my mind, I'm on the hippie beach, spiraling into the surf. I feel the waves, the wind. Beside me, the blonde in the crocheted bikini hugs my shoulders and tells me everything is going to be okay. The shells strung through her hair sway and clack in the wind.

It's not until Travis wheezes into my face and falls atop me that I realize the pain has subsided. I am raw, cut open, but the violence of it has grown numb.

A flash of lightning fills the skylight, reminding me of the moment the sun disappears below the horizon—that bright green flash I've never seen. A lie. A grand falsehood fabricated by my father.

A crack of thunder soon follows, and I think of speeding down the Seven Mile Bridge so close to the other cars that the mirrors click as they pass, a mere inch from collision, from plummeting into the ocean. Unlucky.

And as the thunder fades away, a reverberation is left behind, filling the band room. All around us, the instruments begin to ring and hum like wine glasses stroked by wet fingers. As though in the sudden absence of sound, they have begun to panic.

~

Richard Quinn docks the Valkyrie at the Duck Key Marina and sits in his car, watching the squalls paint the Atlantic.

Water pools from his body and soaks the gray seat black. The next time Miriam takes the car, she will complain that her dress is wet, ruined, but Richard doesn't care. Danni's at the Halloween Dance, and waterspouts are moving inland, but Richard doesn't care.

He plucks a cigar from the dashboard. It was to be his reward for a job well done. He breathes the rolled tobacco, but tonight, he smells nothing. He inhales the cigar through his mouth to find that his tastebuds have abandoned him as well.

Richard bites the end from the cigar and spits it onto the floor. He lights a match and does not roll down the window.

He closes his eyes and pushes against the headrest. Hail dents his hood. He takes a long drag from the cigar and tries to taste the leaves, the fermentation, the soil creased in the palms of the man who rolled it—*anything* other than the emptiness wafting over his tongue and clogging his throat.

IT CAN'T HURT YOU IF YOU DON'T LOOK

I tug my damp arms through the shawl and dash from the band room, wiping my cheeks against my sleeves. I ignore Travis as he calls after me, stumbling over the pants twisted at his ankle.

I don't look back.

This wasn't about him.

I duck into the restroom and lean against a sink.

Everything hurts.

I forgot my stockings in the band room, but I won't go back. They're gone forever now—a sacrifice to the Virginity Gods.

I can't wait to tell Audrey. Should I tell her it was pure magic? A pastel-colored narrative of tenderness and passion? Or should I tell her the truth? Which version would she like best?

My necklace dangles from my collarbone, the chain now broken and draped around my neck, and I pull it into my palm. I wore this necklace when Eddie first kissed me outside the old lighthouse, and I've worn it ever since.

In my hand, I hold the last tie that binds me to him.

I walk to the toilet and drop it into the water, like mom at the Bahia Honda Bridge, tossing gold and emeralds over the edge. And as the necklace rocks to the bottom of the bowl, its ruby eyes twinkling for the last time, I think I understand mom a little better. Because it's time I stop hoping for things to be different.

I take one last look at my owl necklace and flush the toilet.

My second sacrifice of the day.

I dash through the hallway toward the cafeteria, kicking through the deluge at my ankles.

The chords of a Chubby Checker song waft from inside as I fling open the door.

I'm ready to dance. I'm ready for Audrey.

And I've got one hell of a story.

Before I can locate Audrey, something catches my eye. Right in the middle of the dance floor are Margaret Leech and Ronald Weller, slow dancing. All around them, kids are swinging their hips and nodding at one another's groovy moves, but Margaret and Ronald don't seem to notice that it's not a slow song. Margaret has ditched her astronaut helmet, and has one hand draped around Ronald's neck, the other braided into his fingers.

I can't look away. Margaret and Ronald? So weird. And yet.

The way he looks at her. The way she smiles at him. Like they're dreaming at the same time.

It can't be possible that the first of us to fall in love is *Margaret Leech*.

I jump when I hear Audrey's laugh, and break away from Margaret and Ronald to follow the sound.

From the speakers comes the voice of Chubby Checker: *Three coins in the fountain; through the ripples how they shine; just one wish will be granted; one heart will wear a valentine.*

And then I see her.

Them.

A triangle of girls—one Rapunzel, one Snow White, and one black cat—all laughing and dancing The Watusi.

I've never seen Audrey so happy. I've never made her laugh like that. Everyone in the cafeteria fades away as I watch her, a smear of brass oil on my shawl.

A spot of blood in my underwear.

The weather matches my mood.

I'm outside watching the downpour, and through the percussion, I almost don't hear the music cut off, the shouts and *boos* of my classmates, or Mrs. Berrett announcing that the Halloween dance is over. That everyone must get home without further delay. School staff and chaperones are already putting in calls to our parents.

Because the hurricane has made an unexpected turn.

My bike's been blown over by the wind, and one wheel twists in the rain. The playing card Audrey tucked within the spokes is long gone. Streamers whip and snap with each gust.

Students flood from the cafeteria, eyes wild with both distress and excitement. Cars are already pulling through the gravel lot, forming a makeshift line along the walkway.

It hurts to sit, as though I've been kicked between my legs. I want to shove my hands down there and collapse to the ground, rolling and wincing, like boys do when they get socked during a game.

A strong gale steers me off the sidewalk and right onto US1, but I hold tightly to the handlebar.

It doesn't bother me that Audrey has new friends. Jimmie's my best friend anyway. Honest.

The rain is cold and sharp, and a crack of thunder explodes overhead. I pedal faster.

It doesn't bother me that my gold owl necklace is gone forever. I never really liked it.

Down every street, men rush around, hammering wooden planks to windows, exchanging ropes and hammers.

And it doesn't bother me that I unceremoniously lost my virginity. It's done and over with. I'm not a slut. I'm a modern woman.

I turn onto my street beneath a sinister sky that's nearly opaque. Our apartment building is just ahead, and the water has risen over the dock, sloshing over the grass.

I'm almost to the stairs when I spot dad standing by the water.

A board I can walk on to find my way home.

The water is to my shins now, and a school of Sergeant Majors weaves around my ankles, lost amid the landscape, their silver and yellow bodies darting toward the walkway. I want to rush ahead of them, corral them back to the ocean, but I just stand there, helpless, watching them swim closer to the parking lot, and farther than ever from home.

Dad's facing away from me, staring at what appears to be a concrete wall descending from the sky. Sheets of rain fan him like the pages of a book caught in the wind.

I trip, splashing onto the flooded grass and scuffing my stocking-less knees.

Finally, dad turns. The stump of a wet cigar dangles from his lips, tobacco unfurling like earthworms down his chin.

He rushes forward, lifts me into his arms, and I collapse into his embrace. His skin is warm and moist, and it feels like being underwater in the best way possible.

When dad's broad shoulders arc around me, something inside me cracks open, and I weep into his chest. When he kisses the top of my head, I can smell the liquor.

It's good to be home.

My mind brims until it shatters and overflows, and I can't stop the tremor in my legs, the heaving of my lungs.

"Oh, pumpkin," he says, which makes me cry even harder.

His fingers claw into my ribs. I can't draw a breath, but I wouldn't dare say a word.

"Don't be scared," he says, squeezing the rainwater from my hair. "It can't hurt you. It's only the band of a small hurricane."

POOF

The storm raged all throughout the night and I barely slept.

But it wasn't because of the hurricane.

I kept picturing those Sergeant Majors swimming through our lawn, headed for the mainland and certain death. So much water, and yet they were cursed within it. When the sun evaporates even the most stubborn of puddles, they will learn their fate.

I hope their final adventure was glorious.

The hippies were on the beach by themselves all night. No shelter, no vehicles in which to seek refuge. There was nothing I could do to help at the time, but now that it's morning, I need to know they're okay.

The hurricane may have stolen my Halloween Dance and my decency, but it can't have my hippies.

I step into the morning and images of Sergeant Majors are replaced by those of devastation. Dad was wrong. This was *not* a small hurricane.

The ocean rose so high that the docks have vanished. The water is no longer gemstone water, but a murky, mustard brown. It flooded the lower apartments overnight, and already our neighbors are hauling what they can salvage into plastic buckets or floating tabletops—photo albums, paperwork, clothing, even family pets—and wading them toward higher ground.

I search for my bike in the flood, but it's gone.

By the time I reach the middle of our street, I'm at a trot, the water only a pane of glass over the asphalt.

We were lucky. No broken windows. No leaking roof. It could've been worse. A lot worse.

There's a felled tree across our street, stripped of every leaf. And right where it was ripped from the earth are the Sergeant Majors. Their lifeless bodies are strung around the roots like Katia's rudraksha necklace. If only they'd kept going. Crossing over US1 to the other side of Marathon, they would've discovered Aviation Boulevard, and a number of waterfront homes on docks and canals. They could've arrived safely in the Gulf of Mexico. But they never even made it to the highway.

On a normal day, I'd never run all the way across town. But today is not a normal day.

All around me are cars where cars don't belong— across the center line of the highway, upside down on the sidewalk, dented and shorn, tangled in downed fencing and wires. A boat was washed ashore, its hull splintered like a pack of used matches. Everywhere, unrecognizable scraps of plastic things, metal things, wood things and paper things.

I pass a house without a roof—just a gaping hole to the sky where the storm pressure became too strong. The curtains curl upward from their poles, yanked through the space where a ceiling once was. The curtains dangle over the tops of the walls, lapping the air like thirsty tongues.

I arrive at the beach, breathless.

The mangroves are largely unharmed, but they bow inland, pushed as one by the hurricane's unyielding winds.

I step through puddles, tucking beneath where wind chimes once hung.

Only one remains—a large conch strung by rope and spinning in the breeze. Above my head is a tangle of yarn snagged across the leaves like the web of a Banana spider.

In the water is a tent, looking more like a sailboat run aground.

No hippies.

I want to shake my fists at the sky, call out for them, but I don't know their names.

Love Children! Oh, Love Children!

The remnants of a campfire float past me. Wet towels, shirts and bathing suits are tangled in tree limbs, baking in the sun.

And then I hear voices.

Some of the hippies are standing in a circle, hugging and smiling. How can they be smiling? Their entire camp was destroyed. They have nothing.

There's a noise behind me. Something small, like a lizard tumbling from a branch.

On the beach, a man stands in knee-deep water, holding aloft a small guitar as he plants his legs. He slams his fingers across the strings, over and over, slinging his pelvis like Elvis Presley. I cover my mouth to stifle a laugh.

A hand on my shoulder!

I yelp and spin around to find the tall man in women's panties and the woman in the red crocheted bikini standing over me, their faces obscured by shadow.

I hold my breath and close my eyes, unable to face my captors.

I've been caught, and I don't know what happens now.

"Hey there, lil' mama," the man says.

But his voice doesn't sound mad. Not at all.

"You're safe and sound, I see," the woman says.

Minutes go by. Hours.

"Maybe one of these days you'll stop spying on us," the man says. "Maybe one of these days you'll come join us, and say hello."

Oh.

He laughs. She laughs.

The man puts his whole hand atop my head and rocks me from side to side, just like dad does.

Then they walk past me and into the blazing sunlight without another word.

Their hair is the same color, as though spun from the same golden hay. The man doesn't look back, but the woman does.

Over the summer, Jimmie and I watched this woman spiral into the surf, naked and free. It was the most amazing thing I'd ever witnessed.

I've seen this woman's nipples. I've seen her pubic hair. But I don't feel awkward or embarrassed.

Just a body.

She stands before me, clad in an ill-fitting homemade swimsuit that barely covers her freckled skin.

"Well," she says to me, her voice like a wind chime made of seashells, "you comin'?"

I step out of the shadows before I change my mind. And when I feel the soggy kernels of sand between my toes, I know my entire world is about to change.

Yes, I think. I'm comin'.

Poof.

Part Three

AWAKENING IN THE SEASON OF MEADOW

WINTER IN PIECES

November was the month of the aftermath.

Dad helped with hurricane cleanup, towing stranded boats to shore, roped to the stern of the Valkyrie. Some were salvageable. Others were goners. He stripped them of any material he could use or resell before turning them over to the flatbed trucks on US1, hauling debris to Miami.

I volunteered with the roadside crew, stuffing shingles and other scraps into large trash bags, while men moved besotted mattresses and broken appliances to the side of the road.

Jimmie volunteered as well, and it was like we were best friends again. When he saw how quickly my black hair had faded, he teased that I looked like Granny from *The Beverly Hillbillies*.

I didn't tell Jimmie about the hippies, or that mom and dad failed to notice when I stayed out night after night, listening to drumbeats on the beach.

I didn't tell him about Leaf, the man who wears women's panties, and builds guitars out of coconut shells and cigar boxes. Or about Sparrow, a chipmunk of a girl with breasts large enough to rival Mercy Turner's, and a gnarly scar that runs from ankle to hip —a souvenir from a motorcycle accident when the fringe of her purse caught in the wheel. Or Ziggy, the tallest man I've ever seen, who cleans barnacles from boats at the Duck Key Marina to send money home to Barbados.

Or Meadow. The girl with the red crocheted bikini who likes to run naked into the surf at sunset.

And I *definitely* didn't tell Jimmie about what happened with Travis Misker in the band room the night of the Halloween Dance. He'd never look at me the same way again.

I could barely look at myself.

But Jimmie *did* tell me about teaching Ellie Walker to crawfish, and that they caught forty crawfish in one afternoon. That's $6.00 each! Jimmie said he spent $3.00 on Mary Janes alone at The Sundry Store. When I asked if he'd kissed Ellie yet, he just scrunched his nose, so I guess that meant no.

December was the month of disguises. It seemed everyone had a truth better left concealed.

Our town was looking more like itself again. But just like the asphalt burn on Sparrow's leg, the hurricane left a scar. Fences remained mangled, splintered trees were ripped from the soil, and I never saw my bike again.

I spent a lot of time at Audrey's house over Winter Break, preparing for our upcoming poetry assignment in Mr. Mallory's class. At least that's what I told mom and dad. But I wasn't with Audrey. I was with the hippies.

Every evening, Meadow and the others would cast their clothing to the sand and run naked into the ocean to honor the sunset.

I never joined them.

But I wanted to. Real bad.

"People can see you," I warned, pointing to the high school beyond the mangroves, the window facing the beach.

But Meadow only smiled. "Let 'em watch," she said.

I asked them if they were really called Love Children.

"Where did you hear this?" Leaf asked. "Love Children?"

Leaf has a slight accent that sounds fake, but Meadow told me he's from Amsterdam, and that he's as real as they come.

Meadow spent that evening creating wind chimes to replace those lost to the storm. The campfire illuminated everyone's faces in clips of orange light.

"How about you just call us by our names?" Leaf suggested. "How does that sound, lil' mama?"

"But my name's not lil' mama," I said.

"You can be whoever you want here. You think my parents named me *Leaf*? How lucky are we to be alive in this era of rebirth? Would you like to introduce yourself now, for the first time in your entire life?"

Everyone stared, waiting for me to reveal my soul in a string of vowels and consonants.

I shrugged. "I like lil' mama."

Leaf nodded his approval. "We like lil' mama too. We like her very much."

It was then that a gust of wind shook the mangrove thatch behind us. We heard what sounded like the rush of an arrow speeding through the air.

And then it happened all at once.

The long, fleshy darts of the mangrove seeds began to fall. Miniature explosions all across the beach, one after another. As each seed released, it pierced the sand and water below. Some lodged in the beach, pointing upward like shards of broken glass. Others slipped beneath the surface like a high diver, leaving no evidence of their existence other than a whizzing slice echoing across the roots.

Like green icicles melting from an overhang.

January was the month of The Great Florida Keys Blizzard.

At least that's what Mr. Mallory called it.

Massive cold fronts pushed south, bringing a chill to the Keys most of us Conchs had never before experienced. On the coldest morning, the lawn crunched beneath my shoes and I bent down to discover each blade of grass encased in a thin shell of ice.

Mr. Mallory complained that he escaped from Colorado to Florida to wear shorts in the winter, not coats.

Most of the students were born right here in the Keys, and don't own *real* winter coats. So we sat in classrooms bundled in blankets pillaged from our beds.

Mercy Turner had a violet tufted comforter filled with goose feathers, and everyone wanted to touch it. I heard Timmy Katz got in trouble for pulling a feather from a rip near the seam, but it's hard to believe Mercy's comforter would have a rip anywhere at all.

I still ate lunch with Audrey every day, but we sought shelter from the chill on the circular steps of the band room, where I once kissed Travis Misker and smoked my first joint. But it doesn't feel real. It feels like it happened to someone else. Like I crawled atop the roof to stare down through the yellow skylight, rain hammering the back of my head.

February was the month of the Teachers' Strike.

We arrived at school on a Monday morning to find Mr. Mallory corralling the students onto the lawn by the cafeteria for an announcement. Salary issues. Budget increases. Something about legislature, and how student support was important. But I couldn't pay attention because I was too busy watching the teachers. Every one of them had a piece of paper pinned to their shirts that read: WE ARE NOT HIRED HELP.

They waited in a semi-circle for Mr. Mallory to conclude, and then they all left. They just left!

I ran to dad's classroom to find him alone at his desk, shaking his head. He wasn't wearing a piece of paper pinned to his shirt.

When he noted my confused expression, he just sighed and said, "Let's go home, pumpkin."

March was the month of denial.

When the teachers returned from their strike, they looked happy. I guess they won.

The days were beginning to warm, and I was finally able to ride the new bike mom and dad bought me for Christmas. It's taller than my old one, a dark shiny red. But no wicker basket. Just a metal clamp mounted to the back.

I miss my old bike, but she was a casualty of the storm.

So was Poppy's memorial. I returned with a Troll Doll and a handful of Seagrape leaves, tying them to the post. In the spring, I'll replace the Seagrape leaves with fresh flowers. Every week. And as soon as I save enough money, I'll replace the Troll Doll with a Betsy Wetsy.

I avoided Travis in the hallways. I stomped that memory into the deepest part of my brain, alongside all the other indiscretions I don't want to think about. Travis never told anyone, either. This is such a small town that a rumor like that would be unearthed in no time. Maybe he was embarrassed, too.

I never told Audrey about my new relationship with the hippies. I didn't want to share them. But I had to maintain the illusion of normalcy, so I continued to sneak out with Audrey every Loveday to spy on them through the mangroves. If the hippies knew we were there, they kept my secret.

Audrey was starting to talk about college. Fresno State in California. She said that's where *everything is happening*.

"We're only freshmen!" I told her. "Plus, there's a college in Key West now."

"A *Community* College."

"So? My dad went to a community college."

"And maybe that's why he's still stuck here," she said.

I stormed away after that, and things have been awkward between us ever since.

Dad started drinking more.

Ever since the hurricane, he's been different. Late for school, or sometimes absent altogether. Perhaps his evening with the beautiful blonde woman did not go as planned the night of the Halloween Dance. Perhaps she ended things. There have been no more phone calls in the middle of the night. And no more smile on dad's face. I'll never know what really happened between them. But I know one thing for sure. She's gone.

Mom and I are still here, of course, but dad has yet to notice.

Andy crashed through our door one night with dad slumped against his shoulder. Spittle leaked from the corner of his mouth and puddled on the floor.

Mom just stared in silence as Andy unfolded dad into his special chair in the living room and then left without a word.

I crept closer to get a look at the imposter pretending to be Richard Quinn. I wanted to see him smile. Just once. A big, lopsided grin that looks absurd on his face. I wanted him to put his hand atop my head and rock me back and forth like he used to.

Dad survived the hurricane alongside the rest of us, yet somehow was washed out to sea all the same.

WHAT COULD HAVE BEEN

In a small farming village outside of East Berlin, the weeds have grown wiry and spindly, and Gunter watches them sway with each gust of warm air.

If he squints, the field becomes water. If he covers his ears, the faint lapping of waves. And if he closes his eyes, the entire black ocean opens up before him.

Was Galina on a fishing boat that night, braving hurricane winds while waiting for his ship to pass?

Or was she co-pilot, strapped into the seat of a small plane, finding no brother among the endless waves?

Gunter opens his eyes and no longer sees the ocean. Just a barren field disappearing into darkness.

This is his life now, and it's best he accept it. He has mama to care for. He's the man of the house. And he won't think about what could've been for a moment longer.

But.

If he ever gets the chance again.

If he ever finds himself on a ship in the middle of the ocean.

Even if no one is waiting to rescue him from the water.

He won't hesitate.

Not for a single moment.

No matter how small the lights in the distance.

If he ever gets that chance again, he will jump.

LOVE CHILDREN

I am no longer Daniella Quinn.

I'm Lil' Mama.

"Read it to us," Meadow says, as I clutch the paper to my chest. "How bad can it be?"

I look to Ziggy, and his salted caramel eyes.

"Okay," I say, "but don't laugh. It's supposed to be about what *home* means to us."

Maya is Ziggy's girl, and she tucks in beside him. "What is home anyway?" she asks.

"Ego," Meadow says. "A security blanket."

"Baby dreams."

"Fever dreams."

"You have to give up this idea of *home.*"

"Once you give that up, you're free."

"*Love* is home."

"Yes."

"You are home right now."

"Home is the water right over there."

"And the sand."

"And music."

"*Yes.*"

Leaf grabs Sparrow's hand, and Sparrow grabs Meadow's hand, and suddenly we're all swaying to silent ballads only we can hear.

Meadow is beside me, and when she bops her head, shells sway from side to side, as though the rhythm shifted in her universe, and hers alone.

I giggle, and she opens her eyes.

"Don't laugh at me," Meadow says.

"I won't," I say, my expression growing serious. "I promise."

Meadow winks and nudges me with her shoulder. "*Please* laugh at me, Lil' Mama. How else will I know you like me?"

I exhale and nod because I do. I really, really do.

"Quiet down, everyone," she says. "We have a poet among us. Go on, Lil' Mama. Tell us what home means to you."

I smooth the wrinkles across the page.

Silence.

A clearing of the throat.

A crack of a knuckle.

"Seagulls dive and sandpipers graze, the mangrove leans and the palm tree sways. The ocean is there to comfort me, even on my saddest days."

The paper trembles in my hand, and no one says a word.

Mr. Mallory's right—it *is* terrible.

Last week, Mr. Mallory wrote a note at the top that says, *This is a great first draft, but I have a few suggestions. Meet me after school Monday so we can discuss.*

In a few short hours, we'll be face to face, and then Mr. Mallory can tell me in person how much he hates my poem.

"I don't want to read anymore," I say.

Meadow clasps her hands beneath her chin. "It's a great start. I dig it."

"I bet your mom and dad are real proud." Sparrow says this with an honest smile, and as she looks away, a tear rolls down her cheek.

Behind me, the bell rings, signaling the end of lunch.

"See you around, Lil' Mama," Ziggy says. "Gimme some skin."

I slap my hand against Ziggy's.

"Well, alright," he says with an approving nod.

In Algebra, Audrey bounds into the desk behind me.

"Where were you during lunch?" she asks.

I shrug, and it's as honest an answer as I can give.

When the final bell of the day tolls, it's like an executioner's countdown, the walk to Mr. Mallory's classroom like a death march.

I expect him to be hooded, holding a scythe and standing in shadow. But he's at his desk, wearing the same khaki shorts and buttoned-down flower shirt he wore this morning. His socks are purple with yellow stars.

"Miss Quinn, please come in," he says, indicating an available chair. "You weren't in class this morning."

"Stomachache," I blurt out.

"Can I assume you're feeling better?"

I hand over the crumpled assignment while staring at a coffee ring near the edge of his desk. "You hate it," I say.

"Not at all! This is feedback and constructive criticism. It's not as harsh as you think," he says, spreading the paper flat on his desk. He pauses, then folds his hands atop the page and adjusts his glasses— his impersonation of a *real* teacher. "Your poem is great for a first draft."

The corner fan clicks in the otherwise quiet room, a torn scrap of paper caught in the blades.

"But I think you need to dig deeper. See here," he says, lifting his elbow to peer at the words beneath. "You talk about water and sunsets, but that's only a physical description of *place*. I want to know what's in your *heart*."

Mr. Mallory looks at the page as though it's injured, scraping the sentences with his fingernail until he locates the wound.

"And here—*friends and love and peace and hope.* Is that how you truly feel?" He stands abruptly, pacing before the chalkboard, flinging his hands to accentuate his point. "Love and peace and hope are the easy stuff, but what about *longing*? What about the need to create? To question our own existence?"

"Our existence?"

"If you look hard enough, you can find the meaning of life on the wing of a seagull, or all the hurt you've ever felt in the shadow of a coconut tree. Do you see what I'm saying?"

No.

But when I nod, Mr. Mallory looks pleased.

And then everything gets really quiet.

Too quiet.

Mr. Mallory leans against the chalkboard and runs his hands through his hair. He looks at me as though dissecting a math equation.

He doesn't say anything.

The silence is deafening.

I know this silence. I've felt it before. This tightening of my muscles. This heavy thump in my chest.

Like Andy—right before he first kissed me.

No…

And then my heart stops beating altogether.

Mr. Mallory looks to the floor, and I can hear him swallow. The shadow of his Adam's apple bobs along his collar.

Everyone's gone home, and the school is another planet without students filling the hallways. Everything echoes, and I wonder if my thoughts echo as well. Does Mr. Mallory know that I'm scared right now?

"Danni…"

His voice trails away as he pulls on an earlobe, fiddles with his belt.

He gazes at the window, beyond which my hippies lie on the beach, unaware of what's unfolding behind these four walls.

I shouldn't have come here alone. I should've stayed on the beach today. I should've ditched.

Mr. Mallory steps toward me.

My fingers claw at my thighs.

This can't be happening. Not Mr. Mallory. Not the man who hitchhiked from Colorado to Florida to wear shorts in the winter. Not the man with colorful socks and Clark Kent glasses, who reads romance novels during lunch period in the teacher's break room. Dad told me that, so it must be true.

Mr. Mallory leans against his desk, right in front of me. He's so close that I can smell his cologne.

Like a plague, I must carry the marks Andy left behind. On my very skin. It's a type of pollution, isn't it? And no amount of time can ever truly eradicate the stain. An everlasting disfigurement for all to see.

And Mr. Mallory sees it too. He's a good man, but a man nonetheless, and I'd be foolish to expect anything different.

Please don't make me say no. I don't know how.

"You should know," he begins, his voice hushed.

I want to cry. I want to snatch my terrible poem and run all the way home, not even stopping at the bike rack. Run until the scars on my thighs bleed through my shorts.

"You should know that I see huge potential in you."

"Potential?"

"You're an amazing writer, Danni."

Oh.

The air rushes back into my lungs.

"Your essays are well thought out. Your grasp of spelling and grammar is top of the class. And your word usage is excellent. I would expect nothing less from the daughter of Richard Quinn."

I can't help but laugh.

"I'm serious," he continues. "You have a bright future in writing, if that's what you choose. But I think you're *trying* to stay topical. You know that rainbows can't exist without the storm. I *know* you can do better."

Mr. Mallory hands me the poem and I stare at my topical words.

"Don't tell me what you *see*. Tell me what you *feel*."

I stuff the poem into my bag and rush toward the door.

"One more thing before you go."

I turn to see Mr. Mallory at the open window, staring at the ocean beyond. He nods toward the beach.

"The girl with the brown hair is very pretty," he says. "What's her name?"

"Who?" I ask, panic clogging my throat. "I don't know."

Mr. Mallory locks onto me with his gaze. We're two animals, he and I, waiting for the other to yield.

"Let's trust each other, Miss Quinn. I'm going to offer you a handshake deal. I won't give away your secret. *If* you promise to never ditch my class again."

My teeth clench, preventing words, so I nod.

"Good. Now go be brilliant and amazing."

I push into the hallway and begin toward the bike rack.

But then I think better of it and turn back to Mr. Mallory's classroom.

"Sparrow," I say. "Her name is Sparrow."

Mr. Mallory smiles, looking like a bashful little boy in purple socks.

He places his hand on the windowsill, returning his face to the sunlight.

"Lovely," he says.

$\sim$

Richard Quinn pushes into The Armada and takes a seat beside Peter. The beer he stashed in his desk at school was not enough today—not nearly—and he signals the bartender. Richard is soon greeted by a tall mug of foaming beer and a shot of warm whiskey.

Both disappear down his throat in the time it takes him to buff the scowl from his forehead.

Peter dips his head toward the empty glass.

"Good day, my friend?"

Richard burps. "Yep."

"You've been having a lot of those lately."

"I don't ask you about things that are none of my business."

Peter considers this before turning his attention back to a notebook on the bar. He makes a note, scratches it out.

"How's the Whaler?" Richard asks.

"Still fudgin' with the fuel line. I get 'er started, but she dies on me." He taps the pen on the paper. "Every time."

"Fuck her," Richard says.

"Indeed."

"I'm serious. You don't need the aggravation. Life is hard enough." Richard spins Peter toward him, and the pen in Peter's hand etches a trail across the page. Richard pushes a finger into Peter's chest to accentuate his point. "You think you're doing something good?

Something important? It means nothing. Fuck your goddamn engine."

"I hear ya, Richard." Peter corrects his chair and waggles his fingers at the bartender. "Have another round on me." He returns to his notebook, but every few moments, his eyes dart to Richard.

Boston Whalers. Faulty fuel lines and lousy tiller engines. Hurricanes. Fuck 'em all.

Richard grunts his thanks to an uneasy bartender, who retreats to the far end.

Couldn't get out of school fast enough. Never fast enough. Not these days. Carolyn Saylor droning on about books he hasn't returned. Spilled coffee in the break room that someone was too lazy to clean up, now a thick smear of gritty sludge that clings to his shoes when he walks through it. Every goddamned day.

Richard withdraws a cigar from his pocket. He sniffs it, but still smells nothing, detects nothing. Richard crumples it in his palm and thrusts the remains over the bar top.

"Jesus, Richard," Peter says.

"Fuck off, Peter."

Richard sits in silence, staring out the port windows toward the sky. His skin itches. His feet twitch. He's got to get out of here. He's trapped in this town. Like a goddamned fish in a tank. Like a refugee adrift on the ocean, a firing squad above, at the ready.

Richard shoves the stool from the bar and stands. He then tosses some cash onto the counter to cover his drinks before storming out of The Armada.

By the time Richard arrives home, the apartment is dark. He braces his weight against the kitchen counter and closes his eyes. The room will surely stop spinning at any moment.

Richard spits into the sink. Misses.

"Call me Ishmael!" he orates to a barren apartment, lugging a case of beer purchased from The Sundry Store on his way home.

Tucked against his chest, a second case.

Richard turns and tries to locate the refrigerator.

"Some years ago! Never mind how long precisely!" he cries, jamming his thumb through the latch. His keys scratch the glossy finish.

The fridge door swings open and Richard squints against the barrage of light. He uses the case to push aside a milk carton and leftovers from the week before, relegating his beer to a spot in the back, where it's coldest.

"But look! Here come more crowds! Seemingly bound for a dive!"

Wait. He's forgotten a line.

He looks down at the second case in his arms. He can't let Miriam see *two* cases of beer.

Richard blinks the haze from his eyes and walks the hallway, nudging open the door of his study with his elbow. He searches the bookshelves for a hiding place, but there are none to be found, the shelves already brimming over with leather-bound adventure novels, stories of ocean voyages, tales of uncharted exploration, historic narratives, the classics.

The adventures of other men. *Better* men.

Richard slumps into his desk chair, clutching the case of beer to his chest as though cradling an infant.

He becomes heavy, then weightless. The room twists around him. Random excerpts from Moby Dick waft through his mind like an anesthetic.

Deep into Distant Woodlands.
Great flood-gates of the wonder-world.
One grand hooded phantom, like a snow hill in the air.

He should've been a poet.

The world was waiting for Richard Quinn.

He should've moved to the city when he was still young and unencumbered. Greenwich Village, perhaps. He could've been one of the greats: Kerouac, Ginsberg, Corso.

Quinn.

But Richard did not answer that call. He stayed close to his hometown like his parents wanted. Earned his degree at a community college in Miami, moved his young family back to Marathon as soon as he graduated, and slowly became his father. Richard leans forward on his knees and examines his hands. Thickened skin around the nail beds, just like his father. Rigid, square knuckles, creased leather flesh, bleached nuggets of sun damage. His father's hands, right here before him. So familiar, even all these years later.

His desk drawer. That's where he'll hide the second case of beer.

Richard perches on his chair and slides open the bottom drawer. He jostles the case until it's flat on its side atop his throng of collected phone numbers, his papery harem of unnamed women, and he kicks the drawer closed.

One final line—*I thought I would sail about a little and see the watery part of the world*—flashes through his mind before everything begins to fade. The last thing Richard hears are the keys slipping through his fingers and clattering against the terrazzo like the mirrors of two passing cars on the Seven Mile Bridge.

A WATERCOLOR SKY

A woman who has grown accustomed to warm breezes off the ocean at night sits by a window in her West Virginia home, alone, watching the snow.

What she wouldn't give to smell the stench of saltwater foam.

What she wouldn't give to watch a cluster of seaweed churn and chafe against a seawall.

Galina places her hand on the frosty window and watches the sun rise beyond a distant tree line.

The air carries a scent of fresh-cut oak and wood smoke. The lights from neighboring houses glow orange against the sky, diffused and scattered by the growing haze.

The sky is lightening to a color she can't quite define. Perhaps if she mixed Manganese Violet with a little bit of Yellow Ochre from her fancy American watercolor pan. Yes, that's the color.

She imagines the snow will fall for a great long while.

ONE OF THEM

It's Friday, a Loveday, but Audrey doesn't want to spy on the hippies today. She wants to eat inside the cafeteria with Mercy and Sharon. I examine my sandwich as they justify their eternal devotion to Davy Jones. That dreamy hair. Those deep brown eyes. Those perfectly kissable—*couldn't you just die?*—lips.

"If I ever saw him in real life, I'd grab his cute little face and never stop kissing him," Mercy declares.

"I think we'd really *understand* each other," Sharon says.

Mercy pushes her enormous breasts against the table. "You'd have to compete with *these*."

"Put those monstrosities away," Audrey says, and everyone laughs. "Danni, who would Davy like best?"

Three pairs of eyes stare at me, awaiting my verdict.

From a neighboring table, Travis Misker glances over as well.

Four pairs of eyes.

"Come on, Danni. Just pick."

Audrey arcs toward me. Mercy bats her lashes as though I'm the one she's trying to woo. Sharon pouts her lips and twirls her ponytail.

"He'd choose *me*," I say, gathering my things, "because you all talk too much."

The three of them gape at me. Travis snickers.

"See you in Algebra," I say to Audrey as I walk away.

I hustle through the east wing and toward the beach, where I never have to listen to Meadow or Sparrow or Maya blubber endlessly over Davy Jones.

"Danni, wait up!"

I recognize Travis's voice, his sprinting footsteps.

"Where are you going?"

I stop walking and whip around. "Nowhere."

Travis grasps his knees, catching his breath.

He seems to be waiting for something. But *he* chased after *me*. I shouldn't have to be the first to speak. That's not fair.

I fumble with the corner of an assignment peeking out from my schoolbooks.

"Um," he says.

Great start.

"What do you want, Travis?"

He shoves his hands in his pockets, looks down. "I dunno," he says. "How've you been?"

"Fine."

"We don't talk much anymore."

"We didn't talk much before."

"Maybe," he admits, "but I thought things were gonna be different after."

"After *what*?" I ask.

I know I'm being mean, but Travis took something from me. Something I barely offered. He should've been more respectful. He should've said no. I thought Travis was different, but he's just like Andy and Eddie and all the other boys in the world. They take what they want and just disappear.

Leaf would never behave like that.

Ziggy would never behave like that.

I meet Travis's gaze, and for a moment, I see the Travis I used to know. The cute boy with the dark hair and a shadow on his chin. But then I remember how that shadow felt, scrubbing against my cheek like an abrasion.

"I thought you might want to be my girl," he says, his voice so soft it's almost an apology.

"No."

"Wow, fine," Travis says. "No sweat."

When he turns toward the cafeteria, he walks slowly, like I might change my mind.

But I won't.

I try to imagine what Meadow would say. She always knows exactly the right words.

"I belong to no one, Travis! I belong to the ocean and the drums and the seagulls and no one else. Ever!"

I wait for him to stop, flash me a smile to let me know I haven't been too harsh. But he enters the cafeteria without a glance back.

Travis didn't do anything wrong. He really liked me. It was *me* who stole something from *him*. I took what I wanted and then disappeared. Poof.

Meadow says honesty is the only real currency in this world. That we have to stop lying to one another if we ever want to be free. Lying about money, intentions, hurt feelings, love. Even lying to ourselves.

But I don't want to be honest with myself. Sometimes it hurts too much.

Meadow crochets for what feels like hours, her dainty fingers clutching a hook, creating tiny loops of a fledgling halter top.

"It's beautiful," I say.

"I'm pleased you like it, because it's for you."

"Oh, Meadow, I couldn't."

"You can and you must, otherwise my feelings will be terribly hurt."

Meadow winks at me beneath sun-bleached hair strung with shells and feathers.

I absorb her words and her voice, committing each syllable to memory while watching the shells twist and sway. "I love it."

When Meadow hands me the finished halter top, I hold it like she's offered her first born. She's crafted little balls along the straps, and fringe knots from the bottom ledge. My belly button will show for sure. I hope I can find the guts to wear it.

"Well," Meadow announces as she stands to scan the beach, "time to split." She whistles, and the others sprint toward us.

"What's happening?" I ask.

"Change of scenery," she says. "Wanna come?"

I glance behind me as the bell tolls, signaling the end of lunch.

Meadow sticks out her lower lip. "Come with us, Lil' Mama. We'll show you a good time."

"Where are you going?"

"Bahia Honda, if we can score a ride."

Leaf grabs a knapsack hanging in the mangroves, Ziggy and Maya trailing behind him. Sparrow is the last to arrive. "See you next time, Lil' Mama," she says.

"She's coming with us today," Meadow says.

Leaf looks to me with an approving nod. "Far out."

"Well, alright," Ziggy says, offering an outstretched palm. "Gimme some skin."

So I do.

I pack my things and follow them to the road that skirts the high school. When I see dad lumbering toward the library, I tuck behind Ziggy to avoid detection.

"It's alright, Lil' Mama, we've got you."

And I know he's telling the truth.

We trek to US1, where there's a better chance of being picked up, and cross the highway to where the lane travels south. Meadow extends her thumb.

"Is it safe?" I ask Ziggy.

"Meadow has a nose for people. She never steers us wrong."

In no time at all, a blue Oldsmobile rolls onto the grass. Meadow approaches the car as I haul my school bag from the ground.

"Not so fast," Ziggy says. "We wait 'til Meadow gives the signal."

The driver is young, perhaps a college student from out of town. His large brown eyes are as sweet as Davy Jones', and he smiles—a big lopsided grin that reminds me of dad—as Meadow tells him we're heading to Bahia Honda to meet some friends. He nods, indicates he's got plenty of room, and tells her he's got enough smoke to go around. He's got a little extra scratch, too. If we need it badly enough. Meadow declines, and when the nice man with the lopsided grin drives away, confused, she extends her thumb once more.

"He seemed really nice," I say.

"Those are the ones to watch out for, Lil' Mama."

"The *nice* ones?"

"First rule of traveling the roads," Meadow says, "is never trust anyone who's too eager."

I turn this around in my mind like I'm studying for an exam.

Nice + Eager = Bad

"Are there other rules?"

"The most important rule is to have an agenda—always tell 'em you're meeting up with friends, even if you're not, so they think someone's expecting you. And never get into a car with someone who doesn't take off their sunglasses when they pull over."

"Why?"

"Shades means shady," Leaf says.

"Anything else?" I ask.

Meadow smiles, stroking a feather hanging from her bangs.

"Always look cute," she says, "but not *too* cute."

A brown, rusted Volkswagen Beetle comes to a stop on the highway and Meadow approaches the car.

This driver is older than the first, and he removes his sunglasses as he speaks with Meadow. Unlike the other man, his eyes don't linger. They dart to each of us, one by one.

"If you can all fit," he says, "I'll get you to Bahia Honda."

Meadow gives the signal, and we rush to the vehicle idling on the road.

"Well, alright, Slug Bug!" Ziggy says, helping Maya into the backseat.

The car smells old and musty, but tucked between Maya and Ziggy, I've never felt safer. Leaf is the last to push into the backseat, and Sparrow sits on Meadow's lap in the front.

Ziggy drapes his arm around my shoulders and pulls me close.

As the Beetle rattles down US1, my racing heart is sure to burst from my chest, raining glitter all throughout the car.

Because it's finally happened. I am one of them.

We spend the afternoon lounging in the shallows, weaving crowns of palm frond strands, and drinking the icy cold orange Fantas the driver gifted us from the cooler in his trunk. His name was David. He was nice. But not eager.

I spin tales of Mister Brownstone, the giant hammerhead that patrols the waters beneath the bridge, pilfering tarpon from unsuspecting fishermen.

"Far out," Ziggy says.

I nod, proud of my hometown.

I tell them about the green flash at the very moment the sun disappears below the horizon. It's rare and happens so fast you'll miss it if you blink.

Meadow's eyes grow wide. "And you've seen this, Lil' Mama?"

"All the time."

When the sun lowers in the sky, Leaf announces he's going to climb the bridge pillar and watch for the green flash from inside the train truss.

The Bahia Honda Bridge was once an old railroad that stretched across the waterway to Spanish Harbor Key. Dad says the railroad was too narrow for cars, so they built a road right on top of the old tracks, and now this particular stretch of highway hides a giant steel cave erected high above the water.

Leaf circles the closest pillar. "Over here! There's a ladder."

We climb a rickety ladder—no shoes, no need—to a concrete slab. Leaf stands, ducking when a car passes overhead, the old steel screeching and showering rust all around him.

"Gnarly," he says, before helping me to my feet.

Once everyone's on the pillar, we follow Leaf into the gaping metal cavern.

Somewhere below is where Audrey attended a bridge party without me.

The walls of the truss are solid steel, stained by decades of salty air. Beneath our feet, wide gaps between the rails offer expansive—and precarious—views of the current below.

Ziggy places his hand on my head.

"Come on, Lil' Mama," he says. "Let's play a game."

We sit in a circle, and Ziggy places an empty Fanta bottle in the middle.

"Ever play Spin The Bottle?"

I wish Audrey were here to see this.

I wish Jimmie were here to see this.

Ziggy flicks the bottle, and when it stops, it points directly at Maya.

"Beginners luck," he announces, as he plants kisses all over her cheeks.

Maya's next, and after a long anticipatory spin, it settles on Leaf.

She won't kiss Leaf. She's *Ziggy's* girl.

But when Leaf leans forward and Maya presses her lips to his, they're met by an approving grin from Ziggy, and a few hoots and hollers from the rest.

No one's mad. No one's hurt. *No one belongs to anyone.*

I relax.

Next up is Sparrow, who kisses Leaf.

When Meadow kisses Ziggy, I look away, but can still hear the sound of their lips breaking contact.

Leaf is the last to spin before it's my turn. My heart hammers in my chest.

The bottle points to Sparrow, and Leaf is gentle, planting only a small kiss on the tip of her nose.

"Your turn, Lil' Mama."

My fingers hover above the glass.

"Hurry," Leaf says. "The sun's about to set. We don't wanna miss the flash."

I have nowhere to go. No way to delay.

So I clutch the bottle, steady my nerves. And spin.

Everyone holds their breath, or maybe it's just me.

The Fanta bottle twists and gyrates as decisions churn in my mind. Do I lean toward my inevitable victim? Girls aren't supposed to make the first move. That's the boy's job.

The bottle comes to a halt. Pointing right at Ziggy.

Maya brings her hands to her mouth, hiding her giggle.

"Aw, man," Ziggy says.

"Alright, Lil' Mama," Sparrow cheers, "go get your man!"

Ziggy waves his hands in the air before him. "I can't do it, man. She's just a kid."

"Am not," I say, crossing my arms over my chest in defiance.

"I rest my case."

"She's one of us now," Sparrow says. "No judgement."

"Leaf?" Ziggy asks, seeking backup.

"I'm just glad it's you and not me, man."

My cheeks rage with heat. I blink away tears.

"You're being silly," Meadow says, reaching for the bottle and pointing it at herself. "Fair enough?"

Ziggy relaxes and drapes an arm around Maya. "Fair enough."

I'm not sure what's happening until Meadow leans toward me on her knees.

Oh.

The Fanta bottle falls into shadow as her body moves closer, her face moves closer, her lips move closer. I guess it's okay for a girl to make the first move after all.

And then Meadow presses her lips to mine.

I'm frozen. The shells in her hair clack beside my ear and I feel the sound in the soles of my feet.

I expect her to pull away, her duty satiated, but she lingers.

Her lips are sweetened by ChapStick, and I want to taste them.

So I do.

I take her bottom lip into my mouth and place my hands on her cheeks so she can't pull away. She doesn't try.

She's powder-soft and syrupy and like a hit off Travis's joint all at the same time. I try to memorize the suction of her lips, the taste of her breath as I take it into my lungs, swallowing her.

Meadow glides her tongue against mine—just a little, and just once. But it is everything.

Afterward, we all bask atop the pillar, facing the sunset and waiting for that elusive green flash. The ocean below us is a shiny oil slick seething with flames of orange and pink and purple.

Meadow clasps her fists beneath her chin in anticipation, and her eyes glint with the rays of a sinking sun. Sand kernels dot her temple and traverse her ear before vanishing into her blonde tangles.

"Here it comes," Leaf says.

"The sun's almost gone, Lil' Mama. Are you watching?"

A tulip shell hangs from a lock of Meadow's hair, twisting in the breeze. Her cheeks are sunburnt, her lips coral.

"Almost."

Suddenly, everyone erupts in applause, and I jump.

"Far out!"

"Unreal."

"Superior and righteous."

"What a treat. Did you see it, Lil' Mama?"

Leaf nudges my shoulder with his whole body. He looks over at me, his eyes illuminated by the sky.

"Yes," I say. "I saw it."

But I lied. I didn't see the green flash. I saw only Meadow.

DEATH OF A LEGEND

Mister Brownstone. Found dead on Sombrero Beach.

Bloated and smothered in sand, he washed ashore just down the road from the hippie beach.

Dad got the call early this morning but declined the request for assistance.

I hop into my overalls, fastening the clasps over Meadow's crocheted halter top.

Everyone will be at the beach. Everyone will want to get a look at a real sea monster.

When I enter the living room, dad's standing at the window, gazing at nothing in particular.

I don't know why this occurs to me as odd. One might think it a natural position. But he's simply there, a rigid corpse propped against the window. His arms hang straight toward the ground, unyielding.

I want to go to my dad and hug him, tell him I love him. I want him to put his large hand on my head, rock me back and forth, tease me about brainsuckers. But the man standing in our living room is no longer my father. He's a stranger. So I turn away, skulking through the front door and into the morning.

The whole town must've heard about Mister Brownstone. The lot at Sombrero Beach is full, some vehicles parked on the grass, or on the sand. I drop my bike against a thicket of Slash pines and run toward shore. This may be my only chance to see the giant hammerhead shark I've heard about my entire life.

The first thing I notice is the throng of people, crammed shoulder to shoulder, by the water. The second thing I notice is the smell. Like rotting seaweed. Or the Yearling's hut, in need of a good scrubbing.

I look for familiar faces, hoping to see Jimmie or Audrey, but they're nowhere to be found. I recognize a few kids from school. Timmy Katz and Scott Waller stand on the coral bluff that darts into the water, trying to get a better look back at the shore. I see Mr. Lovitz and Miss Mason standing on the beach and shaking their heads, sadness painted across both their faces.

I creep closer, seeking a gap in the crowd.

And that's when I spot Andy and Dottie. But they don't see me—their attention is on the creature tucked within the gathering.

Mister Brownstone lies in the surf, fins reaching toward the spectators as though begging for help, the waning tide forming craters in the sand beneath his body.

He's smaller than I imagined. In my mind, Mister Brownstone was massive—the length of a ship, with teeth the size of conch shells. But I see now that those are the fantasies of a child.

The shark is old. Propeller scars are engraved through his hide. His eyes are yellow, plugged with a pale liquid that's begun to pool in the sand below.

Maybe it's best that dad didn't help with removal. He's told folks that he's clashed with Mister Brownstone on many occasions, but I know the truth. And I wouldn't want dad to see him like this. Let Mister Brownstone stay fantastical. If nothing else, dad deserves that one small courtesy.

I make my way toward the pines, looking for a bike with rainbow streamers and a white wicker basket before remembering that she, too, was ravaged by our fickle waters.

As I locate my new red bike and pull it upright, I notice the ice cream truck parked on the grass. It's always here on the weekends, strands of lights blinking in the windows, silly tunes blasting from the speaker. But this morning, the vehicle is idle. No lights. No music.

Everyone, it seems, is mourning the death of a legend.

I return home and enter the apartment expecting solitude, but what I find is my father. Still at the window. Arms by his side.

"Dad?"

Nothing.

I stand in silence beside him and peer at the ocean beyond. Today, it's dark, serene. We stay like that for a while, dad and I, watching the waves. Seeking the hulking shadow of a ghost through the water.

A SECRET WAR

Meadow hands me a small shell and shows me how to create knots around it with my fingers until it's suspended within a web of colorful yarn. Hers looks like a work of art from a big city museum. Mine looks like a bait net.

"You'll get it," she says. "You just need practice."

"How do you know what it's going to look like when you're done?"

"I start with a single knot and trust the rest will reveal itself. Don't worry about where you'll end up. Just begin."

From the corner of Meadow's swimsuit, I spot the delineation of smooth, untanned skin. A private glimpse of her, just for me.

I want to tell her she's pretty.

So I do.

But Meadow doesn't respond. She doesn't even look up.

"You're pretty," I say again. "Honestly, I think you're the most beautiful woman I've ever seen."

Meadow looks at me with a pinched expression, as though I've said something wrong. But I haven't. Not even close. I'd give just about anything for someone to say that to *me*.

"Did you hear what I said?" I ask.

"I heard you." Meadow returns her attention to the macramé in her hands. "And it's very kind of you to say."

This is far from the response I was expecting, and my face flushes with mortification.

Ziggy and Sparrow emerge from the mangroves in the distance and walk toward us. A distraction from my embarrassment. Good. Hurry.

"It's just that," Meadow begins, dropping the wind chime to her lap. "I didn't earn being pretty. I just got lucky is all."

Oh.

"Like you," she adds, placing her hand on my knee and giving it a little shake. "That's what people see, but they're not really seeing *you*, are they? I didn't work for it. I didn't create it. So it doesn't count." She holds aloft a bundle of knotted shells. "But I created *this*. It didn't exist in the world until I made it, and that's what really matters. This is the real magic. So tell me, Lil' Mama, do you like my wind chimes?"

I look to the mangroves and the peach and white shells tucked within, interspersed with pinecones, driftwood fragments, sea glass, and feathers. Their ropes are like fine lace tapestries, intricate and bewildering.

"They're amazing," I say.

Meadow beams.

"Lil' Mama!" Ziggy greets as he throws down his hand. "Gimme some skin. We're gonna miss you this week."

"Miss me?"

"We're headed to Memphis," he says. "Splittin' real early."

"What's in Memphis?"

"Dr. King!" he cries out, prancing in place with a boyish smile on his face. "Dr. King is returning to Memphis."

"He's speaking at the Mason Temple up there," Meadow adds. "We missed Selma and Stanford, but we're not missing this one."

"When are you coming back?"

"Thursday. Maybe Friday. Depends on how the rides pan out."

"You're *all* going?"

"Well, all but Sparrow. Our little bird here is staying behind."

Sparrow shrugs and looks to the ocean, hiding an expression I can't quite define. Something between elation and contentment. Maybe both. I've only known the nostalgic Sparrow. The sad Sparrow. I like this new version much better.

Meadow turns to me. "You should come, Lil' Mama."

Yes. Yes. A million times, yes!

Ziggy puts his hands on his hips, studying me. "Wait just a minute. What do you know about our Dr. King, Lil' Mama?"

"Lots of things."

Please don't ask.

He strokes his chin.

"She's one of us, Ziggy, so if all of us are going, that means *all of us*."

"Ain't no field trip," Ziggy says. "We're not goin' to the zoo afterward."

I hug my knees. "I know."

"You make the call, Ziggy," Meadow says, returning to her wind chime.

I look away, drawing patterns in the sand. Awaiting his decision.

"I'll keep it real simple, Lil' Mama," he says. "Here's the situation in Memphis: The sanitation workers are on strike because two of our fine African brothers were crushed to death by a garbage truck. If you can tell me why everyone is angry about this, I'll give you my blessing."

Everyone is angry?

A low wave rolls onto the beach, delivering a cluster of lush seaweed, fresh for the picking. But I just sit there, mute.

"Stay in school, Lil' Mama. Memphis ain't no place for kids right now." Ziggy's voice is apologetic, and he places a hand atop my head as he walks back to the water.

Meadow taps my knee. "I don't think that was very fair of Ziggy. Everyone has to start somewhere. We leave tomorrow at dawn. If your folks say it's okay, pack some clothes and meet us at the top of the road. You know the place."

I nod.

"Pop quiz," she says. "Why don't we trust a driver wearing sunglasses?"

"Shades mean shady," I say.

"Good girl. And we *never* get into a car with…"

"Someone who's too eager."

"That's right, Lil' Mama. That's right."

I wake before dawn and pack an overnight bag, stashing it by my door. Atop the bag is the note I scribbled for mom and dad last night.

Big test in Social Studies this week.
Staying at Audrey's for a few days so we can study.
I'll be back by Friday.

I haven't forgotten that dad works at the high school and could easily inquire about the upcoming test that doesn't exist. Or that he might discover my bike stashed in the pines by the school. But dad doesn't notice much these days.

Plus, Meadow says not to worry where you'll end up. Just begin.

Memphis, Tennessee. Wow.

I can't wait to tell Audrey.

I can't wait to tell Jimmie.

I take a final glance out my window, toward the horizon, and in my head, I hear dad's voice: *Red sky at night, sailors delight; red sky at morning, sailors take warning.*

The sky is still a nighttime sky, and I don't yet know what the morning will bring as I snatch my bag and step through my bedroom door.

The kitchen light is on, and mom stands at the counter, grinning at me.

"Good morning, sunshine!" she says in a voice entirely too loud for this hour.

In one hand, I clutch my overnight bag. In the other, a worthless note.

"I'm making breakfast, silly," she says, as though I've questioned her motives. "It's going to be a beautiful day. What do you think about playing hooky, just this once? I hear the tide will be particularly low this morning. It's not to be missed. We can pack a picnic. Make a day of it. What do you say?"

No. No. A million times, no!

"Put your schoolbooks away and help me with the eggs. These shells are breaking into bits. I fear this will be a disaster."

Of all days, mom chooses *today* to be happy again.

I want to say, Go back to your catalogs. Your candy-colored appliances. Your fickle melancholy.

If you loved me at all, today of all days, you'd just disappear.

Movement on the sofa catches my eye. Dad slumbers in the dark living room, kicking a cushion onto the floor. He wheezes, coughing something thick and wet into the upholstery. The living room smells like The Armada.

I hate him.

And I hate mom, smiling at me like she's happy. This is fake happy. Manic happy. And it could be gone in the time it takes me to blink the remaining sleep from my eyes.

"C'mon, silly goose."

How fast could I run through the kitchen and out the front door? Would she chase me? Would she holler, waking dad who would stagger after me in an alcohol trance, tumbling down the stairs in my wake?

Don't worry about where you'll end up. Just begin.

One step toward the door.

I'm going to do it.

Right now.

"Shucks, I've missed a piece," mom says, digging into the bowl with the edge of a broken shell.

Dad burps in his sleep and mom looks to the sofa, her smile dipping at the corners as though connected to her mind by strings and pulleys.

And I don't run for the door.

I step backward, depositing my overnight bag inside my bedroom, and when I take my place beside mom in the kitchen, she wraps her arm around me.

"That top is simply lovely on you," she says. "Is that new?"

Meadow's halter top. Crocheted just for me.

I smile and hope it's enough because I have nothing left to offer. On this particular morning, she's already taken everything.

Mom stuffs a picnic basket with containers of scrambled eggs, sausage, toast, and a thermos of pear juice.

The last time I was at Sombrero Beach, I watched pink liquid seep from the gills of Mister Brownstone. Andy was there, too.

Two different beasts on the same sand.

Mom and I carry our breakfast bounty onto the flats, and when I finish my juice, I rescue small fish from tidepools, collecting them in my thermos and returning them to deeper waters.

As the morning drones on, mom insists she can still do a cartwheel, just like when she was a little girl. She proves it until she's out of breath, collapsing onto the flats with an uproarious giggle.

I shouldn't be here. I should be tucked between Leaf and Ziggy in the backseat of a stranger's Slug Bug.

I look to mom and all I want to do is hurt her.

I'm going to do it.

Right now.

I'm going to tell mom the one thing she would never want to know. The one thing that will ruin her forever.

"I saw Dottie the other day," I say, "when that shark washed ashore."

"Oh?"

Mom has no idea what's coming. This is pure payback. If I can't have my friends, she can't have hers, either.

I pull on my fingers, stretching my knuckles one by one. I breathe deeply, planning each word in my mind.

What I want to say is: Mom, I know Dottie's your best friend, but you need to know that Andy kissed me. He touched me. I was just a kid, and he touched me, mom. *What are you going to do about it, mom?*

But mom smiles at me, and like always, the confession dies on my tongue.

When we arrive home, dad isn't in the apartment, even though mom had the car all day. I picture him walking all the way to The Armada, stumbling south on

US1, his shoulders slung forward, his brow scorched red from the sun.

I sulk into my bedroom and kick my overnight bag beneath my bed, where I don't have to see it.

Before long, mom's voice slices into my bedroom as though my door were made of skin and muscle.

Lunch is ready.

In the kitchen, mom sways back and forth in a frilly apron while stirring a lumpy something atop her glossy cream electric skillet.

After lunch, I wash each plate, and mom takes the dish, wiping it dry with a hand towel. She's still wearing that frilly apron. She's still wearing that stupid smile.

I seize the opportunity.

"I've been thinking about college lately," I say. "What do you think about Fresno State?"

Mom traps me in her gaze, and my world turns to stone.

"It's in California," I stutter, handing her another plate, my arm bobbing in the air.

"We have a college in Key West now," she says, her voice girdled by disapproval. "No need to go any farther than that."

If this is a battle, I'm one step from victory.

"But California is where everything is happening."

Mom yanks the plate from my hand and lobs it into the cabinet with the others. She unties her apron, launching it across the counter. "You can finish up."

As mom passes, she sticks a finger under the strap of my halter top, lifting it from my neck and rolling the stitches between her fingers. "Not much to it, is there?"

The last thing I hear her say as she disappears down the hallway is, "You look like a slut."

And with this final blow, mom declares her victory.

I drop the plate into the sink and run to the bathroom, locking the door behind me.

And then I snatch the razor from the sink and bring the blade onto my thigh.

SHIPPING COMBINE

In the chaos of the shipping combine, there are many smells, and Gunter has memorized them all.

There's the oily sludge that pools on the ground in a continuous feed from the machinery. In the morning, the smell is sweet, but as the afternoon wears on, it becomes foul and sticky, dripping from his nostrils in a black sort of fermentation. There are plastic smells and metallic smells that wage a daily war in his sinuses. Bird shit and rat shit. Moldy bread and old meat—the rotting remains of discarded lunch remnants in unemptied trash receptacles.

Even when home, Gunter can still recall the feel of the combine against his skin. The heat that soaks into his blood, creating an itch in his flesh that's never satiated. Sweat that builds on his scalp throughout the day, collecting grease and dirt as it drips down his nose, his neck, behind his ears, in a slurry that doesn't ever fully wash away. An ache in his arms and the swelling of his feet. The sharp tinge of a torn nail, or a broken toe, engraved in his mind.

And the tastes. The salty tang of sweat mixed with blood. Solvents, oils, burning rubber. Ashes on his tongue when he inhales, the warm spice of bile when he belches.

There's a plethora of sound in the shipping combine as well. The clang of metal pipes, steel chains, and rusted hardware. The never-ending clunk of wood.

Collisions of crates and machinery. Steam valves and sledgehammers. A sudden outcry of pain as somewhere across the factory, another nail is torn, another toe is broken.

Today, Gunter hears all of these sounds.

And a new sound. One he hasn't heard in many months. Heavy footsteps approaching behind him. His name called, brisk and urgent.

"Gunter, halt."

A man thrusts a note against Gunter's chest, and he grasps it before it falls to the floor to be consumed by the black sludge below.

Gunter waits until the man walks away before reading the words printed within. It's a letter from the union requesting his immediate presence.

Gunter powers down his machine and advances slowly toward the front of the building, a knot like a bundle of steel chains unraveling in his gut.

A KING, DETHRONED

I wake Thursday morning trying to channel Meadow in my mind.

Last night, Dr. Martin Luther King Jr. spoke to a crowd in Memphis, and I wasn't there. So instead of having a grand adventure in Tennessee, I worked on my poem for Mr. Mallory's year-end assignment. I swiped dad's thesaurus so I could write something truly great.

I read the first line aloud.

"Oh, blasphemous encampment of blue above me, you've drawn your line in the sand. You've promised me treasures and riches of favor, but nothing has turned out as planned."

Mr. Mallory will be so impressed.

When I get to the top of my street, I look around for Jimmie before remembering that he bikes to school with Ellie Walker now.

In English class, I turn in the new draft of my poem and rush to the window before taking my seat, seeking a glimpse of the hippie beach beyond. But it's still vacant.

Mr. Mallory moves slowly today. Dawdling. His voice is lower than usual, his words drawn out and lingering, as though sweeping from his tongue in cursive.

Margaret Leech and I exchange a look. She dips her head toward Mr. Mallory and mimes bringing a joint to her lips.

Maybe Margaret Leech isn't so bad after all.

In Social Studies, I examine the giant wall-sized map of the United States, finding Memphis. Then I follow every highway through Tennessee, Georgia and into Florida, tracing the roads that will lead my friends home.

After supper, mom and dad sit on the sofa to watch the news, and I'm about to retire to my bedroom when I hear the booming voice of the newscaster: *"Doctor Martin Luther King Junior, Civil Rights leader and Nobel Prize winner, was shot and killed tonight in Memphis, Tennessee."*

Mom says, "My God, Richard."

"In Washington, at the White House, the news reached President Johnson…"

"Richard, what will happen now?"

Dad is silent as I rush into the living room, colliding into mom.

"Oh, dear," she says to me.

OH, DEAR?

The man on the television says, *"Doctor King was in Memphis to lead demonstrators in support of…"*

I know this.

I know because Ziggy told me. Sanitation workers on strike. Two men crushed to death by a garbage truck. Two of our fine African brothers.

"He was standing on the balcony of the Lorraine Motel on the second floor when a single shot came from across the street…"

"Richard, turn this off," mom says. "Danni, go to your room."

"No!"

"What did you just say to your mother?" Dad's voice cuts across the small space, sharp and violent.

His eyebrows swell, and in his gaze, an unmistakable threat. *Red sky at morning.*

I become small, my body small, my voice small.

"I want to hear—"

"This is not for children!"

"I'm not a child!"

In the distance, like an echo from another room: "*...since riots a week ago yesterday that broke out after Doctor King led what he hoped would be a nonviolent demonstration...*

Dad marches to the television and switches off the power. The screen flashes once and goes black, displaying nothing more than a reflection of dad's stained pants.

"To your room," he orders. "We'll talk about this in the morning."

"You'll be passed out on the couch in the morning."

I bring my hands to my mouth and take a step backward. But no amount of concealment or retreat can retract the words I've just spoken to my father.

Mom gasps.

Dad looks as though I've struck him. His face turns purple and his frame expands beside the couch until he blocks out the light from the lamp on the side table. He grows until I can no longer see the window behind him, until he has to hunch to avoid the crush of the ceiling above. He's a monster lumbering toward me.

I take a step toward the dining room table.

And I run.

I dash through the kitchen and out the front door, and don't even look behind me as I plummet down the stairs and swing my leg over my bike. I pedal faster than I've ever pedaled before.

And I don't even think about where I'm going.

My feet know the way; I barely look up.

I know I'm close when I smell the crab traps.

The hut grows larger as I pedal, the scent of smoked fish like a lighthouse guiding in a ship. I drop my bike and peer through the Yearling's open window.

Inside, illuminated by the black-and-white screen before them, Jimmie sits on the couch between his parents. Mrs. Yearling's hands are cupped to her face, and I suspect she's sat like that for a long time.

Dr. King was shot, and my hippies were there. Do they know? Are they safe?

Dr. King is dead, and mom asked, What will happen now?

Something bad, but I don't know what, or why. Because Ziggy was right. I'm just a stupid little girl.

I almost knock on the window but hesitate.

This was a mistake. The Yearlings are Jimmie's family, not mine. I shouldn't be here.

As if sensing my sudden arrival—and impending retreat—Jimmie turns. "Danni!"

The smile on Mrs. Yearling's face tells me everything I need to know.

She opens the door, and I collapse beside Jimmie on the couch. Mrs. Yearling wraps her arm around the both of us, and we watch in silence as the newscaster speaks of Dr. King—his life, his fight for civil rights, his tragic and unexpected death.

I turn to Mrs. Yearling. She smells like fresh-baked cookies. Her legs are wrapped in a long, pink skirt. Her lips are painted maroon.

"Thank you for having me over," I say.

"Of course, Danni," she says. "You're family."

And I know she's telling the truth.

DEADLINE: JUNE 7th

Gunter disembarks the train and rushes past empty farmlands and gravel streets grown weedy and dusty, past rusted vehicles and factory stacks, where in a home that hasn't been repainted in years, under a roof that leaks during a dense fog, his mother waits for him.

"Gunter! Du bist früh zu hause!"

You are home early!

"Ja, mama," he says, stuffing a folded piece of paper into his back pocket. "Die Züge waren früher als geplant."

The trains were ahead of schedule.

Gunter rushes to his bedroom and shuts the door, listening for his mother's footsteps. When he's sure she hasn't followed, he withdraws the paper from his back pocket and unfolds it atop his dresser, reading each sentence again and again.

He slides open the top drawer, thumbing through his identification papers, a microfilm of his diploma, and a small stack of photographs still bound in plastic. Still encrusted with salt.

He digs through the drawer until he finds a pencil, the blank pad of paper, and the watercolor pan stashed at the bottom.

His hands tremble as he hashes words across the blank page.

Sister, we've been given a second chance. They are sending me once again to Cuba. Scheduled to port June 7th. Please tell me, will you be there?

ADVENTURE ON THE HIGH SEAS

Richard Quinn heaves the Valkyrie into the swells. Just ahead, the old Sombrero Lighthouse rises and falls on the waves.

Seawater coats his face and he licks his lips like he's tasting a lover. The salt of her. The warmth of her. The intoxication of her. He swallows it all.

The Sombrero Lighthouse, a floating relic in the middle of the ocean, is the sole marker for the barrier reef. Below the rocking fortress is an underwater rainforest of living coral and sea life, great and small: Parrotfish, Trumpetfish, Starfish, Sergeant Majors, Barracuda, Sea Turtles. Even sharks.

At Richard's feet, a mesh bag of snorkeling equipment rolls from side to side with the waves, and he peers down at his daughter.

"Not long now, pumpkin," he hollers.

She doesn't answer.

Richard knows he's been a bear to deal with these last few months. He's not hiding it as well as he thought. But a day on the water always makes things right with his little girl.

He surveys the horizon, glancing to the islands behind him. Marathon, Duck Key, Big Pine Key—mere gashes across the horizon. He's not far enough. Not nearly.

The lighthouse grows larger, and Richard cuts the engine of the Valkyrie as she approaches the boundary of delicate coral. There's only one other boat on the reef today, yet Richard already feels claustrophobic.

He descends the helm to stand behind Danni, and puts a hand on her head, worming his fingers behind her ears.

"What's this?" he asks.

"Dad, stop."

"It's a brainsucker! And what's it doing?"

Danni flings his hand from her head and walks to the railing, peering at the reef below.

In the distance, gray clouds form, the sky and ocean darkening as one. Richard unspools the anchor from the anchor cubby and is about to toss it overboard when he spots something on the horizon.

A large freighter. Heading right for the storm.

He drops the anchor to the deck.

Richard recognizes the bright red hull and can already taste the beer on his tongue.

He shouldn't take Danni to dangerous waters. It's no place for a young woman, no place at all.

But if he'd had a son, he wouldn't hesitate.

Richard turns to his daughter.

"How about a little adventure?"

Richard nearly topples from the helm as the Valkyrie launches from the crest of a mighty wave. The vessel plummets into the abyss, throwing him forward, and he submits to the wooden spindles of the wheel.

"Hold on!" he yells to his daughter. "Stop moving! Stay down!"

Her blonde hair is a tangle of twisted roots whipping across her face.

Maybe this wasn't such a good idea.

But the daughter of Richard Quinn can handle anything.

The Soviet ship is just ahead, more beast than boat, red paint dulled and bleached by saltwater. Wide cracks traverse her coating, like aging skin. Richard studies the wake patterns—where they disperse, and where he should steer the Valkyrie.

A fresh surge pushes the boat into the air, and for a moment, all Richard can see are storm clouds. The Valkyrie nosedives into a deep trench between the waves, and a fishing pole dislodges from its holder, vaulting into the darkening sky.

This isn't the first time Richard has piloted alongside a Soviet freighter. He's done this many times before. To feel dwarfed. Insignificant. Like gazing into the night sky to experience your own mortality. Because in that impotence, there is freedom.

And within freedom, there is power.

The sky splits, and rain pellets his face like gravel. Sailors gather along the railing, monitoring his approach, and when Richard waves, the men cheer and shake their hats into the wind. No Russians. No Americans. Just fellow passengers on the sea.

High above the amassing sailors, a colossal flag clashes with the wind. Only short clips of a golden hammer and sickle can be seen through the onslaught.

Danni stands against the railing, gaping at the bright red leviathan before them.

Richard steers the Valkyrie closer, and though safer within the freighter's wake, this is not still water, and he keeps a constant hold of the wheel to avoid collision.

Rain hammers the thin roof, and seawater lashes from beneath as the sailors push one another aside to get a look at the crazy American accelerating beside them.

Richard holds a hand to his mouth, tipping it to his lips, before waving to the crowd. Again, he signals for a drink.

A man sends a bottle overboard, where it's swallowed by the cold Atlantic waters. His comrades jeer and steal his hat. The man gives chase and is quickly out of sight.

Another sailor throws a bottle to Richard, and it clatters to his feet before losing its cap, spitting foam across the boat. Richard scoops it up. The beer is warm and salty, burning the back of his throat. It's glorious.

"One for my daughter!"

He points to Danni, grappling to stay upright at the bow.

A downpour of beer spills from the Soviet ship, many destined for the bottom of the ocean.

Danni covers her head as glass strikes the deck. One bottle explodes on impact. Another rolls into the empty anchor cubby.

Danni falls backward as a third bottle detonates against her ankle, spraying beer and blood across the deck.

She screams, and Richard cuts the engine.

The Soviet ship quickly sails on, and Richard gives a farewell salute before hustling to the bow.

Danni looks up, cradling her leg as another wave sends the Valkyrie into the sky.

Richard braces for them both as his boat crashes back down.

"Let me see," he hollers, and Danni moves her hand.

"It hurts!"

"Can you move your foot? That's good. Wiggle your toes."

Again, the Valkyrie is aloft. Until it isn't.

Danni moans as her head bashes against the deck.

"Sit up," Richard commands.

By the jagged line across her skin, he knows the cap is what got her, and not broken glass. She'll heal. No hospital visit today.

"Come into the cockpit with me. It's safer."

"I wanna go home," she says.

"Stand up!"

Danni clings to her father's wrist.

The deck sloshes with rainwater and spilt beer. The rescue float comes unhooked from the side of the cockpit and glides back and forth with the swells, tethered to its own rope.

The Valkyrie is suddenly in flight, and Richard feels the rudder leave the water as if he and the boat are one, his own legs being yanked from the depths.

Lightning cracks above them and Danni screams as the boat falls, colliding with the ocean as though colliding with concrete. Richard crashes to the floor, and Danni slides from his grip, skidding toward the stern.

Richard tries to right himself.

He tries to grab her hand.

He kicks the deck, following her closer and closer to the boat's edge.

Her eyes are panicked, her mouth brimming with water, as she screams for her dad.

One foot slides overboard, and her arms are askew, grasping for the railing as the waves pull the Valkyrie in every direction at once.

Danni folds in half from the force of the wind ripping through the boat. She grasps at the anchor sliding across the deck, but the weight pulls with her, forcing her closer to the edge.

And then the wayward anchor pushes Danni off the stern and into the churning waters of the Atlantic.

～

It happens so fast. The water hits my skull like a foul ball and everything goes fuzzy. No one ever tells you how hard it is to fight for survival when faced with death. When that moment actually arrives—and it's no longer just *something that might happen someday*—the mind goes dormant. It tucks into a ball, like a little kid crying under the blankets.

Sometimes I'm high in the air, gasping for breath that's more sea water than oxygen. Sometimes I'm in blackness, caught in an underwater tornado that yanks my limbs from my body. My teeth clamp together so tightly I fear my jaw may crumble from the pressure. And there's nothing I can do to stop it.

I hope water takes me one day.

I said this once.

Beautiful, peaceful drowning.

But it's not beautiful.

It's not peaceful.

Rain. Wind. Rolling. Choking. Up. Down. I can't tell anymore.

Dad screams somewhere in the distance. So far away. Like a memory. Like it's all in my head. Like he's not even there.

∿

Richard pushes the rescue float through the waves.

An image of the child he pulled from the water— that poor little girl who was washed out to sea when her family crashed into the Vaca Cut Bridge—flashes through his mind. Pallid. Bloated. Sightless.

No.

Not again.

Not Danni.

He throws the rescue float and uses the rope to pull himself closer.

"Daniella!" he screams, the words garbled and drowning on his tongue. "Daniella!"

Richard kicks and one shoe dislodges, dropping away, then the other. The rain has begun to lessen, but it's of no comfort. He must be faster. He must be stronger.

Finally within reach, Richard throws his hand toward his daughter but misses, grasping only the waves.

⌒

My brain screams—not my mouth, but my *brain*. Fighting the inevitable. Stubborn thing.

I think about dad. My irresponsible dad, just like Mr. Yearling says. Our *adventures*.

My mind races with thoughts, disconnected and unrelated. Flashes of images that mean nothing and everything at the same time. My entire life.

Eating Mary Janes with Jimmie at the Vaca Cut Bridge. Smoked fish spread in the hut. Audrey's color television. The flash of lightning through the band room skylight. Andy's hand on my knee, tracing circles. Meadow's voice, a wind chime made of seashells. My gold owl necklace, gone forever.

And Poppy.

Dead, like me.

And I hear my father in the distance. His voice calling, Daniella. He never calls me that.

The waves bolster me toward the sky. No more plummeting. No more choking.

No more thoughts.

Just rising.

"Daniella!"

I feel something like a hand around my wrist, forcing my body to follow. Like an arm around my waist, buckling me in half. Like the warmth of my father holding me as a baby. The scratch of his whiskers, the scent of his skin.

And his voice whispering, "Daniella."

Maybe it's real. Or maybe I'm dreaming. Either way, I smile as everything fades to black.

Richard Quinn collapses to the deck of the Valkyrie with his daughter in his arms. Danni's conscious, but barely, and when she grins up at him, he hates himself.

Richard scoops her into his arms and ascends the cockpit. He's out of breath, as if all the oxygen was swept away with the storm. The cut on her ankle weeps, staining his shorts red.

He positions himself behind the wheel and folds her onto his thighs. No longer a young woman, here in his lap, she is once again a child.

By the time they reach calmer waters, Danni is fully awake, her troubled face to the wind and to the shoreline drawing closer. Richard cuts the motor.

"Let's have a look at you. Show me your ankle."

Danni props her foot against the seat. "I'll be okay," she says.

Richard laughs.

"Is this funny?"

"The last time you were on my lap, you were a quarter the size."

She smiles. She tries.

"Walk with me," Richard says, leading her down the stairs and to the bow, where he takes a seat on a fiberglass cubby.

Danni sits beside him, tossing a glance to the islands.

He wants to apologize, chastise himself, beg for her forgiveness, but he doesn't know how. This emotion is unfamiliar to Richard Quinn.

Danni shivers, and Richard wraps an arm around her, pulling her close. This, at least, he can do.

He appraises the Valkyrie. Puddles of seawater and rain collect in the corners. Broken glass litters the deck. His rescue float is missing, likely blown away. Its torn rope waves in the wind like a nautical flag.

He spots a beer bottle glinting from the corner of the anchor cubby. A silver lining.

Richard dislodges the beer and pops the cap against the railing. He hands the bottle to Danni.

"I don't want it," she says, looking away.

"You've earned it."

Danni accepts the beer and examines the label. A small circle of tan. She runs her fingers across the paper, tracing the red and gold letters neither of them can read, before tipping the bottle to her lips.

She hands it back, and Richard downs the rest in one long gulp.

"Adventure on the high seas," he says.

They sit in silence as the Valkyrie bobs closer to a sandbar.

The sun sinks lower on the horizon.

"Look," Richard says, pointing to a school of Nurse Sharks swimming under the boat. "Sea puppies."

She doesn't respond, and the conversation vacates as quickly as the sharks.

Richard spins the empty bottle in his hands and considers his words, testing different versions in his head, before settling on, "Let's not worry mom, huh?"

Richard eyes Danni's hunched shoulders and trembling fingers.

From the chill, he tells himself.

He unlatches a storage compartment and withdraws a beach towel, wrapping it around her shoulders.

Danni's barely spoken to him all day. Barely looked at him.

She's just tired, he tells himself.

Her feet are wrinkled from seawater, knees already blooming with shades of purple. And her thighs…

"What happened there, pumpkin?" Richard asks, pointing to the marks peeking out from beneath her shorts.

Danni jumps, tugging the stiff fabric down her leg. "It's nothing," she yelps.

Richard kneels. "Let me see."

"It's old."

"Doesn't look old."

"I fell off my bike."

"How many times?" he asks, reaching for her leg.

"Can we go now?"

Richard places a hand on her head, rocking her from side to side, and she shrugs away.

As he fires up the engine for the last time today, he considers the marks on her thighs, still raging pink.

Those injuries could certainly be the result of a bicycle accident. Rocks are hazardous in the Florida Keys. Tiny shards of shell and coral, sharp as daggers.

A bicycle accident and nothing more.

Kids are clumsy, he tells himself.

～

When I turn away, the tears finally fall.

Not from the cut on my ankle, or because I almost drowned. And not because dad saw the scars on my thighs, or because I nearly confessed the truth of them. It's deeper than that. And the tears keep falling.

Dad's behind me, high above the ocean. Even out here, atop the endless blue, his presence is expansive, filling the gap between every wave. Like a tether. A board I can walk on to find my way home.

I used to think that board was limitless, dependable, but now I fear I could step off the edge at any moment, blindfolded, a harpoon at my spine.

We skirt the shore, passing beaches and mangroves, canals capped with houses big as my school and pools large enough to rival the sea. Waterfront restaurants. Waterfront motels. Waterfront gas stations. Waterfront bait shops. And boats run aground, their masts twisting evermore atop the sandbars.

We pass Marathon, heading to The Duck Key Marina. I wish dad were able to dock the Valkyrie at Quade's Boathouse. We would've been home already.

When we pass the Vaca Cut Bridge, I look away and hold my breath—because that's what you do when you pass a graveyard.

TENDER MERCIES

Richard Quinn stumbles out of The Armada and lumbers toward the old abandoned lighthouse with his leather-bound copy of Moby Dick in his fist.

His breath is thick with spirits, and he probes his lips with his tongue, searching for a remaining drop of whiskey.

As a boy, he would sneak in through the door of the lighthouse, ascend the nautilus staircase and sit beside the giant faceted bulb. Sometimes he would watch the sunset, sipping a beer stolen from his father. Sometimes he would climb the railing, scale the pitted wall until he stood atop the roof, startling incoming fishermen as they neared the shore.

When Richard was young, the lighthouse was a castle to storm. A dragon to slay. It was an empty train station, a jail cell, a secret spy fort. Anything he wanted it to be. But now it's just an old lighthouse, with faded paint and rusted steel. Any dragon who once sought refuge here has long ago turned to rot.

In just over a month, on the last day of school, Richard will recite the first chapter of Moby Dick to an eager classroom. As he did last year. And every year that came before. Like goddamned clockwork.

Anticipation is already building. Just this week, Mrs. Berrett cornered him in the break room.

"I've heard I should stick close to your classroom on the last day of school," she whispered, giving Richard a wink. "They say you turn Ishmael into Paul Newman."

Richard staggers along the edge of the serrated embankment and spits into the foaming seawater at his feet.

Yesterday's adventure on the high seas was supposed to bring them closer, bridge this growing expanse that's formed between them. But once again, Richard Quinn was unable to complete his mission. He may have pulled her from the water, but he's no one's hero. Danni simply got lucky.

He stares at the book in his hand, tracing the gilded embossed title.

No one will write books about Richard Quinn.

No campfire stories about his seafaring journeys, his battles atop the great blue yonder. Or his death-defying confrontation with an East German freighter on the dark ocean, somewhere between Key West and Havana.

He's clutching the pages of his book, searching for the courage to tear them from the spine, condemn them to a watery grave, when Andy grasps Richard's arm and pulls him back from the edge.

It sounds like the beginning of a joke: three fishermen sit in a boat.

But this is how Richard Quinn will spend the rest of his night—in a small, mustard-yellow Boston Whaler skiff with a tiller engine and a faulty fuel line, tethered to a dock at Quade's Boathouse.

"You ever fix the motor on 'er?" Richard asks to break the silence.

"We still argue from time to time," Peter says. "But I usually win."

Richard sits on the bench by the motor, staring into the infinite black, while Andy and Peter perch at the stern. Studying the back of his head, he imagines.

"You can talk to us, Richard," Andy says, "if you need to get something off your chest."

And there it is.

Richard says nothing.

"Never seen you this bad, buddy."

Richard huffs and belches a splash of stomach acid across his tongue. He watches a large boat idle by the marina, and the wake left behind is enough to jostle the small skiff burdened by the weight of three grown men. Richard grasps the ledge to keep from rolling overboard.

"What's the problem, Ishmael?"

"You don't *want* to know my problem," Richard mumbles.

The longer he stares into the night, the more brilliant the moon and stars reflecting off the water, like a drowned city in the ocean grasses.

"Why are we here?"

"Thought you could use a change of scenery."

Richard considers this, generates a comprehensive argument in his head, but ultimately acquiesces. He grunts his consent.

Richard still grips his special copy of Moby Dick, and he thumbs across the pages. How long has it been since he's ventured beyond chapter one? He flips through the book and stops at a random page. He reads the first line to reveal itself.

Abominable are the tumblers into which he pours his poison.

When I enter English class on Monday morning, a substitute sits at Mr. Mallory's desk. And when I see each and every student crammed against the open window, seeking a glimpse of the beach beyond, I stop dead in my tracks.

"Hippies! In our hometown!" says Sharon Wolinski.

"Far out," says Darlene Kipp.

I swallow a rock in my throat. A brick. An anvil.

Our substitute stands and commands everyone back to their desks with a few claps of her sun-spotted hands. I peer through the window on the way to my seat. To anyone watching, I'm just another curious student, nothing more.

Meadow lounges in the surf, her hair sweeping to and fro with the waves. Beyond her I see Leaf. I look for Ziggy and Maya but they're nowhere to be found.

As our substitute attempts to locate chalk for the board, I take my seat and feel a tap-tap-tap on my shoulder.

"*I* could be a hippie," Margaret whispers.

I don't have the energy for Margaret Leech today.

"No foolin'!" she says. "When I graduate, I'm moving to San Francisco. Like Audrey."

"No you're not, Margaret."

"I might," she whines. "Darcy Eagen says they're nudists. Darcy's sister's boyfriend is a boating instructor, and he saw them naked yesterday. *So* weird."

"Just bodies."

"Grody. I don't want to see that."

"So don't look."

"What's wrong with you today?" Margaret asks. "You're shakin' your feet like you've got fleas or somethin'."

I force stillness into my legs, though all they want to do is bolt from this classroom and run all the way to my friends.

When the bell rings, I wait until every student has exited the classroom before peering out the window.

Beyond Meadow and Leaf, I spot Sparrow emerging from the mangroves, wearing a tiny bikini and a scar that runs from ankle to hip, plainly visible in the sunlight.

But Sparrow isn't alone.

I clasp my hand to my mouth to keep from crying out in shock.

It's Mr. Mallory! No socks. No shoes. No shirt. Just swim shorts, his Clark Kent glasses, and a dazzling smile I could spot from space. He wraps his arms around Sparrow from behind, kisses her neck.

And then Mr. Mallory plucks Sparrow from the sand and stumbles back to the mangroves, away from the beach and out of sight.

After school, I run to the hippie beach for the first time since they've returned.

"Lil' Mama!" Meadow calls, her voice like a wind chime made of seashells.

I spend a whole hour helping her weave complicated rope designs around a large conch shell. Sparrow joins us, displaying a small, pink shell she gathered along the beach.

"It took me all day to find just the right one," she says. "Look at this circle." Sparrow points to a tiny hole boring right through the center. "It's so perfect, like God carved it especially for me."

"Of course she did," Meadow replies.

I learn of Sparrow's new sweetheart: James, a recent transplant from Colorado who teaches English at the high school.

"I think he loves me," Sparrow says.

"Why do you think he loves you?" I ask.

Does he write you love letters? Sing you songs? Declare that you're the most beautiful woman he's ever seen? *Tell me the secret code.*

Even Meadow has stopped knotting to learn the answer.

Finally, Sparrow speaks.

"He kisses my scars."

Meadow nods as if anticipating this answer all along.

Sparrow admires her shell, no additional explanation required.

"So, Lil' Mama," Meadow says, "you *must* know James."

I consider this.

"No," I say. "I don't know him."

And I'm being honest. I don't know James. I know Mr. Mallory. And that's not the same thing. There are different people living inside all of us. Faces we switch between like the sheared facets of a lighthouse bulb.

I can feel the joy crackling from Sparrow's body like static electricity, and I wish I knew James. He sounds wonderful.

But James is only for Sparrow, and I can live with that. Mr. Mallory isn't too bad, either.

I help Sparrow craft a thin rope from string, holding taut the end as she weaves a tight and delicate braid, threading it through the small hole of her shell. She holds it up to the sun and the shell glows even pinker in the light, like the dainty helix of a lady's ear. I expect her to tie it around her neck, but instead, she tucks the necklace into her pocket.

We're soon joined by Leaf, who spent the afternoon fishing with a handcrafted cast net. The knot work is as unique as Meadow's own fingerprint. A feather dangles from the corner like an artist's signature.

As the sun begins to set, Leaf builds a roaring fire and we bask in the smell of smoldering wood and roasting mullet as he tells me all about their trip to Memphis. How Maya wept during Dr. King's speech. How they learned of the assassination from a radio broadcast in a rusted old Studebaker somewhere outside Birmingham. And that when they arrived in Miami, Ziggy and Maya thumbed a ride to the airport, flying home to Barbados.

"I guess Ziggy's had enough of America."

And with this statement, the sun seems to sink even lower on the horizon.

"I know what'll cheer us up," Meadow says, untying her bikini top.

It flutters to the sand like a fallen petal, and I force my gaze away from the rosy haloes of her nipples.

"Right on," Leaf says as he, too, stands and disrobes before rushing into the surf.

But Meadow lingers, crouching beside me instead.

"Join us this time, Lil' Mama. Please?"

I run my fingers across the sand, crafting spirals and hatch marks. "People can see you, ya know. From the window."

Meadow stands and faces the school in the distance, spreading her arms. She then bends over and offers a full view of her backside to whomever may be spying from afar. I can't help but laugh. She winks at me. "Let 'em watch."

When Meadow sits beside me on the beach, I tug on my shorts to be sure my scars are covered.

"I know why you don't want to take off your clothes," she says.

Oh.

"We all have pain, Lil' Mama. We all suffer. But it's the bad things that make us who we are in ways you can't see right now. Can you try to understand that?"

I shrug, and it's an honest answer.

"I've been hurt too," she says. "More than you could know. So has Leaf. Sparrow. Everyone. But do you know why I still have love? Why I'm still happy?"

I shake my head.

"Because I like *me*. As I sit here right now, I wouldn't change a thing. If I went back in time and fixed everything bad that's happened along the way, it would trickle down and change everything about who I am today."

"Butterfly Effect," I say.

Meadow looks surprised. "That's right. How'd you know that?"

"Science class. If a butterfly flaps its wings on one side of the world, it can cause a tsunami on the other."

"That's pretty heavy, isn't it?"

I nod.

"So you really just have to ask yourself one question, and all the pain starts to heal. You don't even need to answer it out loud, only in your mind. But you have to be honest. We can't lie to ourselves. Ever."

Ask me anything; I'll tell you anything.

"Do you like yourself, Lil' Mama?"

HOW NOW BROWN COW

On Friday, the 3rd of May 1968, a package arrives at the Deutsche Post warehouse in the small port town of Warnemunde. It's nondescript, flat and already tattered from days tossed about and stacked in the stale interior of a German postal vehicle.

It travels an inspection line, and a man with knuckles like acorns plucks the package from the pile of recent arrivals. He shakes it. Scowls. Examines the return address, and the address of the recipient—Key West, Florida, United States.

The man pries open a corner before signaling to a guard.

"Buch drinnen," he says. "Stift."

Book inside. Pen.

The guard accepts the package from the man with the acorn fingers, and the worker crosses his arms atop his broad chest.

The guard withdraws a blade from his belt and slices open the tattered package. A pencil clatters to the floor.

"Es ist ein Bleistift, du Idiot. Kein Stift."

It is a pencil, you idiot. Not a pen.

The guard withdraws the remaining contents, spreading them onto a nearby table: 1 brush, 1 pad of paper, 1 box of paint, and 1 poorly painted picture of a brown cow. The grass below the cow is brown as well, the sky purple. He plucks the pencil from the floor and adds to the tallied items: 1 pencil.

The guard chooses the pan of watercolors first. Deciding it is insignificant, he trades it for the blank pad of paper, but this, too, is neither interesting nor worthy of his time. He tosses it to the table and snatches the painting, leaving dirty fingerprints along the bare edge.

Look at this piece of shit, he orders the warehouse worker. Would you give this to your mother? Your wife?

The guard examines the destination address.

I wouldn't even eat this cow, he says, but someone in America will hang it on their wall. Idiots. Get it out of my sight. It's hurting my eyes.

And with that, the worker repackages the items, stretches tape across the gash in the box, and slaps an inspection sticker along the edge before pushing it down the line to be wheeled into a waiting cargo container bound for America.

The package travels north, along the coast of Denmark, before making a southwestern turn through the North Sea and into The Atlantic Ocean. The ship travels slowly between continents, the captain having made the decision to run the engine below capacity to conserve fuel consumption.

There's a small notch in the roof of the shipping container, and heavy rains along the northern edge of the Bahamas drench the freighter, causing a constant drip of moisture to dampen the package. Purple paint blooms from one corner.

When the package arrives in Key West, it's swiftly cleared through customs by a boy so distracted by thoughts of his sweetheart that he doesn't notice the purple watercolor stain that's ruined the cuff of his favorite shirt.

The package is released to the shipping line and placed in a tub en route to the Key West Post Office.

On Thursday, the 16th of May, the package is delivered to its final destination—a small motel outside of Mallory Square—where a girl chewing a lavish quantity of Dubble Bubble signs for it before remembering to check the list of current guests.

She examines the name on the package before checking the registered guests, finding none by that name.

The girl blows a large bubble, and when it pops, it flutters across her lips. She licks it away.

Her manager would be angry to discover she's signed for a package without first checking the guest list.

She looks around to be sure no one is watching before dropping the package into the trash bin, concealing the evidence of her workplace blunder under a few pages of a discarded newspaper.

THRESHOLD

I meet Mr. Mallory after school for my second poem critique.

"Oh, blasphemous encampment of blue above me," he reads aloud.

His pinched eyebrows tell me I should be grateful there's no one else in the room.

"I assume you're talking about the sky, but can you tell me what 'blasphemous encampment' means to you? How is the sky making you *feel?*"

"I used a thesaurus," I offer.

"I have no doubt about that, Miss Quinn."

Mr. Mallory scans the page, but I can't take my eyes off his neck.

Right there, at the base of his throat, is Sparrow's pink shell necklace.

"Writhing waves of plunder conceal an internal plague," he continues, before placing it on his desk. "It's interesting, Miss Quinn. I'll give you that."

"Interesting means bad."

"Not at all. You get a resounding A for effort on round two."

I trace the shadow below his Adam's apple. A delicate line of braided rope. And that shell with the perfect hole, carved by God herself.

"The word *blasphemous* means to go against something sacred," he says. "Writhing waves of plunder conceal an internal plague. It sounds like something is happening just under the surface. Like an allegorical hell hides beneath everything."

I resist the urge to ask what allegorical means.

What I want to say is, I don't know what the poem is about. If it's allegorical, it's a deception of the thesaurus, and you've been thoroughly fooled.

But instead I say, "Thanks?"

"I suggest one more revision," he says. "These are fancy words, but great writers don't hide behind fancy words."

Mr. Mallory fingers mindlessly at Sparrow's necklace.

"*You* control the poem, not the other way around. Don't write from the head. Write from the *gut*. Bleed onto the page until you can no longer see the words. Then wipe that blood away and bleed all over it again."

"Bleed?"

"Home can be messy. Scary. *Bloody*. Don't wrap it up in a neat little bow."

I collect my second draft as Mr. Mallory walks toward the window.

"One more thing before you go, Miss Quinn."

I take a deep breath. What now?

He smiles. "A poem doesn't always have to rhyme."

When I retrieve my bike from the rack, I spot something secured to my handlebar. A piece of paper with words printed in pen.

A note from Audrey.

It says, simply, *I miss you.*

The next day, Audrey and I escape through the exit doors, toward the mangroves.

When I found her note strapped to my bike, I had to be honest with myself, like Meadow says. It wasn't Audrey who pulled away. It was me. But Audrey's a true friend and refused to accept my apology. Her only request was that we reinstate Lovedays, just her and I.

But I can't rebuild my friendship with Audrey on a foundation of lies, so today, I take her onto the beach for the very first time, and introduce her to my friends.

Everyone loves Audrey, and I'm not even jealous. I knew they would. But I'm relieved when they don't give her a special name.

We stay with the hippies all afternoon and into the evening.

Here, on the beach, I never question what I say or how I look. I just *am*. And it's always enough. Here, I'm not a child. I don't require protection from the world. Or a board to walk on to find my way home. Because I already am.

So when Meadow tells me they're leaving for good on Sunday, she should've lobbed a rock at my temple. It would've hurt less.

I'm barely listening as Meadow says, "We'll be living on a little ranch in the woods, in a little town called Siskiyou County. In northern California, there are so many trees and mountains, Lil' Mama. It's unlike anything you've ever seen. You'd really flourish up there, I just know it. We're gonna miss you so much. You *must* visit us sometime."

The cruelest words ever spoken, tumbling from her mouth like spilt marbles. I want to chase after them and shove them back inside, pinch her lips shut.

Leaf plucks at his cigar box guitar, strumming the first chords of a Joan Baez song.

"If you were a carpenter," he begins, his voice high and reedy, "and I were a lady…"

I'd laugh if I weren't about to cry.

"Talk to me," Meadow says. "What are you feeling?"

Dead inside.

"What's in California, anyway?"

The flames dance in Meadow's eyes, and her expression is one of pure contentment. It's at this very moment I know she won't change her mind.

"Free land for free people," she says. "Something special is happening out there, and we want to be a part of it."

Audrey places her hand on my knee in solidarity, but she doesn't insert herself. She knows this conversation is only for me.

I stare at the horizon, to the clouds sagging with russet underbellies.

"Something bigger than us," Meadow continues. "A family. An opportunity to live honest lives, reconnect with the earth."

"Can you dig it, Lil' Mama?" Leaf asks.

No.

"Everyone's trying to find their place in this crazy world," Meadow says. "Well, *almost* everyone." She gazes at Sparrow. "It seems our little bird here has already found hers."

Sparrow grins, pushing her toes into the sand.

"Where is it again?"

"Siskiyou County," Meadow says patiently, weaving her fingers atop her knees. "California. We leave Sunday."

Someone passes me a joint and I accept it immediately, inhaling deeply like Travis Misker taught me. I hold it in my chest until I'm coughing so hard I fear a piece of lung may dislodge. Audrey plucks the joint from my fingers and takes a hit. She doesn't cough once, and I wonder if she smokes with Mercy and Sharon.

"Meet us here Saturday night," Meadow says, "and we'll have a proper goodbye. We brought a little something back from Memphis. It'll really open your mind, Lil' Mama. We're all connected. You'll see that California isn't so far away after all."

My head is already swimming from the one hit I took off their joint.

"I don't want to smoke again," I admit.

"It's not a smoke, Lil' Mama. It's a *test*."

I scowl, and she laughs.

"Just be here Saturday night. And bring Audrey. It'll be a blast."

Meadow appraises my expression in the firelight. My confusion over the word *test*.

"Do you trust me, Lil' Mama?"

"Yes."

And I don't even have to think about it, because I do. I really, really do.

GOOD DEEDS

Six days ago, on Sunday, the 19th of May 1968, an older man with a slight limp carted his cleaning supplies through the lobby of a Key West motel near Mallory Square.

He dusted the fans and the lamps, then used wood oil to make the counters gleam *just so*, before mopping the floor twice over. He concluded his final walkthrough of the lobby, dumping the overflowing trash bins into a large plastic receptacle.

When he collected the bin from the front desk, it was heavier than usual, and curiosity overcame him. He handpicked papers and tissues from the bin, paperclips, a broken coffee mug, until he located an unopened package lodged at the bottom. The man used a piece of tissue to pull a wad of bubblegum from a customs stamp, whistling when he saw it had been sent all the way from Germany. He noted the stain of purple at the corner. His favorite color.

The man took this as a good sign and placed the package on the front desk before gazing one last time across the lobby. Satisfied with his work, the man carted his cleaning supplies out the door and into the night.

The next morning, a woman who almost called out sick—though she was merely hungover—clocked into work and took her seat at the front desk, popping an aspirin.

The tattered package was hard to miss, bound with two types of packing tape, a plethora of postal stamps, and a giant purple stain at the corner.

The woman traced the recipient's name with her finger.

She'd heard that name before.

She walked to the filing cabinet and located guest records for the previous month. When she found nothing, the woman continued her search because puzzling over a mysterious package was more enjoyable than rearranging her pens in an effort to look busy.

When she reached a drawer labelled "Oct-Dec '67", she discovered a checkout record for the guest with the unusual name and pulled the file. She taped a piece of paper over the motel's information and transcribed the woman's West Virginia home address.

When the mail carrier arrived later that afternoon, the woman handed him the package and asked that he please forward to the correct address. When he left, the woman smiled, pleased with her good deed, before swallowing another aspirin.

When the package arrived at West Virginia's postal hub, it was loaded onto a truck bound for the recipient's county, then sorted into a bin and transported to the post office that serviced the neighborhood of its final destination.

And this morning, Saturday, the 24th of May 1968, a package that endured a vigorous inspection in Germany, a voyage across two oceans, a burial at the bottom of a trash bin, and a journey through six states, finally lands on a residential doorstep.

The woman who receives the package is not prone to optimism. She notes the return address, the watercolor stain, and the slashed edge that's been re-taped and covered over with a German inspection sticker.

It doesn't look good, but optimism is hard to shake once it has its claws in you.

"Bruder," the woman whispers, clutching the tattered package to her chest.

THE TEST

For the first time in months, Richard Quinn wakes with the sunrise.

The sun is different today. The hue, perhaps. Or the brilliance of it.

He enters his study and locates a beer hidden in the bottom drawer of his desk, stashed among his collection of telephone numbers. He opens it, muffling the sound against his shirt, and walks into the kitchen.

Near the front door, he spots Danni's school bag slumped against the wall, a crumpled sheet of paper protruding from the zipper. Richard tells himself he's only being helpful when he wrestles the page from the zipper's teeth, but he doesn't hesitate to scan the poem once it's in his hand.

If it weren't for Danni's meticulous handwriting, Richard might assume these were the tortured words of a classmate. Maybe that girl with the short black hair, whatever her name is.

It seems someone has stolen his little girl and replaced her with an unknown woman who wears halter tops and writes brooding poetry.

He hears the click of the bathroom door, and considers slipping the poem back into her bag, but Danni moves quickly into the dining room.

She's taller than Miriam now, no doubt about it. Her cheekbones are higher, more defined, and he notes the thick swatch of eyeliner smudged against her lashes. Upper *and* lower.

"That's not yours," Danni says, snatching the paper from his hand.

"Is this your final assignment for Mr. Mallory?" he asks.

Danni walks toward her bedroom.

"Where do you think you're going?"

"Am I in trouble or something?"

"Of course not."

She leans against her door and crosses her arms. A challenge.

Richard must be cautious if he wishes to continue chatting with his daughter, so he takes a step back, gifting her the space she's demanding.

"Your poem is well written," he offers.

Danni studies him, searching for cracks in the facade.

"Mr. Mallory will be very impressed."

"He hated it," she spits out.

"Impossible. It's lovely, pumpkin. Would I lie to you?"

"Yes."

Richard drowns the lump in his throat with a swig of his desk-warm beer. "Teachers are always hardest on the students with the most promise."

Danni chews her lip, and Richard senses she's offering him one final comment.

"He must see something special in you because your poem is very good. You have real talent."

Danni shifts her weight from one foot to the other.

"You could be one of the greats."

And with this, he's said too much.

Danni rolls her eyes, slips into her bedroom, and slams the door behind her.

We're supposed to meet at sunset but are too excited to wait any longer.

Audrey doesn't have a bike, so she balances on my handlebar like I once did—last summer, as Eddie pedaled to the haunted house.

Everything seemed so easy back then. Like happiness could be found in a single kiss from a cute boy, and I'd wanted nothing more.

Thoughts of Eddie are always followed by thoughts of Poppy. I haven't looked for her memorial at the Vaca Cut Bridge. I don't know if the Troll Doll I left after the hurricane is still there. I never swapped it for a Betsy Wetsy like I'd promised. I never replaced the Seagrape leaves with fresh flowers.

We skid to a stop and stash my bike in the mangroves. When we reach the roaring bonfire, everyone stands and waves like they've spent all day waiting for us. Meadow, Leaf, Sparrow.

And Mr. Mallory.

"Ladies," he says, rising from his seated position.

"Hi, Mr. Mallory," Audrey and I sputter in unison.

"You *do* know each other!" Sparrow squeals. "How wonderful!"

Mr. Mallory wears only tiny blue swim trunks that expose the topmost muscles of his thighs. His leg hair is thick as a stuffed animal. He may as well be naked.

"Call me James."

Audrey and I exchange a look.

"Tonight, we're not teacher and student," he says. "We're just *people*. Let's allow one another to be exactly who we are. Just this once."

Mr. Mallory says this with passion, like when he speaks in front of the chalkboard.

"So there's no test?" I ask.

Everyone finds this amusing.

I do not.

Mr. Mallory winks. "Not the kind you think."

Leaf walks toward us sporting the women's panties he wore when I saw him for the very first time. I don't think I'll remember Leaf any other way.

"Stick out your tongues," he says.

I look to Mr. Mallory—James—as he pushes a fist against his lips, hiding a smile.

When I open my mouth, Leaf places a small square of paper against my tongue, no bigger than a fingernail.

~

Richard Quinn sits at the helm and powers up the Valkyrie.

He aims the bow at the bare horizon and takes it slow. He's in no rush.

The waves are dense and lethargic, rolling without haste toward shore as if they, too, are in need of reflection.

Danni is becoming a woman, and there's nothing he can do to stop it. She's on her own path now.

It's a separation as inevitable as death. And just as worthy of mourning.

Richard looks to the sky. He can already detect the gleam of Saturn and Jupiter rising beyond the clouds. Soon enough, the stars will join them.

Richard has no destination in mind, only a voyage. Just he and his ship.

But the water doesn't call to him like it once did.

Perhaps that time of his life is over.

The water batters the hull of the Valkyrie as he pushes the motor further, faster. But still, the sirens do not sing for him. He's no Ishmael, no Captain Ahab. He's just a middle-aged man in a boat, searching the ocean for a beast that doesn't exist.

Richard cuts the motor and descends the helm as the Valkyrie drifts along a broad swell.

He hears a splash and turns toward it, finding nothing.

He scans the waves.

And then he hears it again. This time from the other side of his boat as something glides beneath the Valkyrie.

The thump of a fin.

The scrape of a tail.

Richard pictures Mister Brownstone, and rushes to the railing before remembering that the giant hammerhead shark that's eluded him all these years washed ashore weeks ago.

A spray of water explodes from the glassine surface, and Richard stumbles backward, wiping the saltwater from his eyes.

And then he spots her.

Gliding through the still water of the Atlantic is a single dolphin.

⁓

The ocean is a lady. I know that now.

She emerges like a waterfall before me, but I'm not frightened. She regards me kindly, as though trying to understand my existence as much as I'm trying to understand hers. She opens like a cloaked angel, her edges bristling with glorious sea foam.

Beside me, Audrey watches her hands.

Gravity pulls me further into the sand, and I'm sinking. I've never been so aware of my own weight before. The sand creeps up my feet. It's to my ankles now. My thighs. My waist. I will surely disappear at any moment. Slip right through the sandbar and be washed out to sea.

"Wow," Audrey says.

My beautiful Audrey. Dark and light at the same time. Her cheeks pink as the blush of a conch shell. She looks at me and her eyes grow larger, spherical. Her smile spreads like oil across her face. But she's not deformed. She's not a monster. She's magnificent.

Audrey waggles her fingers.

"Do you see it?" she purrs, her voice dreamy and dispersed.

Colors ripple from the tips of her fingers like wind chimes spun from metallic spiderwebs, sticky and glistening.

"Tell me I'm not crazy," she pleads.

I grin at her, and by the look on her face, I know my smile is spreading like oil as well. But I'm not deformed either. And I'm not a monster. I'm magnificent.

I place my hands on her cheeks and touch my nose to hers.

"No," I say. "You're not crazy. I see it too."

"This is Far. Out."

"Far out."

The sand rises to my elbows. My chest.

"I feel like I could do *anything* right now," Audrey says. "Like every limitation I've ever felt was only in my mind. Does that sound crazy? Tell me I'm not crazy."

"You're not crazy. I feel it too."

Audrey grins as she spins into the water. The splash she leaves in her wake unfurls like a sprout seeking sunlight. She collapses in the shallows, and I wonder if she can see the ocean looming above her, protective and maternal.

"Can you see it?" I ask.

She doesn't ask what I'm referring to, but she coos, "Yes."

I peer across the beach. The bonfire smolders with pink and orange flames, tipped in flecks of royal blue. By the fire, Meadow and Leaf lie beside one another, staring at the sky. Holding hands. I can't tell where one hand ends and the other begins.

No one else is on the beach, and I sling my heavy head from side to side, seeking Sparrow and Mr. Mallory.

But then I remember.

We were all sitting at the shoreline when the sand started crawling up Sparrow's arms.

She was screaming, "I can't get it off!" Over and over. "I can't get it off! I can't get it off!"

The sand was such a comfort to me, soft and warm, swaddling me like an infant. I thought she was pretending, so I laughed at her joke. Everyone else laughed, too.

Even Sparrow.

She laughed and laughed. Until she wasn't laughing anymore.

Her chuckle turned to choking. Her smile turned to tears.

She swatted her arms until scratches bloomed across her skin. And that's when we knew Sparrow wasn't pretending.

Mr. Mallory helped her stand. He washed away the sand and led her to a tent tucked in the mangroves. He supported her like a child who had only recently learned to walk. He spoke to her with soft, gentle words.

I stretch my arms out before me, examining the thick sheen of sand sparkling across my body.

Freckles swim across my arm, like amoebas under a microscope.

Moonlight drapes across my collarbone and I feel the weight of it like an owl necklace.

I bury my feet in the sand.

No shoes. No need.

"I love you, Danni," Audrey says.

And I know she's telling the truth. I just know.

Richard watches the dolphin weave through the water, her dorsal fin slicing the waves before descending.

He can see her entire body beneath the surface. Her flesh is creamy gray, nearly blue, and she glistens as though a constellation lives within her skin. When she crests once more, a geyser erupts from her blowhole, transforming into a fine mist.

Richard leans over the railing to admire her slow retreat.

There's no shortage of dolphins in the Florida Keys, but it never fails to take his breath away.

Tonight, Richard has found more contentment in this single dolphin than he could ever chase across the Atlantic. He could watch her all night. Maybe he will.

He's looking to the sky, searching for a scorpion in the stars, when he hears another splash behind him.

A second dolphin emerges from beneath the Valkyrie.

Two in one night.

A third splash. Another small geyser.

Richard spins around.

Blinks.

Forces his mouth shut.

When the moon is full and the skies are clear, one can see for miles over the water.

Tonight, Richard can see for miles.

And what he sees are dolphins.

Hundreds of them. Perhaps a thousand.

He rushes to the other side of his boat, clutching the railing as the ocean becomes a teeming unrest of fins and tails and blowholes. All around him. Emerging from everywhere and nowhere at once.

Like threads stitched through fabric, their bodies crest the surface, one after another. A vast mountain range of creamy gray peaks and valleys.

Richard was alone with the sea only moments ago, but is now a stone in its current, the horde breaking around him. He feels every breach of the water like a warm breath against the back of his neck.

They glide toward the Valkyrie as if there were no boat at all, plunging beneath it, skirting around it.

A few pause to study Richard, lifting their heads and peering at him with giant doe eyes, petite teeth glinting in the moonlight.

Richard stands in reverence until each and every dolphin has passed.

He stumbles to the other side of his boat and leans against the railing to watch their retreat, trying to memorize it all.

He watches until he no longer sees their fins flashing in the light of the moon. Until he no longer hears the sound of their blowholes echoing across the ocean.

The moon is different tonight, Richard thinks as he peers into the night sky. The hue, perhaps. Or the brilliance of it.

～

I don't know how Audrey and I ended up on a sandbar in the middle of the ocean. I peer back at the shore. It looks so far away.

Audrey follows my gaze.

"It's closer than it looks," she says. "Don't you think so? I'm not crazy, am I?"

"No," I say. "You're not crazy. It's closer than it looks."

Audrey relaxes into the sand. "Meditate with me," she says.

We lie on our backs, and I'm instantly lost in my breath. The rushing tornado of an inhale, the watery gush of an exhale.

I find myself thinking about dad, and the distance that's formed between us. As palpable in my mind as the sand between my fingers. A tether, cut. A board, warped and splintered.

We're just two strangers now, a vast ocean growing wider between us.

When stars begin to form in my vision, I'm grateful for the distraction.

Galaxies bloom before me. Optical nerve explosions like fireworks. Clouds in geometric shapes. First, they're flat—triangles and hexagons. But then they become three-dimensional—tetrahedrons and prisms.

Some people marvel at the Milky Way, at planets and galaxies. They spend their whole lives looking up.

But I have it all right here inside me.

I smell everything at once, picking apart the fragrance like a recipe I'm trying to deconstruct. Audrey's apple pie perfume. Smoke from the bonfire. Sea salt drying on my skin. Distant rain carried on a breeze. And from across the beach, the scent of Meadow's tangled hair.

I hear everything, too. Audrey's slow breaths, the gurgle of her empty stomach, the waves lapping at the shore. Even the moon migrating across the sky.

And something else.

A small splash.

I open my eyes and sit upright.

All around the sandbar are dolphins.

Hundreds of them. Perhaps a thousand.

They're circling us, surfacing and diving. When they leap over one another, water spirals from their tails and dorsal fins like bouquets of Christmas tinsel.

I can't speak, so I grasp Audrey's knee and shake her until she opens her eyes and sits up beside me.

"What is it?"

I point to the dolphins.

"Danni, what?"

Finally, I find my voice. "Dolphins," I whisper. "All over. Look!"

Audrey spins her head, searching the sandbar.

"I don't see anything."

I try to catch my breath but my heart is racing, my skin slick with sweat.

They're everywhere! Here. There. All around.

Audrey looks again, one eyebrow raised. "Are you okay?"

How is she not seeing this?

"Dolphins!"

Another surfaces, but I blink, and it disappears as quickly as it arrived.

And then there is nothing.

No dorsal fins. No blowholes. Not even a ripple on the glassy surface, as far as the eye can see.

I run my hands across the sandbar as though searching for proof.

"Don't pull a *Sparrow*," Audrey warns with the hint of a smile.

"They were here!" I insist.

I try to stand, but my knees wobble, and Audrey catches me before I crash into the shallows.

"The tide's really coming in now," she says. "We should head back."

I feel my eyes bulge, my lips tremble. I'm going insane. There's no other explanation.

"Tell me you saw them! Tell me I'm not crazy!"

Audrey places her hands on my cheeks and touches my nose with hers. She lingers for a long moment, and sighs, lowering her voice to a whisper.

"I saw them," she says. "I promise I saw the dolphins."

But I know she's lying. The dolphins were just for me.

FREE PEOPLE

Audrey leaves at dawn, so I follow everyone to US1, helping Leaf arrange a pile of bags at the curb.

Sparrow flings her spindly arms around Meadow's neck. They share kisses, laughs. Meadow wipes a tear from Sparrow's cheek.

I can't watch.

"No more sadness," Meadow says to her. "And no more motorcycles." She points to Mr. Mallory. "Take care of our little bird."

He brings his palms to the center of his chest as though in prayer.

I can't stop them. I can't make them stay.

I wrap my arms around Leaf and breathe him in, trying to memorize his scent.

"There's something different about you, Lil' Mama."

Leaf squeezes me so hard it's a challenge to move, and my fingers claw to stay attached when he pulls away.

"You're not the same girl we found hiding in the mangroves."

"No," I confirm, "I'm not."

And then I hear, "Lil' Mama," behind me. That voice.

I close my eyes.

"Lil' Mama."

I'm not ready.

I want to throw up. Make myself hurt. Punch my thighs and watch the skin blanch. Blade against flesh. Release.

And then she's standing before me. I can smell her. Feel her hands on my arms.

I open my eyes.

Meadow's hair sways in the morning breeze, shells and beads clanging against one another. A living, breathing musical instrument.

Her eyes are wet. Her lips flecked with sand.

"Siskiyou County," she says. "Repeat it back to me."

"Siskiyou County."

"Promise me I'll see you again."

"You don't have to go," I say.

Meadow dips her head against mine. "This little adventure of ours has come to an end. The next one is calling. Can't you hear it?"

Meadow grabs my shoulders, pulling me against her, and we sway back and forth to drumbeats only we can hear.

"Come find us," she says, her voice muffled against my hair, "when you're ready for your next adventure."

"I'm ready now," I say, more plea than statement.

"No," she says, clasping my hands. "But when you *are* ready, nobody can tell you otherwise."

My chin trembles and I can't stop it. I don't try. "Shades mean shady."

It feels good to make Meadow smile, even if I've lost my own.

"That's right, Lil' Mama. What else?"

"Avoid anyone who's too eager. Have an agenda."

"And?"

"Look cute. But not *too* cute."

She nods. "One more thing."

I'm searching my brain for a forgotten rule of the road when Meadow reaches down and places her fingers on my thigh, on my scars, and I lose my breath.

No one's ever touched me there.

I feel her fingers like a torch against my skin, the heat penetrating my shorts, igniting the hatch marks beneath. And then they're as cold as a frosty bottle of Fanta pressed against the small of my back. I want to run away, but she has me. I'm hers. I always was.

"Never again," she says.

"I won't," I say, and I know I'm telling the truth.

Meadow extends her thumb, and when a white sedan rolls to a stop, she appraises the driver.

It's happening too fast.

Kiss me.

One last time.

Meadow gives a quick nod to Leaf before reaching down and plucking her bag from the curb.

I can't see her eyes. She's avoiding me.

In her mind, she's already on the highway, crossing state lines, en route to California, her next adventure. I try to gather as much of her as I can in these last moments we have to share. But I've already lost her.

I remember her mouth against mine. A hint of ChapStick.

Atop the crumbling pillar of the Bahia Honda Bridge, the current churning beneath us. Like we could fall in at any moment, be washed out to sea, unlucky. But we didn't care, *we didn't care.*

Kiss me.

But she doesn't.

Meadow offers one final smile as the white sedan rumbles north on US1 and disappears. Poof.

I pedal slowly because the road is no longer asphalt. It's a wound, raw and bleeding. Miles of damaged skin struggling to heal.

When I arrive home, the apartment's dark, the curtains drawn to block the rising sun.

The *old* dad would've been up by now. It's Sunday, and the weather is beautiful. A perfect day for fishing. But this *new* dad is probably passed out in his study, coughing stale beer into the sofa cushions.

I want to see it. I *need* to see it.

I push open the door to his study, but the room is empty.

I creep further down the hallway and toward my parents' bedroom, pushing against their door.

Illuminated by a ray of sunlight breaking past the curtain, my mother lies asleep in her bed. Her hair is in curlers, hidden beneath a headscarf.

And dad lies beside her, his arm draped over her torso.

Oh.

I study the curve of his body, melded perfectly to hers.

In his sleep, dad's fingers twitch. Without waking, mom strokes his hand until he settles.

Everything is as it should be, and I've never been so grateful to be wrong.

I edge the door shut and tiptoe back into the living room where I belong.

When the telephone rings, I rush toward it to relieve the sound.

Don't wake them. Don't break the spell.

"Quinn residence," I whisper into the mouthpiece.

"Richard, please. I need to speak to Richard."

I know that voice, even all these months later. That beautiful blonde woman from The Armada.

I cover the mouthpiece with my hand as I listen to her plead for my dad.

"Hello? Hello?"

The sound of her words. That slight drawl I can't place.

"Are you there? Hello? Please."

That voice ruined my father. Nearly destroyed him. And mom and I were the casualties. Innocent bystanders mutilated in the crossfire.

I think of mom smiling in her sleep, dad's embrace tightening around her.

"Hello?"

I listen to the woman's voice one last time. Commit it to memory.

And then I return the handset to the base and unplug the cord from the wall.

SALTWATER COWBOY

It's been a week since Meadow left. Seven whole days.

At least I still have Audrey.

Last week, I told her about Poppy, and my failure to maintain her memorial despite my promise. So this morning, Audrey meets me at the Vaca Cut Bridge with a handful of Katia's flowers.

I accept the bouquet, counting five large hibiscus flowers. I pluck one from the bunch.

"For Eddie," I say, and Audrey nods her approval as I toss it to the wind.

The flower twists in the breeze, spiraling toward the horizon as though strapped to a paper airplane. It sails away from the bridge, over the ocean, and I don't see where it lands.

Audrey reaches for the ribbon tied around the post.

"The Troll Doll," I say, searching the ground that borders the road. "It's gone!"

"Down here," she says, pointing to the slope that leads straight under the Vaca Cut Bridge. "I see it."

It's not as mountainous as the slope beneath the Seven Mile Bridge, but one wrong move and Audrey could slide right off the hill and into the current, washed out to sea.

She sits and scoots across the grass.

"Be careful!"

I bite my lip, preparing to call out for help, but Audrey grabs the doll and quickly crawls uphill. Disaster averted.

We tuck the Troll Doll into the ribbon, but it doesn't hold, and the knot won't budge.

Audrey takes the flowers from my hand. "We can use the stems to take up extra space."

One by one, she wedges the flowers around the doll. It slips a little, but ultimately stays.

We clasp hands, swinging our fists back and forth between us.

"June 7th," she says, long and drawn out. "Last day of school. Secret party. Under the Seven Mile Bridge."

I scowl at her. "The last time you invited me to a bridge party, no one was there."

"Honest mistake! This time it's an end of the year celebration. It was Mercy and Sharon's idea, and only a select group of people are invited. Don't be mad, but I told them about the hippies, and how you've basically been living with them for the last few months. I told them we dropped acid last weekend, and they think you're the grooviest girl in school. They want to hear *everything*. It's basically in your honor."

I roll my eyes and bite my lip to keep from grinning too much.

"We can go stag," she says. "Just you and me."

My chest swells. I nod because I can't speak.

"You're my spirit guide!" Audrey hollers, loud enough to be heard by the entire diner behind us. "I wanna be *you* when I grow up!"

Mom is bustling about the kitchen. Her cheeks are rouged, her body encased in a powder blue pant set.

On the shelf behind her, her appliance collection sparkles. Someone's been dusting. There's a pink hand mixer next to the old olive hand mixer, an electric skillet in shiny cream, an electric tea kettle boasting sage and silver, and a brand-new Sunbeam Mixmaster.

"How do I look?" she asks, twirling before me.

Her smile blazes, but I don't yet know if I can trust it.

There are sandwiches on the counter, and she steps away from me to cut them into triangles before tucking them into a picnic basket.

"Are you going somewhere?"

"Darndest thing," she says. "I haven't heard from Dottie in *days*, and then who do I run into at the Cash & Carry? Dottie! She's been trying to call me all week and assumed our phone must be down, though I assured her our phone was working just fine, thank you. But then I come home, check the phone, and sure enough—no dial tone!"

She plants her hands on the counter and looks to me, disbelief painted across her face as vivacious as the coral painted across her lips.

"I almost ran down to the phone company, but then I had the good sense to check the line, and would you believe it? Disconnected. Right from the wall. But the telephone is up and running again, you'll be happy to know."

"Are you having a picnic?" I ask.

"Silly me, yes. Dottie and I are going down to Bahia Honda today. Won't that be lovely?"

I try to imagine mom at Bahia Honda. Climbing the old railroad bridge in her powder blue pant set. Playing spin the bottle with Dottie atop the pilings.

What I want to say is: Mom, I have to tell you something. I don't want it on my conscience anymore, and I know Dottie's your best friend, and I am so sorry for being selfish right now, but you need to know that Andy kissed me. We have to stop lying to one another if we ever want to be free. Don't you want to be free, mom? Do you still love me, mom?

I clamp my lips shut to prevent everything from flooding out.

I can't do it.

Not when she's dressed so nicely and planning a picnic with her friend.

Mom places two folded napkins into the basket and fastens it closed.

She's so beautiful. Everyone says I look like her, and at times like these, I hope they're telling the truth.

Mom kisses me on the forehead and walks out the door.

Her scent lingers in the air, even in her absence. A little bit of hand lotion, a little bit of hairspray. A hint of ham and bread.

I tuck a stray lock of hair behind my ear and take another whiff of mom's fragrance.

And then I unplug the phone cord from the wall.

Later that afternoon, mom and dad argue in the living room, and the happy couple who slept beside each other all night become something else altogether.

Mom's tone is sharp and bitter.

I push my ear to the wall so I can hear better.

"Where were you all day, Richard?"

"Where were *you*, Miriam?"

"I had lunch with Dottie. Who did *you* have lunch with?"

I step away from the wall, transforming their jagged words into soft, indistinguishable lumps.

I pace my room, then lie on my bed and try to meditate, like I did with Audrey on the sandbar. But this time, I can't see the galaxies.

Cabinet doors slam. Feet clomp through the living room.

I sit up and try to work on my poem, but I can't concentrate.

Mom and dad are still talking, but now their exchange is calm, measured. If I were listening to only their tone, and not their words, I might be fooled into thinking everything is going to be okay.

"You disappeared, Richard. You up and left, right after the hurricane. You've been gone for months, but you're all better now. Is that what you're telling me?"

I've heard mom speak words of jealousy, anger. Even manic ramblings designed to wound. But something in her has come undone. She spits words lined with blades, sharpened and honed over years, angled to draw blood. And aimed directly at my father.

"You're a fraud, Richard. A drunk little boy pretending to be a man. You think you're a hero? You're no hero. You're nothing but a goddamn saltwater cowboy."

The last day of school is less a week away, and Mr. Mallory gives us the entire class to work on our poetry assignment. I stare numbly at a page that's been scribbled across, erased, crumpled up and smoothed open a few times over.

My thoughts return to mom's words, and the way she spoke them. She called dad a little boy. A saltwater cowboy. I mull this over, trying to decode the meaning. I write it across my paper.

Someone taps my arm, and I don't need to look behind me to know it's Margaret Leech.

"What is it, Margaret?"

She passes her notebook over my shoulder.

"Will you read it? Tell me if it's any good? I'll read yours, too."

I look at my paper with nothing but *saltwater cowboy* scribbled across.

"It's not ready yet," I say, accepting her notebook.

Margaret's poem is about Ronald Weller.

Gross.

She knows she's home when he curls his fingers through hers. He's taught her to see the beauty in things she's always taken for granted. She's never before understood the meaning of home until she fell in love. And that home is everywhere, as long as they're together.

The poem is poorly written, but I'm happy for Margaret Leech.

I twist in my seat and return her notebook.

"Well?"

Margaret's eyes brim beneath her brows. When she bites her lower lip, her front teeth don't seem as imposing as they once did. Maybe she's finally grown into them. Or maybe I just don't notice that kind of thing anymore.

She's waiting for my verdict. And I don't think it has anything to do with her writing.

"Do you really feel that way?" I ask.

Margaret lets out a breath. "He says he's gonna marry me someday."

Her cheeks flush, and she looks away, embarrassed.

"Don't do that," I say. "You're lovely. Your poem is lovely too. And when that day comes, I hope you'll invite me to the wedding."

Audrey won't stop talking about the bridge party as she walks me to the bike rack, and I watch Jimmie ride out of the lot with Ellie Walker.

Audrey says, "Can you grab candy after school on Friday?"

And Audrey says, "Mercy's bringing soda and Sharon's bringing Bugles and Travis is bringing his fishing gear and his dad's grill."

And Audrey says, "Can you at least *pretend* to be excited?"

I try to be more accommodating. Travis and I haven't spoken since he asked me to be his girl. If nothing else, the bridge party will be a good excuse to reconcile our friendship.

"What kind of candy?" I ask.

"Mary Janes. They're my favorite."

They're Jimmie's favorite too.

I wave goodbye to Audrey as she slides into the passenger seat of Katia's car. They're wearing matching bandanas.

"Bye, *Lil' Mama*," Audrey mocks, blowing me an exaggerated kiss as they roll out of the lot.

I grasp the handlebar of my bike and pedal behind them until they're out of sight. It feels good to ride. And it feels good to hear someone speak my true name.

FIVE STATE LINES

Galina latches closed her suitcase, and her fingers tremble as she checks her documents. She touches each item laid across her bed to be sure she hasn't forgotten anything.

She considers the pad of paper, and the pan of watercolor paints, below which is Gunter's last letter—she can see the diluted stain of a brown cow—but she doesn't want to bring it. Their watercolor correspondence represents one thing to her, and one thing only: separation.

Galina wipes a sheen of sweat from her forehead. She's called Richard every day—sometimes twice a day, three times, four. Still nothing.

But Shane is expecting her. Everything is ready. She has only to get there.

Gunter's ship is scheduled to port in Havana on June 7th. She has six days to make it from West Virginia to Key West.

Five states lines.

She can travel on highways for much of the drive, but a large portion will be spent on county roads, many unpaved. She takes a deep, calming breath that calms nothing at all.

Once she's on the road, she'll stop at a pay phone in Virginia and call Richard. If she still can't get through, she will try again in North Carolina. Then South

Carolina. Georgia. She will call from every phone in Florida until she reaches him.

Because without Richard, there can be no rescue.

Without Richard, Gunter will leap from a German ship and die alone, swallowed whole by a vast, black ocean while she watches from the sky.

Galina reaches into her pocket and withdraws the Polaroid, tucking it against her dashboard.

Six days.

Five state lines.

~

Somewhere on the Northern waters of the Atlantic Ocean, Gunter presses his lips together to stem the nausea, and draws open the thick curtain in search of fresh air.

Across from him are the stacked bunks of fellow passengers.

Three men lean toward one another, speaking in hushed voices. Upon Gunter's emergence, the men grow silent.

He regards their clothes, their shoes. One man wears a belt tied in a knot around his waist, reminding him of Christoph, the man who threw himself overboard and swam toward a mirage in the distance, only to be met with a bullet.

He considers offering a small hello, but the furrowed brows and flared nostrils of the men convince him to stay silent. Plain-clothed officers? Possibly. Gunter turns to watch a ship guard stroll down the narrow corridor, but he can still feel the gaze of all three men biting into his skull.

He chances one more glance in their direction. There's a similar slope to the bridge of their noses. The same dark eyes mantled by heavy lashes. It seems to Gunter they may be of relation to one another.

He looks away.

It's best to stay isolated. Fewer questions. Less chance of his plan being discovered. Less chance of seeing a new friend shot dead in the water.

Gunter has no way of knowing if Galina will be waiting for him at the jump point. He did not receive a letter from her before he departed. But plane or not, boat or not, Gunter will wait no longer.

The plastic-wrapped documents press into his flesh, strapped under his shirt. He feels them like a crooked finger to his ribs. The men can surely see them beneath the fabric—their eyes say as much—and Gunter hooks his fingers into his collar, loosening his shirt before tucking into his cubby and drawing closed the curtain.

Part Four

METAMORPHOSIS IN THE SEASON OF LIL' MAMA

WHAT WAS SAID (AND WHAT WAS SILENT)

Richard Quinn surveys his sparse classroom.

The bell has rung, but with finals over and only two days remaining in the school year, many of his senior students have already vacated their post.

He slides open his top drawer and sips quickly from the coffee mug hidden within and then pushes his knuckles against his lips to disperse the unmistakable aroma of straight whiskey.

He returns the coffee mug to the drawer, beside a bottle of mouthwash and tin of Altoids.

Sara Racine takes her seat, and though she wears a demure shift dress in stiff cotton twill, he can tell she hasn't yet discovered the modesty of a brassiere.

"Good afternoon, Sara."

She doesn't respond, but instead cracks open a book. He sneaks a peek at the cover, reading the title aloud.

"*The Feminine Mystique,*" Richard states. "Romance novel?"

Sara glares at him for a long moment before saying, "No," and returning to her book.

Carolyn Saylor pokes her head in the door. "Preparing for your big day?"

Richard questions her with the lift of an eyebrow.

"Tomorrow!" she says. "*Call me Ishmael!*"

Richard's nearly forgotten about his final day performance. Moby Dick, Chapter One. He searches his mind for the first line, but after "Call me Ishmael," everything goes blank.

"I invited my book club," Carolyn says, adjusting her glasses. "I told them they're in for a real treat."

Richard leans his face toward the fan.

"Well, I'll let you get back to it," she says, departing his doorway.

He should skip these last two days, like many of his seniors. Time served. Early release for good behavior. Just get on his boat and never come back.

Richard buffs his hand across his face.

At the beginning of the year, Danni asked if she could come to his class on the last day of school, watch his Moby Dick monologue, and he told her, No.

Don't skip class, he said. Freshman year is important, and you don't want to start high school with a sour reputation among your teachers.

But just this once, he hopes she ignores his instruction.

Because he could do it for Danni. Stand tall. Orate to a grand crowd of one. Just to see her smile again. Just to see her proud of her old man.

～

When I arrive home, I find mom sitting at the dining room table, organizing a sewing box.

She wears the hint of a smile, but her eyes are glassy and vacant as she buffs a pair of shears to a mirrored shine.

She nudges the sewing box with her wrist. "Dottie's sewing curtains today and needs an extra pair of hands."

I trace the phone cord from the receiver to the wall. It's been replaced, and I have half a mind to cut it in half with mom's' sewing shears.

But there's something else on my mind. Something more important than a beautiful blonde woman who's probably already given up on dad and found another family to destroy.

Dottie. I see her in my mind.

On the couch beside my mother, sharing ice cream.

On the beach, standing before Mister Brownstone.

And I feel her.

A lead weight on my conscience every time I remember kissing her husband.

Meadow says honesty is the only real currency in this world. That we have to stop lying to one another if we ever want to be free.

I sure hope she's right.

Because mom deserves to know the truth.

And I need to be strong enough to speak it.

"Mom," I say, studying the terrazzo beneath my feet, "there's something I need to tell you."

"Mom, please say something."

She wrings her hands, rolling each knuckle, one by one. She scratches an imaginary itch.

"And this went on right under our noses? Why would you do that?"

I shrug and it's an honest answer.

"You're a pretty girl, Danni. You have to be more careful."

Mom fumbles with a seam ripper, and it clatters to the table. She picks it up, wriggling it into a small drawer in her sewing box.

"I don't want you wearing that halter top anymore," she says. "It shows too much. You're still a child."

Mom looks down and shakes her head.

Go ahead, I think. Slap me, like you did once. Call me a slut, like you did once.

Do it.

Say it.

I want her to put away her sewing supplies. Sit beside me and tell me she understands, tell me she's angry. That she's never been so enraged in her whole life to learn that a grown man took advantage of her only daughter, a mere child at thirteen years old. Tell me he should've known better. Tell me it wasn't my fault.

Mom reaches across the table and grasps my hands, stroking my fingers with her own.

For just a moment.

And then she withdraws, organizing thread spools on designated spikes, and straightening pins on a tomato-shaped cushion.

She stands, smooths the wrinkles of her skirt, and lifts the box from the table.

"You're leaving?"

Mom stares at the floor, at nothing at all.

The skin above her cheeks has begun to thin. Her eyelids are dusted with violet shadow, but it does nothing to hide her sadness.

"I'm going Dottie's," she says, her voice unburdened by emotion of any kind. "We're making curtains today."

I sink into the chair.

"Why didn't you tell me when it first happened?"

I want to collapse at her feet, beg her to stay.

Don't go.

"Because Dottie is all you have." I swallow hard, barely able to cough out the next words. "I didn't want you to lose your only friend."

Mom walks toward the door and pauses, looking back.

Ask me anything; I'll tell you anything.

"Thank you," she says. "that was very thoughtful." Mom fluffs her golden hair, fixing a curl at her shoulder before adding, "It's probably best not to mention this to your father."

And then she is gone.

I watch the door for a long while, and the place where she stood, as though her body left a stain, a clue to be decoded before it fades.

It's a strange moment—the first time you see your parents for exactly who they are.

I couldn't stay at home a second longer.

I skirt dried clumps of seaweed and a sun-bleached buoy washed ashore as I approach the small strip of beach behind the haunted house.

A breeze surges in from the Gulf, and a discarded bottle rolls across the deserted mansion. I appraise the tall, glassless windows. The stacked slabs of a staircase within.

I'm not as enchanted by the haunted house as I once was. Did it used to be bigger? Scarier? This was once a destination for adventure. For romance. A mysterious land where dueling ghost stories rivaled for supremacy.

But now…

Now it's just an old house made of rock.

Quiet and abandoned.

Where many years ago, a husband and wife died in a fire.

I haven't seen Sparrow on the beach since my friends left for California. I hope she's happy. I hope she drifts into blissful sleep every night, tucked safely within Mr. Mallory's arms. I hope he still kisses her scars.

Sometimes it's hard to breathe without Meadow. Not because I want to *be* her, or because we once shared a kiss on the Bahia Honda Bridge. Meadow was like a spell. Her magic transformed the sun into a prism, rainbows shimmering from every damp surface.

Without her, the landscape has dried and withered, and the sun has disappeared completely.

I shouldn't have let her go. I should have clung to her ankles, begged her to stay. If I could turn back time, I would do so many things differently. I would go to Memphis. I would make a hundred macramé wind chimes. I would go skinny-dipping with my friends at sunset. I would be bold, like her.

Afraid of nothing, like her.

A car rolls to a stop beside me on US1.

"Daniella," Andy calls. "Let me give you a ride home."

I halt, inching my bike backward.

"C'mon," he says, opening his door and hobbling closer to the sidewalk. "I'm heading to your place now. It's not a problem."

I appraise the driver. Nice + Eager = Bad.

I study Andy's eyes and the wrinkles at the corners, deeper every time I see him.

He pauses, crossing his arms and leaning against the car, studying me. There's a stagnancy between us, as though even the air is hesitant to move.

"It's good to see you, Daniella," he says.

I say nothing.

"I've actually been wanting to talk to you for a while now. I didn't expect it'd be on the side of the highway, but it's as good a place as any, I suppose."

I wait.

"I want to apologize," he says.

The Slash pines sway in the wind, rustling the early morning shadows cast across the road. It's all I can see as I search my mind for a response.

"It never should've happened," he continues. "You were just a kid. Hell, you still are." Andy pauses, clasping his hands together at his knees. "So, for the record, if it means anything, I'm sorry."

Andy exhales and relaxes into his stance as though accepting the forgiveness I haven't offered.

He smiles. "You're gonna be a real heartbreaker one day."

I don't want to talk to Andy.

I don't want to look at his crow's feet.

And I don't want to force pleasant conversation to alleviate a grown man's guilt.

"I already am," I say, stomping on the pedal and biking away. I don't look back.

～

By the time Galina emerges in Key Largo, the roads are dark, cloaked in a dense gloom that's not quite evening, not quite night.

But she has arrived.

Galina called Richard many times along her route, with no success. But she knows where to find him.

She presses down on the gas, and the engine pulls her south on US1 until a small sign welcomes her to Tavernier.

She leans forward, her fingernails carving crescent moons in the steering wheel.

She has one final stop before arriving in Key West: The Armada.

HALLOWED GROUND

I'm standing before the mirror, lining my eyes in black, when I hear conversation from the living room.

Mom sounds like she's crying.

"I'm alone, Richard. Every day. So alone."

"You have Dottie," dad says. "And me and Danni. We're here too."

I lean toward my reflection, stretching my eyelid toward my temple, and draw a thick, crisp line.

"The bar is your priority, Richard. Not me. Not us. You're not the man I married. I barely remember that man. I sometimes wonder if he ever existed at all."

The razor stares at me from the ledge of the sink. I reach for it with shaky fingers…

…and put it in the medicine cabinet.

"Miriam, I'm begging you. Don't do this. Please."

Silence.

I, like dad, await mom's decision from behind the safety of the bathroom door.

And I, too, beg.

Her footsteps skirt the kitchen counter. She leans upon it, and I swear I can hear her hands folding together, unfolding, palms flat on the countertop.

"I need you to stop drinking, Richard."

"I will, my love. I swear it."

Dad's panicked. It's evident in his voice. Did he even listen to mom's request before considering whether or not he could honor it?

"The school year's almost over," mom says.

I picture her standing there, chewing her lip. Choosing her words.

"I'm serious, Richard. No more bar. Not another drop. I need you sober. I want to remember the man I married."

"I want that, too."

"Starting today," she says.

And dad says, "Done."

Home is so different now. If someone asked me last year to write a poem about what home meant to me, I may have written about deep sea adventures with dad. Crawfishing with Jimmie. Key lime fights at the haunted house.

I wipe away a tear and fix the smudges below my eyes.

And suddenly, I'm ready to write my poem.

I slip into my bedroom unnoticed and pull a notebook from my school bag, turning to a crisp new page. I grab a pen—not a pencil—because this time it's not a draft. This time, I know exactly what I want to say.

I hear Mr. Mallory's voice in my mind: *Bleed onto the page until you can no longer see the words. Then wipe that blood away and bleed all over it again.*

I wield my pen—mightier than the blade of a razor —and bring it to paper.

And I bleed.

〜

Galina expects to be met with a cool, salty breeze when she arrives at The Armada, but the night air is warm and viscous, the wind off the ocean doing nothing to dry the sweat from her neck.

She pleads with the bartender to give her Richard's home address. *Begs*. But the scowl on his face convinces her that if she continues to loiter, she'll be greeted by an officer of the law, so she takes her leave, opting to wait in her car.

Hours from the nearest city, nighttime in the Keys is opaque. The sun has long ago set behind The Armada and the barren lighthouse beyond.

Tomorrow night, Gunter's ship will pass south of Key West, and they will fail without Richard Quinn.

Galina cracks the window and pushes her head into the seat. She closes her eyes.

If Richard won't come to her, she'll go to him. First thing in the morning. He's left her no choice.

Galina knows how to find the high school—she spotted a sign the last time she drove through town. It's down the road that's lined by the Slash Pines.

And it's the last place where she may still find her madman.

UNRELIABLE NARRATORS

It's the final day of school.

Richard Quinn clenches his fists, shakes his fingers through the air. But still, the tremor persists. He could blame it on anticipation—or even a nerve disorder—but the truth is much more grim. Richard searches his desk drawer for a forgotten beer or whiskey bottle, but no matter how many papers he overturns, the drawer remains stone cold sober.

It's early, the day hasn't yet begun, and already the sunrise outside his classroom is a brilliant hue of red.

Red sky at morning, sailors take warning.

In an hour, his classroom will be filled with eager students, faculty, and staff, awaiting his practiced rendition of Moby Dick, Chapter One.

Richard grabs the trash can, placing it between his legs in case the nausea wins.

At least he has an hour. Any sooner, and they may receive a performance of a very different kind.

Richard's classroom is as stuffed as a well-fed tick. Even those seniors who were absent at the commencement of the school week have made an appearance. If nowhere else, on this one day a year, within these four walls pinned with posters and scrawled with the quotes of literary greats, Richard is a luminary.

And though he does not see his daughter, Richard can delay no longer.

He knows this routine by heart, and what's expected of him. Richard pages through a textbook, feigning preoccupation as though oblivious to the nervous chatter of those packed three or four to a desk. Sitting atop. Leaning behind.

His big moment is fast approaching, and Richard reaches into his bag, trading the textbook for his special, gilded copy of Moby Dick.

Whispers echo through the room, followed by insistent hushes. The hum quickly abates as Richard stands.

He paces before the eager room, his footsteps heavy and dramatic. He licks his finger, turns the first page.

A student sneezes, and is met with, "Quiet," from the boy beside her.

A chair briefly screeches across the floor.

Somewhere in the back, a girl stops chewing her gum.

Richard looks once more for Danni, but her face is not among those who stare back.

He closes his eyes, picturing himself on the bow of the Valkyrie.

Winding. Pulling. The clacking of the reel.

Deep swells of a black ocean, gray arcs of dolphins weaving through the water.

He sees Mister Brownstone, robust and fierce, his fin slicing through the current.

And then he is ready.

Richard opens his eyes and snaps the cover closed.

The room is so silent it may as well be empty.

He's on stage. Standing at a podium. A breathless audience before him.

Richard slams the book on his desk, sending a plume of chalk dust into the room, and the crowd erupts in applause. "CALL ME ISHMAEL!"

〜

Dad's classroom is on the other side of the school, yet his voice fills every hallway, every corridor. My ears lead me more than my eyes.

"Here come more crowds," dad orates, hidden behind the throng of people spilling from his doorway, "pacing straight for the water, and seemingly bound for a dive!"

Dad's voice is deep and commanding. My pace quickens.

I push past Mr. Mallory and his first period class clustered outside dad's door. Mr. Mallory smiles and creates an opening for me to tuck through.

I study the students first. Their rapt attention, expressions of awe across each face.

Behind me, a woman whispers to Mrs. Saylor, "So handsome."

Mrs. Saylor says, "Don't remind me."

And then I turn toward my father.

He's so large, standing before his classroom of onlookers. Imposing as a movie star. He paces deliberately, one hand in his pocket, the other stroking his chin, or striking the air as he speaks.

"Deep into distant woodlands winds a mazy way," he continues, his voice and footsteps slowing to accent the introspective note of the sentence, "reaching to overlapping spurs of mountains bathed in their hill-side blue."

And for just a moment, I see him the way everyone else does. The stoic man chiseled by the sun, veteran of the sea. His intense gaze, unrivaled intellect.

And for just a moment, I see him as a liar.

Because I see something else, too. Something no one but me would notice. The shadows blooming beneath his eyes, exhaustion draining every sentence.

And the growing tremor in his hands.

Richard spots Danni by the door and pauses.

She's here.

And so grownup. Her hair is long, cresting over her shoulders, just like his Miriam. Same lips, same stance. But unlike his wife, Danni hasn't yet acquired the empty gaze of disappointment.

Richard takes a deep breath, renewed. He pushes his shoulders back and belts the next verse. He can hear his own voice echoing down the vacant corridors of the school.

He grasps his pockets to give his trembling hands something to grip.

With Danni present, the room is brighter. The air cooler. The sentences flow from his tongue like the very tide along the shore, pulled forth by the moon.

"The great flood-gates of the wonder-world swung open…" Richard pauses, his gaze roaming the sea of faces. The students, the teachers.

But every word spoken is for his little girl.

～

I watch dad's performance, and think, that's precisely what this is: a *performance*. An act. Regardless of how loudly he speaks, he cannot hide the sheen of sweat across his forehead, the sickness in his skin.

I feel like I've emerged from a dream, or have recovered from a long illness that had me seeing mirages. Like I've had a ringing in my ears since birth and am only now experiencing clear sound.

In the back, two boys snicker and mock dad's movements, their arms fluttering through the air like clumsy conductors.

My father is evaporating before my eyes. A hero, enfeebled. A soliloquy, abridged.

When did this happen? Was it the death of Mister Brownstone, a crusade forever unfulfilled? Was it mom, and her perpetual state of delusion? Or was it me, no longer a little girl in need of dad's tether?

And suddenly, I don't want to watch dad's Moby Dick speech anymore.

There's a poem in my bag to be turned in, and Mary Janes to buy for the bridge party tonight.

I push through the crowd to emerge in the blinding sunlight, and rush to retrieve my bag from class before the bell rings.

But I can't outrun my father's voice bellowing after me.

"And, mid most of them all, one grand hooded phantom, like a snow hill in the air!"

~

"You can't sleep here," a man scolds Galina through the inch-wide gap of her window.

She opens her eyes, shielding them from the sudden brilliance of daylight, and blinks away the haze. She sees the lighthouse by the water. The Armada. The Polaroid on her dashboard.

Galina bolts upright. "Please, what time is it?"

"Time for you to leave," the man says, "before I call the police."

Galina fumbles with her keys and the man turns away, shaking his head as he storms toward the bar.

She checks her reflection in the rearview mirror. Her eyes are bloodshot, bulging from dark, cavernous shadows. She slaps her cheeks, wipes her teeth, and tries to stroke the wildness from her hair before spinning out of the dirt lot and onto US1 toward the high school.

She must get to Richard right away.

She's out of time.

Because tonight, boat captain or not, her brother will plunge into the Atlantic.

THE EDGE OF AN OCEAN TRENCH

Mr. Mallory is gazing out the window when I enter his class, and I clear my throat to pull his attention.

"Hello, Miss Quinn."

Miss Quinn. I guess we're back to formal titles.

I place my poem on his desk.

"I enjoyed your father's reading this morning," he says. "Quite inspiring. It's no wonder you write so well, surrounded by all that literary passion."

Today, Mr. Mallory wears yellow and orange checkerboard socks.

"I'm not staying," I say.

Mr. Mallory takes his seat, reaching for my assignment.

I don't offer an explanation for my early departure. Mr. Mallory and I have an understanding now.

"I see," he says. "Because it's the last day of school, I won't tell if you don't."

Around his neck is Sparrow's pink shell necklace.

I lean against the wall outside Mr. Mallory's class until the halls are empty.

It's done. Freshman year.

Soon enough, we'll all be sophomores, and a new freshman class will rise to take our places. I've seen the eighth graders coming and going from the middle school wing. They look like children, yet they'll be ninth graders in a few short months. We didn't look that young on our first day of high school. No way.

I peek through the door to see if Mr. Mallory is reading my poem.

He is.

Mr. Mallory scans to the bottom of the page, then starts over at the top, reading it again, slower this time.

He holds up a hand as a student tries to ask a question, and covers his mouth. For a moment, I think he hates it. But then he laughs, which is odd, because there's nothing funny in my poem. When he finishes, he puts a hand to his chest and stares toward the open window, nodding to himself.

I smile. Because I can tell by the look on Mr. Mallory's face that he didn't hate my poem this time. Not one little bit.

I spend the rest of my scheduled classes on the hippie beach by myself.

No shoes. No need.

I sit in the very spot Leaf pranced around the campfire, strumming his cigar box guitars. If I close my eyes, they're all right here beside me.

Something jangles in the mangroves and I turn.

Meadow's wind chimes sway in the breeze, shell clanging against shell.

She left them for me, I'm sure of it.

And I don't need a poetry assignment to know that right here, on this beach, I am home.

—

Richard Quinn accepts his ovation. The nods and the whistles. But when he looks to the door, Danni's no longer there.

Carolyn Saylor approaches, her hands clasped to her chest, a smile splitting her face.

"Richard! How wonderful!"

"Carolyn," he says, gathering his papers, his bag, his special copy of Moby Dick, "I need you to watch my class."

Richard pushes through the confused crowd and hurries out the door after his daughter.

He thunders down the hallway, spilling into Mr. Mallory's classroom.

"Mr. Quinn! What a lovely surprise."

Richard scours the room, finding a dozen startled children and one empty desk in the back. Blood pounds in his ears.

"Can I help you with something?"

"I'm looking for Daniella."

"Yes, of course," Mr. Mallory says, his eyes shifting to the empty seat. He wrings his hands.

"Is she in class today?"

"Is she in class…"

"This is her scheduled class, Mr. Mallory. Yet here I am, and I see neither my daughter, nor her school bag."

"She was in your classroom just a few minutes ago. A powerful performance, Mr. Quinn. Truly inspirational."

"Goddamn it, James, where the hell is my daughter?"

A wave of gasps and whispers surges across the seated students.

Richard takes a deep breath, listens for the clacking of the reel, but all he feels in his chest is that familiar growing emptiness.

Mr. Mallory leans against his desk and motions for the class to settle down.

"She handed in her assignment and then she left. I'm sorry, Mr. Quinn. I know nothing more."

Richard nods his thanks before exiting the classroom of stunned students.

He searches each hallway, inside the cafeteria, and across the lawn.

Richard digs his car keys from his school bag and rushes across the gravel lot.

He has to find her.

He must mend whatever has become unraveled between them before it's lost forever.

～

The hallways are funhouse mirrors, stretching and compressing around Galina. A tall, young man rushes past, leaving her spinning and clutching a pillar to regain footing. A cluster of giggling girls cascades by, and Galina pushes from the pillar to stand in the middle of the gushing crowd. She perches on her toes, shielding her face from the sun. But she does not spot her madman.

"I am looking for Richard Quinn, the boat captain," Galina announces to a group of boys who scowl at her as they pass.

She turns to the next child.

"Please," she says. "I am looking for Richard Quinn."

The girl turns to her friend and laughs.

A boy rushes past her, dressed in nothing but socks, underwear and a football helmet. Across his back is painted: *Class of '68*. The hallway erupts in whistles and applause.

Galina grasps her knees, taking deep, steady breaths. Her vision pulses. She is gone. Adrift.

"You're looking for Mr. Quinn?"

Galina stands and faces a thin woman with vibrant orange hair, haloed by the sun.

"Yes," she says, grasping the woman's arms. "Richard Quinn. Please, is he here?"

The woman takes a step back, peeling Galina's fingers from her flesh.

"Yes, dear. His classroom is right down that hallway," she says, pointing with a long finger. "First door on your left. Are you a parent? Be sure to get a Visitor Pass from the office."

Galina turns away from the woman with the carrot hair, and toward Richard's classroom, where the door is propped open with a chair. Students bulge from the doorway.

And somewhere inside is her boat captain.

"Richard?"

It takes a moment for Galina's eyes to adjust. A corner fan casts cool air across her balmy skin.

Galina is highly aware of the scrutiny of the students. She stands straight, smooths her hair, and clears her throat.

Seated at the desk is a middle-aged woman wearing cat-eye glasses.

"Can I help you with something?" the woman asks.

"I thought this was Richard Quinn's classroom."

"You're in the right place, but I'm afraid you've just missed him. He left early today and hasn't been back." The woman laughs. "I don't think we'll see him again until August, unfortunately."

Galina takes a step back, catching herself against the door.

August is two months too late.

"Do you have a student here?" the woman asks.

Galina stumbles away from the gaping doorway and into the grass. She plaits her hands atop her head and contemplates the drive ahead of her. Key West. After all this time, all this effort, just one more hour on the road. And for nothing.

"Don't forget to stop by the front office for a Visitor's Pass," the woman says from the doorway.

Galina nods her head and holds up a hand, but she's not listening.

She's wondering if she'll be able to detect from shore the very moment her brother's body hits the water.

～

"Hiya."

I turn around to see Jimmie, and there's no better feeling in the world.

He sits beside me, and together, we watch the incoming tide.

A cluster of seaweed rolls onto the beach, teeming with an entire ecosystem of critters ready to tumble into our hands.

But we don't reach for it.

"How did you know where to find me?" I ask.

"*Everyone* knows where to find you."

I look back at the school and the English classroom window that faces the beach. "Let 'em watch."

Jimmie laughs. "You're weird," he says.

And I say, "Thank you."

There's something to be said for silence. Not every breath needs to carry a sentence. Not every thought needs to be voiced. Sometimes the most meaningful conversations happen when no words are spoken.

Behind us, the bell rings, concluding the end of the final day of school, but Jimmie doesn't move.

"Don't you have to go?"

Jimmie leans closer.

"Can I tell you a secret first?"

"Always."

He peeks over his shoulder as though the mangroves might be listening.

"I'm gonna kiss Ellie tonight," he whispers, "at the old lighthouse. For first time."

Jimmie grimaces as if he's said something awful, and lets out a breath, the air whistling through his teeth.

I think of kissing Meadow.

"Be gentle," I say. "Go slow. Pay more attention to her lips than her tongue."

Jimmie looks at me with a raised eyebrow, so I continue.

"Don't touch her body," I say. "Let the kiss be enough."

He shakes his head, adamant. "I would never."

And before I can say more, we hear, "Jimmie?" behind us as Ellie Walker steps onto the beach. "Are you ready?"

And suddenly Jimmie and I are out of time.

"Almost," he says. "Give us one more minute."

Ellie volunteers a genuine smile, which I return, before walking back toward the road.

Jimmie stands, wiping sand onto his pants. "You're still my best friend, you know."

I swear I see pink splotches bloom across his cheeks.

"I know."

"Any final advice, best friend?"

I see Ellie in my mind, standing on the coral bluff below the lighthouse. Young, beautiful, illuminated by the lights of passing boats. On her face, pure innocence. A hopeful smile. I envy her.

"Don't rush into it," I say. "Wait for the right time. But if you think you hear the words, *Kiss me kiss me kiss me*, raining down from the sky, don't wait a moment longer. Just kiss her already."

I stay on the hippie beach until the sky turns pink, but no matter how forcefully I squint my eyes, I cannot detect Meadow and the others frolicking in the water.

There's no one left to honor the sunset.

Well, no one but me.

I unbutton my shirt, folding it atop the sand.

I unzip my jeans and kick them off, draping them atop my shoes.

My underwear, too.

And I step toward the waves.

For Meadow.

The water is warm, hugging my ankles, my knees, my thighs, soothing the scars engraved on my skin. A saltwater compress over my wounds.

I disappear beneath the surface, naked as the day I was born. I emerge new. Free. And I don't care if anyone is standing at the classroom window, spying at me.

Let 'em watch.

LET THE WATER RUN DOWN

"Where were you today?"

Despite his promise to mom just last night, dad's drunk.

He steadies himself against the counter.

"You weren't in class," he continues.

"It's the last day of school so—"

"You weren't at the lighthouse or the haunted house. You weren't at The Sundry Store. I drove all over town looking for you. It's like I don't even know you anymore, Danni. You're just a stranger living in my house, eating my food."

Mom emerges from the bathroom, her robe creased with moisture. "What's going on?"

Dad buffs a hand across the stubble on his chin and lowers his voice.

"Nothing to worry about, my love."

"Were you at the bar?" Mom steps closer. "You were, weren't you? I can smell you from here."

"Andy bought me a round. One round is all, my love. Just a little *last-day-of-school celebration*," he says, glaring at me, his gaze sharp. "No harm done. Isn't that right, *pumpkin*?"

I feel the scales in my hands. The weight of evidence and decree my father has given me. But it's a minor offense, and with the dismissal of his charges, I'm clearing my own.

"Right," I confirm. "No harm done."

He nods, slow and deliberate.

Mom sighs, placing a hand over my father's.

"Danni," she says, "why don't you get cleaned up. I'll have supper ready shortly."

And with that, she retreats down the hallway and vanishes into the bedroom.

I look to dad, seeking a wink from him. A lopsided grin. A joke about brainsuckers. Anything that will prove my father still loves me.

That despite our mistakes, we're going to be okay.

"Go on," he says, scraping dirt from the corner of the counter. "You heard your mother."

~

Galina sits in the cockpit beside Shane, listening to mindless chatter rattle from the VHF radio. Something about marlin. Something about beer.

Galina and Shane spent the afternoon searching all of Key West for a new boat captain.

But as Galina feared, no one would touch it. No one said, Yes.

Too dangerous. Too drunk. Death sentence. A family to think about.

Cowards, all of them.

"Why are we here, in your plane?" Galina asks, watching a drop of dew slide down her reflection in the window.

Shane's hot breath fills the cockpit. "We can't just give up. We can fly out, locate his ship. And if he jumps, we can radio a distress call that someone's in the water. Maybe harbor patrol will hear us. Or the Coast Guard."

"They will never get there in time."

"A civilian craft might be nearby."

"If there is no plane, Gunter may change his mind. But if he sees us in the air, he will jump, and he will die."

Galina leans forward onto her knees, studying the indecipherable labels of the instrument panel.

"You should call Richard one more time," Shane says. "There's a phone inside the hangar."

"I have called a hundred times."

Shane punches his chair. Galina doesn't even flinch.

Across the VHF radio, two fishermen debate the proper throw of a cast net. Galina turns the knob, pausing briefly on a channel giving current weather conditions before moving on. Clips of conversation crackle in and out. A word here. A sentence there.

"Wait," Shane says. "Go back."

Galina reverses the knob, scanning through past channels.

"Stop!" he says. "Right there."

Shane lurches forward, adjusting the squelch before turning up the volume.

At first, there is only silence over the radio, but then a conversation resumes.

Yeah, I see it now, Ocean Holiday. Wow, she's a beast. Over.

That's the biggest ship I've seen come through here in a long time. Russian? Over.

Maybe Russian. Or German, Man, you don't see something like that every day. Over.

She's lit up like a goddamn Christmas tree. I can feel her wake from here.

Shane falls forward and onto his knees, wrestling the mouthpiece from its holder.

"Ocean Holiday! Ocean Holiday! This is Wailing Bird, are you receiving me? Over."

Shane holds up a hand. Galina counts her breaths.

Receiving you loud and clear, Wailing Bird. You in the sky? Over.

Galina wants to scream. She wants to pound on the windows. Tear off her skin. Her brother is on the water right now. He exists. And she's stuck here in this godforsaken airplane.

Shane holds the button on the mouthpiece. "What's your twenty? Over."

"About a mile off Tavernier. Over."

Shane looks to Galina with enough optimism in his eyes for them both.

"You remember his number?"

"Yes."

"There's a phone just inside. Can you try one last time? For me?"

Galina nods.

"Atta girl. Go get our madman."

The phone rings.

I barely hear it through the water cascading over my face. And I think nothing of it as I plan my outfit for the bridge party tonight: Meadow's crocheted halter top, the flared jeans Audrey gave me because they were too long, ponytail.

I step out of the shower and wrap my hair in a towel atop my head. The scars on my thighs are lightening, the purple ridges now rosy pink.

Mom answers the phone. "Quinn residence."

A moment later, dad's heavy footsteps plod into the kitchen. Words are exchanged before the phone receiver slams onto the base and dad quickly returns to his study.

"Richard," mom cries, "what's going on?"

"It's not what you think," dad insists.

I try to drown them out and focus on the bridge party attendees. Audrey will be there. So will Sharon and Mercy. Travis Misker and Timmy Katz. Margaret and Ronald will be there for sure, sucking face all night under the pillars. Mary Janes have been purchased, as requested; they're currently bundled in paper atop my bed. Soon, the setting sun will be hot against my skin, the breeze cool and salty. And tonight, under the bridge, I will eat grilled fish, drink cold Fantas, and share a bag of candy with my friends.

A slamming door pulls my attention.

"Who was that woman, Richard? Who was on the phone?"

I freeze.

Everything spins around me.

"Please don't go, Richard," mom says, and I feel her words as though they're lashed across my own heart. "Please don't leave us."

I bolt from the bathroom to catch my father at the door. Holding a brown twill suitcase.

A decision has been made.

Dad wrestles keys into the pocket of his boat jacket.

"My love," he says, reaching out to mom.

She shoves away his hand and he takes a step back, burrowing his fingers through his hair.

"It's not what you think."

"Don't tell me what to think."

Dad glances at the ceiling as though pleading for help. And then he turns to me. His eyes search my face, my soul, looking for something. Forgiveness?

I study him by the door. Mute. A puddle of a man grasping a suitcase.

Here he is, ladies and gentlemen. Esteemed literary professor, ocean adventurer, and small town hero. The great Richard Quinn. My dad.

He looks to me as though I'm a tether. A board he can walk on to find his way home.

And then he looks at his watch.

Apparently, there's a time limit on abandoning your family.

Don't go.

"Pumpkin, there's something I have to do tonight. I promise you'll understand very soon."

I look away, wedging the towel tightly beneath my arms until it burns.

"You're an extraordinary young woman, Danni," he says. "And I am so very proud of you. If I've had even a small amount of influence over who you are, you've already made me the proudest father in the world."

Don't go.

"Go!" mom screams.

And then dad rushes out the door.

As soon as dad leaves, mom begins searching the apartment. Under stacks of books. In drawers. In the pockets of dad's clothes, heaped in the laundry basket.

I step into my bedroom as mom sprints down the hallway toward dad's study.

Papers shuffle across his desk, and a squeak echoes through the apartment as mom settles into his chair.

I quickly dress.

And then I hear the chair rolling away from dad's desk and slamming against the wall.

I step out of my bedroom to find mom in the hallway, skin and eyes gone pale. Even her hair seems to have grayed in the last few minutes.

In her hands, a pile of paper scraps and bar napkins, falling through her parted fingers to land like snow drifts at her feet.

I pluck one of the napkins from the floor.

A woman's name. Telephone number. Motel room.

"I told you, didn't I?" she says. "I told you."

FOOL'S ERRAND

Dad's probably already in the car. Turning the key. Pulling out of the lot.

The bridge party will have to wait.

I hurry into the kitchen, skirting mom huddled on the floor in the hallway.

"Danni!" she cries.

I fling open the door and step into the night, rushing down the stairs toward my bike.

No shoes. No time.

Richard Quinn tunnels north on US1 toward the Duck Key Marina, where the Valkyrie waits for him.

Tavernier. That's where the ship was spotted. Galina's voice was frantic, her sentences fractured, but the word Tavernier rang out like a foghorn. So close, but he's already lost too much time. It could've passed south of Marathon by now, and Richard is heading *north*.

So much to do once he gets to his boat: warm engine; check gauges, temperature and oil pressure; unhitch from dock. Did he fill the tanks the last time he took her out? He doesn't remember. If he didn't, that will only consume more time.

Richard crushes the brake and his car lurches to a stop in the middle of US1.

He looks to the suitcase on the passenger seat. Within the brown case is a towel and change of clothing. An extra windbreaker. Nothing more.

He shakes his head, trying to erase the image of his wife and daughter standing in the hallway.

Tomorrow, they'll know the truth. By morning, Miriam will remember who she married. By morning, Danni will understand that her father was destined for greatness.

Richard rattles the wheel, screams into the dashboard.

A car approaches from behind and honks the horn before pulling onto the sidewalk to pass him.

Tonight, his family hurts. But he will spend the rest of his life making it up to them.

If he isn't shot down in the middle of the ocean.

If he walks through that front door with this one final adventure to regale, he will settle into his golden years with grace. He swears it.

Richard peers up the dark road before him, checks the rearview mirror. He's running out of time.

And he's going the wrong way.

"I'm sorry, girl," he says to the Valkyrie. "Not this time."

Richard cuts the wheel, spinning in the middle of US1. He takes a breath to still his heart and then pushes south, flying down the highway toward The Armada.

Richard enters the dark bar.

"Ishmael!" Andy calls out, struggling to stand.

Richard rushes forward, reaching over the counter toward the bartender. "I need your phone. Now."

Andy slaps an arm across Richard's shoulders. "What's goin' on, buddy?"

"Call Quade's," Richard orders as the bartender lifts the receiver. "It's an emergency."

The man passes Richard the phone. "It's ringing."
"Emergency?" Andy asks. "What emergency?"
Richard holds up a hand as the line rings again.
"Is it Miriam? Daniella?"
Still ringing.
"Dammit, Richard, what's wrong?"
This can't be happening. He needs a boat and he needs one fast. Peter Quade is his last hope, and yet his call remains unanswered.
Richard shoves the phone at the bartender and bolts toward the door.
"Hey," Andy calls behind him.
But Richard is already gone.

There's only one place to look for dad: The Armada.
I push my weight into the heavy wooden door and stumble into the smoky room, scanning the bar for my father, but he's not here.
And then I look for *her*. The bitch who called my dad.
But there are no blonde women in the bar tonight.
"Daniella! Is everything okay?"
Andy ushers me closer.
"Where's my dad?"
"You just missed 'im."
"Was she with him?"
Andy pulls back, peering at me. "Who? Your mother?"
"I have to go," I say, retreating from the counter.
The door is heavier than I remember, and I shove my weight into my heels, hauling it open.
"Try Quade's," Andy says.
I look back, and Andy smiles at me. Like the Andy I used to know.
"Is that where he went?" I ask.

Andy shrugs. "I know nothing."

I could hug Andy right now. I could cry with gratitude.

But instead I offer a curt, "Thanks," before slipping out the door.

Richard Quinn stands before the towering boathouse with a suitcase in his hand.

He's met with only the sound of lapping waves beneath three stories of dark storage compartments.

"Peter? You here, buddy?"

Richard circles the boathouse, runs down each dock, checks the front office, but Peter Quade has long ago locked up for the night.

He peers down the docks illuminated by warehouse lights. A small fishing boat rocks against a piling, and Richard vaults into the abandoned vessel, searching the console for a key. Empty. He checks the storage hatch for a spare. Feels beneath the cushions.

When he finds no key, he tries another boat, parked on the neighboring dock. Then another. All empty.

And then he sees something tethered to the back of the warehouse, in the owner's slip: a mustard-yellow Boston Whaler skiff with a tiller engine. No key required.

Richard climbs into the old boat. It's small, but it'll do.

As long as the motor turns over.

"C'mon, Peter," he pleads, attaching the fuel line. "Tell me you did it, buddy."

Richard stands before the motor. He reaches for the starter.

The boat rocks beneath his weight, and Richard takes a moment to steady his footing before pulling the handle.

The engine ignites, and Richard hoots into the air. He searches for the power switch, finding it rigged below the wooden bench seat. He flips it on, and the boat illuminates. A green light on the starboard side. Red on the port. And the white anchor light behind him.

Richard clamors onto the dock, tossing the suitcase into the idling boat. He spots Peter's fuel tanks, filled and stacked by the warehouse, and snatches one. Two. A third to be safe.

And then Richard climbs into the skiff and twists the handle, exploding out of the slip.

As he skirts the southern tip of Marathon, passing beneath the Seven Mile Bridge and into the Atlantic, he spots a few kids climbing atop the rocks and unfurling blankets. One of them is setting up a small charcoal grill.

He looks for Danni among the party-goers, but she is not there.

I careen into the lot of Quade's Boathouse. Rocks lodge beneath my wheels, forcing the handlebar to one side, then the other. I throw down my legs, dragging my feet through the gravel to prevent a fall.

Dad's car is in the lot, so I drop my bike to the rocks.

The front office lights are snuffed out, the door locked.

When I enter the dark cavern of Quade's Boathouse, the waves rock and crest beneath my feet, and the clacking of swaying chains and rope lift the hair on my neck. It's spookier than the haunted house.

It's also just as abandoned.

Beside the boathouse are rows of docks jutting into the Gulf, and I run toward them. Dad's here somewhere, and it's only a matter of time until I find him.

But I arrive at the stack of fuel tanks just in time to see dad's anchor light fade as he speeds into the night.

I stand there for a while, watching the water crash against the pilings. And just like that, dad disappears. Poof.

Mom was right. She knew the truth all along.

~

Gunter stands against the railing and watches America, her lights glistening across the ocean.

Passengers fill the deck as the ship draws closer to land, clustering against the railing, pretending not to covet the lights along the horizon.

A shadow falls over Gunter as the three men from his cabin file in beside him. They speak in hushed whispers, but Gunter tries not to listen as he obscures the documents beneath his coat with his arm.

"Guten Abend," says one of the men.

Good evening.

"Guten Abend," Gunter says, staring at the wake boiling from beneath the hull of the ship.

Beautiful, yes? the man asks, nudging his head toward America's lights.

The man who spoke is the taller of the three. The other two men linger just beyond, shifting their weight from foot to foot. Once again, Gunter makes note of their similar noses, their matching dark eyes.

Gunter offers an appropriate response: Not as beautiful as Germany.

And the man says, Perhaps not, but still, are you curious?

Gunter takes a step back from the railing. He's being tested. These men are clearly Stasi, quizzing him on his intentions.

No need to leave, my friend, the man says. We are all comrades on the water.

Gunter stiffens, tightens his coat around his body.

I am sorry, the man says. I meant no harm.

No harm done, Gunter says.

He skirts the men and begins toward the bow where he can be alone.

Where no one asks questions.

And where he can watch America in silence, seeking the light of a plane through the clouds, a fishing boat speeding across the Atlantic.

ATONEMENT

I hover at US1, staring down the dark corridor of my street. There was nothing I could do to stop him. I was too late.

Nothing good will greet me when I walk through my front door. It's the last place in the world I want to be right now.

There aren't many cars on the highway tonight, and I could ride up the center line all the way to Jimmie's house.

So I push north, passing my street without a glance back.

There's enough love at Jimmie's house to go around, and for just one night, I want to nestle on the couch beside him, tucked between Mr. and Mrs. Yearling, and pretend that it's *my* house. That they're *my* family. A place where no one's depressed. No one gets drunk. No one has affairs. And no one ever disappears.

I hope Mr. Yearling wraps me up in a bear hug when I get there.

As I tunnel up the dark highway toward Key Colony Beach, I approach the Vaca Cut Bridge and Poppy's memorial. A drooping hibiscus flower sags from the pole, illuminated by a flickering yellow streetlight.

~

Richard Quinn stays just offshore, shoving the tiller handle inland, and sending his small skiff careening out to sea.

Tonight, the ocean is flat and calm. The russet clouds retain the memory of a setting sun, now long gone.

The German ship looms in the distance, obscuring the horizon. A leviathan on fire amidst the endless black. The lights from the vessel blaze like spotlights probing the vast Atlantic. The wake churns from its hull like a grand hooded phantom. A snow hill in the air.

Richard pushes the engine further, racing the freighter south, toward Key West. He searches the sky for a plane, but there are no crafts darting through the clouds. Not yet.

He's without a VHF radio, but this is of no concern to Richard. All will go as planned. It's written in the emerging constellations above him.

The engine handle rattles in Richard's hand.

As if it, too, smells impending victory on the salty breeze.

The ship grows larger before him, and the clouds drop lower in the sky.

As though they, too, can taste the spoils on their golden tongues.

Faster.

Closer.

A grinding sound rattles forth from the motor, and the skiff makes a sudden deceleration before laboring ahead in irregular, defiant spurts.

The boat slows, then lurches forward, and Richard loses grip of the tiller handle, sliding to his knees.

By the time he regains his footing and grasps the handle once more, the engine has died completely.

The German freighter sails on, leaving Richard and his stolen skiff alone on a calm, black ocean.

I'm pedaling closer to the Vaca Cut Bridge, closer to the remains of Poppy's memorial, when my tire hits something on the road.

The handlebar lurches from my grip and the wheels twist beneath me.

And then I'm airborne.

Everything is in slow motion.

The bridge spins ahead of me.

The sky rolls around me. Above. Below.

My shoulder slams against the pavement and I'm sliding.

The spokes of the wheel catch my foot, and we careen as one entity across US1 and into the grass beside the bridge.

I open my eyes to see the Troll Doll roll to a stop in the middle of the highway.

That's what I hit.

That's what sent my bike catapulting out of control.

That stupid Troll Doll that kept slipping from Poppy's memorial because the ribbon was too old to fix, and the flowers Audrey wedged within have died.

The Troll Doll is the last thing I see as my bike cascades down the slope beneath the bridge, taking me with it.

And the last thing I hear before the current takes me out to sea is the clap of water against my ear drums as I succumb to the wild waters of the Vaca Cut.

～

"Pequod, this is Wailing Bird. Do you read me? Over."

Galina presses the headset into her ears.

"Pequod, this is Wailing Bird. What's your twenty? Over."

Static.

"You spoke to him?" Shane shouts over the cacophony of the plane.

"He said he was leaving right away."

Shane presses the button once more. "Pequod! Goddamn it."

Galina closes her eyes, pressing her knuckles to her mouth.

"Galina," Shane whispers.

She holds her fist against her forehead, pushing against the blossoming headache.

"Galina, open your eyes."

Outside her window, the clouds part before them. And just below, the brilliant glow of a German ship on the water.

Galina falls forward against the console.

"Is that…"

"Hold on," Shane says, pushing the plane higher and into the clouds.

Galina drops back into her seat as the ship vanishes from view. "Go back!"

"We need to wait for Richard."

Galina wants to clutch Shane's neck, force him to turn the plane around. Her brother is *right there.*

Bruder.

She peers through the window, but all she can see are the wispy threads of nighttime clouds.

She lunges forward, ripping the mouthpiece from Shane's grasp.

"Richard!" she screams. "Richard! Where are you?"

The current yanks my body, and my bike dislodges from my ankle, sinking to the ocean floor.

But I don't sink.

I bend and fold at the whim of the angry water. It launches me toward the sky above—just long enough to gasp for air—before buckling me under once more.

I've been here before, but unlike last time, my brain does not go dormant. It does not tuck into a ball like a little kid crying under the blankets.

I flail my arms and fight, kicking the water, punching my way toward a surface that's always out of reach.

I will not end up like Poppy, stolen by the current and washed out to sea.

Unlucky.

I hope water takes me one day.

I said this once, long ago, when I was young.

I never meant it, not really. It was an act, scripted and performed for the benefit of my father. And he smiled when I said this. He *smiled*.

But what did I know back then? I was just a naïve little girl assigning romance to tragedy.

Like seeking restoration from the blade of a razor.

Richard Quinn wrangles the fuel line from the engine and disconnects the filter.

Fuel splashes across his feet, and he thrusts the hose overboard, draining the remainder into the ocean.

"Dammit, Peter."

Richard holds the filter beneath the cold, white anchor light. Clogs are visible within: rust and debris in a dark, oily sludge.

He bangs the filter against his thigh and holds one end to his mouth, giving a solid blow and painting the hull with gritty brown globs.

On the horizon, the German ship continues south.

The fuel filter slips from his grip, rolling to the bow of the boat. Richard lumbers forward, steadying his weight on the small vessel to prevent a fall overboard.

He drops to his knees, his hands fumbling across the wet hull. Dirt and salt coat his fingertips, and he wipes the sweat from his eyes with the back of his hand. There's fuel in his mouth, in his lungs.

And then he sees the filter, illuminated by the red port light. He scoops it from a pile of discarded work towels and twists the clean filter onto the line.

He pulls the tiller handle.

The cord trembles in the air between the engine and Richard's fist, as the motor sputters with the last bit of air trapped in the line.

Richard pleads into the night, "C'mon, Peter. You did it, buddy. I know you did it."

And he pulls the handle.

The engine explodes back to life, and Richard laughs into the sky.

"Not tonight!" he yells across the water. "This is *my* goddamn night!"

And then Richard Quinn is careening toward the freighter, the lower Keys a blur in his periphery.

TRIAL BY WATER

Richard Quinn draws closer to the freighter, spotting dozens of bodies lined against the railing.

He slows, cutting the lights to avoid detection.

The massive ship towers above him, and he navigates the small skiff, staying just outside the barrier of light emanating from the vessel.

Richard hears a sound—the low rumble of a small plane.

He searches the sky but sees nothing.

Though it's a calm night on the water, deep swells are inevitable this far from shore, and Richard bends forward, clutching the edges for stability as the freighter's wake pushes more waves toward him, spinning him like a nickel across a bar top.

Clouds move in from the Gulf, thick nests obscuring his view of the sky.

Richard starts the motor, following the freighter as it slows, approaching the shallow Cay Sal Bank southeast of Key West.

And then he hears the low rumble once more as a plane emerges from behind a cloud.

It's time.

But Richard has no way to contact the pilot. No VHF radio to call out, *Wailing Bird, Wailing Bird, now, NOW!*

He's just a man on a skiff in the middle of the ocean.

Richard searches the boat for a flashlight, a flare, anything that could signal Shane of his arrival.

The vessel is empty, save for a few fuel tanks and a small brown suitcase.

But he has the boat lights.

Richard fumbles below his seat for the rigged switch and flips it on. The skiff illuminates with green and red. The white anchor light above him blazes.

He toggles it off.

On. Off.

Over and over.

But the plane shows no sign of acknowledgment. It doesn't approach the ship. It doesn't swoop low above it, providing signal and distraction.

The plane lifts higher, disappearing beyond another cloud.

∼

To be lucky or unlucky under the Vaca Cut Bridge. The fates have yet to decide.

I catapult down the Vaca Cut, past the empty diner and into open water, the waves more mudslide than current.

Seawater floods my throat, and my head explodes with pain as salt paints my sinuses.

Trees stand at attention along the coastline, a unified horde denying my reentry.

I'm gone. Drifting away. Just a speck of dust wafting down an empty hallway.

I jerk my head from the surface and gasp for air, seeking land or lights. But all I see is a vast watery tundra.

∼

Galina hollers into the mouthpiece, "Richard? Richard?"

"Have faith," Shane says.

Galina lobs the mouthpiece at him.

The plane crests through another cloud, emerging on the other side, and Shane makes a wide turn through the air. In the distance, Galina spots the ship once more.

"Pequod," Shane calls, "do you read me? Over."

He points out the window.

"Watch for Richard," he says. "It's a big boat. Can't miss it."

Galina clings to the console, scanning the black ocean for the Valkyrie.

"Pequod, we're about a mile north of the Cay Sal Bank. What's your twenty? Over."

Static fills the cabin.

"Pequod?"

Galina searches the ocean for a boat, but is fooled by every whitecap, every silver reflection of the moon.

"There is nothing, Shane."

"Pequod?"

As the plane moves closer to the freighter, Galina studies the ship below. From the sky, it looks like a child's toy, and she plasters her face to the window.

"Try these," Shane says, handing her a pair of binoculars.

Galina scans the passengers atop the deck, magnified through the lenses. She sees guards with weapons strapped to their chests, maids bustling about, and a growing crowd along the railing, watching the lights of America pass in the distance.

"Can you see him?" Shane asks, his voice gentle. "Can you see Gunter?"

Shane knows she cannot recognize individual faces at this altitude, but she smiles anyway. "Yes," she says, "I see my bruder."

"How does he look?"

Galina takes a long, wistful breath. "He looks happy."

As the plane approaches, Galina scans the deck once more, counting the guards. She studies the bridge and the cargo containers stacked along the bow. The lights from the ship are blinding, and she moves the binoculars toward the ocean, away from their glare.

"Shane," she says, placing her hand on the window. "Shane, I see him."

"You see Gunter?"

"I see blinking lights. On the water, just past the ship. Green and red lights. Shane! Green and red lights!"

Galina tries to stand, but the ceiling is too low, and she falls back into her seat.

Shane bolts upright beside her, straining to see through her window. "Is it him? Is it Richard?"

Galina locks the binoculars onto the small boat hiding in the darkness. The green and red lights flash quickly, then stop. They flash again.

"Yes!" she cries. "It's Richard! Go!"

Shane punches the instrument panel.

"Hold on," he says, pitching the nose downward and tunneling toward the unsuspecting ship below.

Madness erupts across the deck, as overhead, a plane dips and dives toward the ship.

Gunter grasps the cold metal railing and watches the crowd disperse and reform beneath the airborne commotion.

Armed guards hurry to the bow, following the path of the plane.

Spotlights erupt from the ship, scanning the sky, but the plane has already departed.

Gunter knows it will return.

Behind him, guards shout orders to one another, but they are confused, disordered.

Gunter turns back to the ocean. He stays quiet, slipping his fingers beneath his coat to check that his documents are still strapped firmly in place.

And then he sees it—a small boat coasting just beyond the lights of the ship. It crashes into oncoming waves, veering in and out of the freighter's wake.

Gunter looks away, afraid of calling attention to the rescue boat. But the guards are not watching the ocean. They're watching the sky.

Just as Galina said they would.

It isn't until he hears the plane's impending return that Gunter wants to run back to his bunk, close the curtains, cover his ears. There are armed guards behind him, spotlights all around him, mama still in Germany, awaiting his arrival home.

And those three men from his cabin.

They're beside him once again, but unlike the guards and passengers, they're not watching the sky.

Like him, they're watching the ocean.

And the boat.

Gunter steps away and all three men turn toward him.

They know.

They will surely alert the guards at any moment.

Gunter nods a quick acknowledgment, but the men return no such pleasantry.

He's caught. Trapped.

The thunder of the plane is deafening as it returns, soaring above the ship.

The guards run to the stern, following the path of the plane.

A guard fires into the sky, and Gunter believes his heart to have stopped beating in that very moment. One heartbeat forever lost atop the ocean.

The men turn toward the gunfire, and Gunter is out of time. Out of choices. Out of doubts. And he jumps.

TO THE DEPTHS GO THE FALLEN

I gave it everything I had, but it wasn't enough.

Each rush of air brings a splash of seawater into my lungs as well. There's a rattle in my chest—a click that taps against my ribs when I breathe.

Thick clouds cover the moon, eclipsing the small bit of light I've been granted until now.

Meadow and the others are already across the country. Their new adventure. They'll never know what happened to me this night. I hope they never do. Let me live a long, happy life in their minds. I grow up. I make macramé wind chimes, just like Meadow taught me. With feathers and shells and driftwood dangling from chunky lace. I fall in love. I become a mother to a beautiful little girl who never wants to look like the cover model on a *Playboy* magazine. No one ever breaks her heart. Her middle name is Sparrow.

An object glides along my back, and I buckle, kicking my feet. My heels wedge into something grassy and solid.

I roll onto my hands and knees to find myself kneeling in the shallows, peering up at the dusty old harbor lights of Key Colony Beach.

I crawl my way to shore, collapsing onto the sand and retching into a seaweed trail clustered along the beach. Water cascades from my lungs, and once everything has been purged from my body, I roll onto my side, trembling from the cold and gasping for warm night air.

I lie there for a long while, just one thought flashing through my mind, over and over.

I got lucky.

I got lucky.

I got lucky.

⁓

Richard Quinn watches Gunter plummet from the bow of the ship, consumed instantly by the waves.

He throttles the motor, turning into the lights and toward the splash.

A siren erupts from the ship. It's everywhere and nowhere, tunneling through Richard's ears, into his throat, his chest. The sound explodes across the Atlantic, a screeching train car breaking against the tracks.

He pushes the motor faster, careening alongside the freighter, no longer confident in his stance against the massive ship or the armed guards rushing toward the bow, eyes trained on the black water below.

But there's no turning back now.

The ship slows, and the wake rushes ahead of the vessel, tossing Richard's skiff out to sea.

Richard veers back, following close to the hull until he spots the flailing arms of a man overboard.

He cuts the motor.

The giant ship lurches as its engine powers down as well.

A large crowd has gathered overhead.

"Gunter!" Richard calls. "Take my hand!"

Gunter gasps, saltwater spewing from his throat as he reaches over the skiff, grasping Richard's wrists.

"Hilfe!" the man shouts. "Bitte Hilfe!"

Spotlights ignite the ocean in large, swooping discs.

Richard throws his weight into his heels, hauling the man over the thin ledge of the boat. Saltwater spins in vortexes across the hull.

Overhead, guards push through the crowd, shouting, "Hier! Hier!", but the gathering is dense, sparing Richard a moment to catch his breath and power up his engine.

And then he hears another splash, followed by two more, as three additional men steal their freedom, leaping one by one from the German freighter and into the churning waters of the Atlantic.

Richard is caught in the spotlight, his small boat haloed, targeted.

Three men kick through the water toward the skiff, their arms thrusting forward, pleading for help.

"Hilfe!" they cry. "Hilfe!"

Richard shakes his head. There's no more room. These men are not his problem.

They are not part of the plan.

Gunter tucks into a ball on the boat's hull, trembling. From the cold, or perhaps the adrenaline. Richard feels it, too. His skin buzzes with energy, his muscles flexed and rigid.

The freighter begins to turn toward him, but the movement is slow, hindered by the weight of the massive ship.

Guards fight their way closer to the railing, but the crowd is dense and unyielding. A passenger who refuses to budge takes the butt of a gun to the shoulder.

There are shouts from the guards, and whistles blown, as overhead, the siren continues to scream.

Richard needs to leave right now. His mission was to rescue Gunter, and Gunter alone. Richard has already claimed his victory. He can outrun the freighter. The massive ship could never keep up.

"Hilfe!"

Richard looks to the men floundering atop the sea, caught in the second spotlight, imprisoned within its boundary.

"Goddammit," he mutters through clenched teeth, spinning the boat and coasting toward the men.

The first bullet hits the water beside the skiff, narrowly missing the engine.

Richard falls to his knees and throws his arms over the side. One hand is taken, then the other. Richard is able to haul both men into the boat before the second bullet whizzes past his head, leaving a blaring ache in his ear.

The last man reaches for Gunter, who pulls him in as a bullet rips through the man's arm.

Blood sprays across the hull and the man howls, falling atop Gunter. A pink mist hovers briefly above the boat before migrating with the wind.

Gunter snatches a work towel from the hull, packing it against the man's wound. He glances nervously to the freighter still making its wide turn.

Richard shoves the tiller handle toward the German freighter and accelerates out of the spotlight that's tracing their retreat, and the line of bullets perforating the water behind them.

~

I don't remember the long walk home. My brain remains somewhere under the Vaca Cut, waterlogged and spinning. I blink, trying to rid the haze that's settled in my eyes, and I pull on my earlobes, trying to clear the hum.

I've never struggled so hard to breathe, like my body has forgotten how to function, and is alive through defiance alone.

When I enter the apartment, everything is dark. In the living room, I see dad's wooden oar, ripped from its mount and thrust through the television screen. I can still see the letters etched deeply in the wood. *VALKYRIE.* Below that, in small white writing: *Marathon, Florida, 1963.*

~

Richard does not look behind him.

He forces himself to blink. To breathe.

He does not hear the screams of the men.

Richard hears only the clacking of the reel in his mind, holding it like a metronome in his chest as the pinpricks of light from a distant shore glow brighter on the horizon.

Richard closes his eyes and is on the deck of the Valkyrie, a pole rigid in his hand, the line swaying from side to side.

Winding. Pulling.

He does not hear the plane soaring through the sky, dropping toward the ship one last time. Nor the spray of bullets blasting through the clouds.

Winding. Pulling. The clacking of the reel.

Richard opens his eyes to an ocean turned choppy with the incoming tide.

"Hold on," he says, steering the skiff into a wave.

The boat tosses atop the water, and the men grasp the ledge, bracing their legs against the hull.

The small craft is cumbersome with the weight of five grown men, and it tips severely from one side to the other. Seawater sloshes in from the bow.

When a silence settles atop the ocean, Richard braves a look back.

The freighter remains halted on the Cay Sal Bank, spotlights deactivated.

It did not pursue.

~

The sharp edge of the boat pushes into Gunter's neck as he watches the night. He doesn't mind.

The black sky is like a memory from his childhood. The stars like fading spotlights across a grand ocean.

The craft slows as they approach the southern tip of the Florida Keys, and Gunter sits upright, marveling at her lights, her sounds.

He looks to the men huddled beside him. One is injured, but he'll be okay. The three men from his cabin. They're not Stasi. They're just like him. Desperate.

Lucky.

Gunter locks eyes with one of the men—the man who spoke boldly to him on the ship.

"Jakob," the man says.

"Gunter."

"Schön dich endlich kennenzulernen," he says.

Nice to finally meet you.

The salty air cools Gunter's skin, the breeze like a passing train car.

Do you have family in America? Gunter asks.

No, Jakob says. You?

Gunter smiles, and says, Yes.

Then you are a lucky man.

Tonight, Gunter says, we are all lucky men.

The skiff coasts over a sandbar. Small fish dart away, fleeing the green and red lights of the boat.

Key West grows closer, her splendor glittering in the middle of a dark and silent ocean.

Why did you jump? Gunter asks. You could have been killed.

Jakob laughs.

When a savior parts the sea, he says, you do not look back to the war behind you.

When the others nod their agreement, Gunter spots more similarities. The same tilt of the head. A dent in the top lip.

Are you of relation? he asks.

Yes, Jakob says. We are brothers.

Ah, Gunter says, then you *do* have family in America.

OF GODS AND VAGABONDS

Richard Quinn pilots the empty skiff along the coast toward home.

The water is flat and calm, the sun barely peeking over the horizon. Onshore, some residents are already awake, their windows glowing yellow against a coral sunrise.

The German refugees are under the protection of American authorities now.

The injured man has already been admitted to the Key West Hospital for care.

Gunter is with his sister, where he belongs, and Richard can still hear her voice echoing across the shallows as he approached the dock at Mallory Square, a soft supplication chanting, *Bruder. Bruder.*

Richard played his part, and he played it well.

And he survived to tell the tale; they all did.

By this afternoon, the newspapers will call Richard for an interview—he made sure to leave his phone number to be passed along—and he will be hailed a hero.

Today, Miriam will weep with pride.

Today, Danni will brag about her father to her friends.

When the school year starts, his students will beg him for stories of adventure. *His* adventure.

The town will remember who he is.

Richard takes his time across the shallows. He's in no rush.

He soars away from the coast, to where the water is deeper, and he can feel its power beneath the hull of his skiff.

He charges into waves capped with salty foam that lashes his face. He bares his teeth and screams into the gale whipping in from the Atlantic.

He pulls a cigar from his jacket pocket, lights it and draws the smoke across his tongue. Sweet as honey.

He licks his lips like he is tasting a lover. The salt of her. The warmth of her. The intoxication of her. He swallows it all.

Richard quietly replaces his boat keys on the hook by the door.

The curtains are drawn closed, and the apartment is dark despite the brilliant morning sun outside the windows.

In the bathroom, he splashes cold water on his face, scrubs the salt from his hands, and doesn't notice that Miriam's makeup is missing from the medicine cabinet.

Richard nudges into his bedroom and slides open the closet. He locates a clean shirt and shorts by feel alone and does not notice that Miriam's dresses are missing from the hangers, or that her suitcase is no longer under the bed.

In the kitchen, Richard discovers a single forgotten beer stashed in the bottom drawer and doesn't lower the can from his lips until it's empty.

Adrenaline is still coursing through his veins, and he wishes his family were awake, but he can wait. He's a patient man.

Richard does not notice the oar smashed through the television as he collapses in his special chair in the living room.

Call me Ishmael, he recites in his mind as he licks the salt from his arm. And then exhaustion claims Richard Quinn.

He quickly succumbs to sleep and does not notice the pile Miriam left for him on the dining room table—an assemblage of papers and napkins scrawled with the names and phone numbers of countless women. His collection, unearthed from his bottom drawer, and heaped atop the letter Miriam wrote only hours ago.

On her way out the door.

⌒

Sleep did not come easy, and I wake to a purple sunrise screaming through my window.

A mosquito buzzes past my face, but I'm too weary to wave it away.

My clothes have dried into deep pleats twisted around my body.

I stand and walk to my window.

Last Halloween, the hurricane uprooted a mangrove tree on the apartment grounds, and now I can see straight to the dock. Today, a man is fishing. He flails his arms, nearly tripping over the tackle box by his feet. Tangled in his line is a seagull. The bird had the misfortune of catching a fish that had already been caught, and now the hook is lodged in its throat. This kind of thing happens all the time, but tourists won't see it advertised in glossy color photographs. Sometimes the startled fisherman can save the bird from ripping out its own throat. Sometimes not.

The fishing line wrenches beneath a wing and the seagull drops to the dock, floundering against the wood. His frightened squawks carve straight through my window.

I turn away and draw closed the curtains.

In the back of my closet I find my overnight bag and stuff it with shirts, shorts, underwear. Enough for a few days.

I consider going to Audrey's house, but Mercy and Sharon probably slept over after the bridge party last night. They'll ask why I never showed up. They'll ask what happened to my bike. They'll tell me about all the fun I missed. They'll be giggling and eating millet or fruit leather, their eyes glazed with contentment and bliss as they watch Saturday morning programs on Audrey's color television because none of them have learned to expect anything different.

No. I don't want to go to Audrey's house.

The Yearlings will surely let me stay with them for a bit. I'll sleep on the couch and won't be any bother.

I grab a notebook in case I want to write more poetry. Not for a teacher, or for a grade, but just for me. And then I pack the bundle of Mary Janes still sitting atop my bed, wrapped in paper. They're Jimmie's favorite.

I place my bag outside my bedroom door and am about to walk to the bathroom when I spot my father passed out in the chair, an empty beer can beside his twitching fingers.

He came home after all.

I wonder what kind of fancy appliance he's brought mom this time.

Dad appears older. His hair is beginning to gray at the temples, and the creases between his eyebrows are tunneling deeper into his skin than ever before. His flesh is pale, clammy. He smells like the ocean, dirty and sour. And like always, he smells like beer.

This is the Richard Quinn his blushing students don't see, his mistresses don't see.

And I don't want to look at this man another minute longer.

After a shower, I peer into the mirror, but the glass is cloudy, my reflection nothing more than an apparition.

Dad coughs into the cushion and begins to snore, the sound echoing from the living room.

I lean toward the mirror and press a finger to the glass. A single drop falls down the haze.

I HATE YOU

That's what I write on the mirror.

As something inside me grows solid where once it was soft, I take a deep breath and let it whistle through my lips.

And then I wipe it all away.

I know the way to Jimmie's house. I barely look up.

The trek is longer on foot. But I have no choice. Last night, my bike drowned, and now she rests forever in a watery grave beneath the Vaca Cut Bridge.

When I arrive, I spot the Yearlings through the window, unfurling newspapers and sipping coffee.

I don't see Jimmie anywhere.

But then I hear a splash.

Beyond the hut is the dock that juts into the shallows —and Ellie's bike, leaning against a piling.

I shuffle through sand and pine needles, making my way closer to the dock. In the water, Jimmie and Ellie are catching crawfish, and I tuck into the cover of trees to watch.

The sun is higher in the sky now, the water a vivid jade above the sandbar.

Jimmie's successful, holding a squirming crawfish aloft in his net. Ellie rewards him with a kiss.

I reach into my bag and pull out the Mary Janes, tucking the paper tightly around the bundle. I lean them against a dock piling.

"Bya," I whisper.

And I walk away.

As I approach the highway, a conversation replays in my mind. Something Meadow once said: It's the bad things that make us who we are, in ways you can't see right now.

She was right.

You really just have to ask yourself one question, she said, and all the pain starts to heal.

I remember what she asked me. I'll remember it forever: Do you like yourself, Lil' Mama?

And I do. I really, really do.

I stand at the intersection, watching the cars.

It's early, but our small highway is already clogged with people coming and going.

To my left is Key West, what everyone comes for. They breeze through Marathon on their way to bigger and better things, and don't even know the name of the town they're driving through. We're just a smudge across their window that's wiped away as soon as they hit the Seven Mile Bridge.

To my right is Duck Key, Islamorada, Key Largo. And then the 18-mile stretch, a narrow road edged with mangroves and water, and nothing else. Our own little purgatory to endure before the highway ushers us into Florida City and Miami. Beyond that, the rest of the world.

I choose my place atop the curb and drop my bag to my feet where it slumps across the soft grass.

And I stick out my thumb.

The man who pulls over is young and handsome. He smiles nervously as I approach the window.

He removes his sunglasses.

"I never do this," he says.

"Neither do I."

"But you looked like you needed some help, so I turned around. Are you okay?"

I wipe the tears from my eyes and peer south along the highway, toward home.

Maybe I'll miss it when I'm gone. Maybe not.

Only one way to find out.

"I'm going to be," I say.

I appraise the man in the car. He's nice. But not eager.

"I'm visiting some friends for the summer," he says. "I can get you as far as Miami if you need a lift. No sweat either way."

When I look at him, his eyes don't falter. And they don't roam.

"That's a good start," I say.

He plucks textbooks and empty soda cans from the passenger floor, tossing them to the back seat.

"What's your final destination?" he asks.

I bite my lip and take a deep breath, settling into the worn upholstery.

"Siskiyou County," I say. "California."

HOME

bridges like stitches connect each island
I hold my breath over graveyards
and seagulls strangled with line

a wasteland of barflies and saltwater cowboys
lighthouses cracked and pale with age
like the faces of native Conchs

shoreline grasses purple as a man-o-war
familiar buildings reach for me
like the spindly fingers of storybook witches

highway asphalt stretches like miles
of damaged skin struggling to heal
a saltwater compress over her wounds

but between tangled mangroves and waterfront hovels
private-beach estates and crab trap mountains
glimpses of the water that birthed me

- Daniella Quinn
(Lil' Mama)

Epilogue

California is more beautiful than I could have ever imagined, and I saw it all. Craggy rock formations that dropped hundreds of feet into the Pacific. Endless redwood forests stretching as far as the eye could see. Giant waves that roiled and crashed, each one dwarfed by the next. Vineyards that swooped along valleys like mom's golden hair. I saw animals I'd never before seen —chipmunks and bald eagles and sea lions and seals. And the mountains. Some are choppy and arid, like giant sandcastles in the sky. Others are smooth and languid, like the nude body of a woman.

I've been in many different cars and met many different people. I followed all of Meadow's rules.

I'm gazing at blue-tipped mountains when my ride informs me that we've arrived. I peer over the dashboard at a broken gate, beyond which is nothing but field and forest.

"I don't see anything," I say. "Are you sure?"

"Lots of new faces around here lately," she says. "Rumor has it they're all living here in the woods. What's going on out there, anyway?"

I shrug, and it's an honest answer.

She points to a dilapidated farmhouse in the distance. "Maybe that's it."

My fingers hesitate on the door handle.

Don't worry about where you'll end up. Just begin.

I step out of the car, clutching my bag to my chest.

The driver waits until I navigate through the broken fence before driving away, a plume of dust in her wake.

And then I'm alone.

The surrounding forest is dense, casting generous shadows, and there are horses on the other side of the grassy clearing. We don't have horses in the Keys, so I watch them for a while, running and playing in the sunlight, before beginning toward the farmhouse.

It's been a long journey. My skin is sunburnt, my throat parched. It's difficult to swallow.

I spot trucks and construction materials—small houses are being built all across the property, and tents have been erected, tucked into the shadows of the forest.

Blisters break against my heel. It hurts to walk.

I hear what sounds like a drumbeat. Or maybe it's the gallop of a horse.

A cluster of people gather before a large teepee, but they're so far away, and I'm not sure I can take another step.

Then someone laughs. A woman. Her voice like a wind chime made of seashells.

And I run.

AUTHOR'S NOTE

Bands of a Small Hurricane is a work of fiction
loosely inspired by true events.

On the 27th of November 1971, Bob Lowe of Marathon, Florida rescued a German man from the Atlantic Ocean after he leapt over the side of a German ship between Key West and Havana.

Bob was recruited by the man's brother who was already living in America. Together, they secured a pilot who would buzz the ship as both signal and distraction.

On the day of the planned rescue, the ship was delayed, and when Bob finally received the call around 5:30am, he did not have enough time to reach his charter boat, the Pequod, opting instead to steal a small skiff from a local marina. The engine failed twice due to a faulty motor, but Bob managed to keep it running.

When he reached the ship, the German brother jumped…

…followed by three others.

Everyone survived the ordeal.

The local papers called Bob a hero.

Bob Lowe lived in Marathon until his death in 1990. He was 61. Bob was a husband, father of three, high school English teacher, charter boat captain, and an avid reader who could recite on command the first chapter of Moby Dick.

And he was my grandfather.

~

Richard Quinn *is not* Bob Lowe. And the specifics of Galina and Gunter are *not* an accurate representation of the rescue that occurred in 1971. This is merely a fictional tale inspired by a real man and the family folklore he left behind.

Bob passed away when I was 9 years old, and I know very little of the man he actually was. But in creating Richard, I feel as though I've created a fictionalized version of the grandfather I never knew.

I like Richard Quinn very much. I think he would like me too.

IN THE WATER FOR THE FIRST TIME

HISTORICAL ACCURACIES & CREATIVE LIBERTIES

Bands of a Small Hurricane references many historical points of interest. Some have been rendered accurately, while others have been given a bit of literary "flare" for storytelling purposes.

Below are a list of mentioned locations and facts, in order of appearance:

* **The Humps** are a popular fishing destination in the Florida Keys, and are a series of underwater mountain ranges or "seamounts". The current funnels around the peaks, creating a unique and diverse habitat for sea life.

* **Mister Brownstone** was inspired by a real hammerhead shark that is rumored to patrol the Seven Mile Bridge and surrounding waters. She is known as Big Mo (short for Big Mother). Locals claim the shark to be upwards of 18' long, and weighing a ton (which would make her the largest hammerhead on the planet). I grew up hearing tales of Big Mo, and she is still very much a part of local mythology. Whether she is real or legend has yet to be determined.

* **US1** (also known by locals as The Overseas Highway) is the only road that connects the islands, running from Miami to Key West. Presently, this is a booming highway filled with vehicles coming and going, but in the sixties, traffic was sparse, hence why Danni frequently rides her bike up and down the center line.

* Those born in the Florida Keys are indeed called **Native Conchs**. I am a Native Conch, and was born at Fishermen's Hospital (now called Baptist Health Fishermen's Community Hospital), which is located just past the turnoff to Danni's high school.

* **Red sky at night, sailors delight; red sky at morning, sailors take warning** is a common adage spoken by boaters, and is based on the moisture particles in the atmosphere. At night, a reddish sky means stable air and usually indicates that good weather will follow. At morning, it indicates high water content in the atmosphere, which is often a predecessor to rain.

* The **Playboy magazine** mentioned in the book is the issue for July 1967.

* **The Vaca Cut Bridge** is, in fact, a dangerous passthrough for boaters. The severity and frequency of accidents were embellished for storytelling purposes.

* **The 18-mile stretch** is a long span of US1 that connects Florida City/Miami area to Key Largo. It is a 2-lane highway with vast ocean views and little else. Stunning for visitors, but can be drudgery for locals.

* In reality, **The Botel** as described in the book is not a singular location, though many places of lodging in the Keys have large floating structures that act as rooms for travelers. They are usually docked behind the main buildings and are frequently called…botels.

* There *was* an abandoned coral mansion in the Keys that the local kids referred to as **the haunted house**. It was not, however, located on Boot Key. The structure stood on what is now called Fiesta Key, and was originally abandoned due to a laundry gas explosion. It was further destroyed by a hurricane some years later.

* **Mallory Square** and **Duval Street** in Key West are currently booming visitor attractions, filled with bars, restaurants, shops, street performers and a nightly sunset celebration. Mallory Square and Duval Street were much more subdued in the sixties, but I chose to include the crowds and revelry it is now known for.

* There *was* an **abandoned lighthouse**, though its location varies from that in the book. It did indeed have a large, faceted bulb and precarious upper deck railing.

* **The Armada** is fictional, but loosely based on *The Buccaneer Lodge*, a Marathon bar frequented by my grandfather. The description of The Armada is from my hazy childhood memories of sitting beside my grandfather, drinking Shirley Temples and eating pretzels.

* Danni's **high school** is based on my personal recollection of *Marathon High School*, complete with a separate middle school wing, yellow skylights, open-air hallways, sticky gymnasium and the wide, circular band room steps. Though it was near the water and beaches, I don't recall having a beach view from any of the windows. This was embellished for storytelling purposes. The Marathon High School that I attended was torn down and rebuilt in the early 2000s, and now resembles nothing of the small campus I once knew.

* **Coco Plum** and **Key Colony Beach** are individual "island communities" situated within the boundary of Marathon. The grandeur of Coco Plum was embellished for storytelling purposes, though many of the houses *are* quite grand and include ownership of portions of the beach.

* The unnamed **hurricane** is a work of fiction. There is no record of any hurricane making landfall in Florida in 1967.

* **The Bahia Honda Bridge** is accurate as described in the book. The bridge was built over an existing train track that once stretched across the water to Spanish Harbor Key. The abandoned trusses are still present.

* **Sombrero Beach** is accurate as described in the book, located past the high school, and does in fact have a coral bluff that juts out from the sand and into the water.

* **The Sombrero Lighthouse** is located about 8 miles offshore from Key Colony Beach, and sits above a barrier reef. I have many childhood memories of leaping from my father's boat to snorkel its waters.

Acknowledgments

First and foremost, I have to thank my parents for allowing me to pillage their memories of growing up in the Florida Keys in the 1960s. Everything from Key lime fights to clicking mirrors on the Seven Mile Bridge to chasing down Soviet ships in the middle of the ocean (and a hundred other tiny details) brought Bands of a Small Hurricane to life, and came directly from them.

A special thank you to everyone at Creative Pinellas, who saw fit to honor me as a literary grantee after reading selected passages of this novel. Thank you for supporting my vision, and for all you do for our local creative community.

A number of people contributed their time and insights to the creation of this book: Logan Zahner for lending her beautiful face to the cover; Joe Flores for his knowledge of shipping routes and postal industry specifics; Susan Cole Marshall, Jennifer Ragsdale and Sally Manz for offering their insights as beta readers; Angie and Vinnie Neaz for sharing their memories of a divided Germany; and Rene Schlegel for his assistance with German translation and pronunciation.

And my biggest cheerleader, Gabriel Cole, whose time, influence and support during the writing and production of this novel was transformative. Thank you for being in my life.

Reading Group Questions

1. How does the isolation of the setting contribute to the larger story? Would Richard still be a hero if he lived in a big city? Would Danni still have been so intrigued by outsiders?

2. How does Danni's home life contribute to her search for love and approval beyond her family? There is no lack of love between Danni and her father. Why do you think this was not enough?

3. What is it about Audrey that initially intrigues Danni? And what ultimately pushes her away?

4. Danni has many people in her life, yet finds something unfamiliar in her relationship with the hippies. What is it that Danni seeks from Meadow, specifically?

5. Danni loses her virginity in a very unceremonious way. What were her true motivations? Will she regret this later?

6. Examine Miriam's response when she learns of her daughter's molestation. How does her reaction serve her character?

7. How do you feel about Richard's decision to keep the rescue plan a secret? How does this choice support his ego rather than his family?

8. Had Richard never attempted the rescue, would he still have lost his wife and daughter?

9. How do you think Danni's childhood experiences will enhance her new life in California? What might haunt her?

10. What are some of the key moments that change Danni throughout the story?

11. Examine the different roles that water plays in this story.

12. Would you consider this a sad ending or a happy one?

13. There are a number of purposeful repetitions in this book: *red sky at morning, sailors take warning; no shoes, no need; kiss me kiss me kiss me; I shrug, and it's an honest answer*, and many more. Does this writing style detract from the story or contribute to it?

14. Did the inclusion of the illustrated map impact your experience as a reader?

15. One of the more remarkable biographical elements about the author is that she dropped out of high school after tenth grade. How does this knowledge impact your own impression of secondary and postsecondary education? Does a formal education stifle an artistic mind or expand it?

ABOUT THE AUTHOR

Shan Leah's debut thriller, *Thieves, Beasts & Men*, was a Finalist for the 2021 American Fiction Award, a Finalist for the 2021 Shelf Unbound Award for Best New Fiction, and was shortlisted for the Somerset Prize for Literary and Contemporary Fiction, Chanticleer International Book Awards 2021.

She's also an award-winning fine artist, and lover of dark literary fiction. Surrounded by an endless supply of pens, papers, paints, and clay, Shan grew up in the Florida Keys and was taught proper wheel-throwing techniques before mastering her shoelaces.

She currently lives in Dunedin, Florida, with her brilliant kid and small herd of cats.

She finds beauty dreadfully boring.

www.ShanLeah.com

For more information on this book, plus past and forthcoming titles, visit

ShanLeah.com

Or *Instagram at @ShanLeah*

There is no better endorsement than a happy reader! If you loved Bands of a Small Hurricane, please consider leaving a review on Goodreads, Amazon, B&N, or social media.

None of this is possible without your support!

9 781958 164020